William Hope and The Princess

Princess

Part One - "For England, Yar!"
Chris Vance

ISBN : 978-1-0683434-4-5

For William...

Come find me when you're old enough to read this...

Contents

With the Grace of Providence,
I am able to present the,
Loves and Adventures,
That maketh,
The most Satisfying,
The most Swashbuckling,
The most Entertaining,
And by no means,
The most Veritable tale of...
William Hope and The Princess
Part One
"For England, Yar!"
With a fair portion of sincerity,
An equitable splattering of wit,
And by no means,
An honest measure of humility...

Chris Vance Esq.

1

Heart of the Charms

29th October 1577

William and Katherine were about to discover that time would forever be relative to their unwavering accord in true love.

The twins were facing each other, eyes-closed, sitting cross-legged in the centre of an elaborately designed chalk circle etched onto the blue slate floor of the rooftop of the southeast corner tower of the Fountain Courtyard of their home.

William held a silver ring with an emerald gemstone in his upturned right palm. Katherine was holding a silver necklace with an opal gemstone pendant in her right palm and a small scroll of parchment in her left hand.

They were three floors up and surrounded by a stone capped, waist-height parapet and four ornate red brick and stone turrets that marked the corners of the southeast tower. If one were paying attention and considered that there were three other corner towers about eighty yards apart,

1

each with four turrets, that constituted the corners of the huge open courtyard they framed, one might be able to consider that William and Katherine's home was not your average run of the mill, one room, one door, two windows, one chimney, two dogs, three cats and a goat type of home. Indeed, and it perhaps doesn't bear a mention, but William and Katherine's home had a fuck-ton of corners, stone capped turrets and towers, multiple scores of rooms, multitudinous doors and windows, chimneys up the wazoodle, several packs of dogs, innumerable cats, rats, mice, chickens, horses, cows, sheep, pigs, badgers, squirrels, pheasants, deer, foxes and copious numbers of whatever other fauna decided to reproduce every spring.

And William and Katherine's home was still being built.

Construction had been in progress in earnest for ten years or more. The kids couldn't remember a time when there were no holes in the ground for new foundations, or scaffolding for new towers, bastions, loggias, walls, and roofs.

It was their thirteenth birthday.

Their mother, Mildred, was dashing around below, organising some sort of celebratory affair to be held in the North Parlour later that evening.

Boring...

They were thirteen now, and, for all intents and purposes, grown-ups whom, as such, should finally be able to present or not present at their parents' parties for reasons of their own. *Should* be able to realise such decisions and choices. Not quite how their father, William Cecil, saw it though, which did place a damper on spontaneous play occasionally.

There were times when Katherine had pressed their father on the conditions of her independence directly – such moments increasing in frequency, almost in parallel with the development of Katherine's newly forming bosom William had noticed – but after several defeating counter arguments, Katherine was lately employing a subtle round about approach to sequester her wishes. She would engage in discussions of architecture to soften the old boy up somewhat, prior to any given want on her part.

Lord Burghley, as he was known to many, which had always been funny to William and Katherine, estimated future expansion and development of the house and grounds would probably take eight further years or so. Then, as he sometimes insisted, Theobalds House would finally be an estate worthy of Queen and of England. Katherine suspected that her father's formative answer was, at best, political sidestepping and, at worst, complete and utter bullshit, and that the house would never be finished. William didn't give a burst-goat's-bollock how long it took for construction to be completed. He and Katherine could run free and explore every new passageway, cellar, tunnel, staircase, and turret, that was being installed in the roaming house and grounds, for none would ever remain 'secret' to them, and William simply loved that.

He also loved Katherine, but that, or rather she, was complicated.

Further complicated now that her breasts were beginning to show.

He would have to talk to his father about his feelings soon, for as little as he knew about girls, he was dead set fucking certain he shouldn't be having at least some of his private thoughts in regard to his own bloody sister.

"I don't believe the magic is working," said Katherine.

William's eyes snapped open and landed directly on Katherine's tits.

Shit.

The bodice of the dress she was wearing was squeezing the makings of a cleavage. William had never seen this on Katherine, largely because she never wore dresses, or at least rarely, and she hadn't for some time. She was always content running around in her dungarees. That was normal. This wasn't.

William quickly raised his gaze to find Katherine staring straight through him, "Errm... I don't know. Maybe I wasn't concentrating on the budding elements."

"What are you talking about?" questioned Katherine.

"The... the... you know... the heart of the charms," said William.

The vibrations of William's bashful attempt at deflection were a cacophony of fragmented, confusing chords with imperfect intervals in a vaguely minor triad of complete horseshit. Katherine was improving her abilities to listen to the musicality of the world around her day by day. In changing winds. In people's moods. Strains in animals. Refrains in plants. None of that was scary. It was all a fascinating study, really. Her ear was keener with each passing month and season. Recently she thought she could even discern some elementary notes and arrangements in pieces of her parent's antique furniture, but, on the flip side, it was sometimes easier and less tiring to believe that her pubescence was just an essence of her growing to become a bat-shit-crazy adult, much like the rest of them.

William was a frigging nightmare for her to understand. He was light, kind, funny and thoughtful, sometimes to a fault. Placing everyone's and anyone's needs ahead of his own. No matter who they were. But there was a darkness and volume of silence in her brother that Katherine could never hear to see him clearly as one. It was sometimes as though he were made up of two different orchestral movements, battling for predominance in the hall of his heart and being.

"You'd better get used to them. Female anatomy regarding mammary glands dictates that they will one day serve a greater purpose than your silly fascinations of late," said Katherine.

"I don't have fascinations," said William.

"It's fine dear brother," said Katherine, smiling, "at least we know you're not fashioning your nature after Francis."

Katherine was referring to their gentle sixteen-year-old cousin, Francis Bacon, whom some of the family suspected was embarking on a period of... confusion... in his development.

"My bum is numb," said William, totally and utterly deflecting by jumping up from the blue slate floor and taking a pace southward.

"No! Wait! You can't cross the circle yet," said Katherine, bouncing up to her feet and grabbing William's arm.

She was referring to the elaborate three ringed chalk circle in which they had been sitting. The outer ring was nine feet in diameter, the inner ring approximately eight feet. In between rings, Katherine had drawn in celestial symbols that she had come across in some of their father's old books on magic and mysteries, elements, forces of nature and all sorts of good stuff that neither she nor William believed in or understood in the slightest. But it was fun. Tonight's incantation was intended to install a charm linking the emerald on Katherine's ring with the opal pendant on William's necklace. Aunty Liz had been the inspiration for the idea. The Monarch had suggested that a charm existed – if they were pure of heart and could study enough to learn how to form it – that would bind the ring to the pendant, thus if either William or Katherine ever got lost, the bejewelled trinkets would guide them back to one another when help was needed most. Brilliant.

Tonight, the night sky would see a Hunter's moon. Perfect.

And it wasn't raining. Even better. The chalk circle would remain intact.

Unless of course William got embarrassed about involuntarily perving over his sister's squished up bubbies in her stupid party dress and tried to walk out of it before the spell had fully been installed and sanctified.

"You said it's not working," snapped William, "I believe you."

William pulled away from Katherine and stepped away to the southern parapet of the tower. He rested his hands on the stone capping and looked out. Directly below him a large formal garden was in the early stages of development. Stone pathways separated nine squares, each seventy feet to a side, that would ultimately all be planted and maintained. Sculptures would be added per their father's whims. Possibly fountains or some such. Hedges, flowers. Whatever.

Katherine stepped up beside William and placed her hands on the parapet. The twins stood in silence for a long moment.

"What do you make of that?" asked William, pointing out in the distance, south along the main road from London to Ware. The unmistakable shape of the White Tower could be seen some thirteen miles away on the north bank of the Thames River. It wasn't what William was focused on.

"Make of what?" questioned Katherine.

"There," said William, moving closer to Katherine and encouraging her to aim her sights as though his arm was the barrel of a musket, "on the old road, moving this way."

Katherine strained to capture William's intended target. The descending sun was casting long shadows flickering through the trees of her father's extensive hunting grounds. Staff had begun the rounds of lighting torches lining the paths of the unfinished gardens. Lanterns were popping up in the windows of one of the newest complete extensions to their home, which was an eighty yard long, three-storey loggia arrangement that would connect the new buildings of the grand Middle Court to the Still House Chamber, which was the furthest building to the southeast. After several beats of considered patience, she clocked what had to be the movement of two or three carriages in a closed line formation, flanked by several horseback riders. It was hard to define the exact number as they were two miles away at least.

"Hard to say, except who gives a shit," dismissed Katherine. "Come on, we must try again. Mother will be summoning us any time now."

"Alright, fine, but last crack at it for tonight," said William, "if I promise not to look at your tits in that stupid dress, deal?"

"Easy deal," said Katherine.

William peeled away from the parapet and entered the chalk circle once again. He sat down cross-legged on the floor facing east. His face was in shadow from the west side parapet of the tower. Katherine sat down opposite him with the last rays of the sun across her eyes.

"Now, we should start..." began Katherine.

"Can I make a suggestion?" asked William.

"Alright."

"I'll hold the ring and the amulet. You do the chanting thing," said William.

"Elizabeth said it would be better..." said Katherine.

"Bessy isn't here, is she? And her way isn't worth a shit. We've tried it three times."

"Yes, and all the while you were looking at my boobs."

"I'm not looking at them now. And I'm sorry I did. Give me the ring," said William.

"You don't like my boobs anymore?" said Katherine.

"Katherine," admonished William, "ring."

Katherine smiled and pulled her ring from the third finger of her right hand. She tossed it across the circled space to William who caught it. He placed it in the upturned palm of his left hand alongside the necklace with the opal amulet and cupped his right hand over the gems.

"Ready," said William.

"Ready, ready?" questioned Katherine.

"Like you wouldn't believe," said William.

"You must believe," said Katherine.

"Uh, huh."

Katherine understood the vibrations of the composed descending scale of William's resigned efforts in their attempted bewitchery. Her brother had been very patient. And she'd taken all the piss out of his innocent lechery that was modestly acceptable. It was time. Then they could run downstairs and eat cake. Maybe even cocoa cake if they were lucky.

Katherine positioned her scroll of parchment on the floor. She unravelled it and weighed it down top and bottom with two polished stones, one white at the top, and one black at the bottom of the handwritten charm. She placed her hands on her knees and drew a long deep breath. She exhaled and began to read:

"In absence of evil spirits,

In presence of light spirit.
In absence of man and politics,
Or in presence of man and politics.
In friendship and truth,
We commit to binding these jewels.
In absence of time..."

Katherine slapped her hand down on the parchment, and stared straight at William, "That's why it's not working!"

William opened his eyes from his pretend concentration. He purposely avoided direct eye contact with any part of Katherine's dress.

"Is it? What is *that* exactly, pray?" asked William.

"Well, why should it be we reference only man and politics? Why not man, woman, and politics? Men are crap at politics. Just look at father. He gets all worked up all the time about politics. Mother doesn't."

"Ergo, women are better at politics, is that it? It's getting late, Katherine," said William.

"I know but it's got to be important, doesn't it? If we don't include women in the spell. I mean I'm a woman. I'm half of this spell, aren't I?"

William stared at Katherine for a beat, then burst out laughing and shaking his head.

"Don't you laugh at me like that. I hate it when you do that. Idiot," said Katherine.

"I'm not. I'm not laughing at you. I think you're right. That's what's funny."

"It's not funny at all," said Katherine.

"Alright, what do you want to do about it?" asked William.

"I don't know. Change the spell," said Katherine.

"So, change it. Here," said William, pulling a small, thin stick of charcoal wood from the hip pocket of his doublet and offering it across the circle to Katherine.

"What shall I change it to?"

"Errm... well, shit. Umm... say man, woman and politics," suggested William.

Katherine began to scribble corrections on the parchment.

"Politics is bullshit also. Can we leave that out?"

"Sure. I agree. Then how does it read?" asked William.

"Well, if we remove politics as a social baseline and replace it with woman, it reads, In absence of man and woman. In presence of man and woman, and on... In friendship and truth works. The next lines are fine. The end is still good."

"Great. But if it's in absence of man and woman, then what are we hoping to charm these gemstones about?" questioned William.

"But it's... in presence too, of man and woman. And it's about all things. Isn't it? Everything is linked. That's how we can find each other. Not even in things, it is life, all around us. And the spirits. But we only want the light ones," said Katherine.

"Give me the thing," said William.

Katherine handed the scroll and the charcoal stick to William. He slapped it on the ground and struck a heavy line through two lines of supposed enchanted verse.

"There," said William, "Man, woman, politics, all gone, the same way. Vanquished."

William handed the scroll back to Katherine, who perused her writing as now presented.

"Alright, let's try it," said Katherine, sliding backwards on her bottom and repositioning herself cross-legged with the parchment scroll on the ground.

"Can we cut straight to the Latin? I'm getting hungry," said William.

"Alright. So am I. Latin it is. Pencil," said Katherine.

William tossed over the charcoal stick. Katherine traced her index finger down the lines on the parchment and crossed out two lines, just as William had done with the English language version at the top of the scroll. She positioned the white and black stones to hold the parchment down on the floor once again, before relaxing back with her hands on her knees. William cupped the ring and the necklace in between his palms once again and closed his eyes.

Katherine began reading in Latin, in a three/four-time chant with an even tempo. She used no punctuation between lines:

"In absentia malorum spirituum
In conspectu lucis spiritus
In amicitia et veritate
Haec monilia ligare committimus
In absentia temporis
In conspectu temporis
in omni tempore
Ut nos his signis latores
Invenies se semper..."

William was listening to Katherine's voice, but her words fell away into the background of his mind. His thoughts were concentrated on the two gemstones cupped tightly in his hands.

"...In absentia malorum spirituum
In conspectu lucis spiritus..."

William thought about losing Katherine. Not being able to find her. What would he do? How would he change such a circumstance? He would absolutely have to. He knew that. He would die for her. He knew that. But how would he find her?

"In amicitia et veritate
Haec monilia ligare committimus..."

If Katherine had glanced up from her reading and chanting, she would have seen William's eyes closed and his brow began to furrow in confusion.

"In absentia temporis
In conspectu temporis
in omni tempore..."

William quelled a weird sort of fear that was beginning to constrict his lungs and he focused harder on the task at hand; it was very strange, as though the jewels were heating up intensely, but the stones weren't burning the skin on his palms. He could still feel the ring, the amulet, and the necklace attached to it, but they were enveloped in a weightless ball of fever.

"Ut nos his signis latores
Invenies se semper..."

The slamming of footsteps behind him and over his left shoulder prompted William to open his eyes. The first thing he noticed was a weird-arse scarlet and emerald light leaking from his tightly cupped hands. He jolted backwards, throwing his arms behind him, dropping the ring and the necklace on the floor in between his legs.

The second thing William noticed was the first thing Katherine noticed when she looked up from the parchment and desisted in the reading of her spell, which was Francis Bacon tripping over the top step of the tower's circular stone staircase and flying out of the small doorway onto the roof top holding a lantern. The second thing Katherine noticed was the third thing William noticed which was Bacon's arse crashing straight into his face.

The two boys tumbled over under Bacon's momentum and sprawled out on the blue slate floor. Katherine took a moment to fully process what she was seeing before her. Much of her concentration was still framed in Latin three/four timing.

Bacon sat up. He did so, proudly holding up the wrought iron handle of the lantern, which curiously enough, had survived the tumble.

"What on earth are you doing, Francis?" cried Katherine.

Bacon made a serious and contemplative effort at answering her, but words didn't escape his opening and closing lips. Intakes of breath came next. Staggered intakes, intermittent with spluttering exhales.

William sat up, "What the fuck, Francis?"

"I... wheeewwww, I... whooooww, we must..." attempted Bacon.

"Francis, head between your knees!" exclaimed Katherine, jumping up, crossing to her breathless cousin, and lifting the weight of the lantern. She pushed the crown of Bacon's head towards his splayed legs.

"They... have," cough, splutter, "The guards," splutter, cough, cough, "We must hide," gasped Francis.

William and Katherine couldn't make head nor tails of what the hell their delicate cousin was talking about, and, in fairness to them, it wasn't unusual for Bacon to become overexcited in any given moment of observation in his life. The trick to deciphering the meaning of his considered scrutiny on any given topic was to calm him down, encourage him to breathe and then, and only then, cut directly to the chase of whatever matter Francis considered paramount to his panic. This was not yet a practised craft for William and Katherine, for they were young and on the cusp of learning the full meaning of Bacon's being, but one thing was certain; Katherine was better at handling all things pertaining to states of fluster.

"Breathe Francis. I'll count. You breathe," said Katherine, "and a one, two, three and four, breathe in."

Bacon inhaled as instructed.

"And a one, two, three and four, let it go. Two, three and four," instructed Katherine, calmly and methodically, as if Bacon's shaking condition was a perfectly normal state of behaviour.

Two more rounds of the same exercise saw Bacon's heart rate lower, his lungs oxygenate, and his pupils centre from cross-eyed mania to a frightened central focus.

"Good. Relay information. We shall then conclude a course of action," said Katherine.

"Guards. Queen's guards are coming here to arrest William," said Bacon.

"What are... what?" said Katherine.

"William, you have committed Treason, apparently, according to Sir James of Bon," said Bacon.

"Treason?" questioned William, "What the fuck are you talking about?"

"Sir James knows you haven't. I stated the facts incorrectly. He commissioned me to present here to you ahead of a group of guards that Elizabeth has sent to arrest you tonight and take you to the Tower. The charge is Treason," said Bacon. "Am I now making complete sense?"

William recoiled a fraction in abject what-the-fuckness? Katherine, though similarly stunned with Bacon's utterance of events ongoing, had the presence of mind to take an objective view that more discovery was to be hastened before panic took to blinding solution. She could tell that her cousin was relaying the truth as he had been informed. His vibrations, though dissonant in confusion and in a minor key, were perfectly pitched in genuine concern.

"Sir James sent you to give us the heads up," stated Katherine.

"Yes," replied Bacon.

"Good. Stand up. You too, William," said Katherine, as she crossed from the chalk circle to the southern parapet and looked out over the gardens and hunting grounds. A cursory glance told her there was nothing but shadows and the odd flambeau lining pathways, so she rounded the southeast corner turret and propped her hands down on the centre of the stone capping of the eastern parapet walling. The Middle Court of their home was massive. The central courtyard was approximately one-hundred yards to a side, framed with three-storey brick-built chambers constructed in her father's favoured loggia arrangement, lending itself to the sprawling prodigy architecture. The main entrance was now on the eastern most face of the courtyard, sited between two generous porter's lodges, with a huge stone archway between them. Beyond that were sidings of servant's quarters and simple pathways bisecting grassed areas to be developed into yet more future gardens, vegetable patches, mazes, and whatever else 'Lord Burghley' could fashion in the imaginations of his sleeping hours.

William and Bacon shuffled up to their feet and placed themselves either side of Katherine, overlooking the eastern parapet. Sure enough, roughly a quarter mile or so away, a line of three carriages, each towed by tandems of six horses, with some twenty or more single riders flanking, were fast approaching. The riders all bore the uniforms and arms of the Queen's Body Guards or Yeomen warders. The same uniforms one might see on show on some State occasion or holiday at some bullshit parade commemorating something worth commemorating in as a Regal propaganda measure for the people. More importantly, they were the same uniforms sanctioned as attire for the guards of the White Tower. As in, *that* tower. First established as a timber framed structure, with a crude ditch and palisade, early motte-and-bailey design type thing as described by modern day scholars, but facts being facts it was designed by Guillaume le Bâtard five-hundred bloody years ago. And it worked. Didn't solve his hair loss and paranoia, but it did fortify his position in conquering London as a stronghold. On the night of Bacon's revelation that William was soon to visit the Tower, it had become a notorious and inexplicable labyrinth of stone laden chambers, ensconced with centuries of dark twisted energies born of the guilty, tortured, and condemned, alongside the protestations of the innocent, yet accused, not to mention the scores of souls belonging to long since beheaded political and religious martyrs. The Tower of London on the northern bank of the Thames River.

"What do they want with William?" asked Katherine.

"I swear, I cannot say," said Bacon.

"What did Sir James say?" asked William.

"Hide. Until he and your father get here. They're on their way," answered Bacon.

"Hide? That's it?" questioned Katherine.

"Hide," confirmed Bacon, "oh, and try not to harm anyone in a uniform."

"Sir James said that?" asked William.

"Oh, God no," said Bacon, "that was your father's addendum to my instructions. I understood his use of the word *try* as a verb in a political context, as in; he didn't say definitively *do not* harm anyone in uniform. Just that we would be better placed to try."

"Francis," said Katherine.

"Yes."

"Shut up. What has William done?"

"Nothing," answered Bacon.

"Then what the fuck?" asked William.

"I'm afraid I lack sufficient information to answer that at present," said Bacon, "but the better part of valour dictates that we hide. And swiftly."

Katherine looked to her right and more specifically directly into William's eyes. They shared a timeless accord, the undertones of which were compounded in a simple, yet magically childlike, mischievous; so be it.

2

A Fine Morning

6th November 1587

A blaze of vivid orange ripped through the darkness where the ocean swelled against the sky. It burned the linings of several purple clouds scattered randomly across the horizon. William was fixed. The image was truly breathtaking.

He allowed it to be so for a time.

Instinct ran a shiver through his bones. A story rippled through the picture; an ominous tale, littered with danger and folly, of bad winds and heavy swells, of furled sails and heaving timbers, of lashing rains and smothering mists, and all that done, the death-watch hiding in the calm that would surely follow.

The ship's bell rang softly, closing the distance of his imagination.

William looked upward from the painted warning in the east. The few remaining stars were diminishing to grains of nothingness, as the canopy of day rolled out beneath them.

It was time to slink quietly beneath the decks of the forecastle of the tall ship upon which he was standing.

If he was dutiful, kind, thoughtful, protective and compassionate, this fine morning might just bring William Hope relatively closer to Katherine.

Finally, after ten years, the morning sky had just told him so.

3

Two Good to be True

The Scarlett Buccaneer was, without doubt, the most handsome man in the world. The accolade was first bestowed upon him in the seventh month of his twenty-eighth year, and, though he had revelled in the attention at the time, it had taken several years for Scarlett to fully inhabit the appellation; to let the honour absorb him completely; to live up to it, as it were. From twenty-eight to thirty, Scarlett was just a little too self-conscious for the full extent of his attractiveness to be realised. Through his thirty-first and much of his thirty-second years, his ego thrust a little too often towards arrogance and this detracted from the full impact of his beauty. That said, the title of the world's most handsome man was not to be sniffed at, and, to his credit, Scarlett had taken the time to learn from his mistakes. He was now a wiser, more exquisite thirty-three, and the extent of his handsomeness was no longer a matter of subjective opinion.

Such is the nature of human rivalry; that other men in the world were often sought out as contenders. Marco Conturo of Florence was mentioned on occasion, as was Bradley Pittwater of Leamington Spa. Recently, Domingo del Monterna, from Madrid, was whispered to be in the same league, but, realistically, and even at their very best, they were nothing but pretenders by comparison. One only had to catch a glimpse of Scarlett on a rough day, when he climbed out of his bunk with bloodshot eyes, bed head hair, and stinking hangover in the first light of the morning and anyone would happily concede that his handsomeness was quite simply unparalleled by any other living male in the known world.

Scarlett was all man and perhaps a bit more. His pulchritudinous appeal began with an athletic six-foot frame – a good three inches taller than your average male – that rippled with perfection. A pack of eight proudly defined abdominal muscles supported the generous pectorals of his bronzed chest. His shoulders were broad, and his arms were strong. A wavy mane of thick, autumn blond hair fell down the full length of his sinewy neck, and all this was magnificent, but his face; his face was nothing short of mesmerising. His flawless nose was one thing; his full and wholesome mouth was another; the sharp cut of his chiselled jaw, stubbled to a light, optimal manliness, was yet another; and all were stunning enough, but each of these features paled into relative insignificance when compared to the mysterious depths of his piercing, aquamarine eyes.

To labour the point any longer would not serve to do him justice.

Though, actually, perhaps a modest embellishment may be forgiven, because good looks alone can only carry a man so far. So, the precise truth of the matter was that Scarlett was also, quite possibly, the most accomplished man of his time. The flamboyance with which he distributed his enormous wealth among those less fortunate than himself had made Scarlett the best known, and one of the most respected philanthropists of his generation. He was an outstanding and accomplished musician. At least twice a year performing his repertoire of piano concertos in aid of his charitable foundations, the proceeds of these benefit nights enhanced the lives of some two-thousand orphans across London. He was a well-respected playwright and had been commissioned for several of the Queen's soirées, including, on two occasions, the most prestigious in the Queen's calendar: The annual October Masque at Windsor. He was one of four consults to Her Majesty's government on economic policy. His specialty was 'Naval Expenditure and Racketeering'. It was a personal favourite of the Queen's policies, and by far the most lucrative enterprise contributing to the Realm's coffers. Scarlett's unmalleable and hands-on work ethic in this area had provided for a fair proportion of the Crown's wealth and he had long since been known to immerse himself in the Queen's cause with a vigour that was the envy of many a fellow 'entrepreneur'.

Were it many other times throughout the history of mankind, for often mankind has existed through ages of greater cynicism, the Scarlett Buccaneer might have been considered a man that was perhaps too good to be true. As it was, in this innocent age of daring and discovery, Scarlett was the stuff great fairy tales are made of, and everyone loved him for it...

Scarlett anchored his feet on the bunt of the yard on which he was standing, leaned his back firmly against the Royal Topgallant mast, stretched his hands above his head and breathed in two full lungs of the tropical morning air. His face relaxed as the comfort of a fresh thought reassured him. A proud but secret smile washed across his face.

His thought was, *Maiden Bride.*

He grabbed a cord of standing rigging, swung out two steps to port along the quarters of the yard and looked directly down to take her in. From his position, just about as high as he could climb on the foremost mast of his ship, some eighty feet above the main deck, he had a bird's eye view of her entire length. She was perfect. A full rigged galleon displacing some four-hundred tons with no expense spared in her construction. She was a hundred-and-forty feet along the keel and thirty-five feet at the beam. From prow to stern her gunwales were a rich cream in colour. From the forecastle to the abaft, her decks were a shimmering skin of deep red Jarrah timber. Her bowsprit extended thirty feet and supported three jib sails, all of which were neatly furled. Her foremast, mainmast, and mizzenmast, though made of pine, were stained to match her decks, as were the yards supporting the sails.

Sails that were presently all doused. His darling *Bride* was lying naked.

Scarlett frowned for a moment's concentration, as he did his best to remember; he had laid order leaving his ship lying ahull until the morning watch. It was a command that was not often necessary. He must have laid the order, or else it wouldn't have happened. Scarlett creased his brow a little deeper, punctuating a deeper moment of reflection. His brow remained remarkably attractive, even with the furrows.

She is bare from tip to toe, but why?

The night's weather had presented as rather unruly. The swells had been strong, and the winds had been shifting.

Just like any other night, I'll have it said.

His brow was crinkled to a thinking maxim and yet it simply wasn't doing it for him. Scarlett pursed his lips tightly and screwed up his face; it would still have been the most handsome face in the world, but no longer by a long shot.

Come on Scarlett, old boy, what went on?

Half a keg of port came to mind. Or rather, the empty half of a keg of port. The wine had been eagerly imbibed during last night's mess. The memory prompted a delicate burp from Scarlett. The wine had been enjoyed, from what he could now discern, and it was surely in part to blame for his nude ship, but still.

Nothing else of even remote consequence could be encouraged to aid a conclusion to Scarlett's musing, so he relaxed his face to its beauteous best, gave up on the mystery of his *Bride's* clothing, and cast a critical eye over her details. Not a blemish of mould was to be found on her rigging. Her shrouds and ratlines were stained white. Her forestays and backstays were tarred to watertight perfection. She was bejewelled in golden finery. Every hook and eye, turnbuckle, cleat, and fitting on board was solid brass and burnished to a coruscating brilliance.

She was elegant and flawless; preened and polished to perfection. A lady truly befitting of the most handsome man in the world.

Scarlett and *Maiden Bride* were equals.

The morning watch were appearing from their quarters directly below the foredeck. The steady stream of men appeared one by one, and each took a short stroll aft before gently mustering amid-ships on the main deck.

Scarlett raised another smile as he passed a moment in what he was certain would be the immediate future...

The Boatswain – a man Scarlett had known for most of his adult life – an accomplished and trusted old seadog by the name of Roger 'Paws' Prowse, would await a decent crowd before cracking one of his lesser gags. The men would laugh heartily, and a cheer would go up for old 'Paws', the new day, and for the Queen. The men would then begin to evaluate the measure of truth in 'Paws'' anecdote. An intense but healthy debate would accompany various revelations before discussions would break down. The men would no doubt settle squarely by inventing some ingenious new ways of slagging each other off in the *Bride's Banter*. That done, they would move promptly to the topic of each other's sisters. The first insult rallied upon another man's mother would summon a measure of reprisal from 'Paws', who would swiftly bring said offender into a line befitting a seaman of a Queen's commission. Thereupon the men would duly fall-in, albeit a little reluctantly at first, before casting their attentions eagerly towards the next of the morning's rituals...

The arrival of Master William Hope on the quarterdeck.

William would stumble out from his quarters, stand atop the stairs, and acknowledge the men with a gentle but firm nod of his head. He would walk purposely down the stair to the main deck, hold a single finger aloft and measure the consequence of the morning's breeze upon it, before turning and stepping promptly to the leeward side of the boat. Thereupon, he would about-turn and stand to attention.

All of which is exactly what happened.

4

Swashbuckle Hustle

Scarlett smiled warmly at the familiar sight of his First Mate standing to attention on the main deck, and raised his deep baritone voice to the wind, "Abew yer eyes me hearties, yer Captain's on the foremast!"

He waited for the full attention of his crew. He didn't have to wait long, so he continued, "Are ye lily-livered bilge rats, or gentlemen o' Fortune?"

His chosen vocabulary on this occasion was by no means his usual refined aristocratic English tongue, but this was not an occasion for refinement. "Ye cast no figure o' shape 'til I am amongst ye. Shall I be showin' ye how?"

A firm and familiar shout rang out with considerable gusto from the men below.

"AYE, AYE CAPPEN!"

With that Scarlett swan dived off the yard.

Twelve feet aft and perhaps fourteen feet lower his hands met with a backstay rope and the momentum of his body allowed him to perform a complete loop around the cord before he released his hands and flew out and on towards the mainmast. He landed squarely on the mid-quarters of the main top yard and steadied himself by gently and flamboyantly tickling the shroud ropes with his left hand. His right hand rested firmly on a coiled whip hanging decoratively from his hip.

Another huge cheer went up from the inhabitants on main deck. Scarlett allowed a dramatic pause. He filled it with a smile from ear to ear. His fabulous teeth outshone his snow-white silk shirt. A shirt that he wore unbuttoned from its collar to the red silk sash he wore around his waist. His breeches and boots were black. The breeze rippled through his clothing and waved through his hair. The Scarlett Buccaneer was at his handsome best and a classic portrait of an era was born.

Confident that enough time had passed to heighten the impact of his antics, Scarlett took off and trotted nimbly atop the yard. Whilst he pranced along the spar, he uncoiled his whip with a flick of his wrist and sent it lashing towards the footropes suspended beneath the lower yard on the mizzenmast, some thirty feet aft. When he reached the yardarm, he placed the heel of his whip in both hands and dived off. The whip snapped tight around its chosen footrope and Scarlett spiralled gracefully in a huge arc, out and around over the heads of his men and down towards the main deck. He landed squarely and surely, with just the right amount of *thump* on the boards and released his whip with another flick of his wrist.

William Hope was still standing stoically to attention.

Scarlett approached him purposefully. A beat of considered silence befell the entire vessel and all those aboard.

Scarlett coiled his whip as he spoke, "Master Hope, how fair thee well this morn?"

"Sadly lacking, Captain," William replied, "though naught that may not be rectified, with your permission."

"Permission granted, lad," Scarlett answered, without a moment's hesitation.

"My thanks, Sir," William put forth, before raising a closed fist politely to his mouth. Having done so he gave a modest belch, before he said, "A pardoned moment if you will."

"Duly granted," Scarlett said, with a firm nod in affirmation of the younger man's request.

William took three paces to the side of the ship, leaned his torso out over the gunwale and promptly threw the contents of his stomach overboard. It constituted much of the previous night's dinner and most of the other half of the keg of port he had shared with Scarlett.

A raucous cry of cheering was immediately drawn from the crew.

William straightened up and turned back towards the cluster of laughing bodies. He gave his mouth a firm wipe with a cotton handkerchief then received a cup of water from a young crewman named Richard Bately.

Boatswain Roger 'Paws' Prowse allowed a beat, before guiding the crew's uproar in a direction more to his liking, by throwing his deep Cornish tones into the mix. "A cheer aloft fer the Bride's Hope an' a fair day's sail abound. HIP YE!"

"HURRAH!" from the men in unison.

"Hip ye another fer the Queen of England."

"HURRAH!"

"Hip ye a last fer Cappen Scarlett an' the men ye 'ave become."

"HURRAH! HURRAH!"

As the men's enthusiastic voices carried off into the wind, Scarlett skipped a few steps aft and bounded onto the staircase that led up to the quarterdeck and helm. He stopped midway up the short flight and turned to face his men with his hands resting on the banisters. He waited for William to hand the empty cup back to Bately.

"Are ye quite cured, Master Hope?"

"Aye, aye Sir, you have my word."

"Your word and your courage, Sir?" Scarlett enquired.

"Aye Sir, and more if these good men will allow," William replied.

"What say ye to that, lads? Will ye aid Master Hope in a fair day's sail?" Scarlett asked.

"AYE, AYE CAPPEN!" the men sang enthusiastically.

"And Master Hope, have you rehearsed the day's advice for these good men, such that your..." Scarlett said, faking his momentary loss of words.

"Dream-state, Captain," said William, without hesitation.

"Dream-state, indeed, I'm thankful for the reminder," Scarlett replied, "which of these men are to be singled out, such that their lives matter today, and will be seeing tomorrow unharmed?"

The men of the morning watch stood still, in absolute silence, for this had become a tradition. Or a superstition. Either way, every man aboard had a story to tell about William's morning intuitions for saving their lives. And every one of them was listening.

Really listening.

Not the kinds of listening one does with good intention, patience, manners, or routine acceptance of command. This was, 'I'll-hang-by-the-rope, or, meet-Davy-Jones-this-day-if-I-don't', listening.

"Well, Captain," William said, looking directly around the apprehensive faces, "well, truth is, Captain, it's a tad foggy."

"Foggy, Master Hope? These men are depending on you for an answer. Come to, Sir," Scarlett said. He was frowning again. This was new. William always had an answer. A beat of anxiety thrust through Scarlett's breast.

"Yes, Captain, I apologise," said William.

"None of your sorry for me, Sir," Scarlett snapped, "an answer for the men, if you please."

William held a flush of embarrassment. And concern. Real concern. He quelled his panic and concentrated on the elements around him. Men's hearts, courage, devotion. Their fears. The ship. The smells. The ocean. The weather ahead. His captain. Last night's wine. Scarlett. An infusion of colours, resonating from way beyond the horizon. Beyond time.

"My advice, this day, Captain, is not for the men. It is for *you*," said William.

The entire crew gasped in a subdued unison. This had never happened. Old 'Paws' took a beat to interject, "Alright lads, steady your nerves now," was all he could summon.

All men looked to Scarlett, who was as surprised as any of them. But he was Scarlett. William was telling the truth, as always. He narrowed his eyes towards his First Mate, allowed his left eyebrow to raise marginally, and smiled, "I'll be havin' an answer to your nonsense, lad, for you have much to learn, but I'll be stowing it a while. More important remedies are upon us."

Scarlett knew only too well that what he was about to say next would come as another surprise to his men. And hopefully a considerable distraction, because, judging by the mood, it was well needed amongst his crew. He'd whip William later. Metaphorically. Though he hoped it wouldn't be necessary.

He looked around at the men's expectant faces, steady as they were on the main deck.

He had made this address many times, but somehow, he had never got it right. He had never really got it wrong either, but to date, he wasn't happy with his efforts. As with any orator of distinction, he had fastened several successful moments from past speeches in his head, and finessed his choice of vocabulary, his timing, and, most importantly, his intonation in his dressing room mirror. After a time, it had all come together, and he had watched his speech roll out perfectly from the rather flawless face in front of him. However, every time he came to say the words in public, his throat would become challenged by his emotions and his bloody words would never ring out the way he had intended. His all too merry soul was tipped with a bittersweet sadness and his audience only received a measure of the full value of his intentions.

That's why it was never quite right.

The expectant faces of the men were still staring at him. Of course they were.

Scarlett caught William's eye.

In an instant he was reminded why the *Bride's* sails had been stowed on the night watch; 'The Swashbuckle Hustle'. The idea had come to him well into the previous evening and, more importantly, well into the keg of wine; and, as such, it had seemed like a marvellous idea at the time.

The expectant faces of his men were by now more expectant than ever.

Well, if any man on earth could pull it off, that man was Scarlett. Thus reassured, he abandoned his traditional address, heightened his voice to his theatrical best and gave it a go; "Tell me this, lads, are we ever bound for home? What say ye?"

A stunned silence befell the men of the morning watch. A few looked towards their neighbours for an indication that they had heard correctly, but no indication came. Even 'Paws' let his jaw drop for a moment of surprised evaluation. All were aware that the captain's utterance was a combination of words that were never aired by a captain aboard his ship. Least not aloud, and at the very least, such words would never, ever, form a question from he to his men.

William wondered at Scarlett's choice. All that came to mind was that a large part of his mind wasn't working at all. The bit that was working was only wondering why he had swallowed half a bloody keg the night before. His head thus engaged; it must have been instinct only that drew William's attention away from his personal suffering and he cast his eyes over the length of the *Maiden Bride*. Two things were immediately apparent. Firstly, his eyes were not behaving the way he was expecting them to behave, and, secondly, he would never drink port again. He tried to clear his eyes by scrunching them tightly shut. When they opened again, they informed him that the ship was entirely de-rigged of sail.

Not entirely necessary, surely.

William looked back to his captain. Scarlett's eyes were bright and full and brighter still with mischief. It occurred to William that Scarlett had just tiptoed his way across the mast tops from fore to aft then swung down to the deck using his whip. He wondered if he and Scarlett had been drinking from the same keg. He knew they had, but he wondered it anyway.

Scarlett set his bright eyes smiling and addressed the crew again, "What ails ye lads? Have you no answer for your Captain?" His tone was theatrically provocative. He set his sights on the largest man in the company, "Mister O'Reilly, for sure you have a word to offer on the matter. Let it be shared."

Shamus O'Reilly, an able seaman born of good Irish fishing stock, had a mouth that was often more able than his might. And his might was mighty, for sure. What Shamus lacked as a punster; he made up for in volume. Except on this occasion. His startled expression was enough to say what his voice could not.

Scarlett continued, "You'll need be louder than that O'Reilly, she's a fair wind, but it lacks the strength to carry your tones."

The big man bowed his head rather sheepishly for fear he was beginning to blush.

Scarlett looked to another man, "What say ye John Prior? Are we ever bound for home?"

William twigged what Scarlett was up to.

John Prior was a lean and sinewy Cornishman who was about the age of forty and who was very much keener in his wit than in his personal appearance. He answered Scarlett's question with enthusiasm, "I'll hav' me belly on the capsan an' ole Paws cat upon me arse afore I'll be whistlin' to that tune Cap, so pardon me nerve."

Scarlett laughed at the man's reply.

Prior was relieved and further so when his shipmates accompanied the captain, though at best their laughter was below par in terms of their usual heartiness at Prior's aptitude for the *Bride's Banter.*

William Hope smiled at their collective reservation. He wondered if another man would be singled out as part of the set up.

Scarlett obliged accordingly. He addressed the perfect candidate, "Mister Bately, Sir, it falls to you. Can ye whistle a merrier tune than Mister Prior, for your Captain?"

This was Richard Bately's maiden voyage. Seven months in he had suffered his sixteenth birthday and as such was the youngest of the crew; a burden he had learnt to carry with considerable dignity for a boy of his age, though not without a measure of honest encouragement from his elders. Bately looked about the men beside him. His expression was not without its fair share of innocent hope. They were now over nine months under sail.

Not before time, he responded. His chosen retort was a less than miserable attempt at the first eight bars of the only tune he knew, 'The Blue Doubloon'. His pained whistling brought on bellows from those present, all of whom fell about laughing. His melody was more akin to 'Mary Had a Little Lamb' than anything else ever written. To his credit young Bately continued his dismal performance through the next eight bars before giving up to laughter himself. As the ruckus died down several of the crew landed healthy taps on the young musician's shoulders.

Scarlett addressed the blushing young man, "The Queen herself shall hear of your bravery Mister Bately, I'll see to it personally lad. Your Captain's request was a difficult one and I'm sorry for it."

Bately's suntanned little face lit up at Scarlett's words. Though embarrassed, he was clearly taking pride in the attention. It was cut unfortunately short when Shamus nearly broke his collarbone with a hearty 'Shamus sized' slap on the arm.

Scarlett rested back towards the stairs with his hands firmly grasping the banisters and looked up. The night's gloom was on the run and the sky was changing from grey to blue.

"Well, I'll be, but it's getting high-by-day and your Captain's no closer to an answer," Scarlett said, then faced his crew again. "Mister Prior, I'll fancy your punishment on the capstan will fall on the First Mate if he gives a wrong answer to the same question. What say ye to that?"

Prior was quick to answer, "If Master Hope offen's ye Sir, I'll cop a lashin' in his stead Sir, what an' ever he says. An' old Paws better be up fer it Cappen, or I'll be holla-pottin' him 'til he mends his course."

"Very well, Sir, and well delivered too," Scarlett said, "Mister Prowse, I'll have you heed the warning if you will. It may save ye a world of trouble after all."

'Paws' responded proudly, "There's no savin' me from Prior's troubles, Sir, but I'll have it stand accord."

William Hope looked directly at Scarlett. The captain was in his element.

"Then the duty falls to you, Master Hope," Scarlett maintained his provocative tone. "You ride upon the back of Mister Prior. Will *you* answer your Captain? Are we ever bound for home? And none of your murky advice if you please, we've had enough already."

William acknowledged Scarlett's question with the slightest of smiles, then pretended to make effort towards some serious contemplation. He feigned this state of apparent ponder until he felt the crew's sense of expectation weighing against him, then gracefully played his part, "Forgive me Captain, but I fear you asked me personally, if we were ever bound for home."

Scarlett fought hard to restrain the smile that strained his lips. William had never disappointed. He replied in earnest, "It is a right fear that bears upon you, Master Hope. I'll have an answer, Sir, and a prompt one at that," he glanced quickly to John Prior, "Mister Prior, you should pay particular respects," Scarlett said, whilst indicating William with a passing wave of his finger and a tip of his chin.

"It is my duty to press upon you, Sir, that words of bearing homeward before a captain's own recommendation may be considered rebellious aboard a ship governed by the laws of Her Majesty's Commission," William announced, efficiently.

"Rebellious, Master Hope?" Scarlett enquired incongruously.

"In the way of mutinous, Sir."

"You talk of mutiny aboard my ship, Sir?"

"As punishable by Treason, Sir."

"You talk of Treason aboard my ship, Sir?" questioned Scarlett.

"The worst kind of Treason."

"How long are we under sail, Master Hope?"

"Nine months, fourteen days, and three hours, Captain."

"I am gratefully reminded. A fair sail. Of what were we speaking last?" asked Scarlett, nonchalantly.

"Mutiny, Sir," William delivered.

"Mutiny, indeed. And afore that Master Hope?"

"Rebellion, Sir."

"Aboard my ship. I'm grateful. And afore that if you will?"

"The Captain asked if we were ever bound for home, Sir," William declared unapologetically.

"No such command has been passed aboard this vessel, is that correct Master Hope?" Scarlett enquired almost absently.

"Aye, Sir. The Captain has indeed not passed the mention," William confirmed.

"Then it's about bloody time he did," Scarlett boomed, "Master Hope, consider the order sealed!"

"Aye, Captain. And your question to the men?" William said, whilst fighting hard to check his smile.

"I'm twice grateful of the reminder," Scarlett said, fighting equally hard to remain straight faced. He looked quickly from William to the rest of the crew, and addressed them with gusto, "Tell me lads. Are. We. Ever. Bound. For. Home?"

"AAYYEE, AAYYEE CAPPEN!" the men shouted.

Scarlett was quick to follow up, "Very well. A double share to all men who see Portsmouth afore Christmas and London New Year's Day. What say ye to that?"

Scarlett had expected an abundance of enthusiasm from the men. Instead, he received absolute silence.

"Well, what ails ye, lads?" asked Scarlett, and to be fair it was a quick recovery.

A few heads were turned to adjacent fellows once more, because surely clarification was needed, but the majority turned towards John Prior who stepped forward a half pace. "Beggin' pardon' Capt', but... well, we knows it ain't a three-month sail from Portsmouth round to Greenwich, so I guess, me an' the boys is pointed to ask; whass it yer askin', Capt?"

"Oh, I see and hear, and you make a valid point, lads," said Scarlett. "No fault of yer own. Let me inform you, thus; Good Queen Liz has chosen to experiment with moving the New Year from March twenty-fifth, to January first, sort of in line with the progress of other nations on the continent of Europe."

"Well, she can't do that, can she?" said Jim Dolby.

"She feckin' well can," mumbled Martin 'Mumbles' No-Name.

"Nah, I'm not havin' it, New Year is New Year, it ain't bloody Christmas," from Dolby.

"Well, I'll be saying it don't matter when it is so long as we gets home safe like," said Ned 'Toes' Williams.

"Aye, but Capt's asking, so let's have a vote quick like," said Prior, "yer either a NewYearer for March or a NewNewYears-exiter, for Jan one."

"I'm in accord, dare I say it, with Prior," said 'Paws', "we need a show of hands."

Scarlett and William shared a glance that almost betrayed their inner smiles.

"NewYearers! Raise a han'", shouted 'Paws'.

A modest showing of hands, possibly a fifth of all number present.

"NewYexiters and a shorter safer sail!" hailed 'Paws'.

Another show of hands. Accounting for approximately three fifths. The remaining needed more time to think or couldn't count.

"Aye, thass it then, the NewYexiters hav' it, Capt," said 'Paws'.

Scarlett was quick to follow up again, "Very well. A double share to all men who see Portsmouth afore Christmas and London, New, New Year's Day. January first. What say ye to that, lads?"

"AYE, AYE CAPPEN!" came the shout again. Many of them began to clap each other on the shoulders or backs, "YAR! Homeward we be." A few men tossed hats in the air. Those without hats chucked handkerchiefs or rags.

"FOR ENGLAND, YAR!"

"I'll see me double share, Cappen!"

"Portsmouth ye beauty!"

"An' a drop o' 'Scrumpy Jack' Cappen, Yar!"

One man took it upon himself to throw a broom. It landed squarely on the head of another man standing some three feet aft. He was the only man to cease cheering.

Scarlett turned to 'Paws', "Your swiftest sail Mister Prowse, and bear my *Bride* for England."

"Aye, aye Captain," said 'Paws'.

"Set her flying lads!" Scarlett bellowed, and with that he skipped up the stairs and set a square step across the quarterdeck towards the helm.

'Paws' turned on the men, "All hands alive lads and swift about. Last lubber on the Royals'll have nine tales a tellin' on his back."

Scarlett's Hustle whirled around the *Maiden Bride* with a ferocious velocity. The sixty-two seamen of the morning watch scampered around the ship like rats fleeing a downpour. In an instant, the shrouds on every mast were cluttered with able bodies, all teaming effortlessly upward.

'Paws' began stalking round the main deck and roared instructions at the top of his voice, "Raise 'em parrels and unfurl 'em sheets to the clutches. Prior, shape yourself lad!! I'll have 'em jibs cutting the breeze afore the sun leaves that 'orizon. Bately! Raise 'em scurvy night dogs from their guns an' haul 'em in while they're still livin'. All hands, is *all hands*, you 'eard the Captain, set her flyin' lads."

William Hope studied the men's performance until the course sail rolled out on the mainmast. Scarlett was doing the same. The two men exchanged a knowing glance from their relative positions on the ship.

William smiled. Scarlett had never disappointed. Not once since they had met, or rather, fought, as it had happened – some eight years prior – over a woman. Actually, two women. Well, perhaps one woman and one girl...

'Paws' interjected a question into William's musing, "Master Hope, Sir?"

"Narrow on a starboard broad Mister Prowse, let's give her some room to breathe," William replied.

"Aye, aye Sir. She'll be gaspin' 'fore ye reach the wheel."

'Paws' stalked away towards the foredecks, with his mouth still pounding after the men, "O'Reilly!! Place yer best hands on the main brace, an' station 'em thass with ye on the bumkins. A full amm-wrist off larboard if you please."

William turned aft, stepped smartly up the staircase to the quarterdeck and joined Scarlett at the helm. The two men stood side by side watching the furious running of the crew. Huge swathes of canvas were unfurling one by one on every mast. The lower sails were already snapping and biting at the wind. Every rope and lanyard on the ship was being pulled and lashed and pulled some more by the men.

Scarlett had the ship's wheel firmly in his grasp and was turning it clockwise with a dead slow and measured purpose, as his instinct set the *Bride's* stern to windward.

"How'd you like the speech?" Scarlett enquired candidly.

"It was different," William replied honestly.

"That's all you have to say?"

"It was good."

"Good?" Scarlett asked, the tiniest measure of frustration apparent in his tone.

"Surely you're happy with it?" William said, briskly, before indicating the fury of bodies around the ship with a nod of his head, "Look at them."

"I am," Scarlett conceded.

"Have you set upon a name?" William asked.

"*The Swashbuckle Hustle,*" Scarlett said proudly.

"Mmm."

Scarlett smiled, "My thanks for playing along."

"More luck than wisdom. Could have gone horribly wrong," William remarked.

"For you; yes. For Scarlett; no."

William turned his head to face Scarlett, who was beaming his handsome smile at its widest. It was possibly the most satisfied expression William could ever remember seeing on the face of any man.

"I meant your stunt with the whip," William said flatly.

"Ah. It very nearly did. How's your head?" Scarlett enquired.

"A muddle."

"Mine also. The port was off, you think?"

"Very likely," William said, thoroughly amused, "I took no seawater this morning."

"That chunder was genuine?" questioned Scarlett.

"As is the taste in my mouth."

"Had I known, I would have landed sooner," Scarlett said, not without a measure of genuine concern.

William simply smiled. Scarlett relaxed.

A minute of silence passed between them. Both looked out over the ship's length and the activity still teaming around her. Such moments were always comfortable.

"The fuck was that display on advice?" Scarlett said, "I should have you whipped."

"I'll take it, if that's what you want them to see," said William, indicating the crew.

"I know you would," Scarlett said.

Another moment passed in the winds, tides, and faithful friendship.

"Every one of them will make it," said William.

"Pardon me?"

"It was murky. All hidden in the dark. I couldn't pick out a man."

Scarlett allowed William's comment to hang for a few seconds. "Except me?"

"Stow sail in the death-watch. Wait it out. It's a trap. That's all I've got for you," William stated.

Scarlett considered the possible implications.

"Will you make Portsmouth by Christmas?" asked William.

Scarlett recognised the change of tone in William's voice. It saddened him deeply. "You'll not with me to England?"

"I will wait in the isles."

"I have a month to better your decision, Will."

"I know," William replied.

The two sailors returned their attentions to *Maiden Bride*. As the last of her Skysails snapped open and swelled with air, the men of the morning watch began to sing. Many of the crew had bundled together in small groups at various points along the sides of the ship. The main course sail was on the turn. Tugs of war broke out; men-versus the ship's braces, as the other sails were hauled to match the direction of the main course. The heave-hoes on the ropes quickly settling into a shanty rhythm with their voices.

It was an awesome spectacle.

William glanced to his side. Scarlett was entranced, standing motionless, his chin raised just a little more proudly than normal. Scarlett was born for these moments.

William clocked himself; he was standing on the quarterdeck of the world's finest ship, beside perhaps the finest sailor in the world, alongside some of the finest crew ever to climb a rigging, watching them race to full sail over the warmth of the Caribbean Sea, and, at twenty-three years old, he was standing there as First Mate. He wondered if it was all real. If he was real. He decided that he had better be, or what would be the point. He was just about to wonder at the events that had led him to be there when Scarlett gave out a loud and rather undignified burp.

"Oohhh, pardon. Me belly's not good and me head's not helping. I'd better sleep 'til the fog lifts from me eyes Will, or we'll be heading for Cape Town. Will you mind her as your own?" Scarlett said.

William was in no small measure surprised at Scarlett's self-proclaimed deterioration. His outward appearance held just about everything of his usual vigour. "Aye, Captain, I'll be glad to," William replied, a little suspiciously.

"Aye, Captain your arse, just keep her flying for the morning," said Scarlett. He placed his hand quickly to his mouth. It was clearly a reflex in response to an impulse of nausea.

William smiled, "I can't say where we'll end up any more than you."

"We'll figure it between us when the lads stop singing," Scarlett said as he stepped aside to allow William to take the wheel.

"And Will." Scarlett said, as he placed one hand on William's shoulder and clutched his stomach with the other.

William pre-empted him, "There's a wealth of paperwork needs the captain's attention, now that we're heading home."

"My thanks," Scarlett said, as he tapped William's shoulder and turned aft towards the stern deck and his cabin. "Methinks I'm too old, or you're too greedy with the wine."

William caught the last of Scarlett's words as he disappeared behind a small, elaborately ornamented oak door, "I'll see you in England before I'm sober, I'm certain of it."

5

Let's Blow Some Shit Up

29th October 1577

Katherine picked up her emerald ring and William's necklace from the blue slate floor of their chalked charm circle and followed Bacon and her brother down the spiral stairs from roof to the ground floor and a hallway adjacent to the Great Parlour. Cake was the first order of business. The three youngsters sprinted north along a loggia that formed the eastern side of the Fountain Court, before dog-legging west into the striking luxury of the North Parlour, with its two-storey oak beamed ceiling, polished multi-coloured parquet wood floor, walls panelled in oak wainscotting and a generous bay window facing south with lead-glass stained with numerous coats-of-arms. A long oak table ran east to west, adjacent to a stone fireplace in the centre of the north wall. A quintet of musicians was setting up in the northeastern corner. Mildred Cecil and two female servants were clearly in the process of placing the final touches on a huge spread of breads, meats, cheeses, fruits, nuts, and sundry food stuffs as part of a banquet, but that wasn't what caught the children's eyes first. It was a huge three-tiered birthday cake covered in blue and white icing sugars. That and the half dozen gift-wrapped boxes sitting proudly at the western end of the table.

"Out! All of you, out!" cried Mildred, who was dressed in a striking gold dress with a modest sized hooped skirt that puffed its way to the floor, "Your father's not home yet, and we're not ready. I told you I'd send for you."

"But mother, something terrible has happened..." began Katherine.

"I'm certain it hasn't happened to you as you are standing before me. Now out!" said Mildred, "You may express your concerns when your father arrives."

"Mother, please. You must listen..." implored Katherine.

"So help me, if you don't disappear post-haste...." said Mildred. She didn't have to finish her sentence.

"Come on," said William, grabbing both Katherine and Bacon's wrists and spinning them around facing the door through which they had entered, "Katherine we need a plan. Francis, my gut's telling me we need distractions."

They passed through the door, took a right turn, and entered the eastern loggia of the Fountain Court once again. Outside, ground staff were lighting flambeaus all around the square which was some sixty yards long to a side. It was hellishly pretty in the evening's fading sunlight.

"Cellars. Underneath Robert's lodgings," said Bacon, referring to Lord and Lady Cecil's first-born son. Katherine and William's brother. The lad was fourteen, super smart, yet small in stature, and generally overly modest socially, as the poor bugger had been inflicted with a rather unprepossessing twist in his spine at birth. It wasn't easy for him living in the higher echelons of a society that favored physical beauty above virtuous traits of character such as empathy, intelligence, wit, political acumen, or even just plain and simple kindness of heart.

"You sure?" questioned William, "Thought they moved all that stuff to the crypts under the chapel and chaplain's chambers."

"Try spinning around and saying that three times quickly," said Katherine.

"What?" from William and Bacon in unison.

"Chapel and chaplain's chambers," answered Katherine.

William and Bacon shared a look of mutual bewilderment. William was first to snap out of it, "Katherine, spinning around and speaking tosh should not be part of our plan."

"Sorry. Alliteration. I found it frightfully funny," said Katherine.

"Not funny," from William and Bacon in unison.

"Given present circumstance, time restrictions, and overwhelming numbers of foes," continued Bacon, "we can't let them take William, before Sir James and your father arrive."

"How many guards are there?" questioned Katherine.

"Two per coach. Twenty cavalry. One captain," said Bacon. "Twenty-seven."

"Holy shit," said Katherine.

"I like those odds," said William, "given our home advantage."

"I wouldn't bet on them odds," said Bacon.

"You'd bet on anything," said Katherine, "it's why you always lose."

"Not always," said Bacon.

"We're wasting time, said William, "they'll spread out if they can't find me. Francis, we need diversions."

"Multiple pyrotechnia," stated Bacon.

"Beg pardon," said Katherine and William in unison.

"Fire in alchemy," stated Bacon, as if it was obvious.

William and Katherine stared blankly at their slightly elder, eccentric cousin.

"Let's blow some shit up. How's that?" said Bacon.

"Perfect," said William.

"Right then, see you in a few," said Bacon. He took off running south along the loggia, turned left into the Great Parlour, which was a large room two floors high, with oak wainscoting on the walls, a large bay window overlooking the centre of the southern formal gardens, affectionately pronounced by Cecil to be the Great Garden, and why not, he had designed and paid for it. Bacon didn't care for any of the architectural finishings in the hall. He dashed east, passed by an elaborately carved eight-foot-tall blue marble fireplace, pulled open a heavy oak door, bounded down a flight of stairs adjacent to the newly refurbished chapel and entered a sixty-yard-long crypt beneath the southern range of the buildings surrounding the Middle Court of the house. The first fifteen feet of it was an impressive wine cellar, with elaborately carved racks supporting hundreds of bottles of fine wines, champagnes, brandies, whiskeys, and gins. As he walked forward, Bacon's lantern cast wavering shadows between the multitude of red brick columns supporting an intricate arrangement of groin vaulted brick ceilings. The space was crammed full of building materials; various softwood and hardwood timber, plaster mouldings, sacks of sand and crushed limestone, blue slate tiles, black and white marble tiles, glazed terracotta tiles. Shit the builders didn't want to get wet and mouldy in the outdoor elements.

Bacon made his way east until he happened on several crates that he found very much to his liking. It occurred to him that the evening would be a great deal of fun, win or lose.

*****

Twenty-five-year-old Thomas Wilson was something of a jack-of-all-trades on the estate; gardener, carpenter, animal handler, sometimes barkeep, acting steward on occasion, really whatever was needed of him on any given day or week of the year. Recently married, he and his wife had moved into the southernmost of the two porter's lodges spanning the grand main entrance to the sprawling house. It was a temporary move, but a welcome one. Their soon to be permanent accommodations were still being constructed as part of an extensive servant's quarters located to the north of the main house, surrounding a vast vegetable garden and fruit tree orchard.

Thomas had seen the three carriages and company of armed Royal cavalry guards rolling up as soon as they had passed through the unfinished gateway arch at the east end of what was known as the Dial Court. Young Mrs. Wilson had freaked out somewhat, but Thomas had placed her unusual display of errant emotions down to changes in her blood caused by her recently getting pregnant with their first child. He'd calmed her down with a cup of hot tea and left her be, sitting on the couch with a blanket over her knees.

Thomas closed the front door of the lodge behind him and stepped out ten paces as the line of three carriages pulled up to a stop. He recognised Captain Tarquin Smedley-Smythe-Smythings immediately. Thomas was good with faces, names, and titles. Had to be in his line of work. And who could forget as fucking stupidly pretentious a name as Tarquin Smedley-Smythe-Smythings.

Poor bastard. Imagine living with that. Hope he finds a posh wife with no brains.

"Good evening to you, Captain," said Thomas, politely doffing his cap. He chose to say no more in the moment.

"Captain Smedley-Smythe-Smythings. Queen's Body Guard of the Yeomen of the Guard. We are here on Her Majesty's command. We seek Sir William Cecil's son. The boy named William. We have it on sound authority that he is presently at residence herein."

"Righty oh then. No messin' aroun' with pleasantries," said Thomas, in his usual salt of the earth Devon accent.

Smythe-Smythings slipped his feet from the stirrups and swung down from Raine's back. He landed on the gravel with a firm crunch under his boots. He approached Thomas while slipping off his right-hand glove, "Apologies for my brusque manner, Mister Wilson."

Smythe-Smythings held out his hand. Something was off, but Thomas shook the captain's hand anyway.

"All good, Captain. I'm sure your duties are pressin' hard on your mind."

"Indeed," said the captain, before lowering his voice, "I don't relish my present assignment in the slightest."

"You're 'ere fer young William?" questioned Thomas.

"I am. He is to be detained at Her Majesty's pleasure," said Smythings.

"Tower ain't what I'd call a pleasure, Captain. If I may be so bold," said Thomas, "I assume thass where yer takin' the lad."

"I am not authorised to confirm that information," said Smythings.

"You expectin' him to run or somethin'? What's with the dogs?" asked Thomas. He was referring to a dozen blood hounds tied to the rear of the third carriage. He hadn't noticed them from the window of his lodgings when the guards had crossed the extensive Dial Court.

"Queen's orders merit a degree of overkill in terms of caution," said Smythings.

"Does it now? Well, I wouldn't know a tit from a blackbird about your job, Captain. But I can tell you it's William's birthday today. There's a bit of a shindig goin' on this evenin' fer him and his twin sister, Katherine," said Thomas, "I don't suppose you can come back for him to-morrow?"

"Nice try, Mister Wilson."

"Lady Burghley is gonna be rightly pissed if you set about snatchin' up one of her kids. You know that don't you?" remarked Thomas.

"I don't wish to cause Lady Burghley any upset. Regretfully my orders came from Queen Elizabeth directly."

"Is Lord Burghley aware of your assignment, as you call it?"

"Honestly, Mister Wilson, I don't know if he is or not."

"Well, this is all a tad unfortunate, innit?" said Thomas, "How you figure on proceedin', Captain?"

"I'm not entirely sure, Mister Wilson. Perhaps I could leave my men here and accompany you into the house. I would seek an audience with Lady Burghley to relay my orders directly."

"Yep. That would work, I guess. Best follow me," said Thomas.

Smedley-Smythe-Smythings issued brief instructions to his men to stay put and at the ready. He joined Thomas and the two men passed through the main entrance archway and entered the eastern most loggia of the Middle Court.

*****

William and Katherine watched Thomas disappear through the main entrance with what they rightly understood to be the captain of the Queen's Body Guards. They were standing four floors up on the blue slate rooftop of the northeastern most tower of the estate. Behind them to the north were the servant's quarters, vegetable gardens, stables, and grain stores, as well as a multitude of building materials, timber and iron scaffolding, and piles of mulch, and gravel.

"Bet they're going to see mother," said Katherine.

"Uh huh. She going to freak," said William.

"What now? We need to get you out of here," said Katherine.

"And go where?" questioned William, "With what? I'll need money. A horse..."

"I need to get out of this dress."

"Why?"

"Because I can't move in the damn thing," said Katherine, "and as I'm coming with you, I'll need to be free."

"You're not coming with me," protested William.

"My dungarees. Shirts. Coats. Boots. Our chambers. Let's go before the guards start spreading out," said Katherine. She was already crossing the rooftop to the doorway. She ran down the spiral staircase to the first floor and trotted west along a corridor on the north range with a dozen windows overlooking the Middle Court. She stopped outside William's chambers, "Grab what you need from your rooms. Meet me at mine. Don't fecking dally."

"I don't need anything from there," said William, "let's sort you out."

"You are bloody impossible," said Katherine, before spinning on her heels and dashing further west passing through the middle tower and arriving at her own spacious lodging which was in the northwest tower of the Middle Court, which was to be shared as the northeast corner of the Fountain Court when the ongoing renovations and construction was completed.

Katherine entered her anteroom and bolted through to her bedroom with its antique mahogany furniture, four-poster Queen-sized bed, plush cushions, silk shades and curtains. She continued and dog-legged into her dressing room. William was following but stopped at the threshold of her private space.

"Get in here," said Katherine, "help me out of this bloody clothing."

William entered. Katherine turned her back.

"What do I do?" asked William.

"Untie every tie, bow, and frigging knot you see. Quickly."

William started pulling on bow tied cords, and loosening every rope looking tie he could see. The dress slipped off Katherine's shoulders in fifteen seconds.

"What the fuck is this shit?" asked William, referring to the whalebone lined silk undergarment suffocating Katherine's torso.

"The thing squishing my boobs up to where you like them. Just rip at the cordage. And hurry up."

William did so and half a minute later the full length of Katherine's slender back was revealed from the nape of her neck to her buttocks. Katherine breathed deeply and pinned the loose garment to her chest with her hands before she turned around to face her brother.

"Make sure nobody is coming," said Katherine. It was more a diversion for modesty's sake than a genuine concern.

William got the message. He turned and walked through the doorway into Katherine's bedroom, "I haven't heard mother screaming yet."

Katherine set about dressing in practical clothing; familiar, comfortable, warm dungarees, undershirt, woollen jumper, leather waistcoat, and leather ankle high boots.

William was racing through options in his mind. There was no way he was going to the Tower. Whatever the fuck aunty Liz was up to was beyond his grasp.

Fucking Treason! What on earth is the old girl up to? Has she cracked up? Fallen out with father or something. Politics? Religion? Frigging witchcraft? Locking me up as leverage or the like. Why didn't she summon for Robert? He's first-born. Why is it me? I get why she didn't want to lock up Katherine. She's a girl. Liz's favourite... Ah, fuck this, we need a plan. Think, William. What would Sir James do? Weigh up variables or some shit. Counter. The guards can only arrest me if they know what I look like, right? Or someone points me out. Father's probably on the way home. Need to buy time.

Fireworks diversion? Good. Horse? Easy; Stables. But that's the first place I'd send guards to lock down if I was a captain. Misdirection then. They don't know what I look like... Oh, bollocks, the captain might. Smedley-Smyth-some-stupid-name. He's been here lots before. Avoid that fucker for sure. Misdirection then. What has father gotten himself into? I haven't done anything wrong. Not frigging Treasonable anyway. Ah, there it is... Counter random variables by thought experiments in the improbable... Thank you, Sir James. See, I have been listening occasionally. Hallelujah. That'll do for a start.

"Katherine, are you done? We need to go," said William firmly.

Katherine appeared in the doorway to her dressing room, "Where are we going?"

"The chaplain's chambers. Then we catch up with Francis," said William, before quickstepping across the bedroom, throwing open the door and sprinting east along the corridor through which they had arrived. Katherine slung the strap of a small leather bag over her shoulder and darted after William, who made a quick stop at his lodging to grab a knee-length dark-brown sheepskin lined leather coat, a dagger, and three handheld Y-shaped catapults with rubber bands attached to the prongs. He tossed one of them to Katherine and tucked the dagger and his catapult into the waistband of his breeches. That done, they bolted on to the east once again, hit the end of the corridor and turned right into a room known as the Painted Gallery. One of their father's many eccentricities within the house, it was one-hundred-and-nine feet in length and twelve feet wide with two stone fireplaces and numerous windows on both sides of the room opening onto balconies that overlooked the main entrance and Dial Court to the east, and the Middle Court to the west. The walls were decorated to satisfy Cecil's passions for heraldry, geography, and horticulture. Intricate depictions of all the kingdom of England's cities, towns and villages, counties, mountains, and rivers were intermingled with fifty-two trees representing the counties of the Realm. The branches were adorned with paintings of coats-of-arms and armourial bearings of every family of lords, knights, barons, earls, and nobles that owned significant lands and properties.

William and Katherine didn't hate the room, but they had grown up with its ever-changing, mind-numbing yawn of historical depictions, and given their present priority to avoid capture, they ran the length of the room in less than five seconds, before jumping down a wooden staircase to the ground floor. They swung around a doorway to the right and headed west along the southern range of the Middle Court. They passed through a utility room where William grabbed two oil lanterns and handed one to Katherine. He lit them both with a flint and taper and the twins entered their father's wardrobe of formal gowns and wears. They stopped at an oak door on the west wall and William knocked. He waited a beat and knocked again.

"Don't you think it a bit odd that no one is around?" said Katherine.

"The staff will be in the kitchens or wherever, catching a bite and a pint before mother's party. Anyway, who cares?" said William, as he pushed the door open. They stepped inside the adjacent room which was officially the chaplain's chamber. Shelves packed with parchment scrolls of scripture and historical religious crap were intermingled with countless books of mostly pious, philosophical, sociopolitical, and theosophical natures.

William stepped up to a large louvre door painted with an ornate golden chalice-looking-cup and slid the screen back to its full extent revealing a considerable walk-in closet harbouring long racks of the chaplain's vestments and liturgical dress; multitudes of gaudy cassocks, chimeres, copes, rochets, stoles, maniples, chasubles, amices and cinctures as well as dozens of white surplices and shelves of lurid pointy hats, fancy ruffs and priest's collars.

"What the fuck are you doing?" questioned Katherine, her elevated whisper pitched in a compressed scale of concern, "We should be heading to the bloody stables. As in, right now."

William settled on the end of one of the racks and what he'd been looking for. A priest's informal outer wear as protection from the English winter elements. A dozen waxed wool and cotton habits, four of them grey, four dark brown and four dark green in colour.

"Grey, green, or brown?" asked William.

"What are you talking about?"

"Green. It will go with your eyes," whispered William as he grabbed the appropriate garment from its hangar and tossed it to Katherine. "Put this on."

"I don't understand," said Katherine.

"Misdirection. Trust me. Put it on," urged William, as he took down a second green habit, threaded his arms into the wide sleeves and began to fasten the wooden toggles into leather hoops that extended down the front of the robe.

Katherine was at a loss, shaking her head, before she reluctantly donned her robe. "You want to tell me what the fuck?" said Katherine.

"Told you, misdirection," said William, "Francis will need one, too."

William grabbed a third green habit from the rack and pushed past Katherine, entering the chaplain's chamber proper once again. He approached a substantial outer door which was solid oak pinned with iron studs, unclicked the iron latch, and pushed it slightly ajar. The sun was three quarters below the horizon and the twilight hour was upon them. He pressed his left cheek to the door jamb and looked out into the Middle Court of the house. Two grounds men were raking leaves from the pathways lining the west and north ranges.

"William, please tell me what we are doing," implored Katherine.

"I will. Just wait," said William, pulling the door closer to the door jamb, leaving no more than a slight crack for his right eye. Thomas Wilson and Captain Smyth-Something-or-other were exiting the central arch of the loggia on the west side of the courtyard. They passed between two black and white marble fountains that were attached to the columns supporting the arch and continued walking east down the central pathway of the open space.

"The captain must have spoken to mother. He's returning to his men," said William, "I'm betting the game is on. They'll all be looking for me now."

"Mother wouldn't have given you up," said Katherine.

"I know. She'll have played ignorant, until father comes home."

"I agree," said Katherine, "this is serious."

"First place they'll post is the stables, barns, and outhouses. The captain and maybe four or five will search the house."

"You think mother will give them permission," said Katherine.

"Probably. She now knows what we were upset about earlier, that's for sure. And she knows I'm not going to get caught too easily," said William.

"And she won't obstruct justice," remarked Katherine. "That would be another headache for father when he gets here. He is coming, isn't he?"

"Francis said he was. And Sir James," said William, as he slowly pushed the door wider on its right-hand hinges. Pressing his right cheek against the open door, he saw the captain and Thomas exit the Middle Court.

"Pull your hood up," said William, exiting and holding the door for Katherine before closing it quietly. They proceeded calmly west for thirty yards. The grounds staff ignored them entirely. William arrived at the substantial arched double oak doors to the chapel, unclicked a solid iron latch and pushed the right wing open. He and Katherine slipped quietly inside and closed the door. The interior was relatively plain. Two-storey stone columns and walls, heavy oak beams supporting a vaulted roof, slate floor with two rows of pews on either side of a central isle leading to a stone altar. The stained-glass windows were relatively modest by religious fashions of the time. William and Katherine had seen the chapel more times than they cared to remember and headed directly to a wooden staircase that descended into the wine cellar and vaulted crypts beneath the southern range.

"Francis," called William.

Nothing.

"Francis, you in here?" called out Katherine.

They proceeded east, sidestepping building materials strewn about around the floor. They arrived at dozens of pinewood crates neatly stacked in two rows leaving a central access space. They were stamped on each yard square side with the moniker, 'Peril. Volatile Powders'.

"He must be outside," said William.

"Err, no. He was, but now the fire master has returned for round two," said Bacon, appearing from the shadows of the crypt's southeastern corner, "Great Garden's going to be a blast, I should think."

Katherine smiled. William tossed Bacon a green habit, "Put this on."

"Ah, misdirection. Good thinking, Katie," said Bacon, as he caught the robe and started slipping his arms into the sleeves.

William glanced at Katherine, and they smiled briefly.

"You might need this also," said William, tossing a catapult to Bacon, expecting him to simply catch it. He didn't. The weapon hit him in the chest and dropped to the floor.

"It is not I that am your enemy, cousin," said Bacon.

"Just... it might come in handy," said William.

"Good idea, Katie," said Bacon, as he placed his lantern on the floor and picked up the slingshot device. He stepped forward while toggling up his habit. His face and hands were soiled with mud and grey streaks of what was surely gunpowder.

"Took the tunnels. Safer. I couldn't figure how to appear in the Dial Court with all those guards lingering out front. We need to spook their horses," said Bacon.

They'll be spreading out about now, mostly on foot," said William.

"We think the captain of the guard has had an audience with mother," said Katherine.

"She can't afford to obstruct him in his duties. Headache for your father," said Bacon.

"So, what now?" asked William.

"Help me load up some more of these bangers and fuses," said Bacon, "bundle anything that looks like a tubed firework or a spool of waxed fuse. There are hundreds of them."

"Alright," said Katherine.

"And pick the big ones," said Bacon with a smile.

The three children grabbed hessian sacks from the building materials and started filling them with all sorts of items related to and containing gunpowder.

A dim light appeared at the west end of the crypt, at the foot of the stairs to the wine cellar. It was accompanied by a baritone voice, "You there. Queen's Guards. Lower your wares and present yourselves."

"Fuck," said William and Katherine in unison.

"Run," said Bacon, as he took off towards the south-eastern corner, dragging his sack of explosives. He stopped at a small opening in the brick wall, allowing Katherine and William to pass by him. Bacon yanked an iron lever disguised to look like a simple lantern mounting. A section of the brick wall began to slide, closing the opening. He stepped through and waited. He could hear two sets of footsteps marching up the centre of the crypt.

"Present yourselves freely for the Queen's Yeomen, I say," came the baritone voice once again. The wall/door clunked shut with a 'thud-phissst' and the footsteps and pompous military bullshit could no longer be heard.

Bacon was quick to catch up with his cousins, who were scurrying along a low-ceilinged, wooden-framed tunnel which was about four feet to a side with a solid red clay floor. This was not their first time scampering around the hidden tunnels and passages of Theobalds. Games of 'hide and go seek' in their home had always been a dead fucking loss. No fun at all at parties. It could take the seeking 'It' boys or girls half a bloody day to find even one of the mischievous munchkins engaged in hiding. And guaranteed nobody had stuck around close enough to ever have heard the immortal line 'Ready or not, here I come!'

After a few minutes the three youngsters skipped up a short flight of stone stairs rising to a small square landing.

Bacon remained on the top step of the staircase as the haven was a tight squeeze for three.

"What now?" asked Katherine.

Bacon and William shared a look of concern. Clearly, they were winging it. Katherine listened to the vibrations emanating from her brother and cousin. Two different keys. Bacon, perhaps a C-major, ascending scales in his breathing, with the tempo of his being beating a crazy rate per minute. Perhaps one-hundred-and-sixty, hard to tell.

"What do you think Will?" asked Bacon.

"Spooking the guard's horses is a good idea. How do we pull that off?"

"From where, you mean," said Bacon.

"Yes. Exactly. Must be the roofs. If we present in the open of the Dial Court, we'll be chased down in a minute," said William.

As for William, his texture was impossible to discern. Perhaps a minor, but Katherine couldn't define the key in which he was existing, he was so crammed with chromatic complications. As often there were two competing recitals within him, straining for dominance, yet the tempo of his being was scarcely thirty beats per minute; a cadence of calm, that quite honestly was on the wrong side of fecking scary. Not frightening. But not what one would expect, given the extenuating circumstances.

"Maybe we should just run away. We could row the canal. Disappear in the forests to the south," said Katherine.

"They have dogs. We won't last half an hour on foot," said William.

"Oh, yes. Bollocks," said Katherine.

"Step aside children," said Bacon, passing between the twins and yanking an iron lever. The roof of the landing sprang upwards. Bacon slung his canvas sack over his left shoulder and grabbed the fourth rung of a six rung hardwood ladder, planted his feet, and stepped up. He stuck his head out into the evening's dimming light and looked around, "I think we're good. Come on," said Bacon, launching himself out in to the open. Katherine and William followed, departing the tunnel, and crouching down beside Bacon, who immediately pushed the trap door shut. It was masked in green foliage and moss. If you didn't know about it, there was no way it could be found.

They were in the very centre of the Great Garden, adjacent to a monumental four-tiered white marble fountain with a sculpture of some old geezer looking down on everything around him. And that something was considerable. Nine individual knots, or formal gardens, were arranged in squares, each seventy yards in length to a side and lined at the perimeter with thorn hedges interplanted with elm, sycamore, lime, apple, pear, and cherry trees. They were separated by three wide crushed gravel pathways and one central canal which bisected the entire garden. In total, the space was some seven acres, walled at the outer boundary.

William, Katherine, and Bacon scanned different, but overlapping arcs of view in silence. Three grounds staff were in the process of lighting flambeaus spaced along the pathways. The closest man was a hundred yards away and heading west, making his way towards a banqueting house. Another was in between an ornate wooden pergola and a goodly sized sundial made of alabaster. It wasn't the only garden in the estate. Cecil had designed a whoppingly intricate maze in his sleep, several years prior, and it was fast growing to be nigh on impossible to fathom. He was in the process of adding three more gardens, which he had dubbed the Privy, Laundrie, and Pheasant. Good to know but not what Bacon was focused on; two men in red and gold knee length coats, black hats, riding-boots, and swords dangling from scabbards on their hips were approaching from some eighty yards away. They were checking the row-boats moored along the sides of the canal.

"Oh, dash and bother," said Bacon, "thought we might have had more time."

William and Katherine were quick to focus upon the armed gentlemen pertaining to Bacon's warning.

"Katherine. You and I should walk calmly back towards the house," said William. "We're dressed as priests. Those guards won't trouble us."

"Are you fucking crazy?" questioned Katherine.

"The dogs won't be in the house. We can hide until father arrives. And we should try to see mother," said William.

"Shit... Yes. I suppose so," said Katherine, reluctantly.

"I'm going east," said Bacon, "I'll hit up the stables and unleash the animals."

"They are four-hundred frigging yards away," said Katherine, "you won't make it."

"They are not looking for me, are they? I'm not the one who committed Treason," said Bacon, with a wry smile.

"Oh, fuck you, Francis," said William.

"And I'm dressed as a priest," said Bacon. "My considerable and most honourable virtues shall be made fully apparent to any passing guards. Then I'll blow some more shit up to the heavens."

"What have you blown up so far? I don't see anything," said Katherine.

"Allow me to ameliorate that particular circumstance," said Bacon. He withdrew a flint lighter and waxed taper from the pocket of his breeches, stepped away to the north edge of the garden knot and stooped beside the thorn hedging. Three strikes on the flint and a flame appeared. Seconds later, three separate sparkling trails were running away along fuses lining pathways to the east, west and north towards the main house.

6

Bugger be. It's no Ghost

7th November 1587

William enjoyed a moment of gentle reflection upon Scarlett's nauseous departure from the *Maiden Bride's* helm. He turned, casting his attention over the full length of the ship. All sails were aloft, and she was beginning to ride, cutting chase through the ocean. The spirited melody of the crew flayed around her decks and sounded out between her swathes of canvas sheets. Fluctuations in the wind dictated a sporadic volume to the piece.

William set his hands on the spokes of the sturdy mahogany wheel beside him and span it a turn and a half to starboard. The *Bride* responded with a small but gracious bow across her keel. Her masts began to tip a few degrees, as cloths captured more of the wind streaming across her from the stern. Her larboard gunwale rose by a foot, and she steadied herself.

The sun was stretching clear of the horizon. The ship's bowsprit was dissecting it with each crest and trough of water that swept underneath her keel. William waited for his ponderous head to draw conclusion. By his reckoning he was heading...

North, East, the sun rises in the... West, East. East, it must be.

He was by no means confident. He glanced around neatly then surreptitiously checked the ship's compass for confirmation. East it was.

William relaxed his grip on the wheel. It was enough to stay the ship's course with one hand, so he did. He thought about hailing 'Paws' and telling him to tighten the lifts on the main course yard, but his hangover was persuading him that lethargy might just be the better part of recovery. 'Paws' would not be long in setting it to rights, in any case.

Another hearty chorus from the crew drifted to him on the wind. The song weaved through William's thoughts for a time then diminished as his mind strayed from the Caribbean colours of his present to the English greys of his past...

Katherine...
"You are bloody impossible,"
Spinning on her heels and dashing away.
Further and further. Always further.
She's running west passing through the middle tower.
Lanterns. Flambeaus.

Darkness. Children running scared. Excited.
Katherine's four-poster Queen-sized bed.
The Queen. So called Treason. Fuck.
Plush cushions, silk shades and curtains. Katherine.
"Get in here. Help me out of this bloody clothing."
Katherine turning...
"What do I do?" Fuck me, I was a twat.
"Untie every tie, bow, and frigging knot you see. Quickly."
Pulling on bow tied cord. Loosening every rope looking tie. The dress slipping off Katherine's shoulders after fifteen beautiful hours.
"What the fuck is this shit?" A whalebone lined silk undergarment suffocating Katherine's torso you twat-child idiot.
"The thing squishing my boobs up to where you like them. Just rip at the cordage. And hurry up."
Katherine's slender back. Naked from the nape of her neck to her buttocks.
Katherine's breath. Whispering.
"Make sure nobody is coming,"
Katherine...

"Master Hope, Sir. Master William. Will, are ye bound to the ship or to the spirits?" William was suddenly surrounded by the quarterdeck of the *Maiden Bride*.

Roger Prowse was bearing down on him. "Will! Are ye with me lad?" 'Paws' enquired, in a punishing tone loaded with impatience. He placed one of his enormous hands under William's elbow and continued in a whisper, "The men have sight of ye, Will."

It was true.

The entire ship's company, though spread around their stations on the ship, were staring straight at him.

William suddenly realised that his face was consumed by a smile. And not a something-funny-just-happened kind of smile, but one of those gormless grins one might rightly, or wrongly, associate with an individual deemed to be intellectually challenged.

I'm smiling at the men. All of them... Oh, bloody hell!

William instinctively soured the stupid expression on his face and raised his arm aloft firmly. Having done so, he thought he had better be just as quick to do something equally command-like, so he rallied his thoughts smartly and addressed the men in full voice, "Right lads," he began, "it seems we have a situation." It wasn't a bad effort given the circumstance. Thus encouraged, he continued, "Skeletons on the rigging, four men on the crows, the rest of you on the main deck, and fall in sharply lads."

It was enough. Those men who were not engaged in ready activity began to slip down the rigging and muster on the main deck. William turned to Roger Prowse.

"Are ye back on board, Will?" 'Paws' asked gently.

"Aye Roger, though I'm sluggish with the wine and sorry for it."

"Well, ye 'ave yer chance fer amends," 'Paws' answered, "there's a squall the size I've ne'er know'd on that horizon, and you' been steerin' the *Bride* straigh' fer it since ye been asleep."

"It's certain?" William replied.

"As sure as ye're a drunkard, William," 'Paws' said, "the lads is havin' a piss hard time keepin' sails up with that wheel in yer han's and wanna know whass on yer mind. As the fuck do I, if you'll pardon me frank tone."

William was back on board and understood. He was getting used to episodes like this. Didn't understand it, but the older he grew, the instances grew with him.

"Katherine," William replied.

"What in blazin' barnacles is Katherine?" asked 'Paws', totally at a loss. And being lost at sea was far from his favourite pastime.

"Shit," William responded quietly, "the Captain's at his papers."

"Aye, same as ye're at the wheel. Will I have him woke?"

"No, leave him be for a moment."

William took a beat, ignoring the pressing impatience of the Boatswain beside him and focused on the sea. The air. The darkening shades of doom in the storm ahead. The rise and fall of the *Bride's* figurehead as the bowsprit cut through heavier swells.

"There's a Spaniard's diamond ten leagues off starboard," William said, "she's set on her Royals and bearing north on a full rope of knots."

"What the biscuit weevils are ye' talkin' about lad? Friggin' seagull can't spot ten leagues out even with a hawk up their arse."

"My sister is on that ship, and that's where we're headed," William replied. "What will the men say, Roger?"

"That we're headin' fer Portsmouth I 'spect, on a double share," 'Paws' suggested, "and that ye're gone south in yer friggin' head."

William accepted the comment with a wry smile and pressed forward, "She's set with squares on *five* mastheads, that I can tell you."

William's words carried way too many implications for 'Paws'' foggy head to figure. He replied appropriately, "Bugger."

"Bugger be then. It's no ghost over that horizon."

"In November?" 'Paws' replied, doing his best. It wasn't a bad question.

William looked out over the main deck. The men were mustering quick smart. Too bloody quick smart. He turned back to face 'Paws' and whispered, "Roger, what would you do?"

"Only one thing to do lad. Ye're a man o' Scarlett's same as I. But ye can ask it or ye can tell it, thass the difference. Only, settle yer mind afore you do. Thass me advice fer the day."

William considered 'Paws'' words for a moment and nodded his head, "My thanks, Roger. I'll give you five minutes with the men."

'Paws' nodded in return before moving away towards the stair to the main deck shaking his head. William watched him go as his mind began to race through his options.

A time it was, that the world had seven known seas on which to sail a ship, and there were many ships that sailed upon them. The vessels varied in size, and form, and shape and lived and died the same as the seamen that lived and died with them. Of all these ships, in all the seven seas, only one was rigged with five masts: *Santa Oscuro*.

The winds were steady. The *Bride* was calm. William tied off the ship's wheel in a lock, ambled away from the helm at a snail's pace, and began to prioritise the three things he knew about the *'Saint of the Dark'*.

The lowest priority was her captain. A despicable excuse for a human being, by the name of Alvaro de Bazán. As a captain he was a ruthless, humourless, miserable dog of a man. As a sailor he had been peerless for most of his life. He had never met his equal.

Until he had encountered the Scarlett Buccaneer.

As William reached the top of the stair leading down to the main deck, his mind reached the second priority. Treasure, and plenty of it. The *Santa Oscuro* was the largest of Spain's numerous ocean-going vessels with a keel nearly two-hundred feet long and she was also the swiftest. If it was a whisper, it was a rumour, and if it was a rumour, it was common knowledge; The *Dark Saint* was swift, but she was never without her gold. And gold aplenty.

As William reached the foot of the staircase – he couldn't remember a time when it was so few in steps – he was about to reason the opportunity cost of his third item of note when his thinking was scuppered by the faces of the men in front of him. Most of the ship's company was present already. Those that hadn't arrived were not far from doing so.

The eyes of every man betrayed the same unspoken fact that good old 'Paws' had chosen his words carefully. If his mind was a cutlass, it was not a blunt one. He'd done very well.

William gave the men of the morning watch a few more beats to weigh up their own priorities because the three things they knew about the *Saint of the Dark* were, let's say, more straightforward:

Starting with their lowest; which represented merely danger, moving on to their second; which represented the potential for sure disaster on the *Bride*, and arriving at their highest; which represented the complete oblivion of *Bride* and every man aboard by demons, spirits, and all the monsters of the deep.

William knew the men's priorities were playing out like this:

I) The *Dark Saint* was bad luck.

II) The *Dark Saint* was bad luck.

III) The *Dark Saint* was bad luck.

An impulse struck William: that any 'speech like' effort on his part would now be totally inappropriate. Instead, he stepped forward until he was amongst the men and settled his backside casually to rest against a barrel of drinking water situated beside the mainmast.

"Well, what say ye lads?" William offered up gently.

Though a moment's silence prevailed in response, none of the men were in the least bit surprised by the First Mate's diplomatic approach to their shared conundrum.

John Prior was the first to speak. "Be right nice of you to be about askin' Will, but us answerin' be like coppin' a feel of an empty corset."

"John?" William asked.

"It be a han'some hand o' nothin', Will."

A few of the men sounded their appreciation for Prior's conclusion with snaps of nervous laughter. Others just nodded in agreement. Prior expanded his thinking, "If what Mister 'Paws' 'ere says is in your head is right, an' we all got good reason to trust you Will, well, the Cappen'll hav' wer flyin' aft' that feral fradgeon afore we be blinchin', Will. W'ether we'r for or agin," he concluded, not without a measure of genuine concern.

"Is it possible for you to speak in English then, or have you forgot?" Dye Bant piped up from the rear of the bunch in his proud Welsh tone. Several other men shared empathy with his frustration.

"Tha' be rich, from 'ee," Prior said defensively.

"What d'you mean by that now?" Dye asked, knowing full well what Prior meant.

"Are ye just a prick? Or be ye forgetin' thass a Taffy clacker in yer mouth?" Prior fired back, referring to Dye's Welsh heritage. He gained a few smiles from the company having done so.

"How would I forget? I have a mother to remind me when I goes home to the Valley," Bant delivered calmly.

"Whass ye be getting' at with tha'?" Prior conjectured.

"Well, I know who she is, is all," Bant declared.

"Right lads, pull yer heads in!" Roger Prowse would have interceded sooner, but he was caught off guard by the sparring duo bypassing any mention of a sister before arriving so soon at the matriarchal insult. His comment was enough, but he followed it up firmly anyway, "Master William's time is not yer own."

William was ever so slightly disappointed. He'd been keenly expecting John's response, and the sport had provided him with a little extra thinking time. He addressed Dye Bant courteously, "You have a grief to air, David?"

"If I might, Will? Can we knock it off with the *Banter*, for a time, is all I'm saying? As you've asked, is all."

William considered the Welsh man's point. In fairness the *Bride's Banter* was not conducive to clarity, on any topic. He didn't have to pursue the matter unaided. Shamus O'Reilly interjected in his mighty voice, "Master William? If I might be so bold?"

William responded, "You have the deck Shamus, what are your thoughts?"

The men parted as Shamus stepped forward. "Well now, I sees a conundrum for sure, but my mind falls to this way of thinking; If I'm choosin' to die, then I'm choosin' to be dyin' with a wench in me lap and a beer in me hand. And now the time's not right for them things, so I'll tell you somethin', I'll choose instead to go with a laugh in me belly and an' a sword in me hand."

"The *Bride's Banter* it be then," from John Prior.

"Aye, I'm up fer dyin' with a smile," the philosophical retort belonging to the voice of crewman Jim Dolby.

"What the hell does that mean, dying with a smile?" from Ted 'Tumbles' Turner.

"Aye, see now, he holds a fair point, Jim," Dye Bant coming to the short end of no understanding at all.

"Who wants to die at all, is my feckin' point?" snapped 'Tumbles'.

"How is it then that I'm agreeing with you, and you're still entitled to pipe up? You clumsy goose-fart land-lubbin' rubber-lover, you," the sparkle in Dye Bant's eyes apparent to everyone present. Including William, who placed a backhand gently to his mouth in studied contemplation and hid his smile at the same time.

"Land-lubbin' rubber-lover!" from the normally refined Shamus, who immediately took to a hearty chuckle, "That's feckin' mighty."

"Yar! It's truth alright," from John Prior.

Ted 'Tumbles' Turner turned ashen for a beat in sure acknowledgement of his forthcoming defeat. He had been clumsy all his life. He had fallen from the rigging more than his fair share on many a voyage at sea, and this one had been no exception. Though that was not the defeat that was now turning him pale. His present defeat had come yesterday when he had slipped from the shrouds of the foremast and landed headfirst into an open keg of whale oil. 'Tumbles' looked around at his ship mates for a last chance of reprieve, and, when none was apparent, he embraced his misfortune accordingly. "Ah, feck it," he began, then quickly assumed the newly accepted vernacular of the *Bride's Banter*, and its exaggerated Cornish tones, "I'll take up no umbrage fer now, fer I'll go proudly wif' a smile and a wink, smellin' as I do, like a whale's slimy arsehole, and hence and forth frum now, when I'm standin' proudly in front of Davy Jones at the bottom of the sea, I'll have him sniff my rubber smellin' bollocks and tell him it's ye shower of bastards he should have taken, not me."

The smiles had begun unanimously somewhere around the midpoint of 'Tumbles" chosen retort and now promptly erupted into laughter from all and sundry present.

"Yar! It'll be the *Bride's Banter* 'til our deaths, lads. A show of hands," John Prior voiced up enthusiastically.

"Aye, the *Banter* it is."

"Fer fuck's sake, alright."

"Ye're a sorry shower o' bastards, for sure," said Shamus adding his hand to the majority.

'Paws' was quick to interject, "Alright lads, enough," raising both palms to steady the masses, he stepped beside William. "I'll remind you with the cat if I 'ave to, that your time is not your own."

It was more than enough. The men fell silent.

John Prior was no stranger to first class seamanship, and, for all his jostling, he knew there was a decision to be made and that the First Mate was doing his best to ask and not tell. He addressed William with respect, "Pardon us Will.

But as I was sayin', the Cappen'll hae us flyin' aft that feral fradgeon w'ether we'r for or agin."

"This is an even forum, lads. Scarlett has given the order to return home. It's for us to decide whether we tackle that Spanish dragon or leave well enough alone. I'll stand by our decision before the Queen of England if I must."

"Yar. He would too."

"Yar."

"You would an' all Will, we knows it," Jim Dolby acknowledged.

"A democracy it is then," said William. "The Captain has passed the order for London. He'll back his word. Our commission is at an end."

"Aye. He's the best of 'em."

"Aye, that he is."

"And for the time being it is us," continued William, "that are bewitched by the *Dark*. The Captain's at his papers. He won't assume responsibility for us losing that ship on the Queen's account, or on his account, because he hasn't feckin' seen it, and we're heading for home anyway. Do I need to paint a clearer picture?"

As it played out in the faces of the men surrounding him, William didn't need to offer further clarification on the legal technicalities of their circumstance. The men got it.

"Thass it done then. We'll live our lives and on to Portsmouth."

"Yar! To Portsmouth."

"Yar, an' on to London."

An accord was quickly forming on deck, but it was shaky. And further shaken by the indistinct voice of one Martin 'Mumbles' No-Name. The latter moniker of his legal designation as a human being had been forgotten, for 'Mumbles' was now in his latter years afloat, and a steadfast supply of cheap rum over his years had long since removed a great deal of his mental record.

"There's a lot of gold on that boat," mumbled 'Mumbles'.

"Aye and mischief an' all," 'Tumbles' offered, much to the agreement of many heads present who impulsively nodded. "She ain't never opened her coffers yet, Will."

"He's right be there, she ain't been plundered yet be any ship that I knows of," Dye Bant disclosed truthfully.

A moment of consideration befell the crew and the First Mate. The seabird in their hands was nestled safely in the *Bride's* hold and the calm waters of Portsmouth Bay were less than two months' sail. They had fared well on the voyage. It was time to go home.

"She ain't met Scarlett yet though," Richard Bately stated, innocently.

Silence followed. A studied silence. Followed by another blush from Bately's young cheeks. He wasn't quite sure what he'd just said, but he was quickly doubting its appeal.

To him it appeared that the men beside him were inching away from his sides.

'Paws' seized the rare natural gap in conversation, and made it his own, "They met once, a long time ago."

The revelation landed like an albatross might hit the deck after a heart attack mid-flight.

"Were ye there?" from Prior, recovering first among his peers.

"I was."

"What 'appen'd?" from 'Tumbles', who was as surprised by the revelation as any other of the *Bride's* men, with the exception of William, who was now fascinated as to how this was all going to play out.

'Paws' breathed deep, sucking in an appropriate beginning to his tale, "I ain't exaggeratin' when I tell ye, I ain't never known a night like it..."

"Well, that bodes well dun' it," from Dye Bant, clearly assuming the worst.

Shamus interceded quickly, "Hold your whisht, Taffy, let the man tell it without your bullshit gettin' ahead of him."

"Right you are. Sorry Mister Prowse," Dye said humbly.

'Paws' simply nodded and shrugged himself back into his story, "Well, as I was sayin', I ain't never known a night like it. Blackest night I e'er saw on sea or land. Even the stars was hidin'. Not a lamplight was lit on our decks. Could barely see the han' in front o' me face. I was on the main deck and the Capt' was at the helm, strugglin' hard to keep a line, 'cause we was runnin' full befor' the wind on a gull-wing jib, straight into the black around us and aiming fer the *Dark* that was ahead..."

"Sounds like bloody suicide, that do", from Jim Dolby.

"Was you aboard Master William?" Richard Bately enquired, reasonably.

"No Richard, that was before my time."

"Well, iss differen' now then, what with you being on board," said Richard, seeking reassurance.

"Will's luckiest man I seen, fer sure," Shamus put forth.

"No offence Will, but there ain't a man alive lucky enough to take that ship's gold. Davy himself couldn't take it," Dye asserted, rather ashamedly.

"No offence taken David," said William honestly, before turning to 'Paws', "Roger, the remainder of your tale?"

Old 'Paws' loved a good yarn, particularly his own, and was positively itching to regain his momentum, but in William's eyes he was reminded that they were men o' Scarlett's, and the First Mate was askin' and not tellin' him to anchor his second and third acts in a more appropriate harbour.

"Aw, it's a good tale William, an' one worth tellin' but I reckon we should stow it a while," said Roger, "I think there's more value addin' to this discussion, by me remindin' that Spanish ship, she's sailing in November."

"It's November?" 'Tumbles' mouth moving faster than his reckoning.

"O' course it's November you dimwit, where ye been this last week?" asked John Prior.

"I've been dreaming of your sister, truth be told," said 'Tumbles', "reckon she's the reason I slipped yesterday."

"An' how exactly d'ye reckon about my sister?"

"Reckon the last time I saw her, she smelt just like that barrel o' fish oil, so naturally I couldn't keep myself out of her."

The gag broke the tension, and the men burst into laughter.

'Paws' was straight on top of them, "Right lads, fer fuck's sake I'll not be telling ye again!" As the men suppressed their spluttering, 'Paws' continued, "I'm sorry for them, Master William."

William gracefully took up the apology, "Is it fair to say, Roger, that if the *Santa Oscuro* is sailing in November, it's likely there is something special on that ship?"

"It's said she never sails out of port in November, William, and right now she's a long way from it, headin' home at a sprint by your words."

"She'll be loaded to the guns w'gold."

"I'll bet she must be an' all."

"Aye, and if we're the luckiest men alive in tackling it out of her, it'll be the Queen's gold soon as we make London," 'Mumbles' said.

"Martin, you of all here should know better," said William, "that will only happen if the Captain gives the order to go on the account."

"Wass thass mean, Will?" enquired young Bately.

"By the Queen's law, we have fulfilled our commission. Right now, we're running under the Captain's given order for heading home," clarified the First Mate. "If there's gold on that ship it belongs to who better keeps it. Could be us. Could be the Spanish. Could be Davy Jones if it all turns to shit. But it won't belong to the Queen of England on this or any day."

"All this talk of money is gettin' me down. I got more than enough to feed my family for six month when I gets back. And that ain't why I'm here," said Richard Bately, rather unexpectedly, judging by many of the men's considered expressions.

"What you alludin' to, lad?" 'Paws' presented.

"I'm here 'cause I'm a man o' Scarlett's an' far as I see I got a score to settle on his behalf. An' on behalf o' Old England fer that matter," stated Bately, as if it were more obvious than by half.

"The boy's no more a boy, lads," from Shamus O'Reilly.

"Yar! That's man's talk fer sure," asserted John Prior.

"Thass a man o' Scarlett's," rendered Jim Dolby.

"Aye, a man o' Scarlett's," added 'Mumbles'.

"If I goes to me death it ain't for the money, Will, I'll do it for Scarlett as he's dun by me," announced Richard Bately, proud as punch.

"An' Will gave chunder this morning lads, so what can go wrong?" 'Paws', divulging what he knew to be all but a silly superstition, but a most important one for the men.

"Aye, I'm persuaded. Fer Scarlett," Ted 'Tumbles' said mildly.

"Fer Scarlett it is."

"To a vote o' democracy then," said 'Paws', taking helm of the discussion. "All those who are still bound for Portsmouth raise a hand."

William carefully scanned the crowd. Inklings of apprehension were numerous, but not a single hand was raised.

'Paws' drew the same conclusion, and was quick to move on, "All those fer the account o' that black-spotted Spaniard, say aye."

"AYE!"

"AYE it be, Mister Prowse."

"Yar! Let's draw our teeth on that Spanish bastard."

"Aye, fer Scarlett!"

"Aye, fer Scarlett it be!"

William Hope took stock of the men, and partly wondered if he'd ever live up to expressing the courage which seemed to come so naturally from those all around him. Another part of his brain was taking stock of the fact that the sun was just crossing the fore topsail yard...

As custom dictated at the time, when the sun crossed the yard, toddies of rum were handed out among all present and correct on a ship. The officers would take their ration neat and uncut. The men imbibed theirs in a diluted form in which the spirit was watered down by a measure of fifty per cent or so. Either way, all were content with their late morning buoy up, for it offered sure warmth of encouragement in tackling the day's challenge, whatever it might entail...

William looked away from the sun and back to the men, "Mister Bately, Sir, I feel certain the sun has crossed the yard on this day."

Richard Bately took heed immediately, for it was his job to pass out the rum, and he was even more popular among the crew for his trouble. "Yes, Sir, Master William, I'll attend right away, Sir," said Bately, as he immediately moved towards the stores for the appropriate barrel.

"Not so fast as I can't finish my sentence, Mister Bately," William said with a wry smile. "Each man shall have a double measure this morning, and he shall have it without water."

Bately stood put, in acknowledgement of the First Mate's unusual instruction.

"Well, set about it, lad," encouraged 'Paws', "you heard Master William."

Bately jumped back into action and quickly removed himself.

"Thank you for your time, Gentlemen," William said casually, "we have a heading for the *Bride* and a challenge before us," and, as he stepped away from the barrel he had been resting against, he delivered, "Mister Prowse, you will find me at the helm."

"Aye, aye, Sir," replied 'Paws'.

The verdict was passed. The men stood in silence as a crew. It was tradition. Though few of them prayed out loud, they would be praying for each other now.

7
Step Aside, Sir... Hand Me My Bride!

William Hope walked aft heading for the stairs to the Quarterdeck at an easy pace.

'Paws' watched the First Mate go for a few beats, before addressing the crew with considerable gusto, "Well, you heard Master William lads, we'll down our rum hard and bear down on that Spaniard even harder!"

"SHIP AHOY! SHIP AHOY!"

The voice, thrown from the crow's nest eighty feet up on the mainmast, spread over the main deck's inhabitants as a shadow crying in darkness.

The crew of the *Maiden Bride* set about the challenge at hand. 'Paws' stalked the decks and pounded out his orders. The seamen jumped in accord to make those orders happen and the *Bride* swept into her pursuit of the Spanish ship of doom with five masts and a keel full of riches.

William resumed his position at the helm. He didn't give a rat's sorry ass about the treasure. If Katherine was on that ship, he would find her. Whether it was the fresh morning breeze, or a newfound surge of consternation due to the impending conflict, he couldn't tell, but he was now completely and utterly awoken to the day. Awake and alive and at the helm of the fastest and most beautiful ship that ever set to sea.

The morning came and went with the rise of the sun over the *Bride's* yards and the *Dark Saint* came and went on the horizon with each successive larboard and starboard tack.

As the swells increased and the sky thickened with cloud, it became clear to William that the *Dark* was attempting to skirt the oncoming storm on a southeast heading. It was a good move by their captain, Alvaro de Bazán. Two or three days added for a passage in calmer seas was more than a fair price in men's hearts.

By noon the Spanish ship was in sight from the foredeck of the *Bride* and there she remained in full view. As the sun climbed down from its height and slipped below the *Bride's* main royal yard the two ships were less than two leagues apart, and that distance was closing. William had taken off his shirt, but, that done, he hadn't taken his hands off the helm. Whether it was a long morning under the sodden tropical humidity or a resurgence of his hangover he couldn't tell, but he was getting tired. He wiped another few beads of sweat from his brow with a sodden handkerchief and checked the ship's compass beside him.

"I always knew I could make a sailor of you."

William snapped his head around aft. Scarlett was ten feet behind him, casually sitting on a coil of sturdy rope with his back resting against the stern deck wall. A small ivory chest supported his feet. His stomach was casually supporting his left forearm which was, in turn, supporting his right elbow. His right hand was casually holding a lengthy dark brown cigarillo. "I'm suffering to cast approval on your casual appearance though, Master Hope," Scarlett said, before taking a long drag from his smoke. As he exhaled, he leaned forward and closed one eye whilst scrunching up his face. "Ye be an officer of a Queen's ship, be ye not?"

William smiled, "You been practising?"

"Aye, that I av' lad. That I av'."

"You should keep it up."

Scarlett relaxed his face and relaxed his body to its former position. "Do you think Her Majesty would approve?"

"Is there anything Scarlett could do that wouldn't please her?" William asked dryly.

"I wouldn't like to find out," Scarlett laughed. "Can you honestly put it to mind?"

"Christ, no."

"Neither I," Scarlett said.

Both men put 'it' to mind immediately, shared a change of countenance and expressed agreement on said topic by turning their heads promptly, whilst vocalising a very definite "Eeeoohh."

Scarlett rose and stepped forward. As he did so he gave his cigarillo a firm flick away to his right. It vanished on the ocean side of the gunwale.

"I see you found a heading after all," said Scarlett, indicating the Spanish ship with a quick lift of his head.

"I was heading for Africa. It was the men that gave her a new course." William said.

Scarlett's eyes stayed with the *Dark Saint*. "Everyone has a story to tell, you just have to listen. Isn't that how it goes?"

"I had half a mind to wake you," William shared.

"The half that didn't was the better half, young William." Scarlett took his eyes off the other ship and looked to his First Mate. "You've done well. Whatever prevails, you have my thanks," he was about to say – *"and my admiration"* – but stopped short of doing so. William didn't need to be told. Instead, Scarlett continued with, "The men's choice, eh? And the men alone?"

"I offered no persuasion," William confirmed. "You don't want her?"

Scarlett weighed up his First Mate, his piercing eyes narrowing.

"Bullshit." Scarlett said, "My question to you, and I'll have an honest answer. What is on that ship that *you* are wanting?"

William could feel his blood pressure dropping, but as blood pressure hadn't technically been invented yet, he merely went ashen in the face. An answer couldn't be avoided. He knew that. Not with Scarlett.

"I think Katherine is aboard the *Dark Saint*."

"You think?"

"I told you. It's murky. Only makes sense why I saw you in the dark last night."

"Uh huh. I was content with Portsmouth this morning," Scarlett said, then returned his gaze to the ship he knew as the *Santa Oscuro*.

William watched Scarlett. He knew that the Spanish ship was opening a thousand wounds in his captain's mind.

After a moment Scarlett's eyes widened and brightened with a devilish smile, "Fuck it. The Queen shall hear nought of this one from me, William. Can I ask that she never hear it from you?"

"How would she? I'll hardly write her a letter."

"Fair point. Though I'll see you in England yet." Scarlett pressed William directly, "You should gain an hour's rest, Will. I'll need you this evening like never before."

William responded proudly, "I'll lie down tomorrow, Sir, if the fates will have it, and I'll not catch a wink before that."

"I need you to close your eyes," Scarlett replied calmly. "That is an order. Use my cabin."

"Yes, Sir," William said, suddenly understanding.

"Now step aside, Sir, and hand me my *Bride*," Scarlett said. "Sweet dreams."

William did exactly as instructed and Scarlett took the helm.

"Mister Prowse!" Scarlett bellowed, "Your attention, if you please."

'Paws' stepped across the main deck and whipped up the stairs like a man half his age. When he drew close, Scarlett spoke, "We'll cross her stern in one hour and I'll have you tend the leeward broad harder than I've ever asked of you."

"Aye Sir, cut her leeward hard."

"And Mister Prowse, inform the men that, if the men will do this for their Captain, their Captain shall make them rich men. Every doubloon shall be shared amongst them. The Queen has no share in this venture, for we are on a heading for home. And Mister Prowse, every one of them shall have their fortune by Christmas. Every one of them, by my word, none will miss out."

"Aye, Captain, I suspect they won't be hard convinced."

"Thank you, Mister Prowse."

'Paws' gave a smile and marched down the stair to the main deck. Scarlett tickled the helm and cut a fierce focus on the *Santa Oscuro*.

Before he entered the captain's cabin, William paused and turned back to glance over the ship. Either in recognition of Scarlett's intention, or some inexplicable concession born in magic, William noticed the ship's bowsprit rise three feet higher, and to him, it seemed...

The *Maiden Bride* began to fly.

8

Pyrotechnical Genius

29th October 1577

Ten seconds after Francis Bacon had sparked three separate fuse tapers in the Great Garden of Theobalds House...

BOOM! WHOOSH. BOOM! WHOOSH. BOOM!

Rockets ripped through the evening air from the ground, rising seemingly to the thick layer of low-lying cloud, whereupon they exploded in scintillating, effervescent, multicoloured, glittering illuminations.

BANG! BOOM! WHIZZZ. BANG! WHOOSH. BANG. BOOM! WHOOSH. WHIZZZ...

Fireworks blasted into the sky from all over the gardens. No decorum or rhythm to it. No choreographed display projecting undertones of story or philosophical meaning. No music. Just plain, old-fashioned fucking mayhem in the skies above.

Bacon cracked up laughing, "Fucking pyrotechnical genius! If I do say so myself. Head to the roof and keep out of trouble. I'll find you soon."

Bacon thrust his sack over his shoulder and took off running east, heading for the loggia of the three-storey southeastern projecting range that connected the Middle Court with the Still House Tower.

BANG! BOOM! WHIZZZ. BANG! WHOOSH. BANG! BOOM! WHOOSH...

William prompted Katherine to her feet, "Come on. Act like everything's perfectly normal. We're just two innocent curates out for a stroll in the gardens."

They lofted their sacks and started walking away from the fountain, heading for the path that would lead them to the southern range of the Fountain Court, which was presently shrouded in scaffolding.

"And we have a dinner appointment with the bishop, I suppose," quipped Katherine.

"That's good. But supper with the chaplain's more believable."

BOOM! WHOOSH. BOOM! WHOOSH. FIZZ. WHIZZZ. BOOM!

Katherine shook her head and looked upward. Bacon's fire alchemy was ongoing and if her lungs weren't so constricted in dire panic, she would have considered the lightshow breathtaking, though it was splattered all over with an avant-garde, spontaneously cheeky sort of random what-the-fuck design.

*****

Sir William Cecil, First Baron Burghley, was finally at home. He raced between elm trees, jumped his horse over a small brook and broke through the tree line of the forest he and Sir James of Bon had just navigated on their mounts. He slowed his dappled grey thoroughbred mare, trotted through the southwestern archway entrance to his Great Garden and pulled up to a stop. It was no surprise that his attentions were fully engaged on the multitude of colours and sparkling explosions decorating the cold twilight sky.

Sir Flemington James of Bon pulled up beside Cecil some twenty seconds later. He wiped sweat from his brow with a sodden handkerchief. He definitively preferred sailing to horse-riding. In the moment, he preferred just about everything life had to offer to fecking horse-riding. His arsehole was burning like it had been lashed a thousand times with a cat o' nine tales.

"What do you see before you, James?" asked Cecil.

"Kiddy mischief at its best, I'll venture," said James.

"Will they have the good sense to remain close by the house?" questioned Cecil.

"Better part of valour for us to discover that promptly," said James.

"Indeed," said Cecil, digging his heels into his mare's flanks and pressing forward at a flying gallop.

"Ah, me fecking arse is never gonna forgive me," said James, sotto voce, before spurring his horse on after Cecil.

*****

Mildred Cecil, First Lady Burghley, first saw the fireworks from the loggia in the eastern range of the Fountain Court. She had held it together in her audience with Captain Smedley-Smythe-Smythings, remaining composed and calm, projecting the steadfast dignity her station in English court circles demanded when in public, or in times of crisis. The ever-dependable Thomas Wilson had worked his salty charms into the conversation in sparing but truly effective moments of understanding and faux-goodwill towards the Queen's Guard and his despicable 'assignment'. Mildred truly believed she would have fainted, were it not for Thomas' unflappable interjections on her behalf. As it was, she had managed to remain on her feet to guide Smythe-Smythings out of the North Parlour, step with him halfway along the east loggia of the Fountain Court and wish him well in finding William promptly and safely. As soon as the captain and Thomas had disappeared outside into the Middle Court, she had collapsed onto the nearest wooden bench, and placed her head between her knees whilst fighting a compelling compulsion to vomit on the floor between her feet.

Two of the Queen's Yeomen Guards entered the loggia from the south. They were walking at pace with their left hands perched on the hilt of the swords dangling in scabbards suspended from their waistbands.

Please God, don't let these two throttlebottoms pause for guidance.

"Good evening, Ma'am," said one of the guards.

"Lady Burghley will do nicely," said Mildred.

"Oh, goodness. Do pardon us Baroness. We... er... are tasked with..." spluttered the second of the guards. They were both in their twenties. Generic looks. Military deportment. They could have been twins, or perhaps clones in a totally different era.

Twin ninnyhammers before me.

"Apprehending my son. Yes, I've had the pleasure of being informed by your Captain," said Mildred.

"Quite so. Sorry, Lady Burghley," said the first guard.

"He's surely innocent, Lady Burghley," said clone/twin/guard two.

"I... or rather, if you might be able to narrow our search parameters, Ma'am," said guard one.

"Tell you where he is likely to be, you mean," said Mildred, "hmmm... I'll do my best..." she continued, rising to her feet. "Let me think... If I were a thirteen-year-old boy, who had committed no crime, and I had been verily informed that two-score of the Queen's Guard were intent on arresting me for Treason, in my own home, which happened to be the largest country estate in England, where would I snudge my butt to quietly contemplate these most peculiar ongoing events?"

"Any pointers would be appreciated, Lady Burghley," said guard two.

"His safety is our paramount concern, you understand," said the first guard.

"I'm almost certain, though I couldn't possibly speak for my son entirely, that the complete and utter annihilation of my coming-of-age birthday celebrations would prompt certain residual resentments that may or may not be persuading me to consider hiding out until my father, the Queen's Lord High Treasurer, arrives home to oversee the cutting of my birthday cake. By Jove, I think I have it, gentlemen... Yes... You are quite surely, shit out of luck, but please, feel free to roam the house and grounds as you please. Good evening to you."

Mildred walked away west, out of the loggia. She breathed deeply, and settled beside the central black and white marble fountain from which the courtyard took its name. The water feature was made up of two substantial water bowls stacked atop each other, with statues of Venus and Cupid looking up at a life-sized sculpture of a seemingly wise old man. Mildred liked to think of the figure as her husband's alter ego, the self he was at home, outside politics and all the demands he endured in maintaining the status quo of the Realm.

Muffled bangs, whooshes, and whizzes were still erupting from somewhere in the Great Garden, on the other side of the southern range.

Robert Cecil appeared in a doorway on the northwestern corner of the court. It was one of the external doors to his ample lodgings, which constituted most of the ground floor of the western range of the Fountain Court. He was dressed for a party, in silver-grey doublet and hose, white ruff and stockings, grey slippers. He had a pleasant, albeit fairly ordinary face. Fourteen years old going on thirty-four, he quick marched his twisted little frame towards the central fountain and his mother. He was carefully managing a large tulip shaped crystal glass of his father's most expensive vintage brandy.

"I saw you talking to the Queen's Guards mother. I thought it best not to interrupt and to proffer this measure of support instead," said Robert, holding out the beverage.

Mildred smiled, "Ah, my dear boy. What would I ever do without you?"

Robert handed the drink to his mum, "It seems it is William you may do without. What's he done now, do you imagine?"

"You've heard already?" asked Mildred.

"The whole bloody estate has heard, mother. Get a grip," said Robert. "The staff's whispers are fast fashioning a rebellion. You know how popular William is."

Mildred shivered, yet it wasn't from the plummeting air temperature of the approaching night. She imbibed a long, luxurious, quaff of brandy and steadied herself as the mellow liquid descended through her oesophagus and banished her goosebumps.

BANG! WHOOSH. WHIZZ. BANG! CRACK! CRACK! BANG!

Mildred and Robert instinctively looked up at the fireworks that were exploding beyond, over the Great Garden once again, but that was not what captured their attention. Two figures, dressed in hooded green habit robes were scuttling along a leaded walkway that was the roof of the Great Chamber. They had sacks slung over their shoulders and the fresh gait of youth in their limbs. The two figures paused, stepped up to the stone capped parapet overlooking the court in which their mother and brother were standing three floors below. William and Katherine pulled back their hoods and waved.

"Ah, look there, mother, good oh!" said Robert, "Marvellous misdirection. I must arm myself and join them immediately, do excuse me."

Robert paced away heading for the southeast corner of the courtyard. In truth, Mildred knew her eldest son was heading for the chaplain's chambers.

She looked back up at William and Katherine. Every fibre of her being was demanding that she call out and tell them to come to her, but she didn't. She simply smiled.

2

Fast Fashioning a Rebellion

Neither curious curates nor proper priests were well known to ascend anything but an occasional staircase for lofty parchment rolls of ecclesiastical text, so it came as little surprise to the twins after they had waved to Mildred and Robert, turned and peeked across the limestone parapet overlooking the Great Garden to find that the two canal-boat-checking-Yeomen had been joined by two other house-checking-Yeomen, all of whom were scrambling up the ladders, iron poles and wooden planks of the temporary building works that shrouded the southern wall of the Great Chamber. Scaffolding that they themselves had just ascended.

"Guess we should have entered the house and taken the stairs," remarked Katherine.

"Nah. Where would be the fun in that?" said William, "Besides we need to attract their attentions for a spell."

"Misdirection," said Katherine.

"Precisely. Come on."

William took Katherine's hand in his and led her east along a flat leaded roof. They entered the southeast tower of the Fountain Court and dropped down a flight of stairs, exiting onto the leaded walkway that was the rooftop of the southern range of the Middle Court. They ran on and entered the southeastern most tower of their home, dog-legged left and alighted on the roof of the east range of the Middle Court in a half crouch, half crawling so as not to be seen by the guards stationed with the three coaches sitting proudly outside the porter's lodges adjacent to the main entrance.

William and Katherine slid up to the low parapet wall and peeked over. Captain Tarquin-Smyth-Something-or-other was pointing in various directions, and though his words couldn't be heard, he was clearly assigning instructions to his men to spread out. Thomas Wilson was standing off to the side, scuffing the sole of his right shoe on the gravel, clearly in earshot and on hand if needs be, but pretending not to listen. The dogs tied to the rear of the three carriages were restlessly tugging at their leashes, clearly roused by increasing human tensions and chomping mildly at the bit for some action in pursuit of whatever prey they were assigned to sniff out.

"Right, let's set these fuses..." began William.

"You mean like this," said Katherine, who was holding a lit firework in her hand.

William smiled and shook his head, "Just so."

Katherine casually tossed her rocket over the parapet. It arced towards the central carriage, hit the gravel, exploded, and whizzed off along the floor between the wheels of the coach at a hundred miles an hour. Dogs and guards freaked the fuck out. Several cavalry horses betrayed a flaw in their obvious lack of training, discipline, or experience by rearing up on their hind quarters and throwing their riders to the ground.

Captain Smedley-Smythe-Smythings rolled into a crouch and raised his harquebus. While he was pointing the barrel this way and that in a vain attempt to target a hidden foe, William cracked his flint and lit six more fireworks, handing them in quick succession to Katherine, who deftly launched them over the parapet in various directions. By the third rocket she was becoming a dab hand; her fireworks skidding across the gravel of the Dial Court in all directions. The results on the ground below were mainly based in absolute chaos; horses were bolting, dogs were barking, jumping, pulling free of their leashes, and running away. Coaches were dragged out of their linear formation by teams of panicked horses. Fallen guards were scrambling to their knees, drawing muskets, and shooting at nothing but smoky shadows in the distance. Only one of the horses remained unmoved, seemingly calm and collected in soldiery solace. The captain's mount, Raine. William could have sworn the animal was focused on little else but his and Katherine's masked position on the rooftop.

"Time to move," said William.

"Two more," pleaded Katherine, "pyrotechy whatchamacallit is awesome."

"They're on to us. Look," said William pointing to the leaded rooftop walkways on the southern range. Katherine turned to see the two rowboat-searching-Yeomen and the two house-searching-Yeomen were fast approaching, swords in hand.

"Bollocks," said Katherine.

"Here," said a smiling William, holding up two fireworks with lit fuse tapers.

Katherine grabbed them while instructing William to, "Hook it!"

William bolted off to the north along the second-storey walkway, with Katherine close behind. She tossed the last rockets as she ran and traced their trajectories in her peripheral vision as they exploded in midair.

*****

Beyond those bangs and flashes, some four-hundred yards away to the east, the sky was darkening quickly over the road from Waltham Cross to Chestnut, which was poignant only in as much as it formed the perfect backdrop for Francis Bacon's latest pyrotechnical painting of preposterous pandemonium. Cecil's penchant for architecture had extended to the construction of a sixty-three-foot-long camel stable, two one-hundred-and-nineteen-foot-long conventional stables, and one extensive barn which was some one-hundred-and-sixty-three feet in length, all spanning the main road. Bacon had measured them all, as he had every other inch of Theobalds House at one time or another, such was his passion for possibilities in scientific data. Suffice to say he was fully aware of the size of his canvas when he planted two score and seven fireworks in the ground, spaced them methodically along the lengths of the barn and stables, and linked them all with spools of waxed taper fuses. Naturally, his final brush strokes of bedlam could not be applied without the opening of every door and gate he passed in the framing of his soon to be completed artwork, and he had been relieved that several close appointed Queen's Guards had been distracted by the fiery goings on outside the entrance to the main house, while he sneaked around in his priest's disguise.

'Alms House' had been built next door to the main barn, as housing for local veterans and elderly persons of limited means. It was a fine stone-built establishment, perhaps betraying the heart of Lord Burghley in a way that many would never begin to imagine, as his public perception was oft that of a gruff, old, pinchpenny, privileged, politician. Cecil was not that. Mildred knew it. Katherine and William knew it. Their brother Robert knew it. Francis Bacon reflected upon it when he pulled back the hood of his habit and knocked loudly on the front door of the house.

After a seemingly endless moment in which Bacon regretted his impulse to elicit an audience, a youthful-ish woman opened the door. She was dressed in a navy-blue robe with a black sleeveless scapular over it, tied at the waist with a black leather belt. A simple wooden cross hung from a string around her neck. Her face was framed in the folds of a white linen wimple which covered her head and draped around her neck and shoulders.

"Yes... Father," said the nun, scanning Bacon from toe to head. She had kind eyes. Her smile was quite nice also. Somewhat forced, but pleasant, if you were into ladies in religious attire. Bacon was into neither ladies nor religion. The image threw him momentarily.

"Good evening to you... err, sister," stuttered Bacon, "it has fallen upon me to invite you, err, well your residents, parishioners if you will, outside, to witness a display."

"A display?"

"Err, quite so, miss. Errm, a spontaneous invite from Lord Burghley. A practice display you see, prior to forthcoming yuletide festivities," said Bacon, in perhaps the least convincing tone he had ever mustered.

"Festivities?" questioned the nun. Her smile had dissipated. She wasn't half as attractive to Bacon.

"Err, yes, forthcoming, festivities, good sister," said Bacon. He was now fully regretting his choice. This delay wasn't helping William and Katherine. His ego had bettered him.

"We do not engage readily in festivities in this house," said the nun.

"Err... No, quite so. Surely that would be, err..."

"Yes?"

"Well, foolish, frivolous... flippant, facetiousness, but you see..." stumbled Bacon.

"We are not facetious in this house," said the nun.

Bacon was longing for her smile to return.

"Fireworks, sister. An experiment. At Lord Burghley's bequest," said Bacon. "It should take but a moment of your..."

"Fireworks!" exclaimed the woman in the wimple.

"Fireworks," mumbled Bacon, shrinking down inside himself. He realised in the instance that he was shit at promoting his art. Or himself, for that matter. If it was this hard to draw in an audience now, how difficult would it be in ten years when he was planning to retire from an artistic career? He would stick to philosophy as a life pursuit. There was no money in it either, but still. And he could always chance politics if shit came to a shovel.

"Well, Father. Goodness me. Fireworks indeed," said the nun, before her smile returned and filled the space framed in her linen head dress, "why didn't you say so?"

The sister spun around on her heels and ducked back inside leaving the door wide open.

Bacon heard, "Fireworks! Outside everyone! Fireworks, I say! Quickly now! And bring the rum!! Fireworks!!"

Surprised, yet fully satisfied his artistic adventure was shaping nicely, Bacon pulled away from the Alms House doorway and ambled off towards the barn and stables. To his delight, a decent number of horses, cows, sheep, goats, pigs, peacocks, and dogs had wandered out of their enclosures and were ambling about in the twilight, seemingly a tad disorientated at the change in their routine. About two-hundred yards to the west, Bacon saw three men – presumably some of the estate's animal handlers or grounds staff – dashing away from the servant's quarters at the main house and heading towards him. Their progress was interrupted by four of the Queen's Guards, who were on horseback.

Bacon searched along the wall of the northern most of the stables. He found what he was looking for in the exact place he had left it; a bundle of gunpowder-infused waxed fuse lines tied together with hemp string.

"I'm afraid, I do not know your name, Father," said the nun, after catching up and arriving beside Bacon, who almost fell over backwards, such was his surprise. His adrenaline spiked and his heartbeat increased, but as adrenaline hadn't been isolated as a hormone yet, and Katherine wasn't on hand to count the essence of his being, neither mattered.

"Oh, right, of course, sister," said Bacon, "Father... Bacon. Francis, if it please you."

"Father Francis Bacon?" questioned the nun.

"Francis," repeated Bacon.

"Sister Agatha Templeton."

"Indeed. A pleasure, I'm sure," said Bacon, whose attentions were split between the fuses in his hand, the three grounds staff two-hundred yards away, and, perhaps more importantly, the fact that they were now approaching steadily with an escort of the four mounted guards who had interrupted their progress only moments ago.

"No relation of Sir Nicholas Bacon then, or you wouldn't be out here lighting fireworks in the dirt now would you," said Sister Agatha. Her smile had turned cheeky. It was very becoming. Distracting, certainly.

"Do pardon, sister?"

"Sir Nicholas Bacon," said Agatha.

The mention of his own father slapped Bacon completely sideways. He dropped the bundle of fuses and fumbled the flint striking tool in his right hand for several awkward beats before it dropped to the floor. He crouched down to retrieve it from the unkempt grass beneath his feet.

Why the fuck didn't I lie?! I'll never make it in politics. Fuck.

Sister Agatha crouched beside him, "Where do you want us to stand?"

Bacon looked over Sister Agatha's shoulder. Two dozen or so people were arriving at what might be best described as a leisurely pace. They were all wrapped up in heavy woollen coats, scarves, wraps, and blankets. No doubt in Bacon's mind; the Alms House crew had arrived. Pyro-time.

*****

William flicked up an iron latch on an oak door and slammed it back on its hinges. He and Katherine entered the northeastern tower, and each grabbed a lantern from a number that were hanging from hooks on the wall. Lanterns were on hand in mostly every nook and cranny of Theobalds, particularly on the landings of the staircases in the main towers. During the initial construction phase of Theobalds, their father had learnt that a bruised tailbone was no laughing matter, and that no matter how many windows he chose to include in his design, skimping on illuminations was root cause, not symptom of most tumbles in his home, given that England's average daylight hours were generally fairly fucking dowdy and miserable for about nine months of any given year. Lessons Cecil learnt the bumpy way; thrash limbs to impede momentum, protect head, particularly chin, tongue and teeth, duck and roll instead of landing squarely on your arse at the foot of the stairs, and, most importantly, invest in shit loads of candles, flints, tapers, whale oil and fancy wrought iron, glass encased friggin' lanterns. Oh, and hang the fecking things everywhere.

William struck his flint and lit the two lanterns.

"Where next?" offered Katherine.

"Cake?" suggested William.

"We should try to see mother," said Katherine.

"While eating cake," said William.

"Fuck's sake. Fine," said Katherine, before taking off and bounding up the stone treads of the tower stairs. She alighted on the next level by pushing through a door leading to the roof of the northern range of the Middle Court. William followed her west at pace, as they slammed through two more doors on opposite sides of a middle tower and ran on to the northwest tower of the Middle Court, which was also the northeast tower of the Fountain Court. William paused at the oak door and scanned to the south, specifically the last known positions of the guards pursuing them along the roof tops. He could only make out two of them; perhaps the row-boat-checking-Yeomen, it was hard to say, but they were having difficulty navigating the towers and staircases separating the various levels of the leaded walk-ways. And the dipshits weren't carrying lanterns. William smiled and entered the tower.

Katherine was waiting inside on the landing, "Stairs down or rooftop south?"

William considered for a half beat, but the decision was made for him; the sound of footsteps two levels below bounced off the stone walls and echoed up the stairwell.

"How many feckin' steps is in this bloody joint, d'ya reckon on, Bert?" came a muffled reverberating tenor of voice.

William and Katherine both instinctively shared the international index finger on lips signal for 'shush the fuck up'.

"Whass it cost to heat this place is whass got me," came a second baritone voice, presumably from a chap named Burton, or Herbert, or maybe Albert, Gilbert, Wilbert, Filbert, Humbert, Cuthbert, or perhaps Delbert...

Footsteps growing louder...

"Bloody 'ell, more money than God, I should say, Bert," from the tenor.

William doused his lantern and pointed upwards at the tower's staircase. Katherine nodded and made her way quietly up a series of circular stone steps, which ended at a fourth-storey landing. Katherine gently slipped up an iron latch on the only oak door, which was embedded in the thick southern wall. William followed her through the portal and closed the door behind himself. They were now on the flat leaded roof of the eastern range of the Fountain Court.

The twins crouched down, faced east, and looked out over the Middle Court, tracing the rooftops they had just traversed. No guards were in sight, which was odd, if not somewhat unnerving.

"Holy Moley," said Katherine, rather abruptly.

William looked out in the direction of his sister's attentions. It wasn't hard to discern the measure of her focus; Some four-hundred yards away, in the east, the gloomy evening sky over the stables burst into flame.

10

He's your Twin, for Fuck's Sake

29th October 1587

Twenty-three year old Katherine nestled her violin gently within the crushed velvet lining of the case lying on the chaise beside her. Every sinew in her body was straining to snatch the bloody thing up again and launch it wildly across the ornate gardens in front of her, such that it disappeared into the fast-approaching evening shadows, never to be seen again.

Her mind countered what surely might have been a satisfying proposition with a self-deflating logic; her woeful playing was not the fault of the instrument. With this undisputable fact bearing upon her, she raised herself from the chair, took three paces forward and chucked her bow instead. It flew out of the ground floor loggia and was obliterated upon contact with a marble statue of a riderless horse in the centre of the nearest fountain. Katherine immediately regretted her somewhat childish outburst. Inanimate object or not, the bow had been her friend. Had others been present they may or may not have heard the crack of a twig snapping. The vibration of the bow's demise pulsed through Katherine in a wave of discordant notes screaming at her in perfect pitch, harmonics that would never live again in the frequency of joy. The ensuing silence was deafening.

Servants were lighting the evening's flambeaus at the far end of the garden, some two-hundred yards away in the west, replacing the faded torchlight of the setting sun.

Katherine normally loved this hour of the evening. The magic hour at Theobalds. Though to call it a mere 'house' was akin to taking the overwhelming grandeur of a four-mast tall ship and likening it to a bathtub. She had attempted to illuminate her father on this very point on countless occasions with very little success. Architecture was her dad's passion, and he had designed virtually every aspect of the sprawling estate. She and the house were the same age. Birthed twenty-three years ago. Though that is where any similarities ended. The house was young, and new, and growing still with each of her father's fresh ideas. She was unmarried. Privileged. Educated. Resolute in her situation. Already an old maid. She drove her father crazy. The great Sir William Cecil, the one and only Lord Burghley, Chief Minister to Queen Elizabeth I. A man amongst men. The only thing she and her father really had in common was architecture. He loved it. Katherine tolerated it.

She had other passions, that were best downplayed around her dad for political reasons. Katherine hated politics. And her dad had nothing to do with her broken bow.

Precious minutes remained before she would have to ready herself for the evening entertainments in the Great Hall. It was a trade-off. The solitude she commanded in the southeast wing of the manor – she had made it essentially hers around about the time she had helped her brother William escape from the clutches of the Queen's Yeomen of the Guard, ten years ago to the day – versus the absolute necessity of her appearances at her father's innumerable political soirées. It was an insufferable age to Katherine. A time in which physical beauty was assigned a ridiculous measure of importance in society. Particularly the top echelons of the 'elite' upper classes into which Katherine had the misfortune of being born. She didn't even look like her father. She didn't take after her mother, Mildred, either, for that matter. A fact that had kept her awake at night often during the unnerving years of insecurity and emotional instability that had accompanied those lonely years of her body's coming of age. But Katherine was considered beautiful. Not 'quite' beautiful. Not simply 'ravishing'. Not even drop-dead-gorgeous-indisputably-beddable-exquisite, beautiful. The plethora of toady-inbred-politicians, dignitaries, ambassadors, statesmen, dukes, lords, barons, princes, kings, and queens that normally constituted the patrons of her father's parties, considered Katherine to be way beyond the possible realms of bewitchingly beautiful. Except Elizabeth. Her 'auntie' Liz was Katherine's anchor in the lascivious seas of lechery that were her father's social gatherings. Liz had always guided Katherine through the trepidations of heraldic aesthetics. Especially during those years when her boobs had multiplied, her legs grown longer, and her arse had appeared. And there it was again, heredity. Beauty, if that was indeed how it could be coined in a word, was not Katherine's accomplishment. That had been determined for her. By her parents. Not that they lacked certain physical attributes considered attractive. But where the hell did she come from? And why? Well, the why was quite a different subject, really. And she hadn't figured that out yet, either. But she would. Her passionate study in the universal vibration of all things would offer relief and reward in the form of answers, one day. She and Liz would eventually figure it out. But Liz wasn't attending tonight. So, Katherine would dress up, suck it up, and swan about with a smile. To protect the trade-off.

A spattering of raindrops prompted Katherine to dash forward into the garden. She leapt across two miniature hedges, circumnavigated a geometrically perfect, but wholly unattractive, flowerbed and perched on the edge of the fountain with the riderless horse. Several of her father's recent ornamental curiosities, or additions to the household menagerie, one might say, were swimming lazily beneath the calm surface of the water in the form of Koi carp, that all seemed to be interested in her broken bow, which was floating, enveloped in tiny splashes from the rain droplets. Marginally out of her reach. Physically. Not magically. Katherine placed the palm of her right hand on the surface of the water and closed her eyes.

Forgive me.

Katherine's concentrated thought was rewarded when she opened her eyes, for the two halves of the bow were nudging her fingers, its knotted strings splaying out in a fan shape. Katherine lifted the bow and cradled it as she made her way back to the loggia in which she had previously been playing. She sat on the same chaise and dried off her bow by wiping it with a calf-skin cloth and laid it down atop her violin.

Ten years, on this day.

Katherine gazed out across the gardens again, but her focus was drawn to various points on the southside of the main house. Three storeys high in places, with its multitude of towers and silly turrets. Mostly darkened red colours of brick with grey stone cappings and corners and dressings. She was looking at the southern wall of the Great Chamber. Ten years ago it had been shrouded in scaffolding. She and William had been dressed as curates, and had been scrambling up the ladders, iron poles and wooden planks with two canal-boat-checking-Yeomen and two house-checking-Yeomen chasing after them.

"Guess we should have entered the house and taken the stairs."

"Nah. Where would be the fun in that?"

"Misdirection."

"Precisely. Come on."

He's crazy, but I love him.

Many of the windows were livening up as servants lit torches and candles within. She used to enjoy running around the flat roofs and walkways when she was a child. The more that had been built, the more diverse the games she and William had invented. Simple times, really. Except for moments when William's frequency had fragmented into confusing, complex chords with imperfect intervals and discordant notes that Katherine had either misunderstood or couldn't absorb. Those moments haunted her, still. Sometimes she couldn't get them out of her head. Or heart, for that matter. They made no sense. But they were still magical. Strangely.

Ten years. That night was some crazy shit, William.

Rockets ripping through the air, exploding in scintillating, effervescent, multicoloured, glittering illuminations.

BANG! BOOM! WHIZZZ. BANG! WHOOSH.

A smile swelled, and a tear welled above it. Katherine allowed it to fall from her eye onto her right cheek. She indulged as the salty liquid made its slow progress to her lips.

Katherine hadn't heard from William. She knew nothing of his whereabouts or wherewithal. He'd been a light, kind, humorous boy. Gifted physically. An athlete born within a court which fashioned lethargy the better indication of sound mind and status. He had a nice bum, from what she remembered of him in the few images she had captured in the passing of a half-opened door or occasional midnight swim. Shapely. His torso was crammed full of tight appeal. She remembered that.

Enough Katherine. He's your twin, for fuck's sake. Something wrong with you this evening. And for all, he might be dead already. Enough.

Katherine always chastised herself in the third party. It was something her Aunt Liz insisted upon. "One should only be accountable to Oneself, if another catches you out," Liz would say, with a wink.

You're not dead. I would have felt it.

Katherine glanced left, then right, along the lengths of the open-faced gallery. She was on her own. She slid along the chaise, hung her body out over the armrest and retrieved a crystal glass and a decanter of red wine from atop a walnut chest. She poured a healthy glass of the rich liquid and relaxed into a casual sitting position.

"You are a man now, William. Ten years is quite long enough. I shall celebrate you tonight with a glass. But no more until you make your mark. It is time. You hear me?" Katherine raised her glass to the gardens and beyond. "Cheers, brother. Hope you remember."

BANG. BOOM! WHOOSH. WHIZZZ...

Fireworks from all over the gardens. No decorum or rhythm. No choreographed display projecting undertones of story or philosophical meaning. No music. Just plain, old-fashioned fucking mayhem in the skies above.

William smiling. Bacon laughing.

What did he call himself?

"Fucking pyrotechnical genius! If I do say so myself."

A muffled thump inspired Katherine to cut short her emotional, sadly non-reciprocated toast to William. Though the wine was still very fine, obliging her to linger on the warm glowing sensations of taste, the onslaught of a sudden pressure change in her auditory perception, compelled her to lower her glass, and coerced her head to turn left, such that her eyes were given opportunity to clarify the 'what-the-fuck-was-that?' of things present.

But the loggia was devoid of anything unusual.

The archway to the chamber at the end of the corridor was open and unoccupied. It was the southernmost tower of the building, three floors high, with generous sized rooms some thirty yards square, and a flat lead roof. On a clear day the Tower of London could be seen from it. Katherine rarely spent time on the roof but enjoyed the blend of curious aromas emanating from the distillation processes housed within the chamber. That, and the fact that it was separated from the Middle Court of the great house by a goodly hundred yards or more. Rare was the occasion a soul would interrupt her soul-searching solace in that part of her father's sprawling edifice.

Bacon.

Had to be. He'd sneaked his way in. Or prayed his way in. Same difference, in Katherine's opinion. Shadows were shadows.

Glass shattered. The reverberations resonating three flights up, west facing, some seventy feet away, now flowing out across the gardens, reflecting off marble statues, trees, fountains, and back to her ears. A window. Exploding outward.

Moonstruck fool. What's he done now?

Katherine knew instantly that the next minute would see her stand – decanter firmly in hand of course – pick up her broken bow, turn left, walk, keep walking, trot, keep trotting, break into a run, then a healthy sprint, pass from loggia to tower, turn left, bound up two flights of stairs and alight on the third floor of the Still House Chamber, to take stock of whatever lay before her. She was so confident that she could make it happen, that she poured herself another glass of wine and downed it before she moved her long legs at all. It was a splendid vintage. Overtones of blackberry, mounted delicately on an aged earthly body. Sublime.

11

Burnt Bacon

Francis Bacon was lying in a heap beneath two up-turned tables, three entangled chairs, countless copper and glass coils, tubes, beakers, ropes, pulleys, mirrors, and one very large broken window.

"Francis! What the...?" Katherine dashed across the room, placing her wine decanter on an upturned wooden chest. Her bow was tossed down on a nearby bench, as the urgency of the situation gripped her, and she wrangled her way through the aftermath of what she could only assume to be an unintended explosion. Bacon didn't look too good. In a preliminary inspection she deduced he was still breathing, somewhat covered in scratches of varying severity, and mostly unconscious. Mostly. His eyes were open. Quite what they were staring at was at best subjective, so Katherine bypassed that enquiry and did the first thing she thought would be unquestionably helpful in the circumstance; she slapped Bacon across the face. Hard.

"Francis! Hey in there, can you see me?" she said, before lashing the fallen man's other cheek with a deft backhand. "Jesus, Francis. You in there?"

Bacon's head lolled sideways, and Katherine slid her hand underneath the rear of his skull.

"Francis! Hey, you're alright, it's me," she said, and thought about landing a third blow on her impromptu patient.

"Do not, touch, anything," Bacon uttered, weakly.

"What?" Katherine asked.

"You'll alter the conditions, of the sensory..." Bacon muttered in a whisper. His eyes, though crossed upon each other, were making a valiant attempt to scan their surroundings.

"What the hell are you talking about?"

"... sensory experience."

Katherine scanned the carnage surrounding them, "I'd say from experience that you're not making *sense*, if that's what you are getting at," Katherine scolded, "can you sit up?"

"Don't touch, anything!" Bacon offered, in a surprisingly forceful rattle.

Katherine instinctively did as she was instructed and withdrew her palm from Bacon's head. The mass of his confused cranium bounced down on the oak floorboards beneath it.

"Ow! Fuck!" Bacon protested. His eyes rolled around a bit more and slowly centred on Katherine, who was obediently kneeling motionless beside him. Bacon slowly propped himself up on his elbows and forced his neck to lift the weight of his head. His chin bounced twice on his left clavicle before supporting his face in an upright position.

"You in there yet?" Katherine asked.

"What?"

"What were you doing?"

"Can't hear," Bacon said, sitting up and shaking his head. He cupped his right palm over his right ear and tapped it a few times.

"Good. You're an idiot," Katherine put forth, testing the veracity of Bacon's assertion.

"Yes, I'm fine," Bacon said.

"You are not right in the head."

"I'm not dead."

"Head, you moron. You are not fit for office, Bacon!"

"Contamination, yes, don't move, I pray of you," Bacon said, and rolled onto his side.

Katherine smiled, in relief really, as she watched her slightly elder cousin slithering around the floor, carefully navigating broken furniture and God only knows what, in a clear effort to find an item of his longing in the wreckage around the room.

"You're bleeding on the floor," Katherine observed, "surely that is messing up your experiment?"

"Impediments, yes. The earth metals fought the materia prima. Perhaps the magnesia, yes…" Bacon offered, as he continued his sifting search, "though full assurance… I confess, I'm at a loss."

"What are you looking for?" enquired Katherine, "Perhaps I can be of help?"

"Don't touch…" Bacon said, absently, "a measure of heat remains in the debris field," Bacon raised his left palm towards Katherine. His hand was blackened and bleeding.

"Well, alright then," Katherine replied, in recognition.

Bacon continued his search, further afield now, skirting around the floor on his hands and knees. Katherine sensed Bacon's resonance returning from minor to predominantly major and she began to relax. He obviously wasn't hurt badly. At least not physically. The health of his mind was clearly up for debate.

"You are attending tonight?" Katherine asked.

"Yes, yes, later than sooner, perhaps."

"I do not suppose you'll tell me why you detonated yourself?"

"I should say it's better to be wrong than confused."

"Are you suggesting it worked?"

"The analysis is ongoing."

Bacon was now separated from Katherine by some fifteen feet. He was stretched out on his belly, probing a narrow gap between a stack of wine barrels with a fractured mirror tied to the end of a slight rod.

"Father's probably going to make you pay for the window."

"He shall be disappointed first."

"Penniless again?"

"Again, assumes repeat. My penury is perpetual."

"How can it be so?" Katherine said, then added, "Again."

"Had I two pennies I should wage you an answer," Bacon said. "Ah, ha!"

Katherine watched as her cousin folded himself into a sitting position with his bottom on the floor and his back resting against a barrel. His eyes were crossed again, but focused intently on a small, blackened object held up before his nose, between his thumb and index finger.

"What is that?" offered Katherine.

"The cause is certain. We must now examine the effect," Bacon replied, and stood up swiftly. He stepped forward three paces, and wobbled sideways, "Whoa, head spinning," he said and propped himself with a hand on a large copper pot still in the centre of the room.

"You must sit down," Katherine said, pacing quickly over and lending an arm to the unsteady man's aid. She plopped him down on a nearby bench.

"Head between your knees," Katherine soothed, while guiding Bacon's cranium in a direction best suited to her instruction.

"Acidus," Bacon mumbled

"Pardon you," Katherine said.

"The aqueous solution is required," stated Bacon. He maintained his sitting position with his head down, but held up the tiny, blackened object in his fingers.

"What?"

"It's over there, somewhere."

"Oh, Francis, give it a rest for a minute, be still."

"We must cleanse this ill-digested mass before the unforgiving minute robs us of conclusion. Don't you see?"

"Fine," Katherine replied, even though it wasn't, "what do you need? I'll fetch..."

"Glass beaker, rubbing brush, sanding cloth, and a vial from the three-drawer chest," Bacon rattled off, indicating a long oak bench stretched along the north wall of the room. Various tumblers, coils, tubes, drawers, and instruments of inexplicable determination were strewn along the bench. Katherine set off towards the collection.

"You are impossible," she said, "stay still."

"It's not as though you have better achievements to pursue."

Katherine paused, turned back towards Bacon, "What are you hiding?"

"There are no lies that pass my mind of present."

"Bullshit," Katherine replied, "you are hiding something, because you are no doubt about to cut to what you believe to be the quick of me with that gaslamp of a heart you carry."

"Whatever do you mean, cousin?"

"I see you, cousin. What is that in your fingers?"

"Pursue your task with the aqueous solution and a brush, pray, and all will be revealed. It's the green vial."

Katherine eyed Bacon warily for a moment longer than perhaps necessary for her warning signal to be recognised, then turned, and resumed her journey to the long bench. She began sifting through the implements upon it.

"I worry for you, Katie, that's all," said Bacon.

"Don't call me Katie," said Katherine.

"My hypocoristic diminutive is fashioned to demonstrate my affections for you."

"Yes, well, I am neither a pet nor a child," said Katherine.

"You're not a wife either, thus have no man to defend you from insult, Katie."

"Oh, you sanctimonious prick. You can't help yourself."

"It is the natural order of things; beautiful girls should take themselves to housekeeping at an early age."

"Oh, please. And what of those considered less than beautiful, by men?"

Katherine already had a small wire brush and was stacking three uniform beakers. A 'sanding cloth' appeared in her peripheral vision as the only thing on the table that was cloth-like. It had crushed seashells coating its surface. She made her way towards it.

"They should absent themselves from the ancestral pool, naturally," said Bacon, "and soften their loneliness in the devout study of the Lord's ways. Better for all concerned entirely."

"And what of men?"

"Men should not marry early, regardless of physical attributes. They should master themselves prior to mastering their chosen female."

"Oh, I see. And what of men such as yourself?"

"I fail to grasp your meaning."

"Do you?" Katherine said, "What of men who prefer nocturnal company in other men?"

"Ah, you offer a conundrum," Bacon said.

"Not really," replied Katherine, "merely guiding this conversation to matters you might know something of. Clearly your wits are struggling in comprehension of the fairer sex."

"The fairer sex? Indeed, I have not heard the expression," Bacon said.

Katherine delighted in Bacon's consternation and took her merry time searching through several open drawers of vials and jars. The green jar was bloody obvious, but she wasn't about to relinquish control of the conversation. This was fun. The forthcoming party would be a nightmare of sexist yearnings and unsuitable suitors. The trade-off.

"Your boyfriends never mentioned it at the gambling houses?"

"I feel certain they have not."

"Never a mention, of the fairer sex?"

"Quite so, I would have challenged the philosophy, thereby enacting grounds for recollection. And I don't gamble my riches, I spend them."

"Sorry, of course you do. But you would challenge the proposition that woman is more equitable, lovely, enchanting, desirable, tolerant, reasonable, passionate, caring and loving than man, as a general rule, Francis?"

"In the eyes of the Lord, men are equally fair as a sex, of course."

"And He's a 'he', is he? Your saviour of the flesh and spirit."

"I have accepted that hypothesis, freely."

"As I should, no doubt."

Katherine picked up the jar of green liquid and added it to the ensemble of implements clutched in a folded lap of her overalls. She didn't live in gowns. Cumbersome creations designed by men, for men's imaginations.

"No doubt, at all," Bacon declared.

"No experiment, analysis, conclusion as evidence?"

"His mysteries are beyond our sensory capabilities, at present. Such is the requirement of *faith*, that it fills those quantities of learning and truth that we have yet to invent."

"Is *He* married?"

"Ah ha. I see. Your impudence has a direction."

"Then He *is* married. Is He married to a girl or a boy?"

"I regret to say, I cannot say, with full assurance."

"Is the answer not to be found in scripture, Francis? Come now, surely you have read them all?"

"The glories of the creator are not *all* to be found in scripture, cousin."

"But all men are equal, are they not? Ergo, by extrapolation, all women equal also?"

"Some, perhaps, more equal than others."

"Are you going to marry a man, or a woman? Come Francis, state your preference, said Katherine, as she left the bench and returned to Bacon's seat, listening all the merry while. His vibrations were of healing. Less suspended, more dissonant sevenths resolving in major fifths. Shock from his experiment dissipating. Time to raise the pitch.

"Neither would be acceptable to my present circumstance, financially, that is."

"Love is independent of wealth, Sir," Katherine said, "I have heard you say it."

"I may have suggested such a reasoning, in the past."

"When you had money."

"Quite so."

"And the freedom to love whom you damn well pleased, because you could afford to."

"Because others would accept my choice, if I announced it with money, more likely."

"Ah ha. The charlatan quacks!"

"Dearest Katie, you will never attract a husband. Your intellect is soothing, but your mouth is far too loud."

"Relax, dear Francis, I feel certain the good Lord will bless me with a wealthy master that will provide for my mind and put my mouth to good use when he chooses."

Katherine arrived beside Bacon. "What do we do now?"

"Open the green jar."

Katherine laid everything else she was nurturing in the folded flap of her overalls carefully on the bench beside Bacon. She pulled a cork stopper from the 'green jar' and held it up in front of her cousin.

"Your sister Anne has three children already."

"She's twenty-nine."

Bacon plopped the blackened mess in his fingertips into the jar and the liquid within began to bubble with moderate aggression. Katherine baulked and handed the jar instinctively to Bacon, before leaving him to it. She set about retrieving her crystal decanter of wine, which was waiting patiently as it happened, not five feet away on the oak chest. It was surely time.

Bacon placed the bubbling jar down on the bench beside him with a cursory glance whilst continuing the conversation. "And you are not getting younger by the day."

"And Anne has five children. Two just happen to live... elsewhere."

"Yes, I know, I'm sorry," said Bacon.

"And I shall not be played by the lecherous fingers of an untrained man who plucks the strings of me in the discordant tones of his ambitions. I will not live as a pretty instrument stacked and silent on the hearth of loneliness, Francis."

"I worry for you, is all."

"That my looks are fading. That my womb is growing fallow. Oh, Francis, pray, how do you sleep at night?"

A man appeared in the entrance of the room and rapped his knuckles gently on the doorframe, before bowing his head marginally. He was about the ripe old age of thirty-five, solid in form, dark, tight-cropped-hair and beard and he dressed in a grey doublet and hose.

"Oh, hello there, Thomas. Come on in, won't you?" Katherine said, with a smile.

"Yes, your Grace. Sorry for the trouble. I have a letter for you."

"No trouble."

"It has Her Majesty's seal, see, or I wouldn't have interrupted. Good day to you Mister Bacon, Sir."

"Thomas. Nice to see you. How's... Missus Wilson?"

"Oh, well, I think, Sir. Thanks for asking," Thomas said. He was clearly unsure what to do with the Queen's letter.

Katherine relieved him quickly, "Just put it down there, thank you, Thomas," she said, indicating a nearby barrel. Thomas placed the sealed envelope down with considered reverence.

"Well, you think?" Bacon asked.

"Never quite know for sure, Sir. Times she don't seem right in the head on account of the young uns. But she's always a step ahead o' me, Sir. So, she must be half right."

"Stay for a drink, Thomas," Katherine said, as she took to half-filling one of Bacon's glass beakers from her decanter and offering it up towards the servant.

"Oh, pardon me, Lady Katherine, but I should probably best press on sharpish, on account of the Lord's festivities an' all."

"Thomas," Katherine said, with a coy smile, "you'll set a terrible example. If Mister Bacon here were to see another man place responsibilities ahead of leisure, why I feel certain he would collapse in a fit of despair and self-loathing."

"Oh, well, I suppose...well, we wouldn't want that to happen you, Sir."

Katherine found an appropriate use for the other two beakers on the bench, poured them half full, and handed one to Bacon and the other to Thomas.

"Your good health, miss," Thomas said, raising his cup.

"And you and yours," Katherine said.

The three imbibed in unison. Bacon was the first to speak, "What would you say to a public house tax, Thomas?"

"Sir?"

"It's a measure circulating on the Commons floor, you see. Early days but gathering impetus. A fixed levy on beer and ale in the public domain."

"Can they do that, Sir? In Parliament?"

"Well, we have in the past, you know. Crown needs money more than ever, Thomas."

"On account of the ships, is that it, Sir?"

"You know about that?" asked Bacon.

"It ain't really a secret is it, Sir? Anyone can see the Thames and what's in it. I was just sayin' to the missus the other day, them Spanish ain't going stave off forever, and what's Lizzie goin' do about it? She's gonna build a bunch of ships ain't she, I said."

"And what did your…"

"Gloria," Katherine interjected, quickly.

"Gloria, of course, sorry Thomas. What did Gloria make of Lizzie building ships?" asked Bacon, smoothly.

"Well, now thass you ask, first she set on raving 'bout Francis Drake and young Scarlett and who was better looking."

"Naturally." Bacon winding up charm he mainly reserved for the public masses when in his role as Member of Parliament in whatever jurisdiction he was elected. They were all the same. The district of Taunton, Somersetshire, which he currently represented, was no different. Except they drank more. Bonus of the work, his being a public figure and all. If he wasn't absolutely hammered in public on occasion, his constituents were prone to becoming suspicious.

"Right, and I pointed out that you can't compare 'em like that you see, 'cause Drake's an older bloke these days in't he, not really fair to him, is it?"

"Quite so, quite so."

"And after that distraction, Gloria took to saying how she thinks the world of Queen Liz and whatever, if she thinks ships is best, we should go for it an' that. As a nation under God an' Queen an' that. Bugger the cost she said. But o' course she didn't know about any levies on the beer coming about," concluded Thomas, while eyeing Bacon suspiciously.

"And what would she think of a marginal increase in beers and ales. Across the whole country of course."

"Right, of course, it'd have to be 'cross the whole country, wouldn' it," Thomas said, pondering the question with a finger sweeping his chin. "Well, I reckon Gloria'd be fine with it. Then she'd start drinkin' wine..."

Katherine cracked up laughing. Bacon struggled to retain his politician's smile.

"...and then she'd probably snore herself to sleep thinkin' 'bout Scarlett, I imagine. An' I wouldn't blame her for it either. He's clearly the better looking, ain't he? Bloody no-brainer, wouldn't you say, Miss Katherine?"

"Why should her opinion be paramount?"

"Well, she's a lady, Sir. And given your present condition an' all."

"My condition, Thomas?" Bacon said, fighting a frown.

"Whass Gloria call it? Your public persona. We got family down in Taunton, see, and they thinks the world of your efforts, Sir. All you do for 'em and that in the city with them politics. An' you likes a healthy drop of scrumpy. Goes a long way with the locals that do, Sir."

"Indeed. Well, I never really thought of it that way, Thomas," Bacon lied. He hated cider. Made him angry. Not a 'healthy drop' at all in his opinion. He thought of pressing Thomas to better define his so called 'condition', but interest was as good as admission.

"How might it be in Taunton, Thomas, were Mister Bacon to marry?" Katherine interjected, sensing the resonance of Bacon's inner struggle.

"Oh, I wouldn't do that, Sir, no. That'd open a few blind eyes, if you'll forgive my humble opinion, Sir."

"Forgiveness is for God, Thomas."

"Well, there it is exactly, Sir. Well said. You can love anything you want at present can't you, Sir. Drop o' the good stuff with the locals on occasion, God forgives, and nobody bothers. But you set about tying the knot with a lady, Sir, different bed to lie in altogether."

Katherine was quick to refill Thomas' beaker. This was golden. She couldn't keep her eyes off Bacon's restrained expression, barely changing beyond a passing quiver of indignation. His internal vibrations were off the scale.

"The sacrament of marriage is a profession of love, Thomas. I fail to see your meaning," said Bacon.

"Well, thass it exactly, Sir. Beautiful that is. Live and let live," Thomas said, and winked before downing the remainder of his wine. "Now, I'd best be getting back to work, Miss Katherine. Sorry again for the intrusion."

"Lovely seeing you, Thomas, give our best to Gloria."

"Oh, right oh, miss. She'll appreciate you for sure," Thomas said, placing his empty beaker on a nearby barrel. "And don't worry about the window, Sir. I'll see it fixed first thing tomorrow. Small price to pay as I see it. Your pursuits in that thing of, experiments..."

"Science," Bacon said.

"Right, science. Magical that is. Everyone loves the antics you get up to, Sir. You're a legend."

Thomas bowed and took his leave.

Katherine's suppressed giggling, swelled to laughter. She placed a knuckle under her left eye to wipe the first readying tear.

"I don't think that's funny," Bacon declared.

"I know. That's what's so funny," Katherine spluttered.

Bacon raised himself from the bench and took off towards the Queen's letter, "Oh really, let's see what's funny, shall we?"

"Don't you dare," Katherine warned, her laughter ceasing. "Don't, Francis."

Bacon upheld the letter and waved it provocatively. "Worried Auntie's forcing you to grow up?"

"That's Treason."

"How so? We're family, aren't we? Surely, we have each other's backs."

"Don't you bloody well open that."

"What's the worst that can happen?" Bacon teased, "I'm already condemned by the masses, it seems."

Katherine laughed again, "Outed perhaps. Not condemned. Just don't pick a wife."

"Oh, fuck you," said Bacon, ripping the seal from the letter, and stepping purposely away from Katherine.

"Francis! Don't!"

"Whass Lizzie got's to say these days?" asked Bacon, in a decent Somersetshire accent, while scanning the contents of the Monarch's private correspondence to his cousin, "Oh my... oh, my goodness gracious," he continued, theatrically.

Katherine rolled her eyes and shook her head. Any attempt to fight for the letter at this stage puerile and demeaning.

"Well... I'll be buggered. I might need a drop o' scrumpy after all," said Bacon, maintaining his counterfeit west-country tones.

"If you must, Francis. Please relay a verbatim version."

"Yes, my lady," Bacon said, and promptly cleared his throat.

"Dearest delectable Katherine," Bacon put forth, his imitation of the Queen's speech surpassing his previous farmer's bumpkin talk in accuracy.

Katherine smiled, already knowing where this was heading. The last thing Liz would ever describe her as was, 'delectable'.

"It is with heavy heart We see it fit to address you in this manner, not in person, but in the writing of these inclinations and intents," Bacon voiced, "for your duties to the

Crown of England are pressing and We have held reserve under the eyes of Our Lord since and of a time that is now becoming quickly offensive to the greater of Our Realms."

"Nice. Please, continue, lest Her Majesty should be made to wait any longer," Katherine said, with a smile.

"Let not Our words be considered instruction herein, but mere suggestion in as much as We may offer freedom of personal interpretation of one's own responsibilities..."

"Cut to the rub, Francis, I have a party to go to," Katherine said.

"Very well," Bacon replied, and cleared his throat a second time, "a moment." He pretended to scan the contents of the letter at pace, "Oh, my!"

"What?" Katherine said, warily.

"She wants you to marry."

"Oh, really? And whom has she chosen, exactly?"

"The Scarlett Buccaneer, it seems, would please her greatly."

"You are an absolute toe-rag of a human being, Bacon."

"No, really. I'm just the messenger here," said Bacon, with a sincere tone that was completely in tune with his conscious and subconscious vibrations as an entity. Katherine's heart punched her ribcage.

"Read it," said Bacon, offering the letter openly.

Katherine stepped forward reluctantly and took the letter. She turned and settled herself on the bench beside the jar of green solution and focused on the Queen's actual words. Bacon waited patiently, knowing where this experiment was already heading, if truth were in the making.

"For fuck's sake!" Katherine exclaimed.

Bacon felt sure there was more for her to offer. The scientist within him was pressing enquiry, but he'd already blown himself up once that evening, so he took a politician's stance and did nothing. Safest bet.

"She can't be serious!" Katherine rasped, between her teeth. It was a question in need, for a beloved cousin to answer. In an instant, she was as young and vulnerable as she ever remembered herself to be. The politician absented the room and her friend stepped forward.

"Makes sense for the country."

"Oh, fuck you, Francis."

"Hey, stop. Take pause. I'm with you here."

"Sorry," Katherine offered.

"Quite alright," said Bacon, knowingly. "Practical terms. Perspective. Not me. I just want to help. Elizabeth has a war coming to her. It's inevitable. The Queen wrote the letter. Not the girl. Not the woman. Not your Aunt. Not your mentor."

"I know."

"You are the most beautiful woman in England. Scarlett is the world's most handsome man. A pairing between you two, would provide a distraction for the people. Security.

Hope. Trust. The figureheads of the great British Empire to come. That is her reasoning. Hope."

"Hope, huh?"

"She's clever. Try to think of it her way. Scarlett can't marry a foreigner. And he can't go into a world war without a woman at home defending the people on his behalf."

"That's Liz's job."

"True, but Liz is getting on in years."

"Beauty again. I hate it. It's a curse," Katherine cried.

"To the truly beautiful, maybe. Certainly, a hypothesis worth considering."

"He's a gifted musician, I suppose."

"Scarlett is more than the everyman. There is that," said Bacon, gently.

Katherine lifted her broken bow string from the bench beside her and cradled it in her lap. Bacon was unsure of his next move but reassured in the fact it would be guided by Katherine if he listened. He gave her time.

"Can you fix it?" Katherine asked.

Bacon was uncertain, until Katherine raised her broken bow. He smiled. "I will try. Might not sound the same."

"Nothing will sound the same," Katherine sighed. "What am I to do?"

"I don't know. Scarlett arrives New Year's Day it seems. You have time. The announcement won't be made before the festivities in Greenwich."

"You sure of that?"

"It's best politics."

"I don't want to marry for hope!" Katherine said, "I want to marry for love."

"Same thing, really, if you think about it."

"Are they?" Katherine asked, "Maybe so. Thank you, Francis. What are you going to do?"

"Get laid as often as I can before Liz sends me a letter, I guess."

Katherine smiled and turned away with a shake of her head. Her eyes were suddenly drawn to the beaker of green fluid beside her. A thin layer of black sediment had amassed at the base of the jar. A twisted silver blob inlaid with small emerald and sapphire stones sat forlornly in the middle of the muck.

"You descend from evil itself! You prick to the quick, shirt-lifting, shit-for-lying, toe-rag, stealing bitch!" Katherine suddenly put forth, "That's my ring!"

Bacon leaned in for closer inspection, "It was," he said, smiling coyly.

"William made it! For me!!"

"I wanted to understand how he fused the gemstones you see, impossible..."

"Get the fuck out!"

"Oops a daisy," Bacon blurted, and bolted from the room.

Katherine watched him go, biting her lip the whole time. She breathed deeply and looked back at the tiny, ruined treasure in her hand. Tears welled up and her shoulders started quivering. She swallowed, breathed again, closed her eyes, and willed her shaking core a return to the root note of her being. After a long minute she slowly opened her eyes again.

"It's time, brother. Please, come home."

12

Fighting the Turns of the Gale

7th November 1587

Smoke. Choking. Gagging. Puking. Retching. **Thirty-four** *souls in the gunpowder reek.*

The stench of burning flesh charring the pages of a book. A book.

Twenty men lost to the sea, and yet one found. **Twenty-one** *souls adrift on flaming waters churning and tumbling with froth and fire.*

'Where am I? Where are we? Can't see!'

Relentless, unrepenting torrents sucking in the darkness of the depths.

Smothering mist above. All around. 'Where is she?'

Katherine. A woman. Blue velvet and silver.

Burning heat. The cover of the book. The smouldering cover embossed with spiral closing on darkness. Tighter and tighter the turn.

Thirteen women lost in a maze. Bearing starboard, fire. A turn to port, fog.

Smothering fog. Sweltering, suffocating retreat.

Barnacles crawling over each other. Burying into the ship's hull. Red with blood in churning water, shocked with flashes of scalding light.

The rudder. Huge. Unyielding ropes, frayed with burning tar.

Katherine. Wild, free, incandescent with rage. Wild winds ravaging her long raven hair. At the helm. Cutlass strapped to her side. Fighting the turns of the gale.

Eight men rushing the quarterdeck. Muskets firing. Swords slashing. Choking smoke.

The stench of flesh burning and blackening and falling through the decks in meaty chunks. Below to the sea.

Five sharks in a frenzy. Blood, bone, and charred flesh feeding the ocean's turmoil.

To port. Long, blackened curve. Walls of bones and skulls. Turn to port. Always to port.

Three carracks. The horizon. Explosions of blackened cannon fire lighting the clouds.

Darkness.

Echoes of pain. Cries drowning in waves of salt and surf. 'Close Hauled' by the howling winds. No return. Head to wind. Head to wind. Must breathe... How, when there is no air?

Drink. Must drink. Yet what? Why?

Two *islands separated by a channel. West winds driving the currents between.*

Darkness blinding. Shoals scratching for souls.

One *man crying. Trying to speak. His words meaningless. Blathering in winds behind raving eyes. Trapped. His soul chained to the darkness of his tattered mind.*

Katherine.

One *sword lying on the deck. Blood washing from its blade in the rain.*

Katherine.

Nothing. *Nought. Alpha and Omega.*

BREATHE!

William sucked in a long deep breath and opened his eyes. They were sore. Burning with tiredness. Waking was exhausting. He sat up slowly, twisted, and lowered his feet from Scarlett's bed to the deck. The storm outside was raging. The ship was heaving. The *Bride's* timbers creaking and moaning in objection to the stresses thrown at her by the elements she was fighting.

Fury.

William felt it. It welled up in him as pure, unadulterated wrath.

Katherine.

He sat as still as the ship would allow, while he focused on tempering the storm within himself. Blind, uncontrollable anger was no more constructive than incomprehensible ignorance. And wrong. Only hurt and shame accompanied unmanageable fury. Nothing good. Nothing kind. Nothing of vision.

Pen and paper. Step by step. Map it out.

William rose from the bed, crossed the cabin, and rounded on a teak dresser pinned to the starboard wall. He opened the second drawer down and third from left, for there he knew he would find the required stationery. He quickly snatched up a quilled pen, ink pot and a sheet of parchment paper. He slapped the items down on the sideboard top and began scribbling. Top right-hand corner; a cross, as if indicating points on a compass, but without lettering. The north/south of it yet unknown. From the bottom right-hand corner William drew a spiral curve, wrapping around itself in two decreasing circles terminating roughly in the centre of the page.

What the fuck is that, William?

He stowed the quill and ink pot back in the appropriate drawer, snatched up the paper, dashed to the door of the cabin, threw open the door, and propped himself against the jamb.

Scarlett was anchored firmly at the helm. Soaked to the skin by lashing rain. So, too, the crewman alongside him.

Ned 'Toes' Williams was the go-to man. In rough weather it took two men to handle the ship's wheel and 'Toes' was, without question, the strongest man aboard. He also had the biggest feet. He was smart, in a practical way. Knew his left from right. Apprenticed in Devon as a finishing-carpenter at a well to do furniture maker, before taking off cross country with the owner's three daughters. Good times by Ned's accounts, and, let it be said, the crew rarely challenged him on the validity of his stories.

Both watches, day and night, were up and about on the rigging or on decks, saturated in saltwater and rain. The storm was fierce, yet all the *Bride's* sails were aloft and chomping at the tumultuous winds like a pack of wild dogs ripping into a sack of stray kittens. Spray from the sea scourged the decks. The *Bride's* masts were tilted some thirty degrees to the leeward broad and her bowsprit bounced over every crest rolling in against her.

Holy shit.

William searched out across the waters for the Spanish ship of doom and death, but he couldn't see her at all. He staggered forward to the helm and positioned himself alongside Scarlett.

"Presenting for duty, Captain," William shouted.

Scarlett ignored William momentarily, directing his attention towards 'Paws'. "About for a reach on the beam, Mister Prowse!"

'Paws' stumbled up the stair from the main deck, bouncing off both banisters, and planted himself against the mizzenmast. "Aye Captain, but let's dowse the top sheets for Christ's sake, she'll keel over on the turn, Sir!"

"Mister Prowse, set a beam reach alive and dowse your concerns, if you please!" Scarlett bellowed.

"Aye, aye, Captain," said 'Paws', before reluctantly bouncing his way back down to the main deck. "O'Reilly! You lads. Set a full turn o' the mainsail! Come up on her hard! Bear all hands!"

'Paws'' bellowing tones were drowned to William's ears almost as soon as they had left the Boatswain's mouth, such was the force of the rising winds. But a dozen of the crew, including Shamus O'Reilly, were clearly getting the message, as they set about rotating the lower yards on the mainmast towards a forty-five-degree angle to the beam. Sixty other men about ship followed the lead and scrambled into groups, heaving and pulling ties and braces on other sails to bring them in line with the main. In this weather, it would drive the *Bride* almost directly north at a punishing clip, but vulnerable to a potentially lethal broadside as she traversed the thirty-foot waves rolling in from east to west. Scarlett was Scarlett, but every man on board who wasn't already pissing his breeches, set about doing just that.

The rain darkened clouds were smothering the twilight norms. William saw the first of the evening's lightning flashes, streaking downwards at a point masked by a grey horizon. An island for sure, but which one?

"Captain!" William shouted, "Where is the *Dark Saint*?"

"That way," Scarlett replied, pointing to port and slightly abaft.

William considered the meaning. Scarlett had driven the *Bride* southeast of the Spanish ship which had already been on a south-easterly course, hoping to skirt the storm in which they were now fully embroiled. A fast sail all the while he'd slept. Now, they were coming about fully north. Scarlett now had the windward advantage, if it could be referred to as such in these winds.

"You saw her make the turn north, Captain?"

"What would you do with a belly full of gold and that storm spreading out over the Atlantic the way she's shaping?"

"I'd find the shallows on the western side of an isle and hole up, Captain," said William, "and fucking fast."

"That's what the bastard's doing, I'm sure of it."

"Which isle, do you think?"

"That, Master Hope, is the prize question," Scarlett said, with a broad smile.

"We're gonna have to do the same," William replied, holding up the soaked parchment with the spiral curve in leaking ink.

"What the fuck is that, William?"

"Unsure, yet. Comes with a story."

Scarlett turned to 'Toes' Williams, "Ned, have you the legs to guide her a while alone?"

"Aye, Captain, me and the *Bride* will hold accord 'til you return," shouted the big man.

Scarlett nodded, tapped William on the shoulder and the two men made their way aft, entering Scarlett's cabin. William was quick to lay his sketch on a dining table in the centre of the outer of the cabin's two rooms. He dashed to Scarlett's bedroom and fetched the quill and ink before returning.

"So, what have we got?" Scarlett asked earnestly.

"Again, not sure, but we have a heading."

"North."

"North," William said and, as he did so, he scribbled a large 'N' on the cross in the top right-hand corner of his primitive illustration. "But that said, North is sort of relative."

"Ah," said Scarlett, pausing for consideration, "I see your meaning."

"Isles," Scarlett said, as he took the pen from William and dipped it into the ink pot, before sketching two alternate compass bearings near the top of the crude spiral.

"Isles," said William, "assume our current position is bottom right."

Scarlett immediately began drafting a series of shapes in a line parallel to the spiral curve on the crude, sodden amateur map. Beginning with Dominica in the bottom right corner, the blobs of ink indicated, Guadeloupe, Montserrat...

"No, put Antigua on the east of the line," William offered.

Scarlett did so with the pen... Antigua and Barbuda, Saint Kitts and Nevis... "Anguilla?"

"North. We spiral back before that," answered William.

"Very well," Scarlett said, and sketched Anguilla above the topmost part of the tightening spiral line on the drawing, which, by now, constituted several blobs marking the chain of Isles making up the lesser Antilles, separating the Caribbean Sea from the Atlantic Ocean.

"Now what?"

William closed his eyes for a moment of recollection.

"Katherine. Smoke. Twenty men overboard, but not drowned. One saved. The stern. The dark stern. The narrows. Something about the narrows. The current."

"Narrows?"

"The channel between two islands. Can't see them but they are there."

"Saint Kitts and Nevis," Scarlett concluded, indicating the small gap between the appropriate blobs on the map, with arrows marking the direction of the prevailing winds and waters.

"What else?"

William studied the drawing for a moment and shook his head. "Your sword, washed in blood, falling to the deck."

"That is not helping," Scarlett said, in trepidation.

"It might not be your blood."

"I fucking hope not, Jesus," voiced Scarlett, his smile cutting through any tension in the room. Both men studied the crude sketch once again in silence.

"You mentioned the stern," Scarlett stated.

"I saw the rudder."

"Well, why didn't you say so?" Scarlett beamed, "I'll be damned, but it's brilliant young William."

"It is?"

"Come, Ned'll be tiring at the helm," Scarlett said, grabbing the map and marching to the door.

William followed Scarlett out onto the quarterdeck and the two men approached the *Bride's* wheel. 'Toes' was busting his nuts staying the course in the unruly weather.

"Take a breather, Ned. Go sit down for a spell."

"Thank you, Captain, I'm losing the answer with her. I'm sorry," 'Toes' said, humbly.

"Sorry, my bollocks, Ned, you've done well. Sit down."

'Toes' handed the wheel over to Scarlett and stumbled aft before slumping down on a coiled rope, staying his back to the wall of Scarlett's cabin.

William took up where 'Toes' left off, aiding Scarlett at the helm.

"Mister Prowse!" Scarlett bellowed out over the main deck, "Mister Prowse!"

'Paws' came to sharpish and was on the stairs from the main deck in a heartbeat. One of a hundred such hearts beating wildly aboard ship, for the weather was worsening to hurricane force, and the *Bride* was listing closer to forty degrees with each passing minute.

"She's on her beam ends, Roger," Scarlett cried, "We'll heave to, and haul down to the lower topsails. Half the jibs and settle the sheets. Horse the bloody sails if you have to."

"Aye, aye, Captain!" 'Paws' yelled, holding a fist aloft and punching the air, before turning fore towards the main deck. He had his 'pipe' in his mouth before he hit the main stairs, and screamed through it with all his might, instructing the crew with fierce whistled orders that cut through the raging gale.

William watched as the crew bounced alive and set about lowering all the square sails above the main course, from the Royals down to the Lower Topgallants. Men were dangling from yards and slipping through shrouds and ratlines. As they worked, he and Scarlett began nosing the *Bride's* bowsprit to starboard, closing the reach to windward. After several minutes the ships masts began to tilt increasingly to the vertical, and her decks began to level across the beam. The froth topped thirty-foot swells of the ocean remained relentless.

"Now what?" William asked.

"I fancy the *Saint of the Dark* will make for Saint Kitts, and you'll be waiting for it."

"I'll be waiting?"

"Quite so," Scarlett assured.

"How so?" asked William.

"Scarlett has a plan. Long as you don't mind getting wet," Scarlett said, his smile loaded with bright white teeth and irony. "Remind me again, do you swim?"

"Remind *me* again, can you be a worse bellend, Captain?"

"I'd volunteer myself, but you're younger and fitter," Scarlett encouraged, wryly.

"Oh really, and what exactly have I volunteered to do?"

"This is all about finding you a girl, after all, so step up man. Courage," Scarlett said.

"Aye, aye Captain Bellend," William replied, thoroughly amused. "What do you have in mind?"

Scarlett laid out his plan for attacking the Spanish ship as the *Bride's* crew exercised their skilful seamanship in the battle with the elements. With the sails doused to his satisfaction, and the ship steadying at the helm, Scarlett called his Boatswain to the quarterdeck once again. As 'Paws' made his way aft across the main deck, Scarlett addressed William, "I'll need you to calm a few nerves out there for a time, while you ready the boats."

"Aye, Sir. But who's going to calm my nerves?" replied William.

Scarlett smiled, "And pick the best swimmers."

"Thought had occurred already," William affirmed.

'Paws' was not long in arriving beside the helm. This was a rare occasion when he looked his own age. If you knew him, he was clearly tiring but managing to maintain at least the outward appearance of inner strength.

"Captain?"

"How are you holding up, Roger?"

"Me airs and graces are full o' brass tacks, Captain," 'Paws' said with a smile. "Now, what's our headin'?"

"North again. We'll skirt Montserrat to the west, keeping an eye for the *Dark*."

"Won't find her there, Captain," said 'Paws', "I'll favour Saint Kitts if you'll pardon me nerve."

"It's what I'm betting on. We'll take Nevis on the windward side and come about in a loop to the northwest, rounding the head of Kitts to leeward. We'll drive south on the Spaniard in the witching hours."

"An' if she ain't there, Captain?"

"The First Mate will be saved a long swim in shark infested waters, Roger. And he'll thank you for it," Scarlett said and burst out laughing.

William shook his head, "Come Roger, I'll need a few men off the rigging and down with me on the gun deck for a spell."

'Paws' stepped in alongside William, "Aye Master William. Name them."

Scarlett watched as his two most trusted men descended the stair to the main deck and set about his orders. He wondered if they held fear to their breasts the way he did. They wouldn't show it of course. And he was Scarlett. He couldn't show it. Ever.

Does a man ever get to grow up? I'm thirty-frigging-three and all I want to do is go the fuck home and be alone with my thoughts for a bit. As if I was seven again. When I was allowed to cry. And fuck the gold! I have enough gold. I just want to see these good men home to their families safe and sound and alive. Without scars. Without trauma. Without hurt... was I really allowed to cry when I was seven? Was I, truly? I don't remember. Blacked that one out, haven't you Scarlett? You big baby.

Scarlett's musing was accompanied by progressive turns of the spokes on the helm, slow and steady, in line with whistled commands from 'Paws' to the men as the sails were set for a close reach on a northward heading. A difficult sail, but doable. It would be alright. He was Scarlett, after all.

'Toes' Williams stepped up beside the helm, "Captain."

"Are you well rested enough, Ned?" Scarlett asked.

"That I am, Sir."

'Toes' took his place in aiding Scarlett and the two men looked on as 'Paws' and William separated on the main deck. Having left his instructions behind with 'Paws', William made his way fore of the mainmast and entered the crew's quarters through a door in the forecastle. From there he skipped down a ladder and entered the *Bride's* upper gun deck. She held sixteen cannon to port and sixteen more to starboard, either side of a central isle, in a cramped space with a low ceiling supporting the main deck above with thick oak beams and iron braces and plates. Smells of gunpowder, stale clothing, and the old sweat of a hundred hard working men pervaded the space. He remembered the first time he encountered the same odour. He'd been thirteen years old. And the ship that he had boarded had been named the *Pelican* at the time.

Dye Bant, John Prior, Jim Dolby, Martin 'Mumbles' No-Name, and Ted 'Tumbles' Turner were all waiting patiently. Thirty other men, predominantly gun crew, were moving about the space busy with preparations for the forthcoming conflict. Checking flints, fuses, chocks, tackles, ropes and cleaning the interior of cannon barrels with wet swabs. Powder lads were running back and forth from the magazine stores two decks below, with bags of coarse-grained gunpowder stocks and various types of iron shot.

The hive of activity punched through William's senses, and he concentrated hard at calming the fury of fears attacking him from all the men around him.

Katherine.

As William approached the centre of the room, John Prior was the first to pipe up, "Be a nice night fer a stroll outta the rain, Will."

William smiled, "My way of offering a bribe, John, that's all."

"Well, I'll take it, wha'd'ya need?"

An image of Prior smashed into William's mind. He was plummeting head-first into the depths of the ocean, entangled in ropes attached to a four-foot-long cast iron harpoon gun barrel. The two-inch muzzle bore pressing underneath his chin, John was twisting and turning and fighting to free himself.

"Will, whass the plan exactly?" Prior asked.

William was on the gun deck facing Prior again, "Right. Where's Shamus? And I asked for Richard Bately."

"Left them rounding up the others, Will, we thought we'd get down 'ere sharpish in case you thought we all run out on you, see," Jim Dolby put forth.

"Decent of you Jim, my thanks."

A vision of Dolby pierced William's consciousness. He was swimming hard against a current, choking in a wild surf that picked him clear of the water and smashed his flailing body hard down on barnacle covered rocks, breaking most of the bones in his body.

"Jesus, sorry, Will," Shamus O'Reilly's unmistakable voice booming out with his approach behind William. "Hell of a time grabbing the boys."

Five members of the crew followed Shamus in a line between the cannon having arrived from the lower decks. William knew them to be among the strongest swimmers aboard. Not the sharpest perhaps, or huge in personalities of distinction, but solid, unquestioning types, all in their early twenties. Good men. It was all he needed. For now.

"Right lads, gather round as best you can," William said.

The men did so and huddled up in front of the First Mate, their attentions spiked with adrenaline, but unaware that their emotions were driven by anything other than excitement and fear because adrenaline, cortisol, serotonin, oxytocin, and in fact the entire endocrine signalling system hadn't been invented yet. Much good it did anyone, anyway. Whole bloody thing was way too delicate. These men weren't.

"We need to load up two yawl-boats with as many kegs of powder and shot as they can carry. Bags of langridge.

Any scrap and metal you can find lads," William instructed, "and we'll have ten men to a boat. Divide yourselves accordingly. John you'll skipper one, I'll take the other."

"Aye Cap... I mean, Will," John Prior said.

"And we'll need the harpoons. Three in a boat. Roped and anchored to the prows," William continued, "and extra oars, we'll not be needing sails."

Martin 'Mumbles' was quick to the obvious question, "Where the fuck are we rowin' in this weather, Will?"

"You won't be rowing anywhere Martin. I need you supervising the ammunitions and explosives. I want everything checked and double checked. These men's lives depend on it."

"That I can do, Master William, that I can," said 'Mumbles'.

"Right man for the job, Martin," William said.

"Master William!"

Richard Bately jumped down the ladder at the foremost end of the room. He was followed by a contingent of eight solidly built crewmen, all of them drowned wet from the past few hours on the decks and rigging.

"Master William," Bately continued, as he approached at a clip, "got them down as fast as I could, Sir, sorry."

"Calm yourself Richard, all's well and it'll end well, too."

"Yes, Sir, thank you, Sir."

As he took in the young crewman, William was smacked in the face by yet another premonition. Bately tripping, falling onto a split keg of gunpowder with a lit fuse stick. The conclusion wasn't pretty.

"What have we missed, Master William?" asked Bately, innocently.

"Martin will direct you accordingly in a few," William said. "The guts of the story lads, is that we're taking two boats through the narrows between Kitts and Nevis in these seas, and we're gonna come up on the *Dark Saint* in the shallows."

"Where in the shallows?"

"The reckoning is she'll take to anchor west of Kitts, to ride out the storm," William explained efficiently.

"And where's the bloody *Bride* gonna be at, while we're tryin' to feckin' row about in these seas?" Dye Bant asking the question, masking none of his scepticism.

"Pipe down now, Dye, Will ain't gonna see us wrong in this," John Prior said. "Is you Will?"

"This isn't a suicide mission, if that's what you're getting at, Dye," William assured, "Everyone here is gonna be alive tomorrow morning."

"What about tomorrow afternoon?" from 'Tumbles.'

William smiled. "Let's get to daylight first, shall we, Ted? Scarlett's coming about after dropping us off, then he's gonna bear down on the *Santa Oscuro* from the north."

"In the night?" Richard Bately put forth.

"In the night."

"And whass with the munitions on the boats, Will?" Ted 'Tumbles' Turner asked.

"We're going to tie them to the stern of the Spanish ship and blow the arse end out of her, rudder and all," William said, flatly.

"They ain't gonna expect that," John Prior said.

"If she's even there an' anchored," Dye Bant put out.

"Wait a solid minute here, am I the only one sees a major flaw in this plan?" Jim Dolby asked.

"Probably not, Jim," said William, "but you have the floor. What's on your mind?"

"Well, what happens to us, like, when we blows shit up?"

"It's a good question," Dye Bant said.

"Yar it is," from 'Mumbles'.

"Hellfire it is, where do we end up in this, Will?" Jim Dolby pressed.

"We're going to set the fuses and abandon the boats. We'll rope ourselves together in two teams and wait it out until Scarlett's done over the Spanish, or we'll swim for the *Bride* if we can."

"Fuck me," from Jim Dolby.

"I reckon it could work," Richard Bately mused.

"Yar, it just might," Shamus O'Reilly, thinking on it.

"Now that... see now, it's bloody brilliant, that is," Dye Bant, coming around with enthusiasm.

"Aye, if the bloody sharks don't get us," from 'Tumbles'.

"Sharks would spit you the fuck out with the first bite, man. Least you'll be getting a bath tonight," John Prior, in the set of things.

"What'd mean ye be that then?"

"Well, you been smellin' same as your sister's twat for more than a solid month, now that you bring it up," John Prior, raising his game.

William smiled, and he'd have allowed a few verses in encore, but time was pressing, so he moved things along while he still had the men's full attentions. "The one thing we do not do is swim for land in these seas."

"Any port in a storm, Will," 'Mumbles' said quietly.

"Listen now and mark me. We stay afloat. Jim, this is for you in particular; mark it. Stay out of the surf and away from the rocks," William stressed. "Tempting it will be, but there are ungodly rips off Kitts in these seas and they're stronger than all of us close by the shores."

"Alright, Will," Jim Dolby said.

"Has everyone marked me on this?" William pressed, "Everyone?" The men looked around each other's faces, then back at William.

"I think we all got it, don't we lads?" John Prior prompted-ed.

"Yar! Got it."

"Makes good sense."

"Right wisdom in it, for sure."

"Richard, Stay away from the fuses. You'll be the first man off my boat. Got it?" William said, pressing young Bately with fierce intent.

"Yes, Sir. First man in the drink," Bately responded.

"John, you'll direct your boat from the rear. And stay the fuck away from the harpoons."

"No harpoons, got it, Will, thank you," Prior said in earnest.

"Right lads, any other questions?"

The men looked back and forth between each other chancing that they'd covered enough to be getting on without further ado. It seems they had. No questions were forthcoming.

"See you on deck shortly. Set to it lads," William said. "Richard, a moment if you will."

Young Bately gave pause while those around him mustered away to split into two groups and perform their given tasks.

"Yes, Master William," Bately said.

"Sure you're up for this? I'm asking a lot of you," William said, gently. Truth was, Scarlett had suggested that William take Bately under his wing so he could protect the boy from the ravages of the sea fight ahead. Hand to hand combat between two galleons was no place for a delicate boy like Richard. Least not at his age. He had too fine a young mind to be scarred for life by the sheer brutality of muskets, cannon, and swords at close range.

"I'm, proud you asked me, Master William."

"Call me Will tonight, Richard, just like the others," William said, "and see to it that we have a few things that float loaded over the munitions."

"Empty barrels, cork, and such? Is that it?" Bately asked.

"Exactly right."

"Alright, Will," Bately said, "and I'll stay away from the fuses. I reckon yours and Scarlett's plan is gonna be plain sailing. It's going to be great."

Richard Bately smiled, ran off towards the forecastle and disappeared up a ladder.

Richard Bately was wrong.

Richard Bately didn't know it yet, that every battle plan turns to shit with the first shot fired. If Shamus O'Reilly had still been in the room, he could have asked Murphy on behalf of young Bately, and Murphy would have laughed and told the boy that *if* things can turn to shit, they surely will. And always with the first shot fired. But *that* Murphy hadn't been born yet so, all things considered, it didn't much matter.

William Hope absorbed the energy of the gundeck for a few moments and concentrated on what mattered most to him.

Katherine.

William breathed deeply, taking in the smells and sounds of the room and calmly walked aft towards the stern.

13

Close Hauled, on Fire, and True

Álvaro de Bazán, Marquess of Santa Cruz, Spanish Fleet Admiral, undefeated in a naval career spanning over fifty years, was not aboard the *Santa Oscuro*. He was in Lisbon, copping a whole lot of shit from King Philip II, because Sir Francis Drake had caught the Spanish fleet napping in the harbour of Cadiz and had properly toasted the king's beard by sinking a bunch of Spanish ships. That had been April. This was November. It was definitely on between England and Spain. War was at hand, and a great number of people knew it.

Capitán Juan Martinezde Recalde was one of them. A tall, regal figure of a man, he sported a well-trimmed beard and a thinning head of mousy hair. He was at the helm of the *Santa Oscuro*, tired from the long day's sail in ravaging winds and seas. His weariness had been amplified by the exhilarating hours escaping the relentless pursuit by the English ship *Maiden Bride*, her *bastardo* good-looking Captain Scarlett, and yet another of the bastardo English Protestant winds that had come with him. A mere squall engorging to a hurricane, cutting the *Oscuro's* path to freedom across the Atlantic, and the triumphant return to mother España laden with riches and glory.

As night closed in, Capitán Recalde had given orders to heave to and drop anchor a half mile offshore to wait out the storm in the relative safety of the island mass now fore of the bowsprit. His crew were presently dousing the last of the mainsails on the five masts. One lower jib and one lateen sail aft the mizzenmast, he would leave loose against the turbulent winds. The *Oscuro* was a huge ship. The largest he had ever commanded. She was two-hundred-and-ten feet along the keel, forty-eight feet at the beam, with two-hundred-and-forty-one cannon stored on three separate gun decks. She had a carvel-built hull made of solid oak and she displaced some twelve-hundred tons in the water.

It had been a long voyage since departing his home port in Seville. Fourteen months had seen ports in Veracruz, Portobello, and Cartagena, among others, and, with each passing stop, the *Oscuro* had taken on more cargo, pushing the ship lower on the waterline.

Recalde still didn't know the ship. She was a strange lady. Temperamental. Unkind to the crew at times. He had lost nearly one third of his original three-hundred crewmen to scurvy and influenzas. Gangrene had proven a constant scourge, even though they had not engaged in a single battle on the voyage, the slightest cuts or breaks of skin or bone were proving to be incurable on-board ship. His crew – hand-picked by himself and vetted by his mentor, the great Álvaro de Bazán – experienced, sea hardened warriors, naturally loyal at all costs to Capitán, King and España, were now shadows of themselves. Weary, burdened with superstitions and rumours. Curses they believed were attached to the Peruvian silver and gold and Mexican gemstones weighting the holds of the ship and burdening the souls of her sailors.

Recalde lashed the ship's wheel with rope ties, slowly and methodically securing the required knots. The only heading he would undertake for the remainder of the night was for his cabin and the bottle of vintage port therein. His First Mate, a fine young sailor of Cuban descent, by the name of Pedro Garcia, was seeing to it that every lantern aboard was being quenched. Pedro would head the night watch in absolute darkness. The moon was but a crescent in a storm ridden sky. What the enemy couldn't see, they couldn't take.

Recalde was about to step away aft, out of the rain, and into the warmth of his cabin, when a flickering caught his attention past the port side gunwale, way off on the horizon to the north.

*****

Scarlett and 'Toes' Williams were sharing the load at the *Bride's* helm. A brief spell heaved to in the eastern wash, between the islands of Nevis and Kitts, had seen William and his teams of mercenaries lowered from main deck to the sea in two rowboats crammed with explosives. The relatively short journey northward, skirting the coast of Saint Kitts on the windward side had been nothing short of a nightmare sail. The *Bride* had been forced uncomfortably close to banks, headlands, shoals, and all manner of rocky outcroppings barely seen in the wretched mists and darkness of the storm front. The crew had been amazingly diligent and courageous in responding to 'Paws'' countless whistles and commands. Scarlett honestly felt he'd been lucky. If asked, he would profess he didn't quite understand where half his decisions and seamanship had come from.

Best luck of the devil's English children, Scarlett, old boy.

An orderly turn to port a few hundred yards past the headland reach had seen a relatively plain sail around the north of the island, though running downwind on the limits of a broad reach had very nearly seen the *Bride* driven uncontrollably into the northernmost headland outcropping. It had been the offshore currents that had saved them, the heavy swells literally throwing the ship away from the rocks in an uncontrollable gybe.

"Mister Prowse!" Scarlett bellowed, as he and 'Toes' guided the ship carefully to port once again, bearing down on a south-easterly heading. Spiral to port. They had reached the leeward side of the island, and the seas were calming with each passing crest of the swells.

"Mister Prowse, a moment, if you will!" Scarlett yelled out.

'Paws' was bounding onto the foot of the main stair to the quarterdeck for what seemed to him to be a thousand-and-one times that night. His thighs were burning, and his back was in pieces, but he forced the pain out of his mind and laboured up the steps.

"Aye, Captain, what d'ye have in mind?"

"A keg of port and a fine wench in a warm bed, Roger," Scarlett grinned. "What about you?"

"I'll happily have a go when ye're done with her, Captain, it'll give me a chance to catch me breath," 'Paws' answered.

"Very well, it shall be so," Scarlett answered with a smile. "Have the lads light every lantern aboard and hang them from every spar and yard. If that Spaniard is anchored, she'll be no more than five miles beyond the bow as we lie, and I want her to see us bearing down on them like a devil's angel."

"Put a right fear into them, is that it, Captain?"

"Closed hauled, on fire, and true for them," Scarlett said, "I want their full attention."

"I expect they'll be more than listenin'," quipped 'Paws'.

"I mean to give William every chance by way of distraction."

"Aye, Captain. I see your meaning. I'll have the lads in accord with the lamps." 'Paws' was about to say more but thought better of it. He knew enough. It was a hell of a tactic. Get them killed outright if it didn't work. 'Paws' made his way back down the stair to the main deck. They would undoubtedly be facing a hundred-gun broadside if they were the slightest behindhand in spotting the *Santa Oscuro.*

*****

William Hope had discovered that rowing would never be, from that night onwards, a sport he ever wished to pursue in the future. If he had a future, that is. That had been up for considerable debate for the past hour. Indeed, the futures of all twenty men in the two rowboats navigating the narrows between Nevis and Kitts islands had been traded by Gods and angels for the past four nautical miles. They had maintained as close to a westerly heading as possible. The current was ferocious, hurling them forward between swells. Drifts pulling them nor-by-northwest with each passing crest, raking the shoals and outcrops on the southern end of Kitts. The winds battering them from behind, kicking the heavy laden twenty-four-foot yawl-boats into erratic orientations, and dumping surf in deluges over the gunwales. They were down to eight rowers per boat after the first five minutes in the sea and the *Bride's* disappearance into the storm on her bearing north. Two men were needed in each boat to bail enough water that they would even stay afloat.

William's shoulders were burning with exhaustion, and he wasn't alone. Only Shamus O'Reilly, seated forward in John Prior's boat, appeared to be immune, as the weight of the oars seemingly increased in the hands of the men with each passing stroke. And there was no relief. Fall out of rhythm with the man ahead, oars were clashing, and the sea consumed any control of the boats, tossing and turning them broadside, lashing out to drown all men aboard for the disrespect they showed in playing at heroes in a hurricane.

They were making the slow turn to starboard, five-hundred or so yards from shore, on a bearing roughly nor-east, the island of Kitts only visible as a wall of infinite black rising from the flecks of rolling white froth smashing against the coast.

Three-hundred yards of gruelling strain saw the two boats clear of the western narrow's wash and finally the sea began to lessen, the headland blocking the worst of the prevailing winds and the current sweeping cleaner along the foreshore. The two boats were riding parallel, some thirty feet apart.

"John!" William cried out, "Throw the lines! We'll ride together from here!"

"Aye, aye, Will!" John Prior shouted and hauled himself to his feet. He wobbled between his men and grabbed the first of two cords coiled for the purpose. They were weighted at their ends by four-pound cannon balls fixed in a mesh woven from strands of rope. Prior grabbed a length, set his hands two yards up the strand, and began to swirl the weighted end around his head methodically. When the appropriate momentum was generated, and the boat beneath his feet steadied for a beat, Prior unleashed the weighted end and sent it flying across the gap between rowboats.

"Incoming!" William shouted, for want of a better word.

He needn't have bothered for all men in his boat were acutely aware of the potential energy of a four-pound cannon ball hurled straight at them. That, and all of them acutely determined to deny John frigging Prior the satisfaction of a direct hit on their person. The cannon ball landed amidships and thumped down easily onto one of the sacks of cork onboard. Richard Bately dumped down his bailing bucket and stumbled aft to fetch the weighted rope.

"Lash it to the fore, Richard," William commanded, "and tie it off hard."

"Aye, Will," said Bately, and did as instructed.

Prior was quick to repeat the process with the second rope and once again the cannon ball landed amidships. William grabbed the second weight and lashed it to the stern.

"Can't be far, now lads!" assured William, as he sat himself down at the starboard rear and took up his oar once again. The sea was calming as they progressed slowly along the coast. The rain was easing up on its lateral lashing and falling in a more orderly fashion, almost in line with what one might expect from the laws of gravity. The thought hadn't crossed anyone's mind, of course, because Newton wasn't on board either boat, and if he had been it would have been to very little avail, as there wasn't room to store apples on account of all the bloody gunpowder and shot.

"Jim Dolby!" William called, "what will you do with your share of the bounty? Let's hear your intentions."

It was a welcome question. The boats were under control, finally, and William thought it best to calm the men. The last hour had been a petrifying ride, and conversation was just about possible once again, albeit somewhat weathered.

"Well, if I'm honest, Will, I hadn't much thought about it," Dolby called out.

"Bollocks you haven't!" Dye Bant called out from the other boat. "You're a lyin' little bitch, right there."

"Piss off Taffy, we all knows what you're gonna be at, you ain't got no say in this conversation!" Dolby responded.

"How's that then?"

"Well, you'll be buying a bunch more of them sheep you're always jerking off about in your hammock at night," Dolby said. "No shame in it for your likes o' course."

"Aye, he holds a fair point," Prior said, "I'll fancy you'll be buyin' into a four legg'd orgy soon as we hit Portsmouth."

"Fuck you both, and don't be knockin' it 'til you've tried it," Dye Bant said, as proud as any Welshman might, knowing he'd been squarely bettered momentarily. "It's cheaper than a go on that barrel of a twat hangs down between your sister's legs, Jim, that I can tell ye."

"He knows that already," 'Tumbles' Turner put forth.

Laughter bellowed briefly and was just as quick to carry off in the wind.

"Shamus, what about you?" William asked, linking the two boats with further discourse, while stowing his oar and stretching his eyesight through the limits of the rain and mist in search of anything resembling the *Santa Oscuro*.

"Well, Jesus Will, that's easy," Shamus O'Reilly boomed, "I'll be buying myself a plot o' land back home in Galway. And a pub in the village, for the evenings, when I'm done tending the cows, and shaggin' the sheep."

"Dye Bant, mark it, perhaps you'll visit," William said.

"Aye, Will, but I'll not be having sloppy seconds. They'll be nothing left o' them sheep after Shamus has a go, I'll bring me own."

"Richard, what about you?" William asked, "Let it be shared."

"Well, I thought I'd buy a place fer a university, Will," Bately said, "and some books to read. Good ones, and the like."

"Aye, you should, boy," John Prior said.

"Aye, bloody right idea that is," 'Tumbles' said, "you should an' all, and get yourself a girl who's right in the head to look after you a spell while you're readin'."

"He can't afford that, man!" Dye Bant, interjected, "Woman like that's feckin' priceless, ain't enough gold on any ship to buy one o' those."

"Well, he can try, can't he, he's young enough," Jim Dolby said.

"Aye, don't be disparaging the boy," from 'Tumbles'. "Rats, Richard? Whass is a bunch of rats?"

"A mischief!" yelled Bately.

"Then we got a mischief a' brewin' aboard, led by a taffy rat," said 'Tumbles'.

"Aye, I suppose. Never mind me, Richard! I'm three wives in and just tired o' the bullshit," said Dye Bant, his confession resonating with a few good men on each boat.

William smiled. 'Tumbles' had done well to play his part in calming nerves. His question, on rats of all living things, had been well placed, for it was well known, tried, and oft tested that young Bately knew the right name for groupings of animals of any kind. The boys loved trying to catch him out. It was a stupidly simple thing, that had grown to become part of a complex banding of different characters, all far away from home and crammed together for months on end above and below decks. He knew Bately was smiling now, least on the inside. Thus far on the voyage, he had never been bettered once by his shipmates.

"William!" John Prior cried in earnest from the stern of his boat. He was half standing in a low crouch and leaning forward over the sailor in front of him. "What's your reckoning be there?"

Prior pointed fore of the boats. Some two-hundred yards directly ahead, a huge silhouette was forming in the mist, highlighted by a backdrop of lanterns and flares further to the north.

"My reckoning is you've found our prize, John," said William. "Right lads, you know what to do, let's have these boats lashed together. Stow the inside oars and tie up close."

Starboard rowers on William's boat matched port rowers on Prior's boat in stowing their oars, pulling on ropes to drag the vessels gunwale to gunwale and tying them together. Forward momentum was maintained by the men on the outer sides of what quickly became a twin hulled rowboat.

"Ready the harpoons," William ordered, "and John, stay the fuck away."

"Aye, Will," Prior said, "Dye, set about the loads."

"Aye, John," Dye replied and stumbled to the fore of the boat. He grabbed wads of hemp loaded with gunpowder from a chest and proceeded to carefully stock the long two-inch barrels of three harpoon guns, which he then mounted against the bow of the boat. Ted 'Tumbles' Turner set about doing the same on William's boat. The harpoons themselves were three-foot-long iron spears, with concave indentations on their dull ends, and small ropes tied to their sharp ends with hooks.

"Right lads," William said, "silence aboard from here on in."

As the boats drew closer, the black shape of the *Santa Oscuro* loomed higher and higher above the sea. The *Saint of the Dark* was enormous, ominous, set heavy and immovable on the water, inciting cold, wet, fear into the hearts of the few men set on challenging her.

*****

Scarlett held the *Maiden Bride* true at the helm. Ned 'Toes' Williams was making his way down the stairs to the main deck carrying his orders to ready with the boarding party of armed sailors. Roger 'Paws' Prowse passed him on the stair, "Set your muskets to port, Ned, amidships."

"Aye, Mister Prowse."

"Then join them thass got the flares. Bang 'em off like it's New Year's night and you just got laid by a fine-looking wench whass too drunk to know you're ugly."

"I've been lucky enough with a few o' them, Sir, I know the drill."

"Good man."

'Paws' continued towards the helm without pause.

"Think they've spotted us enough, Roger?" Scarlett asked, his smile beaming in the fractures of red and gold light thrown by the crescendo of shots and flares being thrown towards the dark sky by fifty or so of the crew on decks and rigging.

"Well, if they ain't," 'Paws' replied, "I'll have it; they're blind drunk an' better for it."

Scarlett laughed, then nodded his head out past the *Bride's* bowsprit, "What would you set her range?"

"Eight-hundred yards, give or take."

"Same."

"We're set to cop a full broadside on the nose, Captain. Thass a hundred guns."

"You're a might concerned, Roger? Is that it?"

"Oh, no, Captain. I seen you do worse, when you didn't know your arse from a jib in the Mediterranean 'gainst the French."

"A fair reminder, I'm humbled Mister Prowse," said Scarlett, "I'll make a note in the ship's log tomorrow morn."

"Aye, and I'll feckin' run off to Spain with an English princess."

"We'll harden up fifteen degrees port for six-hundred yards. On my mark, we'll douse the lights and ready about to starboard. We'll find the weather gauge by cutting her stern," Scarlett instructed.

"Aye, Captain. But what of young William and his men? We'll smash them to bloody pieces if we can't see 'em."

Scarlett knew his Boatswain was on the money, but for what he couldn't control he would afford no time.

"Throw down the Jacobs both sides and jerry another aft the bumkins."

"Aye, Captain. I'll see it done."

'Paws' moved off. Scarlett concentrated on the black shape of the *Dark Saint*. It was strange. Strange that her capitán hadn't yet raised sail and made effort to come about. He had the weather advantage.

*****

Capitán Juan Martinez de Recalde was enjoying Scarlett's firework display. Pedro Garcia was, too. The two men were at the helm and for the past twenty minutes they had barked orders to every able seaman aboard ship. The gundecks had seen most of the action. Every cannon on the port side of the ship was packed, primed, and charged. Recalde would have insisted all cannon aboard were in a similar ready state, but for the loss of so many of his crew to disease of late.

He didn't know Scarlett, his nemesis of the night, but he knew the English. Their Protestant trickery with the wind in their delicate little ships. The way they would dance a hundred yards out beyond reach of cannon, while they summoned the courage to attack.

"Esto es nuevo. Los fuegos artificiales," Pedro said, in reference to the lanterns and fireworks exploding from the *Bride.*

"Sí. El Capitán Scarlett quiere que tengamos miedo, ¿no?" Recalde said, suggesting that he was not in the slightest bit intimidated by Scarlett's flashy assail.

"Si Capitán, supongo," said Pedro.

"Levantar las velas mayores," Recalde instructed, his command dictating that all mainsails aboard ship be raised in unison and quickly.

"Sí, Capitán," Pedro acknowledged, and moved away towards the port side stair to the main deck.

"Y Pedro, la milicia en cubierta," Recalde ordered.

Pedro acknowledged his capitán's request to have all military crew on deck. The implication was 'with immediate effect' and Pedro was no slouch in passing the order down the rigid chain of command aboard ship. Within two minutes, Recalde was satisfied that his full company of sixty warriors were present and correct on the main deck, armed with muskets, swords, and knives, their armoured breast-plates and helmets polished and shining in the reds, greens, and yellows of the Scarlett Buccaneer's stupid fireworks. As the first of the mainsails unfurled, Recalde gave order to raise anchor, and a dozen men swarmed the forward capstan to wind in the heavy chain.

The English ship was no more than one-hundred-and-fifty yards off the port bow of the *Santa Oscuro*, on a ramming course directly for amidships. A stupid, yet predictable move in Recalde's humble opinion. Scarlett was guiding his *Bride* very nearly head to wind, and though he was presenting a minimal target in profile, the fore of his ship moved slowly and was face on to a hundred menacing four-thousand-pound cannon.

Imbéciles. Jodidamente imbéciles.

When the English ship breached one-hundred yards and showed no sign of altering its pig-ignorant course, Recalde spun the helm nosing the *Oscuro* slightly to port. He quickly sequestered the attentions of Pedro, his Master Gunner, his Marine Captain and to all he gave the order, *"¡FUEGO!"*

The 'first shot' of the battle constituted one-hundred cannon and some eighty muskets fired in unison. The recoil of the cannon saw the *Oscuro's* leeward gunwale rise by two feet as she listed to starboard momentarily.

Recalde took pause, straining through the smothering cloud of gunpowder smoke, when unexpected things happened that left the capitán wondering if somewhere in the annals of Spanish history there had ever lived a fellow by the name of, *'Señor Murphy'.*

Every lantern, torch and flare aboard the *Maiden Bride* snapped out of existence simultaneously.

A massive vibration trembled up through the stern of the *Santa Oscuro*. Recalde had to fling himself against the wheel to steady his legs, such was the shaking of the quarterdeck. When the quake subsided the spokes of the helm to which Recalde clung, spun freely in his hands, his grip slipped, and he plummeted face first to the floor.

*****

Four decks below Recalde and his impromptu swan dive, the ship's lazaretto could be found, which was rarely, as the dingy little space was reserved for any crew that contracted an infectious disease during the voyage and were indispensable. Yellow fever, typhoid, smallpox, tuberculosis, scabies, erysipelas, anthrax, trachoma, not to mention leprosy, or plague, were generally cured by a bullet between the eyes for ordinary sailors, but, occasionally, an officer might cop a dose and be quickly quarantined while the ship was between ports. The lazaretto was currently occupied by a stowaway. A man. He was about forty years of age. An old man. Very weak. Delicate in form. It had been a long time since he last did push-ups. He used to enjoy those. He had boarded the ship during the previous night. The *Santa Oscuro* had docked for supplies in Puerto la Cruz, Venezuela, prior to the last leg of her journey back to Seville, for that was where she was now heading. The stowaway was of Spanish descent. He knew that much. He had some food and water. The cramped space he inhabited soothed him. He enjoyed the dark. He couldn't really say why he was there, but he liked it. It was warm and dry. He cradled a small leather-bound book in his arms, and this soothed him more than any other person, animal, or thing he'd ever known. He didn't remember where he came from. And that was fine. He didn't need to know. The only name he could remember was Tortuga. He didn't know why. But it calmed him.

At the precise moment that Recalde was slammed face down four decks above him, the stowaway was torn violently from his comfortable little dungeon of disease when the starboard wall exploded. He was thrown out from the ship in a tumble of splintering timbers. He splashed down into a terrifying rage of salty froth. He was still clinging to his book as the sea consumed him.

*****

William had been the first man in the two rowboats to fire a harpoon at the stern of the *Santa Oscuro*. Silence, mist, darkness, and Scarlett's certifiable distraction had protected his crew from detection. Five other harpoons were fired in quick succession and rope lines were drawn upon, pulling the boats in tight to the three-storey looming aft castle of the Spanish ship.

"Lash up," cried William, "and abandon ships, lads. Bately, you're first. Go!"

Young Richard Bately grabbed an empty wooden keg and jumped over the aft end gunwale. His was attached by a twenty-foot line tied securely around the waist of one Ted 'Tumbles' Turner, who was next man in the water. The other crew in the boat followed suit one by one, and were matched for pace by John Prior, Shamus O'Reilly, Dye Bant, and the crew of the second boat. It wasn't an easy or graceful task as the rowboats were slammed repeatedly against the hull of the *Oscuro* by tide and merciless waves. William was on his arse when he threw his first torch into

Prior's abandoned boat. He was stumbling aft of his own boat as he dropped a second torch on a healthy line of gunpowder trailing forward to the main store of munitions in the craft. As William dived from the rear gunwale the whole bloody kit and caboodle exploded, sending a firewall up and over the stern of the *Dark Saint* and ripping the air out of the sky some eighty feet above the sea.

14

A Pretty Pandemonium

29th October 1577

F ather Francis Bacon and Sister Agatha Templeton
clinked copper mugs and imbibed decent swigs of the
rum provided by the senior members of the Alms House
crew, who were all standing in a half circle facing southwest,
with craned necks, straining their fading eye sights on the
spectacle above them...

BANG. BOOM! WHOOSH. WHIZZZ...

Gunpowder tubes were igniting, whizzing, banging, and
exploding in torrents of multicoloured streaks and sparkles,
all showering down over an escaping menagerie of freaked
out farm animals that hadn't the faintest idea which way
was best to run.

"Cheers," said Bacon.

"To Father Bacon's pretty pandemonium," said Agatha.

"Good title," said Bacon.

"Damn fine festivities," said Agatha.

The fake priest and the honest-to-goodness nun clinked mugs a second time and chugged drinks again. Bacon looked down from his scintillating scene in the heavens and scanned the grounds to the west. The three groundskeepers or stable hands – hard to differentiate in the twilight – were chasing cows, sheep, goats, chickens, and whatever beast happened to be closest. They were intermingling with the four mounted guards who were all straining to control their cavalry horses. None were immune to the apocalypse of detonations above them. It soon became apparent that a dozen more grounds staff were approaching, bolting across the Dial Court alongside six more of the Queen's Guards, who had wisely chosen to dismount and ride shanks instead of ponies.

*****

Sir James of Bon slid from the saddle of his mount and joined Sir William Cecil. The two distinguished old boys of the Realm were standing nearby the southeast corner of the Great Garden with an uninterrupted panoramic view of Bacon's light show over the stables.

"Young Bacon, you think?" questioned Sir James.

"Most certainly a Bacon play," said Cecil, "the lad gets around, doesn't he?"

"He has fresh legs and his arse ain't been battered into submission," said James.

"Oh, I wouldn't be too sure of that," quipped Cecil.

James smiled, "House or barns?"

"House. I must find Mildred," replied Cecil.

"Aye, right oh," said James, adjusting the seat of his breeches by tugging on them.

Cecil took off at pace, heading north, leading his horse by the reins. James followed. The two men tied-up their respective mounts to twin limestone hitching posts spanning the door to the range linking the Still House Tower to the main house and turned right into a loggia. They quick marched through the southeastern-most tower and entered the loggia adjacent to the porter's lodges of the main entrance. James glanced to his right and tapped Cecil on the shoulder, causing him to pause. Masked in shadows, looking through the archway, they recognised the captain of the Queen's Body Guard standing beside several of his men outside. He was encouraging order in his ranks and insisting that a line formation should be reinstated with his three displaced horse drawn carriages.

"You should perhaps have words with Captain Smedley-Smythe-Smedley something," said James.

"No. Fuck him. Let's find Mildred. She'll have a handle on things by now."

"What mothers are for," said James.

"How would you know?" quipped Cecil, turning and heading west, exiting the loggia onto the central pathway of the Middle Court.

"I've known one or two in my time, I'll thank your good Grace," said James.

"Yes, but they're different when sober and standing," said Cecil.

James grinned. Two valets, dressed in white cotton shirts and black tunics, breeches, stockings and shoes, exited through the central arch of the western range of the court. Both were tall gents, in their early thirties, carrying the finest deportment, and ordinarily would split shifts to provide for twenty-four-hour service to the Cecil family. The unannounced arrival of the guards prompted a change in their routines, as was the case with the footmen, housemen, hall boys, boot boys, chambermaids, housemaids, parlour maids, kitchen maids, scullery maids and pages, all of whom were scattering to various locations around the house, now formally engaging in whispered communications relaying the particulars of events ongoing, all with William's best interests in their hearts.

"The two Michaels. Just the fellows I seek in this moment," said Cecil.

The valets stopped walking and bowed marginally in unison.

"Yes, my Lord."

"Welcome home, my Lord."

"Enough with the Lord shit. Have you seen the kids of late and where's my wife?"

"William and Katherine were last sighted scampering the rooftops," said Michael I.

"Several steps ahead of the guards, Sir," said Michael II.

"Ha! Excellent behaviour," said Cecil, tapping James, "what did I tell you, James?"

"Master Bacon is creating havoc around the stables, Sir," said Michael I.

"Yes. We bore witness," said Cecil.

"A pretty pandemonium," said James.

"Master Robert was last seen exiting the chaplain's chambers, Sir," said Michael II.

"They are all dressed in habit robes, Sir," said Michael I, "hard to tell them apart."

"That'll be Katherine's ploy, for certain," said Cecil.

"Undoubtedly," said James.

"Lady Mildred is currently in the North Parlour, Sir," said Michael II.

Cecil stepped between the two staff, "Thank you gentlemen. Tag along now."

James followed Cecil, passing between the Michaels, who tucked in behind and tagged along as instructed. The group entered the western loggia of the court and walked straight on through a large central hallway, passing between the

Great Hall and the Winter Parlour. A right turn, followed by thirty brisk steps and a left turn past the upper Great Kitchens led Cecil, James, and the Michaels into the North Parlour. Mildred's personal maids were standing patiently beside the large bay window in the centre of the south wall, alongside a footman and a hall boy. The quintet of string musicians was playing slow, sombre tones, in a rendition that should probably have been entitled 'Ignominy', if it wasn't already.

"Has somebody died this evening?" bellowed Cecil.

"William, thank Christ!" exclaimed Mildred, from her position at the west end of the long table, beside the birthday cake and presents, "It's about bloody time."

"I am sorry, my dear," said Cecil, crossing the room, "rather pressing appointment with Her Majesty."

Michaels I and II headed for a large cabinet in the northwest corner. A multitude of wine and spirit bottles, decanters, glasses, and trays were on display in front of a tall, mirrored backdrop.

"I'll say. Has she lost her bloody mind?" questioned Mildred, rounding the table, and closing on her husband.

"Long since, truth be told," said Cecil.

"Well, she's outdone herself this time," said Mildred, throwing her arms around Cecil's waist and embracing him.

"What have we done to obstruct this folly?" asked Cecil.

"Why, absolutely nothing, of course," said Mildred. "Good evening to you, Sir James."

"Good evening to you, Lady Burghley," said James.

"Ooh, say that again, Flemington," said Mildred, "the only time I can tolerate the bloody title is in your accent."

"Very well, Ma'am," said James, laying on his full Scottish brogue, "'tis a striking wee gown you're sporting tonight, Lady Burghley."

Mildred started giggling.

"Oh, please desist, the pair of you," said Cecil.

The Michaels returned with crystal decanters and glasses on silver trays.

"Brandy, Michael. Thank you," said Cecil.

"Rum, if you please," said James.

"Do you boys have a plan?" asked Mildred, snapping into seriousness, "Tell me you do have a plan."

"Aye, of sorts," said James. He would have added a third 'Lady Burghley' just for Mildred, but figured it was inappropriate behaviour given the gravity of young William's situation. He accepted a glass of clear rum from Michael I, while Michael II handed a generous measure of vintage brandy in a tulip glass to Cecil.

"We do have a scheme in hand, my dear. Though you might not cherish the full extent," said Cecil, before turning to face the string ensemble, "and can we please change that damned morbid tune?"

The musicians immediately desisted from bowing their instruments, closed in shared attentions, and quickly arrived at a unanimous consensus. After a count of four a new tune began in the key of G-major, with a lively bass and engaging upbeat melody. Much better.

*****

William and Katherine were on the move, in awkward-heads-down-bent-at-the-waist sort of shuffling, travelling south along the roof of the range separating the Fountain Court and the Middle Court. Three floors below, to the east, gardeners, groundskeepers, and handymen were amassing in the Middle Courtyard. Several of the guards were instructing the outdoor staff to present and line up for inspection. It was little surprise to the kids looking down that the hardy Theobalds 'green-thumb' ranks were somewhat reluctant to offer full cooperation to the snotty red-tunic-wearing poncy Yeomen patrollers. No obstruction was in play though, let that be stated for the Constable of the Tower's record, but looking on, it was difficult to discern exactly which line was being drawn in the gravel on which to stand. Which way to face was another conundrum. West and the last of the fading sunlight was the lesser of shadow, but if all men lined up as instructed, they would be forming a queue, rather than a line, wouldn't they Governor?

The twins reached the central tower of the range; a striking red brick and stone-capped bell tower with a domed copper roof, which protruded from the eastern wall, overlooking the Middle Court. William and Katherine squatted down and took pause.

"I don't think we should see mother," said Katherine, "we should just go."

"Not without cocoa cake," said William.

"We don't know if there is cocoa cake," said Katherine.

"What are the odds?" asked William.

"Will you be serious, for a minute?"

"Alright, sister. How serious?" asked William, whose attention was mostly on the ground of the Middle Court, "Oh, shit, that's got to be Robert."

Katherine looked down following William's lead. A modestly statured figure, dressed in a grey habit, with the hood covering their head was shuffling slowly east, skirting the court's northern wall, carrying themselves with a gait that was easily recognisable.

"That's Robert," agreed Katherine, before pointing further out, "but who is that?"

A second figure, also dressed in a hooded grey habit, but sporting a green sash around their waist, was standing in the shadows of the northeast corner tower, some ninety yards away. William squinted through the fading light over the courtyard. He couldn't be certain, but it seemed as though the figure had two radiating emerald eyes and was staring directly up at him.

*****

Captain Tarquin Smedley-Smythe-Smythings was finally satisfied that his three carriages had been restationed in a line of order befitting a company of the Queen's Body Guard of the Yeomen of the Guard. His company, hand-picked from the finest available, at short notice, of course. Best he could achieve for the mission at hand. As was his right, by God.

One of his red/gold-livery-wearing, halberd-wielding chosen, exited the archway of the main entrance and approached, "Captain, permission to debrief?"

"Yes, Adjutant Walters. Go ahead," instructed Smythe-Smythings.

"Well, Sir. It seems we have encountered an obstruction," said Walters, planting the foot of his six-foot-long, axe and spike topped pole on the ground beside his feet.

"Obstruction?"

"A deliberate ploy to deceive, Sir," said Walters, clarifying nothing.

"Bloody hell, Walters, be specific man."

"The children of the house, Sir," said Walters, "it appears that they have all taken to disguising themselves as priests."

"Priests?"

"Indeed, Sir. With habit robes upon them," said Walters.

"Fancy dress is hardly a crime of obstruction," said Smythings. "They're rich little twats, and it's a birthday party. Have I not taught you to expect the unexpected in combat, Walters?"

"Yes, Sir. But the men are reluctant to apprehend men of the cloth."

Smedley-Smythe-Smythings slid his ebony stick from underneath his armpit, twiddled it, and propped the bulbous gold topped end on the centre of his Adjutant's chest.

"What? What am I hearing? You said yourself, they are in disguise, did you not?"

"Yes, Sir. We believe so," said Walters, "though, the men... well, supposing one of us apprehends a genuine cleric, Sir? All hell to pay, Sir."

"Walters."

"Sir."

"You think too much when your head is stuck up your arse," said Smythings. "Arrest every posh little fucker in a habit, post-haste."

"Sir, yes, Sir," said Walters, clicking his heels. He was half about-turning when the captain added, "Second thoughts;

follow my lead, Walters. For Queen and for God, we shall not fuck this up."

Smedley-Smythe-Smythings tucked his ebony stick back under his armpit and marched away from the carriages, heading west towards the main entrance. Adjutant Walters followed, half a pace behind.

*****

William and Katherine suddenly found themselves in a tight spot, up on the lead roof of the central range in their crouched positions beside the bell tower. A very tight spot.

Two guards exited the oak doorway of the northwest tower of the Middle Court. It was the same door that the twins had passed through a minute ago. One of those guards was almost certainly named Burton, or Herbert, or maybe Albert.

The two former rowboat-checking-guards exited the oak doorway of the southwest tower of the Middle Court and stepped out onto the walkway. After momentarily looking about, they gained a measure of their bearings, focused directly on William and Katherine, and drew their swords.

"Oh dear," gasped Katherine.

"Ah, shit," said William.

The four guards began to approach in their pairings of two from either side. A pincer movement of accomplishment, for certain, as they were blocking the only exits from the leaded walkway. The kids were trapped.

"What do we do?" questioned Katherine.

William stood up and pulled back his hood, "Ever heard of fight or flight?"

"Don't be stupid," said Katherine, "they have swords, and you can't friggin' fly."

William held out his hand. Katherine pulled back her hood, took William's hand in hers and stood up.

"Don't move. Stay put," said one of the guards to the south, thirty yards away.

"Identify yourselves," said one of the guards to the north, twenty-five yards away.

William watched. Katherine listened. The guards advanced at a measured pace, strangely in unison with each other; one step, and a second step, and a third step, and on the beat a fourth...

"Put your sword down, Bertram. We don't needs be scaring them," said one of the guards approaching from the northern flank.

"Aye, right oh," said the guard called Bertram, stowing his blade in his scabbard.

William realised he hadn't thought of the name Bertram when he was listening to the guard's movements on the staircase minutes earlier. He quite liked it. Not enough to call one of his own kids that, if and when he ever had any, but he didn't object to Bertram in the slightest.

Katherine was confused. Her own heart was racing, growing louder in her ears. William's inner tempo remained at a steady thirty beats per minute, which should have been impossible, given their imminent capture.

Why doesn't he give a shit? How can he not... The Tower, William. The fucking Tower is a horrible place. I mean, I haven't seen the dungeons, but I've read about them.

"Thass the way now," said one of the guards to the south, stowing his sword away, "we don't mean you harm."

"Just doing our jobs, we are," said the second guard to the south; twenty yards away...

"He's right about that," said the guard approaching from the north in step with Bertram, "You boy. Are you William Cecil?"

William smiled, "Nope. Never heard of him."

"Is that so?" from a guard to the south; eighteen yards...

"Well now, what if we all go downstairs and find your parents?" said Bertram.

William made an improvised attempt at ventriloquism, in a whisper, "Katherine. I think I hear bells ringing."

"What?" whispered Katherine.

"Follow me... ready?" whispered William.

The guards continued to steadily approach from both sides; fifteen yards...

Katherine, whose mind was racing faster that her heart, twigged William's intention, "Oh, shit. Really?"

"Go," said William, launching himself onto the eastern parapet. He took Katherine's hand and pulled her up onto the ledge. The gravel floor of the Middle Court lay some forty feet below. William scrambled onto the carved lime-stone façade of the bell tower, hands and feet clambering on the heads of stone sculptures of cupids and angels. Katherine followed his route, as the guards closed in, underneath her feet.

The twins reached the stone ledge of an open bell housing and swung their legs over the parapet. Four feet down inside the tower a framework of thick oak timbers housed a large central bronze bell and six other marginally small-er chimes. All the bells were suspended from thick oak headstocks mounted on iron bearings, with grooved wheels attached, ranging in diameter from three to four feet. Seven ropes wound around and through the spokes of the wheels and descended through holes in the floor into the seeming abyss of the tower's depths.

"Wait," said Katherine, quickly digging into her leather bag.

"Why?"

"These," said Katherine, producing a pair of leather gloves.

The guard named Bertram was eight feet below, and trying to climb the tower, "Don't you move, you two. Nobody needs get hurt, now, do they?"

William smiled as Katherine pulled on her gloves. He launched from the parapet and landed on one of a dozen oak cross-member beams constituting the landing on which the arrangement of bells was situated. He turned quickly and aided Katherine down from the stone ledge. They found themselves face to face, somewhat uncomfortably close, perched on the four-inch-wide oak beam.

"You alright? You're breathing funny," said William.

"Why are you not taking this seriously?"

"Grab the middle rope, it's thickest," said William pointing down and to his left.

The guard Bertram stuck his head over the parapet, "Don't move now. We all know you ain't done nothing wrong, William. We're just doing our duty for..."

"Go," said William.

Katherine carefully stepped over one of the peripheral bells, dropped to her butt on one of the central crossbeams, took hold of the rope attached to the largest of the grooved wheels, and dropped down into the darkness of the tower.

"You should be careful, Mister," said William, looking directly up at the guard Bertram's head, "It's slippery down here."

"Don't move an inch," said Bertram.

Too late. William grabbed the nearest rope and jumped down between the huge bell housings and thick oak beams.

15

Jesus Almighty, Who Put That Fucker There?

7th / 8th November 1587

William was belted by the gunpowder blast that bajaxed the aft hull of the *Santa Oscuro*, before he even had a chance to hit the water. It threw him across the surf in a flailing mess of uncontrollable limbs. He breached the surface of the sea on his side and was immediately sucked under by the powerful rips in the offshore currents driven by the storm. Strangely he wasn't panicked. He found relief swell over him as the sea drove him deeper. The madcap plan had worked, surely. The rudder of the *Santa Oscuro* was blown to shit. And he was tied to nine of the strongest of the *Bride's* swimmers. One and all, bound together, they would weather the sea, the tides, the currents, and this rip now dragging them to the depths of hell.

William righted himself in the water, grabbed his nose and balanced his ears to the increasing pressure. He was doing alright for air. No need to throw a wobbly. The worst thing was the suffocating blackness and the disorientation, but he had a lifeline around his waist and twenty feet away was a good man righting himself, tied to eight others all gaining advantage towards the surface with their strong strokes. William grabbed the rope and pulled hand over hand, expecting a fair degree of tension and resistance. In less than a second it became obvious that no such tension was apparent. All that was to be found was the frayed end.

Oh, FUCK!

Perhaps now was a good time for trepidation.

He could tell from the pressure in his ears that he was still descending to the depths, the riptide straining the sinews of his body. A splutter of precious air spat from his mouth involuntarily. Not good. Though tracing the bubbles as they raced past his nostrils was invaluable in gaining a true sense of what was up and what was surely a downward path to drinking with Davy Jones. William rotated his body in a prone position with his arms splayed at ninety degrees to the current and began swimming horizontally with a furious kicking. Pulling at the water with his arms in an underwater breaststroke. The next full minute felt like an hour. The strain settled in his lungs with a burning desperation. He still couldn't see for shit through the black water. His ears were suggesting he wasn't sinking deeper. Hard to be certain.

Fucking lungs. Shit.

Lactic acid was building in his shoulders and thighs, stiffening his movements as his muscles screamed for relief against the onset of tearing and tissue damage. But William fought on, willing his body to function past its pathetic human limits.

Katherine.

His eyes suddenly began to burn. An arrow of pain struck deep into his brain behind his forehead.

Holy flying fuck, what's that?

William's chest and torso began to convulse, wracking his ribcage with contractions that were crushing his bones together.

Then the pain in his head cleared instantly.

The wild shaking in his body stopped.

He could see.

The ocean wasn't just a black mass of masked oppression and violence. He could see turbulence in the water. The eddies. The drafts. Streams of emerald and aquamarine. The sea floor in grains of sand willowing and waning, drawn by the water's movements.

William looked up. The white crests of surf capping the surface some sixty feet above him, as clear as polarised sunshine on a spring morning in a cloudless sky.

William breathed. Relief flooding his burning lungs with gloriously cool air as purified and fresh as that inhaled on any mountain top in the world on a winter solstice.

How the hell am I doing this? Am I dead?

William checked himself. The rip was ended. The emerald traces of turbulence falling away to his right and down to the deep. The surface above was clear. He kicked for it without taking another breath, for fear it was a one-off, beginner's luck at drowning, type deal. He didn't want to contemplate a mouthful of seawater and the associated choking if his next breath underwater went sideways.

He carefully expelled small amounts of air as he surged to the shimmering surface and when he broke through, he was virtually blind again. His face was lashed once more by the rain and froth of the breaking waves. The sky was black and tumbling with knotted clouds. He breathed again. And again. And rolled onto his back.

*****

Scarlett had come about and was driving his *Bride* on a close haul towards the stern of the *Santa Oscuro*. The ship had taken several direct hits from the Spanish bombardment, all above the waterline. The bowsprit was in tatters and the lower yard on the foremast was split, with the starboard yardarm broken off. The pine timber was now planted at a forty-five degree angle piercing through the Jarrah timbers of the foredeck. Splinters had strafed several of the crew, and the injured were being hauled to the 'chop shop' in the officers' quarters, where Doctor Trevor 'Needles' Neary, the ship's surgeon, historian, naturalist, philosopher, and pastor would be prioritising the wounded on a needs must first basis.

"Mister Prowse!" Scarlett bellowed for the umpteenth time in as many minutes, "On my mark, kedge anchor and come about hard to port. A full turn if you please, and a bloody fast one!"

"Aye Captain!" 'Paws' screamed from the main deck. His voice was lost to the wind, but his captain got the gist.

Scarlett steadied the helm with one hand. His eyes were burning into the hull of the *Oscuro*. Her mainsails had been raised and she was gaining traction on the surface of the sea. But William had done a beautiful job of disabling her rudder. She was a lame duck heading nowhere but straight for the island of Saint Kitts, its shoreline some four-hundred yards off her foremast. Scarlett raised his right arm and steadied his palm in the air.

"Now Mister Prowse!" Scarlett bellowed, and dropped his arm as he did so. The forward capstan was let loose with the freefall of the anchor. Its heavy chain rattled through its placements in the port side of the ship. At the same time a fury of bodies heaved on lines and braces and the yards and mainsails were swung about the masts, dragging the *Bride* about to port in a parallel course to the *Oscuro,* but now with the windward advantage.

Turn made, Scarlett raised his voice again, "Weigh anchor, Mister Prowse!"

A dozen men jumped to the capstan once again, this time reversing their push on the lateral bars extending from the central barrel of the windlass core.

Both ships were heading straight for the island, and Scarlett was beaming. Roger Prowse came bounding up the stairs to the quarterdeck and joined Scarlett at the helm. "Gunners ready below, Captain."

"Good man, Roger."

"Muskets and grapple irons on the make."

"Every man, Roger."

"Aye, Sir, save the Doc and his patients."

"We'll strafe this bastard to the nines in two minutes."

"She'll run aground afore that Captain, she got a draft on her lower than me wife's knickers on her birthday," said 'Paws'. He was pumped to all heaven with excitement and not because he was single again. He had been on his own in that regard, for a very long time.

"I'm counting on it, Roger, ready the men and steady their hearts."

"Aye Captain, I'm all about it," 'Paws' assured and sprinted down the stairs to the main deck where he vanished among eighty-odd crewmen, all armed to the chins with muskets, swords, clubs, spears, knives, and anything else considered appropriately nasty in hand-to-hand combat.

Scarlett tied off the helm in a fixed lock, unfurled his whip. A minute later the two galleons were no more than twelve feet apart, and the *Bride* was gaining ground. A loud scraping and crunching could be heard beneath the *Santa Oscuro,* as she raked her hull over rocks and shoals some hundred yards from the shoreline of Kitts Isle.

"FIRE! FIRE!" Scarlett bellowed, "Fore to aft, all guns!"

Scarlett snapped his whip around a backstay rope descending from the mainmast to the port side gunwale and he dived off the quarterdeck.

The *Maiden Bride,* a much smaller ship, with a fast shallow draft, slid neatly alongside the grounded Spanish monster. Thirty-two cannon let rip one by one from fore to aft on the *Bride's* port side gundecks. Muskets were fired and fired again and again at close range by all able men on both ships. The grappling hooks were unleashed, ladders slammed down between gunwales, swords were drawn, and two-hundred fighting bodies charged into each other in packs of wild animals, cutting, slashing, punching, gouging, kicking, and tearing strips off each other, smothered in blinding jelly reek smoke, splintering timbers, and blazing hot iron shot.

Scarlett had landed squarely on the foreign ship's starboard gunwale just fore of the quarterdeck, and from there he skipped onto the nearest stair. He ran his blade through two Spaniards but had the presence of mind to maim rather than kill them. They were young lads, and clearly shitting themselves. His focus was the helm of the *Oscuro* and her capitán, Álvaro de Bazán, whom he couldn't quite see in the maelstrom of mists, gun smoke, men and lashing rain.

Scarlett twisted clear of another incoming Spanish blade and parried another two, before disarming the fencers of their swords and kicking the men down the stair behind him. He reached the *Oscuro's* quarterdeck, slashing his way through a half dozen men stationed to protect the helm. Capitán Juan Martinez de Recalde was waiting, his back resting against the spoked wheel. He held a musket in his left hand and a cutlass blade in his right.

"Captain Scarlett," said Recalde, evenly.

"Recalde? Where's Bazán?" Scarlett enquired calmly.

"Retirado."

"Ah, shame. Permission to come aboard, Capitán."

"Ortogado," Recalde said, with a humourless smile. Then he fired his musket, hitting Scarlett in the left side of his abdomen.

*****

The big Irish seaman, Shamus O'Reilly, powered his arms through the waters. He was tied to John Prior, Dye

Bant and seven other strong swimmers, all of whom were passionately intent on latching onto the Jacob's ladder sweeping alongside them on the *Maiden Bride's* starboard side.

"Come on boys, now or never, swim ye bastards! Swim!" Shamus yelled at the men bobbing around him on the rough surface of the blackened depths. All souls took their cue and splashed into furious front crawl strokes. Shamus was ahead in closing the gap to the eight-foot-wide mesh of sturdy ropes hanging down from the ship's gunwale to the waterline. Within inches of his target and arms outstretched, a wave hoisted him up and crashed him against the ship's side. It knocked the wind entirely out of his lungs. It was only when his breath returned did Shamus fully comprehend that he was entangled in the netting of the Jacobs. A sudden jolt around his waist threatened to drag him back to the sea, but he weaved all four of his limbs in and around the ropes of the ladder and took the strain of the nine swimmers tied to him. John Prior was the first man to grab hold, quickly followed by the Welshman, Dye Bant, who scurried a few rungs above the water and clung on for dear life. In the same manner that Shamus had nearly been jolted off the ladder, as it was for Dye, when the strain of the next man in the water took its toll on the lifeline lashed around his waist. And so it went, each man foaming at the

mouth in their desperate need to swim for the safety of their
ship.

Safety being a 'relative' term, of course, which John Pri-
or was quickly to discover when he scrambled up some
twenty feet, reached the top of the ladder, launched himself
over the gunwale to the *Bride's* main deck and was nearly
beheaded by a red-eyed Spaniard wielding a cutlass. John
ducked the crazed slashing, tucked himself into a forward
roll, and allowed pure instinct to guide him in striking the
crazed Spaniard's left knee with a viciously sneaky kick.
The man's leg bust on contact, and he fell to the ground
screaming.

John was frantically trying to untie himself from the rope
around his waist when Shamus leapt the gunwale and inadvertently landed with his two-hundred-and-eighty pounds
and two feet planted on the fallen Spaniard's neck, which
broke instantly.

"Jesus Almighty, who put that fucker there?" Shamus
said, stumbling sideways.

"I did," said John Prior from his crouched position, "best
tool up, Shamus."

"Aye," said Shamus, grabbing the Spaniard's sword from
the deck, and stripping the man of a twelve-inch knife.

"Cut me loose," John said.

"Here," Shamus said, and tossed the knife to Prior, who deftly caught it and slashed through the rope around his waist.

"Now what do ye reckon?" Shamus asked.

"Catch our feckin' breath," from Dye Bant, who was scrambling over the gunwale behind Shamus. Dye slumped to the deck, and was joined by Shamus and John Prior, all three with backs propped low against the side of the ship. The men took stock of the scene before them, and all came to the self-same conclusion.

"HOLY SHIT!"

In the dim half-light of a morning sun not yet clear of the horizon, both crews were engaged in a vicious, frenzied melee. Cannon fire boomed from below decks, mostly from the *Bride's* gunners who were extraordinarily well practised and efficient in loading the twenty-four and thirty-six-pound shot into the demi-cannon. The sharp reek of fired gunpowder accompanied the smoke and burnt vapours assaulting the eyes and stinging the sour throats of every fighting man. No one was spared. Muskets were fired off at close range with little or no aiming required as the two ships were no more than twelve feet apart. Men were crowding the lower shrouds on both ships, taking the unrestrained fighting from the decks to the spars on every mast. Swords and cutlasses were thrusting, clashing, and parrying among perhaps one-hundred men still in the fray. Many of the injured simply lay down where they had fallen, others were scampering for cover and repose where they could find it. Men were falling from the rigging and kicked over gunwales dropping limb over limb into the gnarly waters that Shamus, John, and Dye were only too familiar with.

"Best get to the armoury lads," said John Prior.

"Aye, there's gold to be had here," said Shamus.

"Boys are doing well by yere, let's go," concluded Dye.

As the other men from John's rowboat crew were dropping over the gunwale and untying themselves, John, Shamus, and Dye made way to the fore of the main deck and disappeared into the forecastle to arm themselves. They passed 'Paws' who was amidships, a way aft of the foremast with two heavy mahogany clubs in his hands. The heads of the clubs were embedded with ribbons of steel blade and dripping with blood. Whilst ordinarily being one of the gentlest and patient of men on any given Sunday, this 'Paws' was a pirate's pirate devil of an unmanageable, riotous thug, truth be told. Spanish soldiers were lying all about his feet, and his wild eyes betrayed the fact that he was looking for more. When none were apparent, 'Paws' went in search, heading for the *Bride's* port side and jumping up onto a ladder spanning the gap to the *Santa Oscuro*. He nimbly traversed the distance and landed on the main deck of the foreign ship. Anyone with a pointy metal helmet and breast-plate took a belligerent beating from his clubs as 'Paws' made his way aft through the sabre-rattling war-mongering all around him. His goal was his captain, for he knew from experience that Scarlett would be taking on the quarterdeck of the Spanish ship to defeat their capitán, Alvaro de Bazán, and so put an end to the bloody battle, to the relief of one and all.

Three dented helmets and two busted breast-plates aft, 'Paws' hit the first tread of the stairs to the Spanish quarterdeck, and to his horror found his captain stumbling down towards him. Scarlett was clutching the left side of his abdomen with a bloody hand and was clearly in a great deal of distress.

"Captain!" yelled 'Paws'.

"Roger, thank Christ," said Scarlett.

As he fell into his Boatswain's arms for support, Scarlett's knees buckled and the cutlass in his right hand fell to the deck. The steel was awash with blood that began flowing out from the blade across the slippery deck. Scarlett collapsed to his knees. The rain was still pelting down but easing as the grainy fibres of day were weaving an increasingly clear pattern through the last dark hour of the night.

"Captain. Christ. We'll head for the *Bride,* come on," Roger said, as he wrapped an arm around Scarlett's waist in an effort to take up his weight. All anger flooded away from 'Paws' in the instant.

"Bastard shot me Roger, 'twas very unsporting."

"Bazán?" enquired 'Paws'.

"Recalde. Bazan's retired."

"Come on Captain, we'll head home awhile," 'Paws' said, urging Scarlett aft.

"No. Tactical retreat is all Roger, tell me when the bastard is at the top of the stair," Scarlett said, as he had his back to the Spanish quarterdeck with a purpose.

'Paws' took in the glint in Scarlett eyes, and suddenly realised he was now part of a ruse in the art of naval warfare being acted out by one of its masters. He looked up and aft to the head of the staircase. Capitán Recalde appeared in all his misguided glory, standing proudly, empty musket in hand.

"He's there now," whispered 'Paws'.

Scarlett's movement was lightning quick. He withdrew a small dagger from his waistband, sprang up off the deck and out of his Boatswain's arms. He bounded onto a near-by capstan, backflipped, twisting a hundred-and-eighty degrees in the air, while setting fly the dagger straight for Recalde. The knife hit the Spanish capitán midway up his right thigh and buried itself to the hilt. Before a scream could pass the foreigner's wretched mouth, Scarlett was hitting the top three steps of the stairs. In a single fluid motion, Scarlett grabbed the knife, extracted it from Recalde's right thigh, buried it into his left, extracted it again, hit the quarterdeck, smashed his right elbow into Recalde's face and whipped the Spaniard into a grip beneath his elbow, bending him backwards with the knife pressed hard against his throat.

"*Piedad, por favor, ¡piedad!*" exclaimed the Spaniard, pleading for Scarlett to be merciful.

Scarlett pushed up underneath Recalde's elbow even harder. Recalde knew he was going nowhere fast.

"*Por favor*. Mercy, *Señor* Scarlett," Recalde pleaded.

"Call off your men," Scarlett growled, "or I swear to God I'll fucking end you here and now."

Scarlett felt, rather than saw, a movement over his left shoulder, and turned his head momentarily to evaluate the threat. The Spanish ship's First Mate, Pedro Garcia, was inching closer, cutlass in hand, surrounded by half a dozen of Recalde's officers. Scarlett locked his grip and twisted Recalde around a few degrees.

"Don't you... Drop the fucking blade," Scarlett said to Pedro, "*¡Déjalocaer!*"

The Spanish capitán gave a brief motion of resistance in trying to pull away. Scarlett gripped the man tighter, threatening to break an elbow or dislocate a shoulder.

The fear in Recalde's eyes was evidence enough for Pedro, who dropped his sword to the deck and reluctantly stepped back a pace. The officers behind him followed suit, dropping their weapons. Scarlett twisted Recalde back around so that he was facing the full length of his ship.

Scarlett snarled into Recalde's ear, "Call it off. Strike your colours, or I'll cut you to fucking strips in front of your men," his words brimming with menace, hatred, and truth.

"*Sí, sí, esta bien muy bien,*" Recalde said, and sucked in a breath, "*¡Suficiente! ¡Dejar de luchar!*"

"Louder!" demanded Scarlett.

"*¡Suficiente!*" screamed Recalde, across the main deck. "We surrender! *¡¡Nosotrasnos rendimos!!*"

One by one every man on the main deck of the *Santa Oscuro* desisted in their swordplay and bludgeoning and pulled their focus to the two captains at the head of the staircase on the quarterdeck. Scarlett pressed harder into Recalde's neck with the blade of his knife and a few drops of blood began to trickle. Recalde's thighs had a mess of blood running down his hose.

"Again," whispered Scarlett.

"*¡Suficiente!*" Recalde wailed, "*Nosotros concedemos.*"

Roger 'Paws' Prowse looked about warily, in part to identify any sanctimonious little Spanish pricks that might defy their capitán's order and continue fighting, but mostly he was weighing up the general state of his own crew. It would take time. The fighting had been rough, and injuries were aplenty.

Spaniards spread out over the decks of both ships dropped their weapons and placed hands up with their palms facing outward in the universal gesture of submission and surrender.

A single cannon shot fired from the *Bride's* hull.

"Cease bloody fire!" 'Paws' yelled out across the starboard gunwale of the Spanish ship.

"Cease fire... cease fire... cease fire..." echoed a series of fading voices on the *Bride* as the instruction was relayed across deck and passed down ladders and vaults to the gun decks.

Silence held the moment true. Only in the falling rain could any man discern that life was continuing still.

Scarlett held his unyielding grip on Recalde, maintaining the knife at his throat. The fucker was going nowhere. Not yet.

"*¿Hablas Ingles?*" Scarlett whispered in Recalde's ear.

"*Sí señor,*" said Recalde, "*Yo hablo Inglés.*" His adrenaline was depleting and the pain in his thighs was increasingly severe, muddling his mind in shock.

"That's Spanish, Sir. I mean English as in the Queen's noble tongue."

"Ah, yes. Yes, I speak English."

"To the victor go the spoils," Scarlett said, and relaxed his grip a little on Recalde.

"Now what?" Recalde asked.

"Well, the bullet in my side suggests you are not a man of honour, but answer me this, can I trust you in a smooth transition if I remove this blade from your neck?" asked Scarlett.

"You have my word. The battle is lost. I would prefer to live to see the war won."

"An excellent sentiment, and well said."

Scarlett relaxed his grip. A tingling sensation arose in the fingers of Recalde's left hand, as blood swelled in the veins in his arm once more. He was immediately aware of just how vulnerable he'd been in the last two minutes. Scarlett maintained the knife at the man's throat.

"I do not want your ship," said Scarlett, "but the gold is coming with me. Sound fair?"

"You are not taking my ship?"

"I didn't say I wouldn't sink her, but that depends on you and your men."

"What would you have us do?"

"Behave," said Scarlett, "we shall discuss the particulars over breakfast in my quarters aboard the *Bride*."

"Very well."

"Now give order for your crew to muster on the main deck of your ship. Any man that isn't present within five minutes will be executed. Understand?" Scarlett said, calmly.

"*Sí*... I mean yes, I understand," Recalde said.

Scarlett changed tempo, "Mister Prowse, the Capitán and his officers need trussing on the quarterdeck."

Old 'Paws' got the message. He sequestered two of the *Bride's* crew and within minutes the Spanish officers were bound and gagged on the quarterdeck of the *Oscuro*. Only then did Scarlett release his hold on Recalde and remove the knife from his neck. The Spanish capitán relayed orders for his crew to gather on the main deck of his ship. That done, he slumped to the floor, exhausted, defeated, and sore. His hands and feet were bound like the rest of his senior crew.

"Roger, we need boats in the water," Scarlett said, "we must find William and the boys as quick as possible. And I want a full head count on both ships. And we need..."

"Aye to all Captain, I know the drill," interjected 'Paws', "it's already bein' seen to. Now sit down a bit and catch your breath."

"My thanks, Roger," Scarlett said with a wry smile. He plonked himself down on the top step of the stairs and watched as his crew rounded up the Spanish on the main deck. The gunshot to his abdomen would have to be addressed by Trevor 'Needles' Neary, the *Bride's* surgeon, but from what he could see there were many other men in more urgent need than he. The sun was on the rise and the rain was easing to a drizzle. The winds were dropping quickly, and the seas were calming. The mist so dense that visibility was limited to about forty yards. The worst of the storm was heading over the leeward isles to the northwest. Scarlett figured it would be battering Puerto Rico by nightfall, but that was the least of his concerns.

Today was going to be a hot one.

The death-watch after the storm.

Scarlett turned to Recalde, who was five feet from him, sitting, propped with his back to the balustrade separating the quarterdeck from the main, "Capitán Recalde, is your surgeon competent?"

"He is a good man and well trained."

"Permission to set him up in your officer's quarters and have him tend your wounded."

"He will need the support of his team."

"Of course," said Scarlett.

"I am grateful," said Recalde, nodding his head.

"The weather is calming. I intend to transfer your crew to the island in the boats. They shall have supplies but no weapons. Would that be satisfactory?"

"I suppose it must be, satisfactory," Recalde said, the slight confusion apparent on his face and in his tone.

"Better than locking them in the hold," Scarlett said, and was about to say more but honestly couldn't be bothered in the moment.

He turned his attentions to the main deck where the Spanish crew were amassing in numbers, carefully guarded by three-dozen armed men of the *Bride's* crew. They were stationed with muskets, on the foredeck, the shrouds, the capstans, the gunwales, and the decks, all intently concentrating their aim upon the foreign crew.

Scarlett wondered about his First Mate. He would have made it. Surely. He wondered if William would ever have mentioned himself in his morning advice to the men. Could he predict his own demise with his dream-state antics? 'Twas a good parlour trick, that much was certain, and the men adored him for it. Surely, he would make it. Wouldn't he?

16

An Innocent Flock

29th October 1577

Robert Cecil was being rudely accosted, in his humble opinion. Truly, he didn't appreciate the hands-on approach of the Queen's Guard Yeoman fucker that was gripping him by the elbow and dragging him towards the centre of the Middle Courtyard.

Several things were happening around Robert, and he was taking careful note of all; the groundskeepers and handymen that hand been forced to form a line or a queue, or whatever shambles of attempted order had been thrust upon them minutes ago, were having none of it, and had broken ranks in rebellion. The head gardener, a solid man named Giles Winterbottom, was walking away from a pack of halberd bearing guards and approaching. To Robert's left the captain of the red-coated morons was quick marching across the courtyard followed closely by one of his men. What looked to be Francis Bacon was hood-up, incognito, skirting the wall of the southern range of the court along-side a lady dressed as a nun.

That's a nice touch, Bacon. Where'd you find her?

The unknown figure who had been dressed in a grey habit and green sash, standing in the shadows of the north-eastern corner of the court, had completely disappeared. Chaplain Joseph Hardwycke II and his protégé, curate Timothy Killam, were exiting the main chapel doors. The seasoned clergyman and apprentice minister were sporting gold embroidered damask cotton robes, with tall, point-ed hats covering their heads. Lastly of note, bells began banging out from the belfry, with nothing like the high degree of control usually practised in the familiar tuneful change-ringing of the canonical hours of the day. This rack-et was a terrible clash of bongs altogether.

"Unhand me, gaoler, your grip is hurting my spine," cried Robert, pulling back against the guard's clasp on his elbow.

"I'm not touching your spine. Move," came the guard's retort.

"Lord Burghley shall hear of this," said Robert.

The guard took less than a second to think it over and released his hold on Robert's elbow, "Don't run."

"I can't run, you solid buffoon," said Robert, "an afflic-tion upon my birth has rendered..." and he would have continued but he saw William and Katherine exiting the archway at the foot of the belfry, calmly and collectedly, hoods-down, chins-up, as if they had been summoned with every given right of the Lord Almighty, they stayed put and observed the goings on before them.

Captain Smedley-Smythe-Smythings reached the approximate centre of the courtyard, raised his ebony stick, and bellowed, "All present in this yard! Hear me now! You are to remain still, and you shall listen up!"

Head Gardener Winterbottom continued to approach, followed by all the grounds staff present. Chaplain Hardwycke and curate Killam kept walking side by side, closing on the captain's position. Francis Bacon waved to William and Katherine who pulled up their hoods and began striding southwards, skirting the middle range. Robert continued walking towards the centre of the court. The guard who had held him stopped promptly in his tracks.

"Stand still, I say!" cried Smythe-Smythings, "Damn you all. You will desist in your approach, or we shall be forced to counter with force!"

"Would that be that be the Royal We, Captain?" asked Chaplain Hardwycke, "I see no grounds for potency or aggression. My innocent flock are but gentle persons, no doubt frightened and confused by your intrusion into their home."

"I have it on Her Majesty's authority, to conduct a search of..." began Smedley-Smythe-Smythings.

"Your signet warrant, Captain. If you please," said Hardwycke, holding out his hand.

"I... errm.. Well, you see, Father..."

"I'm afraid I do not see, Captain," replied Hardwycke, calmly. "Your missive, Sir. Present it forthwith."

"I have spoken with Lady Burghley and obtained her..."

"Do you hear the Lord's voice in the echo of those bells, Captain?" asked Hardwycke, rhetorically, of course, "No? Neither do I. They are a shambles of inharmonics. Yet the hour is upon us to pray for your redemption."

Curate Killam turned his head and masked his not-so-subtle smile in a fit of coughing.

"To the chapel, everyone!" cried Hardwycke, turning his back on Smythe-Whatever- the-Fuck, and herding his flock, "The Captain and his men are wanting of our blessing!"

The veteran priest took off in the direction he had just arrived and headed for the chapel doors. Curate Killam stepped in alongside. Robert Cecil walked past Smedley-Smythe-Smythings and followed the clerical insurgency.

"You heard the good Father!" shouted head-gardener Winterbottom, catching on quickly, and, addressing his labourers, "We shall down our tools and pray for this lost soul!"

The ringing bells had prompted a good number of the house staff to exit loggia archways and doorways and enter the Middle Court from all sides. All were relatively sober and gathered in groups of twos and threes exchanging whispered opinions on the strange goings on, and all were instinctively heading for the chapel doors. Only the half-company of the Queen's Body Guard of the Yeomen of the Guard maintained their stock still positions around the courtyard, as instructed by their captain.

*****

Mildred Cecil was increasingly vexed with every word progressing from her husband's mouth. The mistimed bells in the belfry had thrown off the quintet of musicians, who were struggling to maintain their upbeat rendition. They seemed to be transitioning back to some sort of default sombre chamber melody, which strangely seemed to exacerbate Mildred's apprehension in the moment.

"It would be wise to see it as a marvellous opportunity, Mildred. One that will undoubtedly expand William's horizons at an age when most children are confined to house chores and possibly books, if they are fortunate," said Lord of the household, Cecil.

"This contrivance is preposterous," said Mildred, "I won't have my son travelling the bloody world with Francis bloody Drake of all people. The man is a renowned pirate, for fuck's sake. No offence, Sir James."

"None taken, Lady Burghley," said James, unable to resist voicing Mildred's formal title in his Scottish brogue this time around. He was hoping to dissipate the increasing tension between the married couple.

"We have no better alternatives, Mildred. Elizabeth will not let William's existence threaten her vision of virgin Sovereignty," said Cecil.

"Then she shouldn't have gotten knocked up should she, stupid cow!" snapped Mildred, "It's not William's fault. This will destroy him. And he's a beautiful boy. The revelation that he's not our child will kill him. He's too young for this."

"He must absent the Realm, Mildred. It is as simple as that. Elizabeth will not rest until he is captured, and silenced," said Cecil.

"He's not going to say anything. He's whip smart and knows better than to betray the bloody Queen. Sail him to the Canary Isles, James, or somewhere close by," said Mildred.

"Aye, that is a consideration of substance, though I fear…" said James.

"Too many spies in the isles, Mildred," said Cecil, firmly. "If William is to live, he must be transported further afield. The decision is made. I'm sorry."

"Just listen to yourselves. Oh, you two pretend to control this Realm, yet you wield influence as gutless, pellucid, servants of a deranged Monarch who harbours no true sense of moral or spiritual decency. This will destroy our son, husband. Mark me on this. I will not agree to this travesty of vapourous ill-thought stratagem."

"He's not our son, Mildred," said Cecil. Though it wasn't immediately apparent to him, he would live to regret this comment for years to come.

If Mildred had a knife about her person, she probably would have cut more than her children's birthday cake. Instead, she breathed in deeply, exhaled, and stepped away.

"Thank you, Michael," said Mildred, grabbing the decanter of vintage brandy that was sitting on the silver tray in Michael I's hands. She ignored any impulse to lift a glass and chugged a long pull from the crystal vessel, while picking up an iced cupcake from one of the many on display amongst the meats, cheeses, and breads.

"You're not getting laid anytime soon," whispered Sir James.

"Do fuck off, Flemington," whispered, Cecil, knowing well that his Scottish friend was on the money.

Mildred skirted the long table, munching on her cake and downing several more gulps from the decanter. When she arrived by the stone fireplace, she grabbed a cigarillo from a mahogany box sitting in the centre of a low-set, oval, oak, and walnut table, slumped into one of four high-backed leather chairs and plonked her feet up on a footstool.

Michael II was quick to dash across the room with a lighting taper in hand.

The bells had stopped clanging outside. The melancholic musicians were strumming and bowing slowly, reciting a sombre melody, which Mildred found to be completely appropriate as she sat back in her chair, chugged another gulp of brandy and chased it with a puff of her cigar.

*****

Theobalds' chapel was flaming in the warmth of two dozen torches burning in cast iron mountings on the thick blue-grey stone walls. Shadows danced among the rafters of the vaulted roof and skipped between the grounds staff and house staff that had filled the pews. More workers were entering through the chapel doors. It was a fine turnout. Chaplain Hardwycke had found a position behind a lectern situated ten feet from the southern end of the stone altar. Curate Killam twisted a small set of ornate sacring bells in his right hand, prompting silence from the softly murmuring congregation. Hardwycke took up his cue, "We are gathered here this evening to give praise to the Lord for the protection of one of our own. One of our home's finest, upstanding children. Unjustly accused..."

Captain Smedley-Smythe-Smythings entered, pushing his way through several maids and gardeners stationed beside the entrance doors. He proceeded up the central isle as Adjutant Walters and three other guards entered, jostling staff aside.

"Desist in your ceremonious rhetoric, Father! Or I shall arrest you and every peasant herein for obstruction to the Crown!"

"Unjustly accused of no less than a matter of Treason!" maintained Hardwycke, ramping up his theatrical manner in defiance of the captain's orders.

I'll give you rhetoric, you prick.

"Treason! Above and Almighty, hear me please, Lord, for both you know, and I know, and all loving souls here know, young William has not the bones in his body to commit Treason."

"Enough, priest!" demanded Smythings, nearing the altar and turning to face the multitude of parishioners present, "Hear me now! William Cecil, you will present yourself immediately! You will stand beside this altar! Or I swear, before God and your chaplain, every one of your people shall be taken to the Tower of London and held for trial. Do I make myself clear, child?"

Silence fell upon the chapel. No one moved.

"William Cecil. You have five counts in which to present!" bellowed Smedley-Smythe-Smythings, "Five!"

Three additional guards entered through the main doors at the northwest rear corner.

"Four!... Three..." continued the captain.

"I most vehemently object to this act of bullying, Captain," said Hardwycke. "The good Lord has no place in his heart..."

"Two!" shouted Smedley-Smythe-Smythings.

William stood from his seated position in the third row of benches on the northern side of the central isle. He pulled his hood back allowing it to rest over his shoulders, though his face remained in the flickering shadows thrown out by the torches, "I am William Cecil."

"Ah, yes... I see you now. You've grown, boy," said Smythings.

A second figure stood up, and pulled back the hood of their habit, in the fourth row of benches on the southern side of the isle. "I am William Cecil," said Francis Bacon.

"'Tis I that is William Cecil," said Robert, now standing, five rows behind Bacon.

"Enough of this nonsense!" shouted the captain of the guard, "Sit down, all of you!"

"Truly, I am William Cecil," said another figure, dressed in a green habit, standing eight rows back, beside the isle. The figure raised hands and drew the hood of their robe back. Katherine's face was revealed to all. She purposely shook out her long raven hair and the congregation burst into fits of laughter.

Head gardener, Giles Winterbottom, stood up, "'Tis I am William Cecil!"

"No, good Sir, 'tis I am William Cecil," said a groundskeeper upon standing. The boy was probably no more than sixteen.

"I'm Billy Cecil," said a page boy standing in the front row.

"Guards!" shouted Smythings, "Apprehend them..."

"I am Wilhelmina Cecil," said a young parlour maid, and the congregation erupted, all standing, yelling they were William Cecil, slapping each other on shoulders, and jostling purposely around one another in feigned attempts to reach the altar and Captain Smedley-Smyth-Smythings, who was suddenly overwhelmed with crowding servants.

Katherine, William, Robert, Bacon, and Sister Agatha made excellent use of the chaos in the chapel by fucking off sharply, shrouded among the assisting bodies of the groundskeepers, maids, pages, and hall boys. They headed west, passing through the Great Parlour, and the loggia of the southern range of the Fountain Court, before turning right and trotting through Robert's lodgings. Another right turn through the northwestern tower had them well positioned to enter the North Parlour from the west. Katherine stepped up to a stone archway, flicked an iron latch and pulled a large oak door open allowing the others to pass by her. She closed the door behind herself and entered. The noise was fearsome. To everyone else, the players within so to speak, it was relatively quiet, but Katherine's coming of age birthday present was apparently a profound change in her ability to listen to the tempo, vibrations, energies, and real-time signatures of every person, chair, table, wainscot panel, window, fireplace crackle and heartbeat in the room. The morbid string section was suddenly filtered into irrelevance, violins, cello, and lute combining in marginally off-tuned extraneousness. William's wellbeing was loudest. He would have to leave. Her heart drummed a triplet base line telling her that her parents wouldn't let her go with him. The adults were on a track to separate them, for no justifiable reason. Katherine heard chords of desperation. Notes in combination from a scale she never wanted to practise. A progression she would never desire to repeat countless times, over and over and bloody well over again, yet in the instant she knew she was most likely facing ten-thousand hours building lonely muscle memory. She impulsively reached into the hip pocket of her dungarees and withdrew the opal pendant and chain that she and William had tried to bind in forever lasting magic.

You'll find me. I know you will. You'd better.

The patriarch of the Theobalds household looked away from his cigar smoking, brandy chugging spouse and opened his arms, embracing the children's entrance, "You all took your bloody time. Been having fun with the fire-crackers, have you?"

"His fault," said Robert and William in unison, both pointing at Bacon.

"Bloody fine show, Francis," said Cecil.

"Thank you, Sir," said Bacon, "may I introduce Sister Agatha Templeton."

Mildred stood up, "Children!" Her motherly intentions were sound, but she wobbled in a nicotine induced head spin, and slumped back into her chair, dropping the de-canter of brandy on the floor beside her. Thankfully it didn't smash into pieces.

"Mother, are you alright?" asked Katherine, immediately crossing the room.

"Yes, indeed, a pleasure, good sister," said Cecil, holding out his hand, "I should have scheduled a visit before now."

Bacon prompted Agatha forward with a nudge. She took Cecil's hand in her own, prepping for a formal handshake but the big man upturned the back of her hand and kissed it.

"Lord Burghley, thank you. The Alms House people thank you, dearly," said Agatha.

"Oh, tosh," said Cecil, "William, you need to be making tracks with Sir James."

"Do I, father?" questioned William.

Katherine knelt beside her mother, who began sniffling and tearing up, "Your father's an arsehole," said Mildred.

"Oh. Well, nothing we can do about that," said Katherine.

"He won't bloody listen to reason," said Mildred, waving her cigarillo the approximate direction of her husband, "He's a pansy, fluttering in Elizabeth's farts."

"Really, mother?" questioned Katherine, rhetorically, while plucking the cigar from Mildred's hand and stubbing it out in an ashtray on the nearby low table.

Captain Smedley-Smythe-Smythings burst through the large oak door in the southeast corner, followed closely by Adjutant Walters and two other guards.

"Lord Burghley. Thank heaven! I insist upon your cooperation, Sir," said Smythings.

"Good evening, Captain," said Cecil, "how might I be of assistance?"

"It's your children, Sir. They are running amok. And we shall not have it."

Three guards entered through the door on the southwest corner, the man named Bertram among them. Both exits were effectively blocked. It didn't go unnoticed.

Chaplain Hardwycke entered, pushing through the guards manning the southeastern doorway. Curate Killam tried to enter but was prevented by the crossing of two of the guard's spiked-axe-head topped halberds.

"Obstruction of the duties of the Queen's Body Guard of the Yeomen of the Guard is a capital, offence, Sir," said Smythings.

"Is it, by God?" said Cecil.

"Lord Burghley, please, Sir. Which of your children is the one named, William?"

"Mildred, dear, which one of them is William?" bellowed Cecil, before casting a whispered aside to Sir James, "A little help here, James."

"Why do you care?" shouted Mildred, lifting the decanter from the floor beside her chair, "You'll never see him again, anyway."

James stepped towards William, Robert, Bacon, and sister Agatha, "William, go with the Captain. He needs be vexed no more this evening. I'll be close by your side."

"Very well, Sir James," said Bacon, stepping forward.

"That one's William?" said Cecil, who began skirting the long table, heading towards his wife, "Well, I'll be, Mildred. He's a handsome boy. Are we sure he's mine?"

"You're doing the right thing, son," said Smythings. "No harm will come to you."

"William, can I cut your birthday cake?" asked William, "We'll save you a piece."

"It's my birthday cake, too," said Katherine, stepping away from Mildred and approaching the western end of the long table.

"Oh, sure. But the cocoa layer is mine," said Bacon, as Captain Smedley-Smythe-Smythings tucked his hand underneath Bacon's elbow and began to lead him eastwards.

"Captain! A pause for a blessing of the child, before you whisk him away into the darkness of the cold night," said Chaplain Hardwycke, stepping in front of Bacon and Smythings.

Sir James turned his head away masking his smile. All credit to the players, he hadn't factored in such outstanding improvisations when weighting the variables of his scheme by the Thames River, earlier in the evening.

"Oh, Christ. Very well, Father. But be quick about," said Smythings, "Men! Form a corridor for transport!"

The guards stationed by the western archway and door, began to approach in an orderly formation, two by two, side by side.

Chaplain Hardwycke stepped past Bacon and Smythings, and walked straight up to Robert, "Best you kneel, William."

"Can we ask the good Lord, if I can cut my cake, Father?" said Robert, kneeling and feigning tears, "And if I have committed Treason, can we ask for his forgiveness?" It was a decent performance.

Hardwycke had to literally bite his lip to hide his smile, "Yes, child. But you must repent of your sins, immediately."

"But I don't know of my sins, Father," said Robert.

"What the hell is going on here?!" shouted, Smedley-Smythe-Smythings.

"Mildred!" bellowed Cecil, "Pray, when were you to tell me we have two Williams? Is that one also mine?"

"I shan't say, as I can't say, Lord Burghley," said Mildred, catching on somewhat.

Maybe her hubby wasn't a complete wanker after all.

"You have three William's, father," said Katherine, from her position beside the real William at the western end of the long table. The twins shared a hold on a long knife, hovering it over the bottom tier of the birthday cake, "Mummy made us promise not to tell you, but I think she's mean. It's not your fault you were away so often, licking Queen Bessy's arse."

"Katherine!" screamed Mildred, "How dare you be so bold!"

"Three Williams!" exclaimed Cecil, "Mildred, what is the meaning of this outrage?"

"Would you like some cake, father?" asked William.

"Oh, curse the bloody cake!"

"I don't do curses, Lord Burghley," said Chaplain Hardwycke.

"Then what use are you, priest?!" stated Cecil, "You knew of these infidelities, I suppose."

"Umm, well, I confess..." lied Hardwycke.

"Damnation fall upon you..." said Cecil, turning to the fireplace, to hide his smile, "Michaels! Fetch me brandy!"

Michaels I and II set about their master's request but were briefly interrupted by James, "And I'll have rum, lads."

Katherine and William cut into their birthday cake and lifted a slice each, "You sure?" whispered Katherine.

"He asked for it," whispered William.

"He did," said Katherine, as she loaded her cake slice into the saddle of her catapult. William was already stretching back the rubber strings on his own slingshot.

"Here's your cocoa cake, William," pronounced Katherine, looking directly at Bacon.

TWANG! TWANG!

Two chunks of iced cocoa cake flew across the room. Bacon ducked, and the cake shots exploded all over Captain Smedley-Smythe-Smything's face, neck, and shoulders.

Robert was surprisingly quick to his feet. He grabbed two cupcakes from the long-table and tossed one to Bacon, who stepped away from the captain, caught the cake and mounted it in the saddle of his catapult.

TWANG! TWANG!

Two disintegrating cakes whizzed over Katherine and William's heads as they ducked behind the west end of the long table. Michael I took the brunt of the squishy ammunition squarely in the chest. Michael II wobbled away laughing.

"Cease fire! All of you!" demanded Captain Smythings, wiping mushed cake from his eyes and nose.

TWANG! TWANG!

William and Katherine returned fire on Bacon and Robert, who copped healthy splashes of birthday cake all down their habits as they dived behind the east end of the table.

"Arrest them, men!" shouted Smythings, "Block the exits!"

TWANG! TWANG!

William and Katherine fired at Smythings, who had the good sense to duck this time, leaving his Adjutant Walters to cop an open mouthful of chocolate and cream coloured gateau.

Bacon and Robert re-loaded and stuck their heads up over the table to fire on William and Katherine once again. Sir James took a full-on broadside as he began to hunch down and reach for William. Cecil had pulled away from the fireplace, stepped past Mildred, and was fast approaching Katherine.

"Desist! Cease firing! cried out Smythings, "Men! Nobody is to leave this room!"

Cecil had his arms around Katherine and yanked her to her feet...

James pulled William up and dragged him away from the table...

Captain Smedley-Smythe-Smythings captured Robert...

Two guards lunged for Bacon, who was quick to bolt off westwards between servants...

"No!! Wait!!" screamed Katherine, digging into her hip pocket, and clutching for the opal pendant and silver chain.

"Katherine, be calm!" insisted Cecil, struggling to shepherd his bleating daughter.

"Wait! Daddy, let go of me!" screamed Katherine.

By the time Katherine had withdrawn the gemstone from her pocket, Sir James had dragged William halfway across the room towards the southeastern door. Bertram and two other guards immediately descended upon them. The struggle wasn't pretty.

"No! William! No! Daddy, let me go!" cried Katherine.

William's necklace fell from Katherine's hand, dropped to the parquet floor, and disappeared under the table beneath their birthday cake.

17

Any Sign of William?

8th November 1587

Martin 'Mumbles' No-Name was finishing the loading of two yawl-boats with food and fresh water when 'Paws' approached him on the *Maiden Bride's* main deck. "How're we fixed, Martin?"

The two rowboats were floating on the waterline some twenty feet below, lashed to the Jacob's ladder on the starboard side of the ship.

"Good to go, Sir," said 'Mumbles'.

"Good man," said 'Paws' and turned about to face John Prior, Shamus O'Reilly, and Dye Bant, who were standing apprehensively nearby. They were accompanied by the seven other crewmen who had braved the night's storm in John's rowboat and dragged themselves out of the water in the last hour.

"Divi' yourselves up lads," said 'Paws', "I don't want you back on board this ship 'til you find 'em. Set 'bout it."

"Aye, aye, Sir."

Prior skipped the gunwale and scrambled down the ladder into one of the rowboats followed by several crew. Dye and Shamus boarded the other boat accompanied by four more men.

'Mumbles' approached 'Paws'. "Hopin' you don't mind, boss, but I was likin' to go with 'em for a spell."

"Well now, that could be a thing, Martin," said 'Paws', "but I got other plans for a man of your talents this mornin'."

'Mumbles', who was no spring chicken, and much the wiser for it, narrowed his eyes in considered suspicion of the Boatswain's response to his reasonable request. He was about to verbalise his thinking when 'Paws' put him on hold with a raised palm and leaned out over the gunwale. "Lockyzee ads, yertiz, get out there an' fin' them, an' be quick 'bout. There's gurt big sharks out there lookin' fer breakfast sure as you babbers ar' betwaddled guddlers back home."

"Aye, aye, Mister Prowse," came several retorts from the men below and the two rowboats pushed out from the *Bride's* hull under oars with the scouting party set on retrieving William, Richard Bately, Jim Dolby, 'Tumbles' Turner, and the remaining crew from the night's demolition teams.

'Paws' turned his attention back to 'Mumbles'. "Right, me old mucker, as I was sayin' man o' your talents, Martin, might be better placed in charge of inventory."

"How's that Mister Prowse?" 'Mumbles' asked.

'Paws' uncharacteristically placed an arm around the elder crewman's shoulder and guided 'Mumbles' slowly towards the port side of the deck.

"Well, as I sees it, it's my duty to put you in a right bobbish mood, fer all ye done on the voyage, Martin, and your duty to get over there...", said 'Paws', pointing across to the *Santa Oscuro*, "get down in her holds and make a true an' fair count of all her bloody gold!"

"By ways of inventory, says you, I'd better I fetch a pen and paper then," 'Mumbles' said with a bright and shining half toothed smile.

"Fetch what's you like, Martin, only keep the tally to yerself fer now," said 'Paws', "and not a sound of it to anyone but me. Or the Captain, of course."

"Right oh, can do. Can do... what about Master William?" 'Mumbles' asked.

'Paws' pulled up short in his steps. The dangers of being adrift in the waters surrounding them cutting through the innocent question.

"Well... yeh, I reckon, of course, Master William too. Soon as the lads fetch 'im."

"Right, there you go then. Thank you, Mister Prowse."

'Mumbles' headed for the forecastle and disappeared through its doorway.

'Paws' steadied his mind for a beat, banishing any negative thoughts. There was much to be done in repairing the damage to the *Bride*, not to mention the wounded men aboard her.

*****

Trevor 'Needles' Neary was hard at it in the officers' quarters below the quarterdeck of the *Bride*. 'Officers' being an extraneous term aboard, as Scarlett detested conventional hierarchy, preferring to treat all crew with equal importance. The established vertical pyramid of managerial organisation was superseded by a robust table of elements portraying lateral divisions categorised by crewmen's particular skill sets. Scarlett, William, and Trevor himself, made decisions and gave orders, it was true, but it was the actions of the men that realised those commands, hence their equal worth in playing parts in their oft chaotic voyages and adventures. 'Needles' Neary loved to examine and cross-examine the differential natures of order and chaos. He was doing it now, leaning over the captain's dining table, while stitching a rather nasty three-inch stab wound adjacent to the groin of a bloodied and beaten crewman by the name of Jonesy, who was, thankfully, unconscious, and behaving as a model patient should.

'Needles' was thirty-five years young, with bright, dark, bespectacled eyes, short afro haircut, neatly trimmed goatee beard, and he lived in a muscular body more akin to a long-distance runner than your customary desk-bound academic. Born in the small town of Arima, on the isle of Trinidad, to an Irish father and an African mother, 'Needles' had skirted orthodoxy his entire life. He was least to say 'unusual' by modern standards, in both race and mind. His father, a renowned luthier from Dublin, had used his gifts in instrument-making to fund his passion for travel around the known world. He had settled in Trinidad, besotted with Trevor's mother and the various music styles of Kaiso, Rapso, Parang, and Creole indigenous to the island. Trevor was the eldest of eight siblings in the Neary family, and, from a very young age, it was apparent that he would forever be the brightest intellectually. To this end, his father insisted in enrolling Trevor in a preparatory school in Dublin at the tender age of thirteen and left the boy in the care of extended family, and the community of teachers that were to exercise their autonomy in determining a suitable curriculum for the brilliant young mixed heritage child. Studies in philosophy, letters, arts, humanities, law, medicines, and theology had culminated in two degrees and a doctorate from the school, before Trevor had turned twenty-two and inherited his father's penchant for travel. He had met Scarlett and William, as it happened, on the island of Cuba some eight years prior, when he had been running a small clinic in the port of Havana.

'Needles' tied off the final stitch stemming the blood from Jonesy's wound and crossed the short distance to a second makeshift operating table in the low-ceilinged room, with its painted red floor, oak walls, and numerous lanterns. He had two assistants, hand-picked from the crew that morning; experienced sailors by the names of Thomas and Johnson, who qualified largely on the basis that they each had four working limbs and, moreover, on the basis that they were the least likely out of the crew to puke at the sight of a busted bone or blood spurting laceration.

The next patient on this table had a bit of both going on. 'Needles' made a quick prognosis and settled his priority on a well trusted old medical adage, 'blood before bone'. Having done so he tore open the man's shirt and staunched a throbbing flow of vital fluid by plugging a wound in the man's right armpit with two deftly placed fingers.

"Arrraagh!" uttered the man on the table, whose name was Powell.

"Steady there, you'll be alright now," said 'Needles' in his hybrid Trinidadian/Irish mongrel accent, before turning to his assistants, "Mister Thomas, ready a half circle and thread it with catgut, eh. And hand me that bottle of rum now, good man."

"Aye, Sir, on it," Thomas replied, and set about foraging through an array of surgical implements atop a wheeled oak trolley, stationed port side of the room.

"Mister Johnson, get that man outta' here and down the line. Ready the next," 'Needles' instructed, indicating the prone figure of Jonesy on the dining table.

"Aye, Sir," Johnson said, before lifting the unconscious patient and carrying him from the room. Several other able crewmen were on standby outside the door, ready to ferry those leaving surgery to their bunks, as necessary.

"Rum, Mister Thomas, rum, man. Don't fall short on priorities now," said 'Needles'.

"Oh, aye, right, Sir," said Thomas, who quickly snatched up a half-full bottle of the spirit and tossed it to the ship's doctor. 'Needles' caught the bottle single handed, took a huge swig of the fortifying nectar within, and offered the bottle to his current patient.

Powell, who was lying on his left side in considerable pain, could hardly move, but passing up a decent drink in his current state was not on the agenda, so he winced his way through lifting his left arm from the table and grabbed the rum from the good doctor. He downed a quarter bottle before handing it back to 'Needles', who, in turn, offered a short length of leather strap.

"Bite down on this for a spell," said 'Needles', "it'll save your teeth."

Powell had been around long enough at sea to have a reasonable idea of forthcoming events and he placed the strap reluctantly between his teeth.

Assistant Thomas was ready with a small, curved needle threaded with catgut suture, which, contrary to popular belief, didn't come from the guts of cats at all.

"My thanks, Mister Thomas, have a drink," said 'Needles' exchanging the bottle of rum for needle and thread. He turned back to his patient and removed his fingers from the wound underneath his armpit. Blood flowed instantly, and the surgeon began his needlepoint cure in earnest.

"The secret is in the connective tissues," 'Needles' began, "you see, we get into the guts of a sheep, or in this case I shaved into the intestines of the Bos taurus, a Black Hereford you can believe it was, and we rip out the natural fibrous strands, twist them together, and grind them clean."

"Aarrraahhhgggh!" uttered Powell, as the needle passed through his skin a second time.

"Ooohh, sorry about that, gotta get in a bit deep just about here," said 'Needles, turning to his assistant. "Pass me over the old zeolite powders, there's a good lad."

"Aye, Sir," said Thomas, and reached for a goat skin pouch on the trolley. He handed it to 'Needles' Neary with considered reverence.

"This is gonna' sting something nasty now Powell, my old mucker, but I gotta stop this bleeding on the inside here," 'Needles' said, as he poured some coarse brown/green power from the pouch into the palm of his hand.

"Bit of potassium, smidgin of calcium, few filings of the right corals cooked nicely on the fire and, hey presto perfecto, we got a nice little powder stops you bleeding out to death. You up for it?"

Powell removed the leather strap from his mouth, "Yeah Doc, whatever, I knows you means well."

"Here, have another skite of rum, man" said 'Needles', handing the bottle of liquor to Powell a second time. The wounded seaman spent no time in downing the remainder of the spirit.

"Brace yourself now," 'Needles' said.

He waited for Powell to return the leather strap between his teeth, then poured a handful of the powdery concoction into his open wound.

"AAAARRRRGGGHHH! Fuck me, Doc! You're killin' me, God damn it!" from Powell. Sweat was pouring from his forehead and blinding his eyes.

"Sorry, it's the sodium. Teach you to not get stabbed the next time, look on the bright side," said the doctor, taking up his needle and thread once more. "As I was saying, so we take the fibrous, tendonous, tissues from the old cow or the sheep mostly, sterilise them in a healthy drop of alcohol and make a twine out of it. Exact same as the strings on a fiddle believe it or not. My old man was teaching me how to make 'em since I was knee high to a leprechaun."

"Is that... is that a fact?" said Powell, through teeth clenched on the leather strap.

"Dead set, that's a fact," said 'Needles', "you can play a tune on this armpit of yours when I'm done here, just bear with me."

"And what tune might that be?"

The question was interjected by Scarlett, who was leaning casually against one of the door jambs to the open door of the room.

"What do you think now Mister Powell, bit of creole in the rhythm, for the Captain?"

"I'd reckon on a twelve-bar reel fer the Capt', meself," said Powell.

"I'll take either," said Scarlett, smiling as he stepped into the room. "How are you holding up Mister Powell?"

'Needles' tied off the last stitch and snipped the catgut suture.

"Bit of a nasty scratch is all, Capt'," said Powell, resolutely.

"And a fractured fibula," added 'Needles', "we'll strap it temporarily, okay now, but you'll be keeping it off it for a while."

'Needles' grabbed an appropriate wooden splint and a wad of gauze cotton bandages from atop the sideboard on the starboard side of the room.

"You trying to tell me Powell's getting a free ride back to Old England, Doctor?" Scarlett asked.

The doctor returned to his patient and proceeded with a makeshift wrapping on the lower half of Powell's right leg and ankle.

"Oh no, Captain, be cheaper to throw him overboard now," said 'Needles', "as his attending physician, I'm merely prescribing that he keeps the weight off his busted leg."

"Sound advice. You hear that Mister Powell?" Scarlett said.

"Aye Capt', a spell in me hammock, with your permission, Sir?"

"Duly granted."

"Thank you, Sir," Powell said, before setting his eyes on Scarlett's abdomen for the first time. "Fuck me, Captain, is you alright? Is you bleedin'?"

Scarlett removed the left hand he had been pressing on the gunshot in his stomach. He undid the red sash around his waist. His white shirt was drenched in blood on his left side.

"It seems, we make a fine pair, Mister Powell," Scarlett said, with a weak smile.

"Jaysus, Scarlett, what the fuck?" 'Needles' cried, "Sit down before you fall down, you bloody fool."

It was evident now as Scarlett stepped closer, that he was ashen pale and sweating profusely. 'Needles' quickly aided him to the captain's dining table.

"Lie down, let me have a look now."

"There's others worse than me." Scarlett said.

"Aye, but they ain't the bloody captain," said 'Needles', as he hastily ripped open Scarlett's bloodied shirt and exposed the wound, "roll on your side."

Scarlett obliged the doctor's request, twisting onto his side, but he remained propped half up on his right elbow.

"Doc's right on that, Capt', so pardon me nerve," Powell said, swinging his legs over the edge of the makeshift table and sitting up alert.

"What d'ya need Doc?" Thomas asked, as he rounded by the doctor's right side.

"It's a gunshot," Scarlett clarified, "short musket, twelve feet."

"It ain't through an' through. We gotta do a bit o' digging here, Scarlett, said 'Needles'. "Fetch a fresh bottle of rum, Mister Thomas."

"Aye, Sir," replied Thomas and dashed to a mahogany cabinet in the port side corner of the room. It was well stocked with bottles.

"I'll not be needing the rum, Mister Thomas," Scarlett said, "I need a clear head for a few hours more."

"It's not for you, it's for me," 'Needles' said, "carry on, Mister Thomas, and be quick about."

"Aye Sir, said Thomas, as he delved into the cabinet.

Johnson entered the room, carrying another unconscious crewman over his shoulder. Heavy bleeding from the hairline on his forehead was evident all down the man's face.

"Doc?"

"On the table," said 'Needles'.

"Heads busted in a good bit, Doc," said Johnson, "reckon he's in a bad way."

Johnson carefully laid the new patient down on the makeshift bed. Powell remained seated but aided in propping the man's head with a hemp-covered pillow pre-stained with numerous blood types. The man's body began convulsing and shaking violently.

"Get to him, Trevor," Scarlett said urgently, "I'm not going anywhere."

"Well, don't." 'Needles' said, as he turned to the makeshift bed adjacent.

Thomas crossed the room with a full bottle of golden rum. He handed it to Doctor Trevor, who immediately grabbed the new patient by his jaw, squeezed his mouth open, and poured in a full third of the spirt. He clamped the man's mouth shut and held his hand over it, while taking a decent slug of rum for himself.

"What's his name?" asked the Doc.

"Tim Darley," answered Scarlett, "crows on the night watch of late. Good man."

"Thass why I don't remember him," 'Needles' said, removing his hand from patient Darley's mouth and offering the bottle to Scarlett. "Drink, now, no more bullshit, doctor's orders."

"Not until the Spanish crew are sitting ugly on Saint Kitts and William and his men are back aboard this ship," Scarlett insisted.

"Watch this fellow for me," Doctor Trevor said, casually.

Scarlett sat up and turned his full attention to the convulsing Darley, as did Thomas, Johnson, and Powell. 'Needles' repeated his 'procedure' of opening Darley's mouth and poured in another solid dash of spirt down the man's throat. Twenty seconds passed in silence. Much to everyone's surprise Darley's shaking calmed, and he lay completely still. Only the rise and fall of his barrel chest betrayed the fact that he was still breathing.

"Papaver somniferum," said 'Needles', "works a charm in a pinch."

"What's that, Doc?" Powell asked.

"My secret recipe, Mister Powell. Completely natural. Common as you like. Poppy plants, don't you know," said

'Needles', with an all-knowing smile, "feckin' education gotta be worth something."

"Will he make it?" asked Scarlett.

"Well, if he don't, he won't care much about it," said 'Needles', offering up the bottle of opiate laced rum to Scarlett a third time, "Doctor's orders, now."

Scarlett shook his head. 'Needles' stayed unmoving with the bottle at arm's length in front of his captain and friend. Scarlett was three shades paler than when he had entered the room, and the sweat from his brow was running down into eyes that drew focus on the bottle and the surface of the liquid swishing within. His mind remained somewhere out over the open seas.

*****

Many miles away from Scarlett and his musing, John Prior was focusing his instincts on the tides from his position at the head of the yawl-boat. Appointed provisional captain of the small vessel, he had discovered the responsibility of saving lives outweighed his natural tendency towards frivolity. He hated it, truth be told, but what could he do but embrace the challenge. He had been stranded in the open ocean more than once during his many years of seamanship, tiring, thirsty, suppressing panic, losing the battle with hope, reconciling personal demons, minute after long minute stretching into hours. He knew how it felt, and he had never liked it.

The dense mist of the previous night and early morning had long since burned off, revealing a cloudless sky, for they were now some eight hours under oar. Since noon the ocean swells had levelled off and the winds had died completely. John figured, quite rightly, that the storm front was heading northwest at a clip and dragging a huge swathe of low pressure behind it. The surface waters were presently akin to a Koi pond in some posh twat's country estate on an airless summer's afternoon. The four rowers in his boat were drenched in sweat from the rabid humidity in the atmosphere, as were the six souls they had managed to retrieve from the ocean. Unfortunately – but lucky for them – all of them were Spanish sailors thrown overboard in the fighting and whisked away from their mothership in the terrible rips presenting in the sea that morning. Foreign enemies they might be, but they were ordinary souls, the same as he, kindness in their hearts for family and friends, inspired to live and let live as best they could in an all too short and often delicate working man's life. One by one they had been spotted, dragged aboard, and given fresh water and bread. What was still rather surprising to John, yet considerably refreshing, was the fact that each one of them had insisted on taking turn on the oars to help as best they could in the search for survivors. Bygones. Humanity. Not a trace of malice lingering from the bloody brawling and savage scrimmages that had taken place for King/Queen, pride, country and feckin' dirty gold.

John had always wondered why men fixated on coin and riches. How the mind was lured, even taught, blackened, over and over in a lifetime, by the hellhounds of greed. The extent to which avarice mired kindness and goodness in a feckin' crazy world whose priorities would never cherish life itself as the greatest treasure. Spend a day and night floating helplessly in the feckin' ocean, alone, afraid, desperate, constantly haunted by your mistakes, possessed by regrets for a life that should have been better lived for others, as the vitality drains slowly from your aching, breath-starved body, and then decide gold is the pinnacle of ambition and reward, spiritual or otherwise.

Guaran-fuckin'-tee you won't. Ever.

The two rowboats forming the search party had long since split up to cover a broader search area. Shamus and Dye in the other boat had followed the storm to the north-west. Prior had set his craft on a heading east-southeast, in a course of half-mile wide overlapping circles he thought would be most effective having learnt from his choking swim back to the *Bride* in the early hours.

John raised himself to standing so to better scan the surroundings, covering three points of the compass in his head; blue-grey to the north, blue-green to the west, navy to the south. He already knew the blues to the east for they had rowed through them. Not a living soul was in sight on the surface of the vast expanse of water. A deep sadness pervaded his heart, and, whilst he would have normally subdued such feelings, shrouded them in play with the *Bride's Banter* and lifted the spirits of the men aboard, he couldn't bring himself to even try. It would somehow belittle the sure suffering of William, Richard Bately, Jim Dolby, 'Tumbles' Turner and the others he'd been commissioned to find.

"Stow oars," John commanded, "rest a while and take some water, I need to hear your thoughts."

The four rowers in the boat did so, two Spanish and two English crewmen sharing a common and welcome repose.

"Night will be upon us soon," said one of the Spaniards in accented English.

"*Sí, entiendo,*" said Prior, "I reckon on twenty-five miles home as the crow flies."

"Three hours at a clip, given the tides?" said one of the English men.

"There abouts," agreed Prior.

"We have food and water, we can stay out a ways in the nightfall," said a second Englishman.

John considered the suggestion for a brief spell. A counter argument to his previous musing popped into his head. Some would say that life wasn't worth living without gold. That existing in poverty was not living at all. You were just dying slowly and hungry and in pain. Stressed to breaking point, day after long and lonely day, the mind collapsing, the body undernourished and withering as your spirit sought its maker. He'd been there. It was a life devoid of light, but it was still a life.

"It's a new moon, we won't be able to see shite," offered a third English sailor.

"You're right about that," said Prior, "I've been thinkin' it, much as I don't wan' ta be."

"Debería mosir al sur," one of the Spaniards said to the man next to him.

"No. Nureste. Triángulo," the other Spaniard responded. *"Sí, claro. Guadeloupe."*

"Muy lejos. Al sur de Montserrat."

"Hey, boys, *en Inglés, por favor,*" said Prior, sternly.

"They say they think we should go southeast. A triangle, from here, to somewhere south of Montserrat," said the first Spaniard.

"I heard that bit, what's your name?" Prior asked.

"Luis Sánchez, Sir."

"Luis, drop the Sir, I'm not one. What's the gist of these boys' thinkin'?" Prior asked.

"Well, the last side, or, leg, as you say, of the triangle would be a straight rowing north back to the ships and Saint Kitts before night," said Sánchez.

"Uh, huh," said Prior, "why?"

Sánchez turned to his Spanish comrades, *"¿Por qué el triángulo?"*

"Se fue un viento del norte, llega una marea del sur."

Sánchez nodded, acknowledging what he kind of knew to be an old mariner's cup of tea leaves, but the saying held some merit. He translated for Prior, "They are saying that because the wind is moving north, the tides will be shifting south. Along the islands."

"What'd you think, Luis?"

"I think it is, an old wives' tale, but I have been married two times and them women, they both knew better than me," said Sánchez.

John Prior smiled. Perhaps even fashioned a chuckle.

"We have a new headin' gentlemen, let's come about southeast an' put our backs into it," said Prior. A curious sense of relief washed over him as all men in the boat took to the oars and turned the small vessel around. This wasn't about gold anymore, it was friendship – '*Fidus Achates*', he was once taught in his few short years of schooling a lifetime ago – and there it was, the treasure of life, and the hope to be found over the horizon.

*****

The sun was three hours lower than the mizzen Topgallant yard, heading down past the aft castle and for the western horizon, by the time Roger 'Paws' Prowse took a break from stomping his orders around the main decks of the *Bride* and the *Santa Oscuro*. He had been back and forth all day, supervising everything. The Spanish crew had all been ferried to what 'Paws' was fairly certain was the uninhabited Isle of Saint Kitts in the *Oscuro's* half dozen yawl-boats, a short trip, only some hundred-and-fifty yards ahead of her bowsprit. The Spanish Capitán, Juan Martinez de Recalde, his First Mate, Pedro Garcia, and their ship's surgeon, Dr. Diego Vázquez, remained behind. They were currently securely locked in Recalde's cabin. 'Paws' had noted earlier that Vázquez was something of an arsehole of a man, but as fine a doctor as he had ever met on land or sea. He had performed several emergency amputations, set dozens of broken bones, stitched up countless lacerations, stab wounds, and punctures from splinters and gunshot. He had run out of suture by mid-afternoon and 'Paws' had turned to his own Trevor 'Needles' Neary for help, which the man gave freely and passionately. 'Paws' was certain the good Doc's enthusiasm for helping Spanish patients was born of the opiate laced spirits he'd been chugging all day, but he couldn't fault the results. Thus far only seven Spanish crew had died on ship. 'Paws' had yet to make a full count of those who had ended up in the water and may well have drowned. Not a soul aboard the *Bride* had died, though many were laid up with severe injury and would very likely remain so for the remainder of the voyage. If they made it, that is.

'Paws' tracked several crewmen climbing the shrouds on the main and foremasts as they made their way to the crow's nests to nestle in for first watch on the nightshift. Confident that all was in order, he made his way aft, trudged up the stairs to the quarterdeck, settled against the starboard gunwale and looked out over the glassy surface of what was now a tranquil ocean. An emptiness ensconced itself in his gut. The death-watch after the storm. Two yawl-boats had set out on a rescue mission that morning and neither had returned. Was it worth it? All this carnage. To some, maybe.

What would it be to live one's life without ever having a fight? Without ever losing a friend. A brother. A child. Even a wife.

Well, the last was perhaps different. There were always up-sides to losing a wife, so long as you weren't dumb enough to marry a second. Or third for that matter. Ah, well. Conclusion is only perception waiting for change. The world keeps turning.

'Paws' made his way further aft and stepped up one of two narrow staircases that led to the *Bride's* poop deck, atop the captain's cabin at the very stern of the ship. The lateen rigged mizzen sail was motionless above his head. The worst of the Caribbean. A windless eve rich in humidity. He nearly missed it in the lowering sun; a yawl-boat heading in from the north. 'Paws' strained his tired eyes, in a bout of sudden excitement. The tiny vessel was crammed with men. Eight rowers among them maybe. Seven or more half in the water, clinging to the gunwales. Holy crap!

"Ship Ahoy!" shouted 'Paws', with considerable gusto for a dog-tired old sea dog.

"Ship Ahoy. Ship Ahoy," the alarm repeated from various crewmen stationed along the lengths of both the *Maiden Bride* and the *Santa Oscuro.*

'Paws' watched carefully as the crowded rowboat drew closer with each passing stroke of the oars. Ten minutes passed in relative silence. Murmurs from a few good shipmates gathering on the main deck in curiosity served as background noise to the sure apprehension plucking 'Paws'' heart strings...

Dye Bant took to standing at the bow of the yawl-boat and waved his arm above his head. They were a hundred yards out and cutting a steady clip through the calm sea as the rowers fired into their final push for the *Bride.*

"Cut to starboard lads," yelled Dye, over his shoulder.

"Aye, aye, Sir," said several of the rowing crew in unison.

"Jesus, will you muffle that shite out o' your mouths. Taffy ain't no Sir and he never will be," Shamus O'Reilly bellowed from the rear of the boat.

"That's where yer wrong be there, see, Shamus," said Dye, "I'm factoring on buying me a title to go with me land and sheep when I gets home to the valley."

"Oh, aye, and what might that be?"

"Baron Bant is what I'm settling on, see, tidy that is," said Dye, his huge smile revealing his stained and crooked front teeth.

"Baron Bollocks 'uld be a better fit, says I," Shamus put forth.

Dye ignored him and cut a new jib, "Right lads, I don't have to tell ye, but round her stern and draw up on the Jacobs," said Dye. "Let's get off this rig with a bit o' dignity. Injured men first."

"Aye, aye, me Lord," bellowed Shamus, and cracked up laughing...

Roger 'Paws' Prowse peeled away from the stern gunwale when the incoming yawl-boat was thirty yards out and made his way fore across the poop, down the narrow stairs, fore across the quarterdeck, past the helm, and down the central stairs to the main deck. He quick stepped to the starboard gunwale and leaned over.

"What d'ye got aboard there, lads?" shouted 'Paws', as the yawl-boat drew alongside the Jacob's ladder and stowed oars. Dye Bant was quick to tie up the bow. Shamus lashed another rope to the stern.

"Twenty souls. Plus the six of us who set out fer 'em," yelled Dye proudly in return. "Seven of 'em is Spaniard's though, so maybe it's not so many souls as I'm countin'."

"Any sign of William and the others?"

"Nothin' doing, Mister Prowse," Dye replied, "this is it. Where's Prior at? Did he not find 'em?"

"Ain't come back all day," said 'Paws'.

"Could use a bit o' help with the wounded," shouted Shamus. "We're all feckin' knackered, by Jesus."

"Aye, right you are," 'Paws' said, and turned to the sailors surrounding him, "Lend a hand here lads, help these poor buggers aboard. Let's have the wounded carried straight to 'Needles', foreign or domestic."

Several of the crewmen snapped to it, jumping the gunwale, and helping the arriving men up the rope ladder and aboard. Five men were helped or carried up to the quarterdeck, aft of the helm and laid down on rugs and blankets. Trevor 'Needles' Neary stepped through the ornate oak door, from his makeshift operating theatre in the outer room of the captain's cabin, to begin triage and prioritise the severity of the wounded. His assistants, Thomas and Johnson, were in tow and on hand.

Scarlett appeared from the same oak door and strode past the helm, taking up position against the balustrade separating the quarterdeck from the main. He was dressed in a fresh set of clothes, white open necked silk shirt, red sash waistband, black hose, and brightly polished knee-high black boots. His coiled whip hung from his right hip and his ornate jewel encrusted sword was nestled in a scabbard that hung down alongside his left thigh. He quietly lit one of his thin brown cigarillos, dragged deeply on the smoke, and took stock of all aboard his ship.

"Mister Prowse, a word, if I may?" Scarlett called out.

'Paws' was quick to attend his captain, scampering up the stairs and joining Scarlett on the quarterdeck.

"Any sign of William?" asked Scarlett, quietly.

'Paws' shook his head and offered, "But Prior's not returned yet, Captain, chances are..."

"Let me know the minute he does," Scarlett said, evenly, then turned his head to the wounded men laying out on the deck. "Set up a reception for Recalde in my quarters, soon as 'Needles' is done patching them up."

"Aye, Captain," said 'Paws'. "By the by, 'Mumbles' ain't done with the count aboard the *Dark*, must be there's a mass o' wealth in that there hull."

"I don't give a shit, Roger," said Scarlett, "I'm going for a walk, find me when we're set for dinner."

"Aye, of course," said 'Paws'.

Scarlett pulled away towards the main stairs.

"Captain," called 'Paws', "William's tough as nails, and a wily bastard with it, when he needs be. He'll make it."

Scarlett reasoned his Boatswain's comment in a heart-beat, nodded his head and continued down the staircase to the main deck.

18

Tigers Gets Hungry Quicker

The young sailor Richard Bately had never been so exhausted. Or afraid. His elder peers Jim Dolby and Ted 'Tumbles' Turner were faring slightly worse physically, but perhaps way better mentally. Least that's the way Richard was feeling. They and six other crewmen were in a huddle, clinging to a motley mélange of empty wine kegs, cork mattresses, and chunks of oak hull that had been salvaged during their swim, and lashed together during a long, suffocating day battling ocean currents. For a time in the morning's early hours, their consensus had been to fight and swim against the will of the sea. It had proven to be a worthy but vain attempt at returning to the sanctuary of the *Bride*.

Richard toyed with the frayed, blackened end of a rope that had previously been tied around the waist of the ship's First Mate, Master William Hope. Given circumstance, his name was something of a sad irony, for all hope had long since faded of finding him.

The morning's fog and mists hadn't helped, and Richard was fairly certain after a day's unavoidable reflection – as there was little else to think about but sharks – that lashed together with rope as the men were, they had all headed off in the wrong feckin' direction after the explosion on the *Oscuro's* hull, when the bloody rip tide had finally allowed them to surface.

Thirst was a bitch. Bately's mouth tasted exactly how he imagined a badger's armpit would taste after the animal had sex for an hour in the desert of the Saharans. He couldn't be certain, as he was still a virgin, but his imagination had always been virtually unbridled. A blessing and a curse. It had been okay come noon, or thereabouts, when the sun had been at its highest. The fogginess had burnt away, waters had calmed to a millpond, and he could clearly see to a depth of several healthy fathoms. Thus far, there had been no sharks, though he'd seen plenty of fish, jellyfish, turtles, and eel-looking-creatures swimming around beneath him.

The waters had turned gloomier with each passing hour, as the sun had fallen towards the western horizon. Clarity of vision had reduced in accord, and now he could only discern perhaps six feet below his own feet, two fathoms at most. Below that, direful, wretched thoughts pervaded into darkening the depths, and the menace of his imagination was doing him no favours. Another hour would see the sun vanish beyond the horizon and the ocean's feeding time begin. Pure panic would be sure to bite him in the arse, if nothing else did.

"Where do you reckon we are?" asked Bately, for the umpteenth time that afternoon.

"A half mile southwest of the last time you asked," croaked Jim Dolby.

"That ain't helping," said Bately.

"Relax lad," said Ted 'Tumbles' Turner, "no point in getting' excited 'bout what we can't control. I keeps tellin' ya, this whole excursion should be a lesson towards your schoolin' when we gets home. Whass a bunch of dolphins?"

"A pod," said Bately.

"Turtles?" from 'Tumbles'.

"A bale," answered Bately, appreciating the men's efforts to calm his nerves with meaningless bollocks.

"Thass it right there," Dolby agreed, "educate yourself, an' listen to the man this time round. Give it a good think on and try to shut the fuck up a bit. Save your throat. Write an essay in yer head, keep yer mind off the Great Whites underneath us."

"And the Tigers, don't forget them," said 'Tumbles', "they gets hungry quicker."

"Oh, that's a fact right there, Ted," said Dolby, half smiling through dry cracked lips.

"And how is *that* a fact right there?" Bately questioned.

"Smaller bites," from 'Tumbles'.

"Smaller bites and they chews more," Dolby said.

"Chews you up good, they does. Smaller bites," from 'Tumbles'.

"Smaller feckin' bites," Dolby said.

"Oh, fuck all the way off, to you both," Bately said, now certain that he'd made the mistake of revealing too many of the fears consuming him, "they'll find us, won't they?"

"They'll be tryin' still fer certain," 'Tumbles' said.

"Stop lookin' down an' write yer essay, lad," Dolby said, "we'll be alright."

Richard had to admire his fellow sailors. Their determined humour, when faced with adversity. Was it courage? Is that what courage meant? Or was it just survival? Or maybe they were just funny? Or maybe they didn't think the same way as he did? Maybe they didn't have much to go home for. Or maybe they did, but understood they'd likely never make it back. Or maybe that was wrong and Jim and 'Tumbles' were seeing possibilities he was just too young to see. Just like the depths below his feet, he couldn't see them, but he knew they were there.

Young Richard Bately stopped looking down and fashioned the beginnings of a philosophical study in his head. Twelve feet below his dangling toes, a lone Tiger shark was cruising in slow circles, patiently undertaking a study of its own.

19

¿Tobago? Cubano

Two three-pronged candelabras were set upon the eight-foot-long table in the outer room of Scarlett's quarters aboard the *Bride*. The makeshift hospital bed, surgical implements, and the rest of 'Needles' medical gubbins had been removed. The cabin had been returned to its formal state of refined opulence. Half a dozen lanterns threw out a warm light that was quickly being absorbed by the oak panelled walls, low ceiling, the dark ruby-coloured floor, and ornate mahogany furniture that constituted the room. The outer door to the quarterdeck was closed, as was the door to Scarlett's inner cabin at the ship's stern.

Capitán Juan Martinez de Recalde, his First Mate, Pedro Garcia, and Dr. Diego Vázquez sat in high-backed chairs along one side of the table, with Recalde in between his officers.

Scarlett and Trevor 'Needles' Neary sat in two chairs on the opposite, port side, of the table. A modest feast was laid out before them on silver platters and china plates. Barbequed duck, lamb, potatoes, vegetables, fruits and several types of biscuits and breads.

Scarlett topped up the Spanish capitán's glass from a crystal decanter with a long pour of rich claret wine, "What of repairs to your ship?"

"As with every other topic this night, it seems I must defer to your judgement," said Recalde, the bitterness of defeat clearly present in his acidic tone.

"No judgement, I assure you, quite the opposite, as I have readily inferred, I have long since admired your seamanship," Scarlett said.

"Gracious of you, I'm sure," Recalde squeezed out, between uneasy breaths.

"Temporary repairs have been made on the stern and starboard quarter. I've seen to it that the *Oscuro* is no longer taking on water, and the bilges have been bailed."

"Though she remains grounded."

"She does," offered Scarlett, "and I propose she will remain so until a wind sees fit…"

"That is poor judgement, it is dangerous to my ship…"

"…until a wind sees fit to aid us in moving her."

"Unacceptable! Put her under tow from the boats. Drag her from the corals under oar and…"

"And what Juan? What?" Scarlett demanded.

"And… and assess the damage under hull, for one," said Recalde.

Scarlett chugged a half glass of wine, placed his glass down, and picked up a small ivory box from the table. He opened the lid and presented the contents to Recalde.

"No, gracias," said Recalde.

Scarlett took a brown cigarillo from the box, lit it on one of the candles nearby, and relaxed back in his chair.

"If you hadn't shot me, I may well be now offering you an accord, Juan," said Scarlett.

"I was aiming for your heart," Recalde said, through gritted teeth.

"I don't have a heart, it's why you missed," quipped Scarlett.

"It's true," 'Needles' concurred, "many is the occasion I've tried to find it, now."

"It's not there," Scarlett said, with a chuckle.

"It ain't bloody there, man," 'Needles' said, with a wide smile. He chugged the remainder of his glass of rum and topped it up from a half-full bottle. The 'full' part representing his general attitude to life.

"Do you ever reflect upon the nature of conflict, Capitán?" Scarlett asked.

"What do you mean?" asked Recalde.

"Dispute, disparity, disagreement, differences and disputations," Scarlett rattled off, "Conflicts among men. *Conflictos. Luchando. Guerra.*"

"Y, ¿y qué?" said Recalde, "It happens. *Siempre sucederá.*"

"First thing we've agreed on this evening," Scarlett said, "we're getting somewhere. But why? Why do men fight? *¿Por qué debe ser así?* Summon your opinion, *por favor.*"

Recalde, who had barely touched his food, picked up his glass from the table and sat back in his chair for the first time since the outset of the meal. He took a healthy slug of wine.

"Your offer of a cigar, does it stand?"

"But of course," Scarlett said, promptly forwarding the ivory box to Recalde, who took a cigarillo and mirrored Scarlett's previous action, lighting the smoke from a candle. That done, he retired back in his chair, as Scarlett offered the box to Pedro Garcia and Dr. Vázquez, in turn, "Gentlemen, please."

"Gracias, Señor," said Pedro taking up a smoke.

"Gracias," said Vázquez, doing the same as his colleagues. Scarlett offered the box in turn to 'Needles' Neary.

"No, man, don't you know that shit will kill you?" 'Needles' said, with a broad smile.

"And your poppies won't?" questioned Scarlett.

"Nah, brother, the good Lord weren't at conflict when he made those beautiful flowers. God bless him an' all," 'Needles' said, with a straight face, before chugging another mouthful from his glass.

"¿Tobago?" asked Recalde.

"Cubano," answered Scarlett.

"Ah, sí. Muy bien," said Recalde, regarding his small cigar with admiration. Several beats of awkward silence pervaded.

"Religion," said Recalde, his seeming non sequitur hanging with the smoke permeating the room.

"I see your point," Scarlett said, where others might have not, "but I would argue that religion is but one of many masks, designed by a scant number of privileged individuals, hiding the true reason for the conflicts in which they are compelled to engage. And that is simply, resources.

"Resources?" questioned Recalde.

"Resources," confirmed Scarlett, "it all comes down to that. Gold, silver, minerals."

"Not power?"

"Certainly, power," said Scarlett, "but let me ask you, how do you maintain power?"

"Stay rich," Recalde said, flatly.

"And get richer," Scarlett affirmed, "so rich, you hand it to your grandkids."

"If the wife don't take it," interjected 'Needles'.

Recalde chuckled for the first time that evening. "Marriage is for fools. *Eso es cierto.*"

"Second time we agree," said Scarlett, "And how do you stay rich and get richer? You round up your fighting men, promise them the world, invade some tribe in a country you're never going to give a shit about, and pilfer their resources."

"That's not entirely true, what about trade? Investment in foreign domains, to the benefit of indigenous peoples, surely. Education, it's not all taking," suggested Recalde, now fully engaged.

"Masks," said Scarlett, "easy to offer sugar with the left hand, while you steal with the right hand behind your back."

"Ah, I begin to see your course," said Recalde, "yet it does not explain religious fervour. Fighting in God's name. In your God's name. The nature of being on the side of the... righteous."

"It's a fair point you make," Scarlett said, "and there will always be lunatics and fanatics hell bent on their one God policy of intolerance and cruelty."

"I know several of the Inquisition. God save me," said Recalde.

"Indeed, I hope he does, you seem a decent fellow. But fundamentally, I would argue that religious conflict has always been because faith itself is a resource."

"Faith? How so?"

"It's the conversion of ideals," Scarlett continued, "look, let's say, for argument's sake, you and I get together, and we want to get rich."

"Richer," said Recalde, smiling again.

"Ha, quite so, richer. So, we plan to invade, I don't know, Brazil. Now, we could load up our ships, sail out and give it a go. We arrive, we invade, we tear into the local tribes, give 'em all smallpox and scurvy and divide and conquer. Then we have all their resources. And a shit ton of resentment from the locals."

"We've gotten pretty good at it since Columbus," said Recalde.

"I know. And our Queen knows it too."

"So does King Philip."

"I'm aware, but let's try to stay on point. Religion. Faith."

"As a resource."

"Quite so," said Scarlett, "you have your missionary priests, going out of their way to spread your Catholicism..."

"The one true religion," said Recalde, the sarcasm in his tone obvious, "according to those zealots in the Vatican, I might add."

"Neither you, nor I care much for man-made doctrine, but the world is filled with peoples that crave some sort of..."

"Faith and perhaps least ways guidance," said Recalde.

"And hope, let it be said, for most, the idea of a better life after this one. As for most this life is hard, gruelling, unfair," Scarlett said.

"Inequitable and discriminatory," Recalde added.

"Exactly so, Capitán. So, those seeking to expand their wealth, use their powers to influence the peoples of foreign nation states, by the conversion of ideals. Offers of freedom from their present tyranny, redemption in the afterlife, wonderful stuff, and the peoples begin to treat them as saviours not invaders, dictators, or autocrats. But why?"

"I see your meaning, now," Recalde said, "offer the sugar and lessen the war. Easier to steal the gold and diamonds if the locals are digging it up for you."

"And not fighting you for it," Scarlett said.

Scarlett topped up the capitán's glass once more, then his own.

Recalde lifted his glass, "To masks, Captain Scarlett, that one day they will be stripped from the affluent few."

"To masks," said Scarlett, raising his glass.

The two men imbibed, downing their respective drinks.

"You know, your weak little Queen is fooling nobody in Spain, least of all King Philip." Recalde said.

"Pardon me?" from Scarlett.

"We had some respect for King Henry, back when," Recalde continued, "his ambitions were at least, realistic. His mask transparent in ways."

"What are you inferring?"

"Your Queen steals our gold. Our jewels. Our minerals, as you put it, from the new world. A world of our invention.

Of our labours and toils. Of our wars. Not yours," Recalde said.

"The new world?" Scarlett said, "Do you not see the blind arrogance? No part of the world is new. It will never be. It has been here long before our Kings and Queens and Bishops. Their insatiable greed and lust for war and wealth."

"Your Queen is no different. But she steals at sea. Hiding behind political veils and denials. Using Captains like you. And El Draque. Mercenaries. With no moral compass."

"Is your compass so shiny, Capitán?" asked Scarlett. "You hold to the course set for you by Philip, do you not?"

"I am but a pawn, in command of a floating carriage of goods. But you steal from me, and you steal from King Philip and the majesty of Spain and the Catholic Church," Recalde alleged, his tone cold and menacing. "Mark me in this Captain Scarlett, if you steal the riches aboard my ship today, it will be the final straw. You and your Queen will have war tomorrow and you will lose everything."

A hammering on the door interrupted the steeled exchange. The door was pushed in urgently by a panting Roger 'Paws' Prowse, "Captain, sorry fer the interruption, would you mind a spell on deck, Sir?"

"Impeccable timing Mister Prowse," Scarlett said, then turned back to the Spanish capitán, "The Queen of England knows nothing of our exploits today. This one is on me, and me alone. And when you kiss the arse of your King on your return, you may tell him that the Scarlett Buccaneer doesn't wear a mask, and he will never pretend to be one of your ungodly saints."

Scarlett pushed his chair back and stood up, "Do excuse me, gentlemen, make yourselves at home a while."

Scarlett paced firmly across the room towards the open door. 'Paws' allowed him to cross the threshold to the quarterdeck and closed the portal firmly behind them.

John Prior stood a pace in front of a ragged looking Richard Bately, Jim Dolby, and Ted 'Tumbles' Turner.

"Mister Prior, welcome aboard. You have a tale to tell, I'm certain," said Scarlett enthusiastically, "let it be shared."

John Prior took a breath and was about to begin, then pulled up short.

"Where's your rum, lads? Mister Prowse, a bottle each for these men," Scarlett said, "it may free their tales of valour."

"Aye, Captain... erm, you see..." said 'Paws', reluctantly.

"Richard Bately stepped forward to Prior's side, "We lost Master William, Captain. We lost him in the explosion and we ain't seen him since. None of us have."

"We looked hard, Captain," Prior said, finding his voice, "all over. Must 'ave rowed fifty or sixty miles or more, Sir."

Scarlett's heart was crushed with the mortifying weight of the men's words. Darkness had fallen, mists and fog were settling in around them and the new moon was seeing to it that very little would be seen over the ocean for the remainder of the long night ahead.

"Mister Prowse, a bottle each," Scarlett said. "You've done well lads and I'm grateful for your efforts. I'll hear the details of your story tomorrow."

Scarlett tapped Richard Bately on the shoulder in a friendly gesture and stepped away towards the starboard gunwale, before turning briefly, "And Mister Prowse, get those Spanish bastards off my ship."

"Aye, Captain, with pleasure," replied 'Paws'.

Scarlett climbed the stairs leading aft to the poop deck atop his cabin and stationed himself under a lantern at the very stern of his ship. He looked out over still blackened waters that were now seemingly devoid of all life. He remained transfixed thus, in an eternal maskless moment.

20

Appreciate your Optimism, Sir

The stowaway, Tortuga, from what he could remember his name to be, was drifting back to consciousness. He had slept for hours draped over the partial upturned hull of a broken rowboat. He knew it had been hours, as the sun had been high in the sky the last time his eyes had been open. And that was fine. It was now dark. And he was dry and warm. The ocean was dead calm. And mercifully quiet. He enjoyed silence very much. He slowly rolled over onto his back. He couldn't see moon or stars. They were smothered in a solid blanket of foggy mist. And that was good. He didn't like stars. Their ever-changing patterns confused and frightened him. They were but a map to man's apocalypse. He'd read that somewhere, a long time ago. When he had read many things. Things he couldn't put a name to. Things he couldn't summon anymore. And that was fine also. The only book he could recollect was clutched tightly against his stomach, but he couldn't think of what it contained. He couldn't open it, for it was locked tight with a silver clasp. He loved it though. It soothed him greatly.

A sudden quiet splashing brought a surge of unwanted panic to his breast. He sat up and turned his head in the direction of the noise to better see the sound. He couldn't. It was shrouded in the night's misty vapours. He waited. Listening. Not brave enough to call out. And that was allowable. He had nothing to say.

The splashing faded a while, then grew increasingly present. And more alarming. Tortuga, if that was his name, strained his eyes to better understand the source of his unrest. The mist was defeating him. And it did so for several unforgiving minutes. Then, a man appeared on the surface of the water. Swimming slow, powerful, rhythmic strokes laced with doom. He was heading directly towards the upturned, fractured hull of the rowboat. The stowaway curled up his knees to his chest and locked his arms around them. His eyes remained on the strange man in the water.

That man was Master William Arthur Hope.

He desisted in his strokes some ten yards out. Treading water, William waved a friendly arm above his head, "Ahoy, there! Permission to come aboard, good Sir."

The stowaway couldn't remember a time he'd been so frightened. And that was permissible, as he rarely remembered anything of consequence. He tightened his grip on his knees. He was amazed to feel his head nodding.

"I'll take that as a yes, I'm much obliged," said William, and stroked forward. When he reached the broken piece of hull, he scrambled atop and rolled onto his back to catch his breath.

A full two minutes passed in silence.

"I owe you," William said, sitting up, "for your kindness in allowing me aboard."

The stowaway raised his chin from his knees, fixed William with a blank stare, then drew his eyes away and lowered his chin once more.

"I'm not sure how long I might have been able to swim. That's the truth," said William.

"*Verdad,*" said the stowaway, in a meek voice, and he burst into tears.

"You are Spanish?"

"*Si. Creo que sí,*" whispered the stowaway, shivering.

"You think so?" questioned William.

"*Sí.*"

"Were you on the *Santa Oscuro*?"

"*No, sé... Un... barco,*" said the stowaway, through fractured breaths and more tears

"*¿Un gran barco?*" asked William.

"*Sí.*"

"Are you hurt?"

"*No lo, se, todavia,*" said the stowaway, sucking in deep breaths to suppress his crying. He raised his chin from his knees and stared out across the ocean, not that there was much to see but varying shades of grey and black. The ocean met the mist some twenty yards away, after that was a void impenetrable to sight.

"Not hurt, *yet*?" said William, "I appreciate your optimism, Sir."

Silence.

"I'm William."

No response.

"What is your name?"

Palpable muteness. Only more tears.

"Okay. No names. Got it," said William.

This wasn't exactly the stimulating company William had been craving over the past fourteen hours, but sometimes, just sometimes, less could be considered more.

Complete silence. Tranquillity. The death-watch after the storm. One windless minute slowly beckoning the next.

"My name is in here," said the stowaway, abruptly, and he held up the small leather-bound book he had been tightly clutching in his lap, "but I cannot open it. I... don't... remember."

William did his best not to raise an eyebrow in consternation. This guy was feckin' weird, let it be said, but one should never judge a book by its cover, so to speak.

"One should never judge a book by its cover," William said.

"Really?" said the stowaway, "Then why do you judge me?"

"What? I'm not. I mean I wasn't," said William, totally taken aback. "Well, maybe I was, but not in a bad way. I didn't mean to, Sir. Each to their own and all that."

The stowaway peered through watery eyes, looking directly at William, and for the first time. He smiled.

"You are one of them, aren't you?"

"Beg pardon. One of whom?" asked William, somewhat unnerved.

"The Dragons," said the stowaway...

A time it was that any man engaged in warfare, at sea or on land, that held a short musket in the belt of his pants or hose was considered to be a dragon. The musket itself could also be referred to as a dragon. Such a time it was that dragons had a very bad reputation. But, as they were only born of myth and legend, the dragons really didn't mind in the slightest...

"Dragons?" William asked, "Oh, no, Sir. I am completely unarmed, as you can see."

Proving his point, William threw his arms wide and exposed his open shirt and torso, down to the emerald sash he wore as a waistband. He had no knives, or short muskets, or weapons of any kind to hide. His boots had long since been kicked off to further his survival in the sea.

"I speak not of muskets in your belt," said the stowaway and turned his head once more to gaze out at the dark ocean mists, "but I see you now. Yet my head does not hurt with you.

¿Por qué tu?" asked William, softly.

Silence again.

William let it be. This delicate little man before him was clearly off his freaking foreign rocker.

"You are a mixed breed. Half lover. Half Dragon," said the stowaway, "I was a lover, I think. But I was never more. I remember... sometimes I remember. When it is dark. Oscuro. *Me gusta la oscuridad.*"

"Just as well. We got a good eight hours of it, by my reckoning," said William, raising his head towards the blind night sky.

"Open it," said the stowaway.

William turned towards the strange Spaniard to find he was holding his little book out at a full arm's length.

"You are one. You can open it," said the stowaway, "*Por favor,* I beg of you. You told me that you owe me. This is what I choose of you, as... *¿cómo?... recompensa.*"

William could do very little to suppress the frown presenting on his brow. He wasn't in the least bit scared of the unorthodox individual before him, but his odd mix of words and themes were somewhat vexing, to say the least.

"I may very well owe you my life. Seems a little trivial that you ask only this of me in return," said William, "but, of course, I will gladly be of service, if I can."

William crossed the short distance to the stranger on his hands and knees, very gently, so as not to freak him out and, more importantly, so as not to rock the boat, or at least the fractured portion of it now saving them from drowning. He reached out and took the book, then sat down with his legs draped across the curvature of the broken hull. His toes tickled the surface of the water.

"It is not to be, destroyed," said the stowaway, "I am mindful of that, I think. It was treated with warmth."

William assessed the book. Maybe five inches in width by eight in height, the worn leather cover was embossed with a spiral curve closing inward from the bottom right corner to the centre. The words *El Libro de Reglas de Amor* were embossed above the spiral.

"The Love Rule Book," said William, "I've seen this book. Dreamed it, I mean."

"Alchemy is love as love is alchemy," said the stowaway, his stare fixed over the sea once again.

William acknowledged the stranger's idiosyncratic comment briefly and returned his attention to what was a quite beautiful little volume in his hands. A four-inch-long silver clasp along the right side held the book locked firmly shut. It was clear that the leather cover was bound to a robust material on the inside. Perhaps some sort of wood. He flipped the book over. The back was leather and similarly worn as the front. There was nothing on the binding. William flipped the book over again, such that the title was facing him. It rattled, briefly. Strange. He shook the book gently. Yes, indeed, rattling again. The muffled sound of a metal bearing against wood. Like a child's puzzle, maybe.

Katherine.

He and she as children. They had solved countless puzzles together, from the mundane, to the extraordinarily complex. Some of them masterpieces of craftsmanship inlaid with silver, gold, and jewels and made of the most expensive hardwoods. Such was the privileged upbringing they had shared. Well, until he'd reached thirteen that is. Then everything had turned to shit.

Katherine. I hope the boys have found her. Or am I as crazy as this lunatic with the book?

"If you live in the past, you're dead in the present, and blind to your future," said William. "Wouldn't you say so, Sir?"

The stranger had stopped crying. His forehead was furrowed in confusion, as though he were trying to make sense of William's words and failing miserably.

"*No sé...* I do not know."

"Uh, huh. Well maybe you're right not to," said William, gently, and refocused his thoughts on the little volume in his hands.

The next hour was spent in relative silence, with only a few comments passed back and forth. William spent the time jiggling, turning, shaking, and rattling 'The Love Rule Book' every which way his flummoxed brain was telling him to try next. The process of elimination was doing everything in its muddled power to eliminate any hope of getting the damned thing open without busting it apart. William had resisted that display of violence out of respect for his newfound, nutcase, Spanish friend, but it was becoming an increasingly attractive proposition.

The air around him changed.

It was barely perceptible, but invisible currents were now cutting through the stillness. William raised his attention from the book and concentrated his senses on the surrounding environment. The stranger beside him, arms locked around his knees, barely breathing, transfixed on the open sea.

No, not him.

The waters, unmoved, serene, glassy. *Not that.*

The motionless mist a wall of solitude. *No.*

The sounds of peace and tranquillity, masking the sporadic ferocity of the animals fighting for survival in the depths below him. *Not them either.*

Katherine. At the helm. Bandana tying back her hair. Cutlass in hand.

William concentrated harder. His eyes began to burn slightly. His head ached. His throat was parched and raw, but surely that was from all the seawater. Perhaps he was coming down with a cold or something. Wouldn't be surprising, given yesterday's antics.

A ship. It's a bloody big ship. Where?

William rose from his seated position and propped himself in a half-crouch on one knee, as if ready to dive from the hull into the water. His sudden movement was not lost on the strange little Spaniard, who asked, *"¿Qué es?"*

"A ship."

"¿Dónde?"

William focused and turned facing southwest. He pointed straight ahead at the mist, *"Por ahí."*

"¿Un barco?"

"Creo que sí," said William, *"Tranquilo. Escucha."*

The Spaniard raised himself to kneeling and listened intently. After a half minute he turned towards William, *"Por favor. Mi libro."*

"Oh, of course," said William, and immediately handed *The Love Rule Book* back to the man without a name.

Somewhere out beyond the darkened veil of mist before them the slightest hint of splashing struggled to their ears through the unstirring, muggy air. A half minute more hearkened in the unmistakable regular rhythm of oars cutting the surface of the sea. Many oars, in unison. A ship! A Galley! Had to be.

"Ahoy! AHOY OUT THERE!" shouted William.

The Spaniard beside him immediately dropped to the upturned hull and curled up into a ball with his arms locked around his knees once more. His eyes grew wide, filled with tears and he took to sniffling again. William thought it strange, but not entirely unexpected by the little he had discerned of the man's overall temperament.

"AHOY! AHOY OUT THERE IN THE MIST! AHOY!!" screamed William, cupping his hands to his mouth to amplify his voice.

"¡Ahoy! ¡Ahoy, ahí!" came a voice wavering in through the fog. A female voice.

A woman? What the..?

"AHOY! OVER HERE!" shouted William, "¡POR AQUI!"

"¡Ahoy! ¿Sobredónde?" came the woman's voice, now clearer.

A Spanish woman.

"¡Aquí! ¡De esta manera!" yelled William, as his heart filled with hope for the first time in two long days of utter chaos, crisscrossed with despair. Whatever was out there, surely it was better than a broken upturned boat and his present certifiable companion.

"*¡Sigue hablando, así podemos encontrarte!*" came the Spanish woman's voice. William nearly tumbled off the fractured hull.

You've got to be shitting me!

"ROSA? ROSA! Is that you?!" screamed William into the fog.

"WILLIAM?! *¿¿Eres tú?!*" came the woman's voice, closer now and closing still, "*¿Qué diablos?* William!"

A huge bird's head suddenly tore through the foggy wall in front of William and the stowaway. The creature's beak was wide open and was soaring in about three feet above the water. It was illuminated from above by two swinging lanterns.

OH SHIT! was William's first thought. As he pounced upon his Spanish shipmate, he voiced his second thought, "Hold onto me! BREATHE NOW!"

21

Bloody Waters Run Deep

William grabbed the quivering Spanish stranger, pulled him up in a bear hug and bounded from the tiny broken hull of their upturned half lifeboat with all his might, at ninety degrees to the massive flying beak that constituted the ram bow of a ship he knew to be named *Doncella Escarlata*. What would have been this his third thought in the adrenaline spiked bid for survival was drowned when he and the stowaway splashed through the surface of the blackened sea. William rolled in the water instinctively protecting the delicate charge in his arms and was rewarded with a blow across his neck and shoulder from the barnacle encrusted hull of the huge ship that had inadvertently rammed into them. It belted the remaining air in his lungs clean out of him.

Bleeding in shark infested waters in the night was about to be William's fourth thought in as many seconds, but he had to put that one on hold when a man appeared, dressed in a grey habit with a green sash around his waist and emerald eyes that were luminescent. Literally.

"You might want to breathe son, be a shame to pass out before saving young Carlos there," said the habit-adorned fellow, and so William did the one thing that most of us might; he recoiled, struggled to get away and was rewarded with a glancing blow from a stray oar that sliced open the top of his head.

More blood in the water.

"Freaking out there a little bit, huh?" said the man in the habit, his words crystal clear in William's head, though all parties concerned were fully submerged in tropical waters. Distracting though that was, it paled into insignificance when William realised that the stowaway in his arms had lost his grasp on the little book he loved so dearly, because he could see it disappearing into the depths below him. Depths that were now illuminated in colours and light that had absolutely no business being there. Currents were defined, fish were everywhere, the sea floor a mass of intricate grains of whirling sands a hundred fathoms below his feet.

"Breathe for heaven's sake!" yelled the cowled stranger. His arm was now resting on the stationary dorsal fin of a very confused twelve-foot-long Tiger shark. Complete suspension of time. Frozen, yet the water was still warm. Bathwater on a good day.

"It's not me you should be worried about," said the weird, but very handsome monk-like figure, as he referred to the shark in his right arm. "It's this little guppy here, he's male, hungry, and becoming very impatient. And you're bleeding. And still not breathing, I might add."

William's diaphragm began to convulse, violently.

"You're lacking nitrogen, roughly seventy-eight percent, bit of oxygen, well perhaps a fifth, small bit of argon, which is a gas, but I suspect you don't know that yet, and carbon dioxide and such. Look the short of it is, is if you don't breathe, you'll die and so will young Carlos there."

William sucked in a deep breath and filled his lungs with the most gloriously fresh cool spring mountain-top air. And he sucked in again. And breathed out. But there were no bubbles. Just nothing. But he was still firmly in water. Its isotropic forces were unmistakable on his skin.

"What... what's happening?" blurted a disoriented William.

"Well, you're drowning young Carlos, unless you step up and blow something into his lungs for a spell."

"What?"

"Kiss him, boy, he's one of the good ones. Blow some air into his lungs!"

William cottoned on, took another breath that shouldn't be happening, cupped the stowaway by the jaw, planted his mouth over the man's lips and blew with all his might.

William breathed again and faced the stranger. "Who, are you? What is this?"

"Name's Arthur."

"What, is happening?" asked William.

"Oh, right. Easy question. Complex answer. Basically, I've suspended the molecular structure of all things relative to saving your sorry arse, so that set of oars above your head there doesn't cut you to ribbons, and this little guppy finds a tastier bite than you later in the night."

"What? Who are you?" asked William.

"Easy questions first. Right. I forget, you're still a baby," replied the curious, habit-wearing stranger, named 'Arthur'. "Shit, Abbey would be better at this. William, the short of it is, I'm your father. You're not dying, actually you're just coming of age, and I stepped in this time because you're doing the right thing, found yourself in deep water, excuse the pun, and you're not committing a stupid act of war over golden trinkets on a foreign ship."

"What?"

"To your point, I'm human, same as you. Just older. Much older," said Arthur.

"How, is this? How old?" asked William, struggling to manage his thoughts.

"Breathe again. Oh, and Carlos needs some more, too."

William did as instructed; he breathed again aplenty, and repeated his mouth to mouth resuscitation of the Spanish chap in his arms.

"Up to this point in time, I'm five-thousand-one-hundred-and-seventy-four years old, give or take. But a little older in some ways. And I can still get it up without pills. To answer your question."

"What?"

"Sorry, late twentieth century gag."

"What?"

"You ask that a great deal? Try listening."

"Am I dead?"

"Do you have a headache?"

"Yes, a bit," said William.

"Then you're not dead. Listen, all this molecular influencing is taxing, so more questions and answers to come. Climb up on Rosa's ship, find Katherine, and we'll talk later, okay?"

"Who the bloody hell are you?"

"Swim, climb, get dry, get Carlos sorted and I'll see you later. It's gonna be great," said Arthur. "Oh, and keep those dream-state things going, that's what you call them isn't it? Fecking funny, anyway gotta go, see you soon."

Arthur's luminescent emerald eyes faded, and he was gone.

The stationary oars above William's head started cutting slowly through the water again. The hungry shark that had been previously tied to Arthur started speeding forwards, and William lunged upward in the water, maintaining his grasp on the man in his arms. He caught the oar above his head and was immediately hoisted out of the water.

"Oh, and don't forget this. It's important."

Arthur was suddenly perched on the upstroke of the oar to which William was clinging and his father was offering *The Love Rule Book* with an outstretched arm and a mischievous smile.

William took it, though by now this entire series of events was proving to be so strange that he couldn't fathom why he'd taken back the book.

A cacophony of voices entered William's ears as his 'father' vanished, and he and the Spaniard, Carlos, if that was his name, were hoisted unceremoniously on-board Rosa's Galley by a dozen tobacco chewing women.

"¡CEASAR RAMOS!" could be heard, as instruction to stop rowing immediately.

"They are men!" was declared, in the Spanish tongue.

"I found him first!" came next, swiftly followed by a rather crass sentiment in William's muddled opinion, *"¡Seré el primero en follarlo!"* which is loosely translatable as "I'll be the first to fuck him!"

All of which were quickly silenced by, *"¡SUFICIENTE!"* from the ship's capitana who had skipped from the helm of the ship to the two bedraggled rescues in record time.

William was on his back, staring up, watching two dozen women backing slowly away. One extraordinarily beautiful woman crouched over him with compassion and concern in her eyes, tie dyed bandana taming her luxuriant raven hair, an array of iridescent black and blue pearls around her neck and an ornate cutlass formed from cold iron, bridged to her left hip.

William knew the sword was made of cold iron and that its magical qualities warded away stray souls, bound to the earth, yet still seeking their maker and prone to inadvertently harming the living.

And William knew the woman who owned it.

22

Adolescents on the Amber Nectar

29th October 1579

Fifteen year old William was stumbling forward along what he considered to be perhaps the most miserable stretch of beach he had yet encountered in the Caribbean. Sure, it had white sand, but it was narrow and mottled with rocks and reefs. Sure, the lapping waters were balmy, but one would need wooden boots to avoid cutting one's feet on the razor corals in the shallows. And sure, the air was warm, but it was sultry, and claggy, like breathing soup. The natural inclination of one's body was to sit and do fuck all for hours. Simply waste away in so called paradise. But today was different. Hence his walk. The winds were increasingly turbulent in what was sure to be an oncoming gale.

Hurricane fucking alley, this shithole.

William raised the leather flagon of rum he was clutching, held the neck of it to his lips, and chugged down the cleansing, mind numbing, pain relieving, spirit warming liquid inside. His legs staggered onwards, while his mind tumbled backwards, perhaps seeking the why of his loneliness, he wasn't certain. Rum was plentiful in paradise, it was strong, and more importantly; it was cheap.

It was his fifteenth birthday. He was fifteen. He was certain. It was sure. He'd been told. Roger 'Paws' Prowse had slapped him on the back several times since dawn.

Where is Paws? Can't see him. Ah, fuck it, he'll turn up before dark.

The suns were now fading in the west. He could see them. Two of them. Dropping down over the low promontory at the end of the shitty beach. He was on the southern coast of the island that 'Paws' had insisted they travelled to for his birthday. Tortuga.

So named because that disease carrying fucker Columbus had all the imagination of a fucking turtle. Ha!.. No, that's not right. Turtles are awesome. They live long and fuck like... Rabbits of the seas... thass what they are. Bet they have fabulous imaginations.

William held the neck of the flagon to his lips again, slugged deep, choked, and cough-spat most of the mouthful down the front of his grungy off-white linen blouse and breeches.

Bollocks. Looks like I pissed myself.

It didn't matter. There was nobody and nothing around to bear witness to a half-cut, half-grown Englishman, on an isle in which the residents all had either hooved limbs or wings.

Taken two damn years to get to this Godforsaken place. For what?

William looked south, over the sea. He should have been able to see the northern coast of Hispaniola, for it was only a league or so away, but darkening clouds of what looked to be a squall forming masked any indication of land.

"Hispaniola, where you at?"

Santa Maria del Puerto, two days ago. On the eastern coast of Hispaniola.

That was alright. Better than this.

Two months before that, Villa de la Vega, on the isle of Santiago. Southern coast.

Bountiful, beautiful. Could have forgotten myself there forever.

Hundreds of miles southeast. Puerto Limón was the harbour's name, in a country called La Costa Rica by Spanish settlers.

Fucking Spaniards own half the world. Something must be done, I say. Paws struck a bargain for our pinnace. Speaking of, where's the bloody pier? It's going to rain, again.

William picked up his doddering pace as he continued west along the beach. At least he thought he was walking faster. His mind was scanning through scattered fragments of his two-year journey halfway round the world in reverse. With Captain Francis Drake. He had learnt sailing. Navigation. All about dysentery. Swordplay. How to get by without sleep. How to pluck weevils from everything he ate.

Nasty. But not her. Bet she's still never seen a maggot in her life.

He was seeking a name. Her name. But she wasn't part of the tall ship *Golden Hind*. Or the same ship as *Pelican* when they left Plymouth Sound and headed for Morocco and Africa. It was before that.

William Arthur Hope... thass my name, and I is now fifteen. And so is she.

Exact same age. Born within minutes of each other. Windsor Castle.

England it was. Her born in silk sheets. Me on a bed of straw. James told me so.

The thick, salt-coated timbers of a pier appeared before him, extending from the shore into the sea. The pinnace 'Paws' had bought in, some fucking place with multi-coloured birds, sea snakes, so many beetles that they would never go extinct, monkeys, bats, wild dogs, lizard-looking scaly, scurrying mini-dragon things, and gargantuan fucking snakes that swallowed people whole. Well, maybe not people, just the dogs and children, was tied to one of the dozen tree trunks that constituted the piles of the structure.

Thank fuck. Wrap me under the mainsail before I get drowned. Where is Paws?

William scanned about as best he could. He covered his right eye with his left hand to gain a sharper image. Sixty yards or so inland sat the one structure on the entire southern side of the isle, as far as he could tell, and it was standing strong. He had marched all around it earlier in the day. It was a single-storey, stone and clay-built barn type thing, with a thatched roof made from leaves of trees and plants he didn't know the name of. It had timber shutters covering what looked to be a large central window on the southern wall. He couldn't be sure. He was no architect, and this was a very foreign land. A deck of cross beams and planks was supported by tree-stumps buried into the sloping ground. It had two sets of stairs leading directly to two sturdy wooden doors, either side of the south facing window, if it was a window. Short of a shot from a demi-cannon, nobody was getting into it. He had tried.

No can do that place for the night, William.

William stumbled onto the planks of the pier, and momentarily he thought of just rolling off it into the pinnace 'Paws' had commanded from... *'Where have we sailed again?'*... but he didn't. He stopped walking/staggering at the end of the pier and slumped down on his arse with his right shoulder propped against one of the two large tree trunks that were the piles furthest out into the water. He twisted, bent his legs at the knees, and let his feet dangle over the surface of the churning surf, ten feet below.

The fuck was her name?

Theobalds House. He could remember that. Pronounced 'Tibaults', by his once supposed father, William Cecil.

First Baron Burghley.

And mummy Mildred. Mustn't forget her. Liked her. Pleasant ducky.

My birthday two years ago. Same day. Her birthday.

Whass was her name? She was fucking fun. Nice dress. Nice tits in it.

"You'd better get used to them. Mammary glands will one day serve a greater purpose than your silly fascinations."

"I don't have fascinations."

"It's fine dear brother. At least we know you're not fashioning your nature after Francis."

Francis Bacon. Gentle boy. Except his firecrackers. Fucking pyrotechnical genius!

Sir Flemington James of... Oh, yes, lest we mustn't forget the Bon part.

Disarming the guards, stealing Captain Tarquin...

Smedley-Smythe-Smythings... fucked up name; Tarquin. Poor man.

Oh, fuck yes; Cocoa cake, in the face!

"Wait! Daddy, let go of me!"

Sir James. William Cecil. Both strong as shit. Guards. Struggling.

"No! William! No! Daddy, let me go!"

Then we're gone, without a trace.

Stealing his cavalry horse and pissing off across the countryside in the night.

Remember all that. Wonder if he ever got his horse back

Avebury Henge, stone circles. Burrow Mump. Me getting sick.

Fuck, I really was sick.

James said I was in shock. No that was later...

Wookey Hole for three nights with those ladies of the night, healing me...

What were their names?.. Ha, that's right; they never told us.

Weird energies in all those places. All connected.

Glastonbury Tor can't forget. Ladies. Half-naked. Or was that the stone circles?

What was her name? Damnation upon it! She used to be my sister.

Hope Cove. Beautiful place. Abbey. My real mother. Pretty as all hell...

Yeah, that was fucking weird. Think of something else...

Grandpa Delbert, and Grandma Flossie. Peter and Connie Chatswood...

Really nice people. Bonkers, but nice. I miss them. Yeah, thass when I got really sick. What did James bullshit about again? I had a what? A psychologically traumatising experience. Fuck off to that then and fuck off now, says I.

Hope's Pies and Pasties. Good pies...

By appointing of... Her Most Honourable Majesty Lizabeth... all spelt wrong, but I wouldn't tell 'em, would I? I remember that. Don't I?.. Grandpa Delbert. Legend.

William looked up from the frothing surf of the darkening turquoise waters lapping beneath his feet, between the piles of the pier. Way out to sea, some idiot captains were sailing two tall ships, closely side by side, about a mile offshore. They seemed to be approaching. Thankfully they weren't at full sail; Royals and Topgallants were furled. But still, in this weather, with this many shoals and reefs to contend with, in fading light.

Idiots.

William covered his right eye with his left palm...

Ah, thass better. It's only one idiot ship, after all.

William raised the flagon to his lips again and cherished a long pull. He was lonely. Had been lonely since leaving Plymouth Sound in December of fifteen-seventy-seven, which had been cold. Grey. Miserable. Everything about it was miserable. He had been lonely, but never could he remember a time when he was alone. Not on the entire disastrous, endless voyage, further and further from home.

Oh, shite upon a biscuit, what was her name?

Footsteps on the boards of the pier prompted William to turn.

There he fucking is. Where the..?

Roger Prowse watched intently as William began to stand up, which was a classic case of balance bowing to drunken intent.

"Where's you fuckin' bee..." was part of the question William intended to ask, but the boy's shoulder slipped from the post he was propped against, and he toppled off the pier, headfirst, into the water below.

Fuck me. Adolescents on the amber nectar.

Old 'Paws' continued walking to the pier's end and looked down, as one does or should when your charge of two years as a babysitter has fallen into the depths of the ocean. As William's head didn't readily appear, 'Paws' considered two options available to him in the moment; He could dive in after William, by way of rescue, in which case he would spoil his attire for the evening's forthcoming event – he was wearing a pristine cream cotton shirt, black velvet breeches topped with maroon silk sash, and brown leather knee-height boots – or he could sit, place the six black kingfish he'd caught that afternoon down on the deck, dangle his legs off the pier, and covet the flagon of nectar that William had so sportingly left behind. 'Paws' chose the latter of the two options.

Not my fault the boy's feckin' lonely, was his thinking, as he lifted the leather receptacle from the deck, upturned the neck of it to his mouth and imbibed.

You know, I don't get it. Why does everyone call me 'Old Paws'? Alright, I happen to be thirty-five, but I ain't thinkin' 'bout kickin' it anytime soon. Gonna 'ave to change people's perceptions, I reckon.

'Paws' set the flagon in his lap and looked out to sea.

Ah, there they are... Righty oh, then, we're on.

The tall ship that William had seen two of earlier was now a half-mile offshore and coursing east to northwest, navigating the relatively unknown channel into the natural harbour in which the pier had been erected.

Wonder what he named her?

'Paws' hadn't boarded that vessel yet, but he knew he would. He'd seen the bones of her hull when she was first being built in Portsmouth, right before he joined Drake's crew in Plymouth for his stint as nursemaid and mentor. And by jolly, she was sure to be a grand home in the years to come. He'd known William long enough now to conclude the boy was special. Not dull special. Special, special. The boy wouldn't let the side down tonight.

If he gets out of the feckin' surf. Ah, he just ain't grown into his own skin yet, is all.

Another smaller ship with furled sail was pulling in alongside the larger; a small low-sided Galley, driven by two-dozen oars.

Brave women, what with this feckin' weather. Fair play.

It was true. The squall shrouding the coast of Hispaniola was northbound for sure. It was heading towards Tortuga. The night would be unruly, for certain, perhaps in more ways than one. 'Paws' smiled, took another swig of rum, and looked down between his knees. William's head finally breached the surface of the lapping waters below.

"You done playin'? We gotta go to work," shouted 'Paws'.

"Work? What work? Where have you been, Roger?" asked William, treading water in surf that was becoming increasingly tumultuous, "I was looking for you."

"Oh, I took a wrong turn and I just kept goin'," replied 'Paws'. "You got a change of decent clothes?"

"Define decent," shouted William, "as if you could."

'Paws' tucked the fingers of his right hand into the open neckline of his shirt and reached for the pendant he was sporting. Two large silver keys were dangling on a leather strap around his neck. He raised them to his lips and kissed them, somewhat overdramatically.

"Unbridled decency, William. I wears it upon me all times," said 'Paws'. "Now get the fuck out of the bath. We ain't got much time."

"Time for what?"

"Your birthday party, young 'un," said 'Paws' upon standing.

A second tall ship appeared through the swirling clouds and tempests of vapours that were the fringes of the approaching storm. She was a mile out and flying on full sail. 'Paws' knew that ship better than the wrinkles on his own face, and her captain was no idiot. He smiled and raised the flagon above his head, "Her bark is blasting, and her bite is barbarous, I says!"

'Paws' picked up his catch, about-turned and walked away along the planks of the pier.

William spluttered out a half mouthful of seawater and began swimming towards the shore.

23

Every Problem has a Panacea

The sun crossing the western horizon had reduced in form from two to one by the time William had joined 'Paws' on the foredeck of the only human-made habitable structure on the south coast of Tortuga.

"I'd say you're wet behind the ears, William. But that's about to change," said 'Paws', dumping the half dozen kingfish on the deck.

"What is this place? I was looking at it..." began William.

"Here," said 'Paws', holding up one of the two silver keys he was sporting earlier, "no man, woman, nor beast can enter 'ere alone."

"That rum's strong ain't it?" said William, indicating the flagon 'Paws' was conveniently still clutching.

'Paws' tossed the key to William, and turned very serious, "You take that door. Put the key in the lock, but don't friggin' turn it 'til I says. Got it?"

"Alright, Roger," said William, knowing better than to challenge his elder on this occasion. He'd seen 'Paws' batter the helmets off the heads of many a Spaniard soldier with the clubs he always chose to wield when Drake had given orders to grapple and board unsuspecting vessels on his round-the-world treasure hunt. William had always hated the violence. Thought it stupid and unnecessary, but men enacted any amount of maniacal madness in their section-able pursuance of gems, gold, and silver. He had never been exposed to it growing up in the confines of Theobalds. Since then, though, he had seen what he thought would be more than his fair share. 'Paws' was holding a silver key. He was holding a silver key. And William thought he recognised the look in the eyes of his mentor and caretaker. He was mistaken, but better to be safe than...

Theobalds; She would have asked what this was all about. She wouldn't have given two shits for the look in a man's eyes. Ka... Kar.. Karen... No. The fuck was her name?

William faced the large wooden door on the southeastern corner of the building. It was set into an arched alcove, mounted on four bulky brass hinges. If it was centred in the alcove, the rock walls were three feet thick, or thereabouts. Midway up, on the left-hand side of the door, was a brass plate with a keyhole in it, which was surrounded with a protruding, decorative, V-shape metal foliage.

Clever. A drunk could open this in the dark.

William studied the key in his hand briefly. The blade was conventional with several marked indentations for the wards in the lock. The bow was embossed with two crossed swords surrounded by an inscription in Latin: *Fratres Maritimi.*

"Ready?" shouted 'Paws' from his position beside the southwestern door of the building. He had the blade of his key in the lock, which was on the right side of that door.

William shoved the key into the keyhole, "Yes. Set. Wait, which way do I turn it?"

"Glad you asked. That swim done you good," said 'Paws'. "Towards home."

"Wait. What? Whose home?" asked William.

"On two, one, turn!"

William took the full two counts to decipher the meaning of 'Paws'' cryptic answer but was just about sober enough to discern that twisting the blade of his key anti-clockwise towards the centre of the building was probably good enough. He felt the chamber of the lock clunk and then; nothing happened.

William pushed against the door. It didn't move. There was no handle to pull. He looked to 'Paws', who smiled, winked, and imbibed from the flagon of rum.

"Did I do it wrong?" asked William.

"Not yet," said 'Paws', before chugging another mouthful.

William felt faint vibrations under the planks of the deck. A soft rumbling could be heard. Or so he thought. The winds were picking up all around. A storm coming.

The door before him started sliding slowly sideways to the right into a pocket cavity in the thick stone wall.

"Oh, grab me key!" shouted 'Paws', "They're a bitch to mend when they gets bent."

William scrambled for the bow of the key that he had left sitting in the keyhole. After a fumbling struggle, the heavy key popped out of the lock, just before the door slid back to its full extent.

William held it up between his index finger and thumb.

"Good man," said Paws, before lifting his batch of fish from the deck. He stepped over the threshold of his door and disappeared from William's view.

The interior of the building was... dark. It had tree trunks for rafters in the trusses that supported the shallow-vaulted, bark-lined roof. It smelled of stale beer and a damp-some-thing-sweet but mildly rotting.

'Paws' lit the first of many lanterns that were suspended on iron brackets all around the walls of the open space, which was roughly sixty feet to a side. Four central columns, also tree trunks, supported the two largest trusses in the roof. The rock walls were washed in a whiteish-grey paint. They were decorated with flags, tapestries of maps, and every type of cutlass, sword, dagger, club, musket, and handheld weapon one could imagine. The floor was made of some sort of exotic hardwood timber planks.

'Paws' skirted the perimeter, lighting second and third lanterns.

Six long wooden table-and-bench sets were strewn around the room in no seeming semblance of order. A dozen tapped kegs were stacked on an upturned split log that served as the backdrop of a modest public-house bar arrangement against the east wall. A low elevated stage filled the northeast corner. It was stocked with tom-tom drums, lutes, fiddles, a pianola, and a cello, among other instruments that William didn't recognise.

She would have known what they were.

'Paws' was having trouble lighting the fourth lantern, "You vaguely sober, yet?"

"I'm alright. What is this place?"

"Light the fire," said 'Paws', as the lantern he was attending burst into flame.

William stepped between tables crossing to the north wall and the modest stone hearth that was embedded in the centre of it. Parchment and kindling were stacked in a neat little bundle inside a cast iron grate that was sitting on ornate legs. A flint striker and wax tapers sat atop a set of iron fireplace tools. Tongs, brush, poker, and shovel, all well used by the look of them. A small stack of logs sat on the west side of the hearth.

"It's too frigging hot for a fire, isn't it?" questioned William.

"Not when you opens the window. You sober yet? You're movin' funny slow like."

"That's cause I'm not moving," said William.

"You reckon this rum was off?" asked 'Paws', holding up the flagon he and William had been drinking from.

"Roger. What is this place? And who is on those ships out there?"

"Friends. If you is friendly," said 'Paws'. "Fire."

William turned his attention back to the hearth. Three strikes of the flint and several rum soaked blows later the fire tanked up and sprang to life.

'Paws' was lighting his eighth lantern, "Get ye behind the bar. Them kegs need turning and check the mugs. Ain't sure if it's beetles what cleaned them or one of the boys washed them proper like."

"What are you talkin' about?" asked William.

"Just get behin' the bar," commanded 'Paws'.

William shook his head but did as he was instructed. He lifted the only part of the bar countertop that was hinged, figuring quite rightly that it was the entrance and egress for serving merriness. It folded up and was designed to be propped against the wall of the northwest corner of the room. William took two paces, crossing the threshold of said bar, placed his leading foot into the air of an open trap door where he had expected solid planks of flooring to be, and promptly tumbled down a set of wooden stairs, landing head over arse on the floor of a cellar, "Ah, fuuuccckkeddy, fuuuck, shit, bollocks, Roger! Arraghhh, fuck! You…"

"Oh, and min' the gap. One of the boys probably left it open. Gets a might musty down below, if nobody's…" said 'Paws', focusing hard on lighting the nineth lantern, "William?"

"The fuck, Roger!"

"Ah, shit," mumbled 'Paws', turning too quickly in the direction of William's voice and bumping against a cello that was sitting neatly in a wrought iron stand. He walked across the stage, half missed the step down to the main floor, recovered well, and better than that, he carried the lantern with him. It was just what he needed to illuminate William's sprawled body at the foot of the cellar stairs.

"Found the gold, did you?" questioned 'Paws'.

William tipped his head back and looked up the stairs. Either 'Paws' was upside down or he was, "Found my arse, is what I found. You're enjoying this aren't you?"

"Aye, somewhats," said 'Paws'.

"You going to tell me what the fuck at some point?" asked William.

'Paws' marched down the eight treads of the stairs. The lantern threw light on the cellar which was a modest sized natural cave. It contained stacks of logs, cut to lengths handy for firewood, a dozen oak barrels, and eight hard-wood chests, capped and tipped with iron fittings, studs and padlocks.

"You needs to quit messin'," said 'Paws', "or my arse'll be in shackles fer not mindin' you right. This bein' your trial an' all."

"Again. One more time," said William, sitting up and twisting to face his friend and guardian. "Hang fire, and scratch that. What trial?"

"Ho there! Doctor in the house!" came a lilting voice from above. The accent was part Trinidadian, part Irish.

"They're here already," said 'Paws', stepping forward, totally missing the bottom step of the stairs and landing on top of William.

"Arrragh!"

"Arrragh, fuck!"

"Alright now, you boys that way inclined, or is help required?" asked the black man appearing the top of the stairs. He was dressed in a white, open-necked cotton blouse, black breeches, and knee-high brown leather boots. He had a maroon sash around his waist. He had bright eyes, toned torso, afro dreadlocks for hair that was tucked into a maroon silk bandana with crossed swords embroidered as an emblem, centred on his forehead. The brightest thing about him was a beaming white teethed smile that many would die for, be they male or female.

"He's drunk. And I'm in the shitter as a nursemaid, Trevor," said 'Paws'.

"Least you made it," said Trevor Neary. "Word is, it was a rough sail fer you boys."

"The rum was off, methinks," said 'Paws'.

Trevor skipped down the stairs like a dancer on coke, "For every problem there is a panacea."

"Trevor, this is William. William, Doctor Trevor Neary," said 'Paws', "one of two men on the earth that don't age."

Trevor held his hand out, grabbed William's wrist and pulled him to standing, "Heard me some about ye, William."

"Err... Nice, it is, to meet you. I hope. I was told, to be... What the fuck was it, Roger?" said William.

"Friendly," said 'Paws'.

"Friendly," said William, "I'm definitely friendly. It's my birthday."

"Heard me that too, friend," said Trevor. "On your feet Roger," continued the doctor, lifting 'Paws' up from the clay floor by the armpits and grabbing his lantern.

"Thanks doc," said 'Paws', "the rum was off."

"Panacea," said Trevor, stepping between William and 'Paws' and heading for a nearby chest. It was the only one without a padlock. Trevor opened its lid and ruffled around inside. He withdrew three glass vials and held them up for William and 'Paws' to see.

"Fish for dinner, then," came a voice from above in the main room.

"Fuck dinner, cider I up," from a second voice.

"Less gets twatted afore the ladies gets 'ere," from a third.

Trevor started shaking the vials in his right hand. Not violently. A measured tipping/shake. He studied the contents under the lantern.

"They don't wants drunkards with your diseases," came a forth.

"They gets whass I'm givin' 'em. Iss free ain't it?" from the third.

Trevor uncorked the vials, passed one to 'Paws' and another to William. He kept the third for himself, "Bottoms up, ye pair of miscreants. Scarlett will be here any minute now."

Trevor necked his vial. 'Paws' did the same. William took heed and downed the contents of his. He crumpled into a fit of coughing, before sucking in a deep breath and exhaling, "Holy fucking shit!"

"Don't worry, be happy, young William" said Trevor, slapping William on the shoulder and skipping onto the stairs. "Nice to know you, finally. Let us hit the good times, now."

'Paws' shook his head to clear the fog within before he followed Trevor.

William coughed some more and straightened up to standing. What seemed to be scores of footsteps sounded from above. The scuffles of instruments being moved. Strings plucked, strummed, tightened, tuned at the head stocks. Tapping of goatskin drums. All manner of voices demanding beer and rum. What was above him? What was he about to climb into? Who were these people? A crushing lack of confidence fell upon him. Squeezing every muscle and bone in his body. His breathing shallowed. His ribcage wasn't round enough for his lungs. His head was lifting, and his legs were sinking. He was dressed in rags and sopping wet from his ocean dip. A musical signature erupted in his ears. It shouldn't have because he was below decks, and the sounds should have been muffled. They weren't. He listened. She would have told him that the tune he was listening to had two parts made of eight bars, and six beats in every bar. Galloping, galloping, galloping, galloping...

"Arrghh me lovelies," came another voice, "There it be now. 'Mumbles', tune up yer lute boy, you're off so flat as you'll ne'er gets it up in her!"

Six beats per bar. Eight bars with a turnaround on the last.

What did I just drink? Shit. What do I do? And who the fuck is Scarlett?

William placed his left foot on the first step of the stairs.

24

Test or Trial

The lead fiddle was owned by a man wearing a yellow cotton shirt and pink neckerchief. 'Black Teeth' McCarthy was his name and he played as though the bow was an extension of his right hand. He sported a greying ponytail and goatee beard, and by fuck could he play. As could all his cohorts on the stage in the northeast corner of the room. The jig was up. The simple joy radiating from Martin 'Mumbles' No-Name's face was to die for, twanging the cello bass notes as though it was the last song he would ever play. It wasn't, and William didn't know him yet, but it was the first thing that grabbed William's attention when he reached the topmost of the cellar stairs, not that it mattered, nobody noticed him tripping on the last riser and closing the cellar door with a frustrated bang. The second thing apparent to him was the amount of people in the room; many. The third was the score of stunning ladies that were among them. Exotic ladies, one might call them if you had never left England, or Theobalds. William had garnered enough soundbites on his voyages with Captain Drake and captain of the pinnace, Roger Prowse, to know that the ladies were probably a mixture of Taíno, African and Spanish descent, most likely gathered and recently arrived from the islands of Cuba, Hispaniola, Santiago, and the Spanish kingdom of New Granada. The most striking among the girls was...

Rosa Brizuela, who was tall, lean, athletic, and twenty years of age. She was darker skinned than the multitudinous horde of pale skinned drunken pecker-scratching pirates surrounding her. She was dressed the same as them. White blouse, black hose, maroon sash, brown knee-high boots. Crossed swords on her silk bandana. She liked the few foreign reprobates she had met in recent months. A man named Scarlett, particularly. It was possible she would settle for him, if, and when, he ever grew up and cultivated marginal degrees of humility. He had asked, and she had agreed to show up that evening. The proposition Scarlett had made had been intriguing. A special boy was to be welcomed into their brethren, if said boy was game enough, tough enough, courteous enough, friendly and brave. She had no idea which one of the men and boys around her was the one named William Hope, and in the moment she didn't care. Her priority was the nine-year-old child hugging her right hip. Aletha wasn't scared, but she was naturally overwhelmed by the noise, the cheers, and the sheer number of ghostly faces in the room.

The Scarlett Buccaneer knew how to make an entrance at a party. Be late, be drunk and, above all, be obnoxious, "Abew ye me hearties!" he said, pacing to the centre of the room, wielding a half-full bottle of rum, "Yer Captain's risin' fer a tune. Shall I be showin' ye how?"

"Aye, aye, Captain!" came the resounding response.

Scarlett trotted over to the stage, stepped up, and faced the crowd, "Let's ye rejoice in 'Black Teeth' McCarthy on fiddle.

"Ohhh, arraghhh, McCarthy!" from those closest in the audience.

The six/eight-time signature continued, none of the musicians missing a beat.

"Martin 'Mumbles' on cello!" announced Scarlett.

"'Mumbles' mayhem!"

"Less 'ave it, 'Mumbles'!"

The oldest, and some, of the musicians, raised a closed fist to the crowd.

"Roger 'Paws' Prowse on…" started Scarlett, before realising 'Paws' wasn't on stage, "Where ye be, Roger?"

Scarlett picked up a lute and held it above his head, "Yer banjo's a beggin' Roger, where you at?"

'Paws' pushed his way through the front row of the gathering nearest the stage and stepped up. He accepted the lute from Scarlett, who whispered, "Is that him behind the bar?"

'Paws' faced the crowd, held the lute up by the neck and took a bow.

"Fer 'Paws', fer Queeny an' fer England, Yar!" came the resounding response.

"Yep. Thass him. Not my fault he's wankered," whispered 'Paws' before passing Scarlett and plonking his arse down on a barrel. Within two bars he was strumming away in time with the others.

Scarlett faced the crowd and continued to introduce members of the band, "Jimmy Wily on the goat skins, ladies and gents!"

The man rapping on the tom-tom drums raised his hand in acknowledgement of the momentary focus.

Scarlett's attention was on the boy looking lost at the end of the bar. His clothes were wet rags, and his long hair was bedraggled with ocean salt. His face was grimy with streaks of island mud.

My word. That form will not do on my ship.

Scarlett continued to point out the players for the audience, while marking Rosa's position among the crowd, turning to the pianola, sitting, and rapping his knuckles over the keys...

Ned 'Toes' Williams was the tallest man in the room. He was also the strongest. He entered the southwest door with his arms wrapped around a fifty-gallon barrel of beer.

He carried the weight of the four-hundred-pound vessel as if it were a cushion. Two other crewmen entered behind him dragging a small, four-wheeled cart with another similar barrel sitting on top. They were puffing and straining. 'Toes' headed for the bar, stepped behind it through the open hinged counter, and shoved William aside, "Mind the way, boy,".

'Toes' plonked the barrel on the floor, "Got me a thirst up, John."

"Aye an' rightly," said a sinewy Cornishman who was clearly barkeep for the evening.

He was wiping a mug with a towel, "Rum, wine, or beer?"

"Those'll do nicely," replied 'Toes'.

"Cocktails it is then," said John Prior, "what took ya, big fella?"

"Got me an eye on two lovely ladies," said 'Toes', "paused fer sayin' hello."

"Sisters, I hope," said Prior.

"Might be same as that, Mister Prior. I'm feeling lucky," said 'Toes'. "Where's this birthday boy we's all 'ere fer?"

"He's the shabby rascal you just shoved out the way like he was a rabid street dog starin' up at ye," said Prior, nodding out over the bar, in the direction of what was fast becoming a dance floor...

William was jostling his way through the foot-stepping rabble. More accurately, he was being jostled by them. He was heading for the southeast door. As he remembered things it was the door closest to the ocean. He needed air. He needed his head straight. He needed to swim. Best cure for seasickness was jumping into the sea. He didn't quite make it to the door. A tall man dressed in a black blouse, breeches, and boots entered. He wasn't wearing a bandana. William knew him. Or had known him. His name was Flemington James. He was from a Scottish harbour village named Bon, and he was followed by a vivacious looking couple dressed in green velvet attire. She was blonde and beautiful. He was dark-haired and heavy set. Sure as shit, they were wealthy. William had heard the tales of Ignatius Jones and his wanton wife Destiny. How they had met on his birthday.

William was in no shape to meet any of them. He needed a swim. Another swim.

"Wench be there!" came a shout from the stage, "Ho now and mark me!"

Loud was the voice and so strong the presence of the man behind it that the music snapped to silence mid-bar of the sixth bar in the first phrase of a new tune.

William turned to see Scarlett front and centre stage. He was pointing at the lady William considered to be the most attractive woman in the room. The exotic skinned stunner with the child of eight or nine years tucked in safely beside her.

"What price for your favours this evening, beauty? For no man here shall have ye before the Scarlett Buccaneer! What price I say?"

"I don't favour pigs or buccaneers, Sir. You appear to be both," said Rosa.

"Ooohhh!" from the crowd.

"She's about right, Capt," from John Prior.

"I'll have you'll know me better before the sun rises, lady. And you shall not be left wanting. What price, I say?" demanded Scarlett.

"A new tune, from you, Sir. And play a new instrument. Your voice is foul."

"Oowww."

"Capsized."

"Scuttled."

"Good on ya girl."

Scarlett beamed. His white smile betrayed the arrogance he was trying to learn, and yet yearning to put to rest. But Scarlett was Scarlett and the show had to continue. He stepped down from the stage and approached Rosa and Aletha, "Then what price for your child? Born out of wedlock I assume. She'll be raised as a fine masseuse, I assure you. When she's of an age to pluck, of course. What price, damn you?"

Silence.

All present focused on the exchange between Scarlett and Rosa.

Tears began to well in Rosa's eyes. She'd agreed to the ruse, but this was beyond disrespectful. Scarlett was being a fucking dick. Was this necessary? Maybe he wouldn't do, even if she was to tame him.

"Leave her and leave her child! You, Sir, are a shameless fucking braggard!"

Scarlett scanned the crowd, quickly catching sight of the bedraggled form of the boy named William Hope, who was pushing his way through the onlookers, approaching.

"A buccaneer? Thass is what you called yourself, isn't it?" said William, shaking his head to clear the squall that was rolling in with Doctor Neary's supposed panacea.

"Who be you, squirt? Are you old enough to drink? Stand straight when you address a Captain of the English Realm."

William ignored him and continued pushing through the crowd. It was unnecessary as the assemblage was parting from his path towards Scarlett before his hands could reach them, but still, it was a bold effort.

"Leave the lady the flying fuck alone, Sir. She's leagues above you," said William, "and fuck the English Realm. And the Queen. She fucked me, didn't she? Or I wouldn't be here."

Scarlett burst out into fits of laughter. Rosa wiped a tear and bit her lip, before wrapping her arm tighter around Aletha and burying her head beside the child in a feigned attempt to mask her giggles. She liked William already...

"No man fucks the Queen of England, boy," said Scarlett...

A gentle coughing was heard from the rear of the room. Ignatius reached past Destiny and tapped James on the shoulder. Destiny, who was standing in between her husband and James, tapped the back of Ignatius' head.

"Shhssh!"

"Yeah, but Scarlett went too far be there," whispered Ignatius, "Rosa's a diamond."

"Shhssshh," repeated Destiny, "James. Don't you dare."

James folded his arms and looked on. In his mind Scarlett had gone too far, but he was more interested in what William would do next. Then it happened.

"He didn't just drop a glove on him," said Ignatius.

"I believe he did," said James.

It was true. Scarlett had plucked one of the gloves from the maroon sash around his waist and slapped William across both cheeks with it before chucking it down on the floor and stepping back, awaiting his opponent's response.

"Ooohhh," from the crowd.

"This ain't good."

"Good, man? It ain't right at all. Let's gets the fuck out the way."

"Aye. After I."

As the closest members of the ensemble to William and Scarlett began shifting intuitively backward, Destiny chirped up, "Your protégé's a wanker, James."

"He's just playing his part," said James in defence of Scarlett's behaviour.

"He's a wanker," from Destiny and Ignatius in unison...

William didn't do anything, at first. His head was a mess of rum and opiates. He also had no idea why the fellow who called himself the Scarlett Buccaneer had thrown one of his gloves on the floor. He clocked on quickly when Scarlett announced, "To the death then," and followed it up with a look towards the bar, "Mister Prior, you shall be the master of ceremonies. Bring the muskets, post-haste, if you please."

William's peripheral vision suddenly became clearer than his direct line of sight...

John Prior reached underneath the bar and lifted a small, ornately carved, wooden box. "Fuck me," said Prior. His comment was supposed to be sotto, but 'Toes' had good hearing as well as big feet and a legendary sized...

Rosa cuddled Aletha and shuffled away. The fireplace seemed the safest direction...

William stood still wondering which way to stand. He had no idea what the decorum of a duel was. No idea what it might feel like when he was shot. Probably in the chest, he thought. Maybe turn sideways...

John Prior presented the box to Scarlett, who opened it. It was lined with blue velvet and contained four pockets. Inside the largest of those were two short muskets. The colloquial name for them being 'dragons'. The two small-est pockets held a tampering wad, a leather pouch with a V-shaped neck made of animal horn, containing gun-powder, and half-inch diameter beads of lead. Scarlett set about loading shot and gunpowder into the barrels of the guns, but he wasn't about to do that without addressing the crowd by way of distraction. The main thought occupying his mind was that he had pushed this whole thing too far by referencing the girl, Aletha, whom Rosa had protected since she had found her as an abandoned baby in Baitiquiri, and thus he had shit on all his chances of ever forming a meaningful and lasting relationship with the most beauti-ful woman in the room. His relationships were always brief and unfulfilling.

"Bear ye witness now!" began Scarlett, holding up both muskets by their handles, "Two dragons. One for the inter-loper in the rags and one for Scarlett."

The response from the crowd was underwhelming. No-body was digging the vibes turned dark, when music, fuckwittery, sex, drinks and maybe sex on the beach were just about all that was on just about every mind in the room, except James of Bon and William. Destiny stroked her husband's codpiece to prove it. Ignatius genuinely appreciated her desire but was focused on...

Scarlett, who lifted the pouch of gunpowder and filled both musket barrels one by one. As he shoved the tampering wad into each upended barrel he said, "Trevor! Come forth good doctor. Pick out two rounds of shot for me from the box. Make sure you know them well. One you shall be digging out of this upstart's chest in five minutes or less."

Trevor Neary was the smartest person in the room. Had been since he was a child. It didn't take long for him to catch on and play his part, albeit reluctantly, but on the opiate upside, improvisation was one of God's greater gifts in life, and he could think of no better alternative than to join Scarlett, make a show of examining the two balls of lead for the crowd's benefit before handing them back to his friend.

"The lead buttons is real," said Neary, for the crowd's benefit, handing the balls to Scarlett, who dropped one into what he knew would be *his* musket, while he palmed the other over the open barrel of William's. It didn't go unnoticed by Neary, who was relieved he wouldn't have to be threading needles that evening, but it did go unnoticed by the crowd of onlookers, who all just wanted the music to kick in again so they could have some chance of getting laid...

Destiny stroked her husband's codpiece again. Being Destiny, it was more of a squeeze than a stroke. This time Ignatius responded. His cock knew full well it was getting some tonight, regardless of the outcome of the duel...

Scarlett made a show of handing the unloaded musket to William, who accepted it in his right hand.

"Mister Prior. A count of pace if you will," said Scarlett.

"Aye, Captain," said Prior. "Back-to-back now, and lets us give 'em some room ye scabbards in the wings."

The crowd made steps as instructed and backed up on bearings that were to the north and south of the line of soon-to-be-fire, which was east from the stage and to west towards the bar.

Scarlett approached William, "Back-to-back is the rules."

William said nothing. He simply did a one-eighty point of the compass turn and held the musket by his side.

"Drums on count, Jimmy Wily, six paces. Slow tempo, the ragamuffin challenger is too young for his rum," said Scarlett, cocking the flintlock on his musket in full show-manship for the audience present.

The musician, Jimmy Wily, rattled off a drum-roll on the goat skin tom-toms, then promptly stopped. He slapped the larger of the three drums with an open palm.

"One!" announced a reluctant John Prior.

SLAP.

"Two!" said Prior...

SLAP.

"Three... SLAP... Four... SLAP... Five... No slap... Six," from Prior.

A last few shuffling bodies behind William's position confirmed what he suspected. He didn't know much about firing dragons other than the flint lock needed to be cocked by pulling it back. After that it was all about pointing the barrel in the direction of the target one intended to hurt. William wasn't about to hurt anyone, so he about-turned with the musket held firmly at his side and faced Scarlett square on.

"Fire," said Prior, but the level of his voice was buried in his lack of enthusiasm for the bullshit ongoing.

Scarlett aimed. He had every sense of knowing what he was aiming for. He lined up the grooves on the hilt and the tip of the barrel on the left side of William's right ear. What he didn't focus on was the curve of a Spanish armour breast-plate pinned to a roof support tree trunk column that was several yards behind William's right side.

BANG!

The musket fire was something Scarlett would regret and yet rejoice for years to come. He shouldn't have pulled the trigger. He was twenty-five, full of shit, and the confidence of his showmanship didn't support the weight of his ambitions. The shot from his gun whizzed past William's ear, struck the captured Spanish breast-plate memento, ricocheted behind the bar, pinged off an ancient heraldry shield sitting amongst the kegs of rum, and obliterated the iron mounting of one of two crossed halberds above the fireplace.

As anyone with an interest in chivalry knows; a halberd is designed to be a weapon. It has a wooden pole, about six feet long, and atop that pole is a metal headstock, incorporating a sophisticated trifactor of tools moulded and designed specifically to maim or kill. A spike. A grappling hook. And last, and oft, the very most damaging; a large, sharpened, very heavy, shiny axe blade.

That very weapon was dislodged by Scarlett's fuck-up of a musket round. Gravity and rudimentary physics dictated that it had nowhere to fall but on the unsuspecting head of nine-year-old Aletha, who had pulled slightly away from Rosa's hip when she had been startled by the gunshot.

Drunken peripheral vision, being what it was in the sixteenth century, wasn't lost behind the ears of fifteen-year-old, out-of-his-box, William, who objected to the decapitation of children under any circumstance. The irises of his eyes spiralled into a luminescence, a sharp pain nearly cut his inebriated brain in half, and the falling axe head stopped in midair, suspended as if time no longer existed six inches above Aletha's thick head of jet-black curly locks.

All present saw the axe floating in suspension above the child's scalp. Scarlett, Prior, Trevor Neary, James, Ignatius, and Destiny were the only people focused on the change in William's eyes. It only happened for a second. A blink of an eye cliché. Nobody was sporting a timepiece that measured seconds, or even minutes for that matter, and there were no hourglasses behind the bar. Only James of Bon understood what was happening. What the change of William's eyes meant; The boy was coming of age too soon. Or not soon enough, perhaps. Either way, he was Arthur's son, for sure.

William leapt to his left and bolted the five yards to the fireplace. He grabbed the long wooden shank of the halberd, yanked it out of suspension, and away from Aletha's head. His eyes had already returned to normal ocean blues and slightly bloodshot whites.

He threw the halberd at Scarlett as if it were a spear. The weapon was never intended to hit the prick that was riling him and insulting the innocent girls he was protecting. It was intended to demonstrate that he could aim if he chose to. The spear whizzed past the left side of Scarlett's right ear. By the time the metal tip had driven into the southeast wall, behind the stage, where no one was standing, William was William fucking Hope again. All that needed to be demonstrated or said was in his surname.

He started pacing towards the southwestern door. The people in his way could go fuck themselves. He needed to be alone.

Didn't happen that way.

Scarlett grabbed him by the throat and five back paces later William found himself pinned to the bar with a dagger to his throat.

25

Treasure of the Finest

First rule in a street fight; hit hard and run fast. Second rule; always keep a knife in your boot. William still had a lot to learn.

Scarlett pressed his forearm hard across William's chest, forcing air from the boy's lungs. Drops of William's blood trickled across the polished surface of Scarlett's dagger.

"Katherine. Her name is Katherine," said William.

The non sequitur threw Scarlett, but not enough to trod on the showmanship required of him when front and centre of the play.

"Katherine? Is this wench worth dying for?"

"She's not my sister," said William.

"Not your sister?!" said Scarlett, before turning to the crowd, "Her name is Katherine and she's not the boy's sister! What say you brethren?"

"Is the wench pretty?" from an attentive onlooker.

"How's her tits look in the moonlight?" from another.

"Is this Katherine worth living for?" asked Scarlett. He'd overdone it on the knife to the throat thing. He hadn't intended to draw blood.

"Yes," said William, who had no idea that his neck was bleeding. He simply wanted to go swimming. His head tingled, and he didn't want to hurt anyone.

"Then welcome to the living, boy" said Scarlett, removing the knife from William's neck and stowing it in his waistband. He knew then that this would be the last moment he would ever be on show before a crowd at William's expense.

"You done being an arse?" whispered William.

"Walk with me, and ignore all else," whispered Scarlett, before addressing the room, "Music, laughter, and shameless behaviour, I says!"

The musicians started stumming. Or fiddling. It was a bit off for the first three bars but fucking awesome thereafter. By the eighth bar Scarlett had all the intention of walking past James, Destiny, and Ignatius, and exiting the building directly, but Sir James of Bon was not a man to dismiss. He paused facing James.

William was already out of the door.

"You're sailing way too close to the wind," said James.

The warning wasn't lost on Scarlett, "I'm aware."

"Fix it," said James.

Scarlett nodded and exited. By the turnaround of the second phrase in the tune, Scarlett had caught up to William, and the music was fading in their ears, "Sorry about all that."

"Are you?" questioned William, stomping towards the shoreline and not slowing.

"Truly," replied Scarlett.

"You got eyes for Rosa, don't you?" said William.

"Guilty."

"She's way better than you," said William.

"That's why I want her," said Scarlett.

"No, you want her to want you."

"Do you think she will?"

"Not if you repeat that shit," said William.

"I shall never. I was wrong. I don't always like being me."

"Good. You're a proper arse when you're you."

It took them ten minutes to row to Scarlett's ship. It would have taken less, but William had taken his swim in the tumultuous waters. Few words were spoken until they had tied up the rowboat and climbed the Jacob's ladder. The ship was bathing in Caribbean waters and the light of a hundred lanterns suspended from masts and rigging. She was shrouded in a magical, celestial aura of warmth and wisdom. Scarlett jumped the gunwale first, landing squarely on the main deck.

"How do you like her?" asked Scarlett.

"Permission to come aboard, Sir?" asked William.

"Fuck's sake, yes, man!"

William slipped his backside from the gunwale and his feet touched down on the main deck of the good ship *Maiden Bride* for the first time.

"How do you like her?" repeated Scarlett.

"She's yours?"

"She belongs to no one. Never will."

"She's beautiful."

"Will you mind her as your own?" asked Scarlett.

"What?"

"Oh, you'll get to know what that means. We need rum."

Scarlett skipped up the stairs to the quarterdeck, marched past the ship's wheel, threw the door to his outer cabin open, and grabbed one of several bottles sitting atop a mahogany cabinet fixed to the starboard wall. Then he thought through his next play and grabbed a second bottle. William was on the threshold of the door, and tentatively entering the cabin.

"About-turn, young 'un," said Scarlett, handing William a bottle as he walked past and exited to the quarterdeck once again.

William followed.

The winds were falling off. It was no longer the squall and storm the sea had earlier promised. Stars were above them.

"How old are you?" asked Scarlett.

"Fifteen, I'm told," said William.

"I intend to marry her," said Scarlett.

"You've got no fucking chance," said William.

"You're likely unfortunately right," said Scarlett, purposefully diverting the importance of his next question by pulling the cork stopper from his bottle and chugging, handsomely, of course. His eyes were on William. "Fancy changing things together?"

"I can't help you change Rosa's heart. I can tell you not to be a dick from time to time."

Scarlett burst into laughter, "And I hope you shall... No, not the girl. Other things."

"What things?"

"Word is, you can sail," said Scarlett.

"Whose word?"

"Doesn't matter. Would you like to become First Mate of *Maiden Bride*?"

Scarlett let the question hang in the air. Then he slugged from his bottle. A cigarillo was missing. He should have picked it up in his cabin. Two cigarillos.

William looked around the main deck, "She's your equal, isn't she?"

Scarlett considered the younger man's observation. His brow furrowed marginally. "To whom, are you referring, Sir?"

William uncorked his bottle and placed it to his lips, "Both of them," he said, before chugging down a mouthful.

"I'll be damned," said Scarlett, "I never once thought of the sentiment."

"Katherine would tell you to break out a cigar and show me around."

"Your sister that is not your sibling?"

"My equal," said William.

Scarlett smiled. His meeting William was pure gold. He simply knew it. It was treasure of the finest. His heart swelled. Things were going to change for the remainder of their lives.

26

Tobacco Piss. Right. Makes Sense

8th November 1587

William had met Rosa Brizuela the same night he had met Scarlett. She was born as a Nitainos – so technically nobility – on the southeastern side of the island of Cuba, in the bay of Baitiquiri, her ancestry was that of the Taíno people, indigenous to the Caribbean, but with some African and Spanish mixed in for good measure. She was tall, lean, caramel complexioned, athletic and spoke with maybe the sexiest accent William had ever heard. Her father had been a chieftain, or a Cacique as it would have been described in Rosa's native tradition. Her mother had been a healer. Both had died from smallpox. Rosa had been orphaned at the tender age of twelve, her family's lands taken by the Spanish. She'd learnt the necessity of fishing for food to survive, the discipline of the Palo religion to mend her broken spirits and lived most of her formative teenage years in dire poverty. Then the fates led her path to cross that of Scarlett and William and her fortunes turned. Now she was the twenty-eight-year-old pirate capitana of a crew of ninety-six fearsome women. Not an easy task. But one she felt was not the worst job in the world.

William was bleeding. Rosa gently stroked his face.

"William. Come. We must patch you," soothed Rosa.

William struggled to sit up but managed to do so when Rosa helped him.

"Is he breathing?" asked William, indicating the Spaniard lying nearby.

"*¿Respira?*" asked Rosa of a nearby sailor named Maria Castella, who happened to be Rosa's First Mate aboard ship.

"*Sí. El esta respirando,*" said Maria, indicating that Carlos was indeed breathing.

"He's still dying!" said another tobacco chewing woman, somewhat elderly, with a gait matching her age, and a huge gold medallion hanging from a chain around her neck. She pushed through a sea of lovelies, to get to young Carlos. "He needs that spirt sent out of him and back across the ocean!"

"Really? Sophia? Really?" said Rosa.

"I'm telling you," said the elderly Sophia, with no messing in her tone, or use of the English language, "patch William's wounds and I'll fix this Carlos boy."

"How does she know my name?" asked William, "How does she know his name?"

"I know things, boy," said Sophia, before she rounded on a half dozen of the younger inhabitants of Rosa's crew.

"Ready my shrine! Ready me some chickens! And fetch me some rum!"

Sophia turned aft, pushed through a few more lady-sailors, stomped off across the deck of the ship and disappeared into an ornate little door that was the entrance to the aft castle. William could have sworn she was a female incarnation of Roger 'Paws' Prowse, but with a worse temper.

Two nearby women hoisted Carlos up between them and followed Sophia aft on deck.

"How's Scarlett?" asked Rosa.

"Erm, alive, I hope." answered William.

"You hope?"

"Long story. But I know he..."

"I miss him too," said Rosa. "What's so important about that book that summoned a man in a habit cloth to make an appearance aboard my ship?"

"You saw him?" asked William.

"We all did," said Rosa, calmly, "he was sitting on one of my oars."

"Wait a second," said William, "that was real?"

"I'm fairly certain."

William's foggy mind was trying desperately to focus on what he knew was probably important, when his attention was drawn to an open oak barrel stationed by the mainmast of Rosa's ship, and, more specifically, to the young woman perched upon it, relieving herself of urine.

"What's she doing?" asked William, "Your crew doesn't piss off the side of the ship, like every other crew in the world?"

"Oh, my gracious, I'm sorry, it's become necessary," said Rosa. "Pirating isn't what it used to be so we're getting into trading."

"Trading?"

"Textiles, to be more specific. You see, we stumbled on a process to make colours more, vibrant, is that a word?"

"Um, yeah, I guess, brighter, maybe," offered William.

"So, the girls chew tobacco, makes their pee sweeter, and we save it for a few weeks. Then we boil it below decks, add a combination of plants, depending on the colour, naturally, and take great swathes of doe-skin wool – again, traded for, not stolen – and we bathe the cloths in the boiled plant coloured wee. Brilliant, bright, vibrant colours. Easier than wielding a sword. I'm assuming you and Scarlett are still at it, given the fact that you are bleeding and stranded in the middle of the sea with a Spaniard."

"No shit?" said William.

"No *caca* allowed in the barrels," said Rosa, "just pee."

"Tobacco piss. Right. Makes sense," said William, though none of anything was making sense.

"Can you stand? enquired Rosa, "We must get you patched."

"Um, yeah, I think so," offered William, and he took to standing. Rosa steadied him through the first wobbles of his spinning head.

"What are you doing with Carlos?" asked William.

"Oh, it's all good, Sophia will work her magic with her nganga and relieve the poor man of the darkness shrouding his mind and spirit. We can't be in there. We're both bleeding. The spirit could harm us."

"You're bleeding?" asked William, finding his sea legs once again, "Shit, where? Was that my fault?"

"No, William. This is a ship full of women and it's a new moon. About a third of my crew are..."

"Oh, right, stupid, I get it."

Rosa, smiled and guided William aft along the deck while she barked a few orders to her crew, instructing them to rest oars for the evening, and prepare the ship for a stationary night watch.

"The girls are tired," said Rosa, "and this death-watch is going to last."

"The ship will be fine," said William, "there's nothing for miles."

"Thank you," said Rosa, "but you always worry, don't you?"

William understood. It took the pair about a minute to reach the aft castle of Rosa's ship, which was eighty-five feet in length, sixteen feet at the beam, displacing just about one-hundred-and-fifty tons in the water. *Doncella Escarlata* was a beautiful hybrid Galley-Frigate, with sixteen oars to a side, and with three powerful women wielding each oar she could cut through the waters of the Caribbean Sea at a top ramming speed of six knots. Scarlett had designed and built it for Rosa several years ago.

Rosa's cabin was ornately finished in balsa woods and pine. It was, if anything, homely. Perhaps even feminine, with a multitude of cushions on her bed, fluffy cream rugs on the floor, candles alight all over the mahogany furniture and an intense smell of flowers, sage, and incense. It had a central dining table, with wicker placemats, china plates and an array of silver and brass goblets.

A slim dark-skinned girl, about sixteen years of age, with long thick dreadlocks and beads woven into her hair, was standing with a small chest in her arms. William recognized both the girl and the chest as Rosa guided him to a seated position on one of the eight dining chairs by the table.

The image of a shiny axe blade nearly falling onto eight year old Aletha's head cut into the forefront of William's mind.

"Aletha," said William, "you're all grown up."

"You don't look so good, Mister William."

"Water and salt," instructed Rosa.

"Sí, Rosa, lista," said Aletha, as she opened the chest which contained an assortment of powders, needles, and threads. She laid it carefully on the table beside William, "Y el polvo."

"Gracias, Aletha," said Rosa, as she turned to William. "Strip from your shirt."

Aletha glided away tactfully to the port side of the room and grabbed a bottle of rum from within a sideboard cabinet. William was out of his bloodstained, tattered white blouse by the time the girl had returned with the bottle.

"Gracias," said Rosa, "three cups this evening, we're celebrating, and I expect you to learn. Not every day we rescue a bloody idiot male from the sea."

"Sí, señorita," said Aletha with a smile, and while she poured three generous servings of the golden rum into goblets, Rosa set about assessing the numerous cuts and scrapes on William's head, neck, left shoulder and back.

"World is changing quickly," said Rosa, "do you mind if Aletha patches you up? She doesn't get much practice and I really think she's gifted."

"No, whatever, I'm good, don't worry about me," said William.

"I'm not, but the coral in these waters is going to give you much grief if we don't cleanse and sew these wounds."

William shook his head, smiled, and received one of the goblets of rum from Aletha. "Muchas gracias."

"De nada," said Aletha.

William took a deep slug of the rum in his cup.

"The *Santa Oscuro*?" asked Rosa.

"Yep," answered William, with a nod.

"You're idiots, both of you."

"Probably."

"I know so," said Rosa, "where is he now? Saint John?"

"Kitts. Last I saw of him."

"Why?" asked Rosa, "How much gold do you need?"

"My fault," confessed William, "dreamt Katherine was on board, wanted to make sure she was alright, I guess."

Rosa, stared at William with blank expression, then turned to her young charge, "Aletha, clean his skin. Don't even try to mend his mind," said Rosa, before placing her goblet down on the table, grabbing the bottle of rum, stepping away to her bed, collapsing back and bursting into laughter.

27

Two White. One Black. What the Cluck?

Two decks directly below Rosa's rum infused giggles, the Bohique lady, Sophia, was holding up the golden 'guanín' talisman that she usually wore around her neck to the low ceiling of a small sanctum at the stern of the ship. She was chanting in an unintelligible language to most ordinary folk, but not for the half-dozen women surrounding her in a ritual dancing trance-like-state that had the stowaway, Carlos, or Tortuga, or whatever he remembered being named, pissing in his wet breeches, and crying again. His arms were suspended horizontally by two powerfully built women, and his legs were entirely numb to his body.

Three cockerels skirted the floor. Two white. One black. All of them, clucking and darting around in a manic dance.

A small table behind Sophia held an assortment of paraphernalia familiar only to priests or healers in the Palo tradition of religion; a nganga, with its assortment of bones housed in a small cauldron, several masks, candles, various figurines, books, paintings, trinkets, and statues.

Still chanting, Sophia suddenly darted forward, grabbed one of the white cockerels and slit its throat with a small white knife made of bone. She poured some of the bird's blood into her nganga, raised the dead creature above her head and approached a petrified Carlos, who was aware of everything before him, but completely unable to move or even breathe. He remained stock still with his arms spread horizontally as the two women holding him released their grip and stepped away.

Sophia spread the bird's wings and rubbed it back and forth across the Spaniard's naked chest. Her chanting now in whispers. The other women in the room had stopped everything and were completely still. The two cockerels whipping around the floor beneath Sophia's feet were frenzied, squawking, flapping, and pecking at each other. Then the two birds suddenly flopped to the deck, quite dead.

Sophia dropped the bird in her hands, stopped chanting, froze, remaining motionless for what appeared to be two hours to Carlos. In any normal reality it was more like two minutes.

Then Sophia's eyes rolled back in her head, her body rigid, and tipped over backwards like a teak plank slamming to the floor.

Tears streamed down Carlos' cheeks, yet still he couldn't move. His head pounded and throbbed, and as far as he was concerned split completely in two halves, left brain, right brain, huge open gash between.

Time simply stopped.

Until Sophia slowly sat up. Her eyes rolled back down from her skull and regained focus on Carlos.

"Heaven and hell," said the healer, "I have never given release to anything like that beasty. That son' bitch is nasty!"

Realising that the woman was addressing him, Carlos said, "What the hell just happened?"

"How do you feel?"

"I'm unsure," Carlos said, honestly, "I... where are we? Where's my book?"

"We released the spirit plaguing your mind and sent it back from whence it came."

"Alcázar."

"Is that it? Spain, am I right?"

"Yes. Segovia."

"What is your name?"

"I am, Carlos, Prince of the Asturias, of the House of Hapsburg."

"How old are you?"

"Nineteen. No. Twenty. No. Yes. I'm twenty-two. You ask a lot of questions."

"Carlos, I want you to sit down gently on the floor beside me," said Sophia, "would that be alright?"

"Yes, I believe so," said the Spaniard, and he slowly sat down.

Sophia ran the fingers of her right hand through her hair, and they came away bloody. "Ah, mierda. That's gonna hurt."

"Are you alright?" asked Carlos.

"I'll be fine," said Sophia. "Now Carlos, I don't want you to freak out, but I have some things you need to know."

Carlos stared blankly at the strange woman beside him for a moment, "Alright."

"My name is Sophia. We have just performed a ritual that has released a very dark and evil spirit that has held your mind captive. Judging by its strength, I think the spirit was many years old."

"Really?" said Carlos.

"Yes. Now don't panic, no harm will come to you," said Sophia, very delicately, "but I want you to look down at the backs of your hands."

Carlos did as he was instructed to and immediately recoiled in terror. "What the hell is happening to me? What have you done to me?"

"It's alright. It's alright," assured Sophia.

"It's not. It's not alright. What have you done?!" screamed Carlos, and he lunged for Sophia's throat.

Predicting his movements, for this was certainly not her first crazy cockerel sea-show, Sophia deftly batted the

Spaniard's hands aside and backed away. The two women who had previously been holding Carlos stepped forward in concern.

"No!" said Sophia, holding up her hands, "Step away, I'm fine. He's fine. Aren't you Carlos? Everything is good. Right?"

Carlos shook his head and sat up once again.

"Just breathe. Let me explain," said Sofia, who turned briefly to one of her assistants, "Fetch me the rum."

"Yes. I demand an explanation," cried Carlos, before softening his tone, "Please. I beg of you."

Sophia paused in her discourse as she received a fresh bottle of rum from one of the nearby crew, uncorked it, and handed it to Carlos. "Drink, it will help."

Carlos nodded, took the bottle with a shaky outstretched hand, and downed a healthy gulp of the rum. He politely offered the bottle back to Sophia. "Gracias. Please tell me."

Sophia took the bottle and drank, before looking squarely at Carlos.

"You have been held captive by a dark spirit for many years," said Sophia, knowing full well how this might sound quite ridiculous to the delicate man sitting on the floor with his old man's body and adolescent mind. "We have taken that spirit out of your body and sent it far away across the oceans. It can't harm you now. It will be seeking the one who created it and return to them. Do you understand?"

"I don't know that I understand, anything."

"That's alright. You will," said Sophia, gently, "you will soon."

Sophia had prepared for this type of conversation her entire life. Her thoughts were not so much of young Carlos, for she knew how to manage this, but more on the wickedness now sailing over the sea into the darkness of night. She was hoping that she had banished it strongly enough to prevent its return, ever.

28

The Fuck do You Make of This, Lads?

Scarlett was fixed to the *Bride's* stern gunwale beneath a lantern, atop the poop deck of his ship, staring blindly out over the dark waters. The mist was thick and unmoving. Suffocating. He was tired, and the wound in his side was stabbing. He wanted to move, but his want for repose and indulgent retrospection was stronger. A single tear fell onto his left cheek, and he wiped it away quickly with the sound of footsteps behind him.

"Beggin' pardon, Captain," said Roger 'Paws' Prowse, who was ambling up the stairs, carrying a lantern, treading carefully.

"Certainly, Roger," Scarlett said, "what's on your mind?"

"Well, do you want the good news or the bad news?" asked 'Paws'.

"Let it be the good. Always the good, on a night such as this," said Scarlett.

The Boatswain, nodded, and continued his approach. He was closely followed by Martin 'Mumbles' No-Name.

"Martin reckons he got the full count fer you, Captain," said 'Paws'. "Reckon he ought' be the one doing the tellin'."

'Paws' stepped aside, allowing 'Mumbles' to step forward. "Beggin' me nerve, Capt," said a somewhat bashful 'Mumbles'.

"Not at all, Martin, what have you gotten to?"

"Well, all of it, I think."

"Quite so. Let's have the tally," said Scarlett.

"Right, Capt," said 'Mumbles', as he fanned through several pages in a scruffy little journal, "where are we now?"

Scarlett, half smiled as he watched old 'Mumbles' decipher his own notes. He had a stubby little pencil in between his fingers, licking the nub before underlining something of obvious importance in his book. "Right, there it is," said the old boy.

'Mumbles' looked up from his numbers, "She's a bloody big ship be there, Capt, that I can tell ye, and she's proper good loaded."

"Is she, Martin?" said Scarlett, holding back his smile, "How so?"

"And I'll tell you this, Capt', she's damn well creepy in her holds. I been shiverin' my way through the count all day," said 'Mumbles' "that's why me notes is a bit wobbly, see."

"I understand, Martin, you've done well. She's carrying gold then?"

Scarlett's enquiry was met with wide sparkling eyes from the old stores man. "Bloody right she is, Capt. I ain't never seen so many little statues, and crowns, and chains, and rings, and earrings and shit that I couldn't figure out what's it's ever meant to be. Here, I drew a few sketches here somewhere..."

"Perhaps, you can show me details later, Martin," said Scarlett.

"Right, Capt, sorry," said 'Mumbles'. "Well, as you know, a Castilian mark is eight and three-eighths pesos, and a peso is twenty-five-gram o' silver, and if you figure there is about a hundred pounds to your average chest, about nineteen-hundred-and-fifty pesos in each, well she's carrying fourteen chests so that's just over twenty-seven-thousand pieces of eight."

"Pesos."

"Right, Capt. But that ain't it, see, 'cause she's got seven chests of marks, eight more chests of coins I ain't never seen before, and I ain't even got to counting how many pearls is in the pearl chests, and there's eighteen of them in total. As well the rubies, and opals, and emeralds and diamonds. And I'll give them Spaniards credit for organisin', because they separated all the jewels out by colours in different chests, but those chests are slightly smaller, I'd say they comes in at about eighty pounds a' piece."

"Right, and how many of those?" asked Scarlett, patiently.

"Oh, there's fourteen and a half of them, Capt," 'Mumbles' went on, "but I didn't count in the necklaces, and pendants, and such because they went in different chests, what with them havin' a mix of different colour stones and pearls and that all together, and there is only five of them chests. And I reckon that was the creepiest bit of the day opening them. Felt like…"

"What? Felt like…"

"Well, I feels like a right kid fer sayin' this, Capt…"

"Go ahead, Martin, you're anything but a child and I'm not judging," encouraged Scarlett.

"Well, it felt like, somethin' was watchin' o'er me shoulder the whole time I was openin' those boxes. Feckin' gave me the right creeps, it did."

"Is that so? I don't suppose you found a young woman down there among the treasures, Martin."

"Oh, haha… brilliant," laughed 'Mumbles' "thank ye fer understandin' Capt, that would have been feckin' creepy. Try an' avoid them women, I does, never knew when they were prone to attack, back in the day, Capt, that's fer sure."

Scarlett laughed.

"I'll second that Martin," said 'Paws', unable to mask his spluttering.

"That's quite the count, Martin," said Scarlett.

"Oh, I ain't done yet, by a long ways, Capt'. There's tons of silks, and tapestries, they got saltpetre by the barrel, tea, opiums, sugar, cinnamon, nutmegs, ambergris, they got plants I ain't never seen afore, all dried out..." said 'Mumbles', as he buried his head down and flicked frantically through the dog-eared pages of his little journal, his excitement infectious.

"Maybe it's best we save the finer points for the morning, Martin, it's getting late," said Scarlett."

'Mumbles' looked to his captain, "Right, Sir, right, that'd be best. It's a lot," he said, "oh, I brought you this, saw it, an' I thought, this'd be best in the Captain's hands, fer all you've done fer us all and that. And Mister 'Paws', he agreed."

"That I did, Captain," said 'Paws', "I'm in accord with Martin on this."

Scarlett looked down as 'Mumbles' pulled out small object from behind his back and 'Paws' stepped forward with his lantern to throw light on it.

It was a dagger. Its handle and scabbard appeared to be made from a multi-coloured pearl like material, inwrought, or mounted within an extraordinarily ornate, silver webbing. Scarlett pulled the knife from the scabbard to reveal a dual-edged steel blade, eight inches in length, mirror polished, with traces of the same intricate web design engraved minutely into its surface.

"It's beautiful," said Scarlett, sincerely. "My thanks, lads."

"Don't thank us yet, Captain," said 'Paws', "we ain't gotten to the bad news."

"Ah, yes, I recall the mention," said Scarlett.

"Martin," said 'Paws'.

"Well, Capt, if you account for the *Dark* is two-hundred an' some feet along the keel, fifty at the beam and she got four decks and a quarter of five, and what with the *Bride's* smaller, and her holds are four fifths full of the Queen's bounty from our travels..."

"Ah, I begin to see your heading, lads," said Scarlett.

"It ain't all gonna fit aboard us, Captain, not a chance," said 'Paws'.

"And, well as that..." said 'Mumbles'.

"Martin, stow that one a ways, or I'll have it..." interjected 'Paws', quickly, then trailed off when 'Mumbles' recoiled back a pace like a six-year-old about to be slapped.

"Roger, enough. Stow what? Let it be shared," said Scarlett.

"Oh, it ain't nothin' Captain," said 'Paws', "it's just... well, some of the boys..."

"I ain't told them anything of what's on that ship, Captain," interjected 'Mumbles, "I swear by it."

"That's true is that, Captain. Martin ain't told 'em nowt all day, though they been pressin' him," said 'Paws'.

"I understand. Thank you, Martin," said Scarlett.

"O' course, Captain," said 'Mumbles', humbly.

"Thing is, Captain, some of the boys... well, they're beginnin' to think that the gold on that ship..." said 'Paws'.

"Spit it out, Roger," demanded Scarlett.

"Well, that some of it might be cursed on account that... well, you know, 'cause William ain't come back to us..." said 'Paws', his words trailing off into the mist.

Scarlett considered the murky meanings for a good five seconds of silence, then he took a deep breath and turned, resting his hands on the stern gunwale, looking out over the sea.

"I understand, gentlemen."

"Sorry, Captain, I knows it's stupid an all..." said 'Paws'.

"I get it," said Scarlett, and he turned back to the two crewmen. "You've done well today, lads, both of you. I mean it..."

The lantern above Scarlett's head began flickering violently, as did the one in the hand of the Boatswain. But the wind remained unmoved. The mist, a solid block of grey vapour, darkened on the starboard side of the ship, becoming ominously blackened, and it didn't go unnoticed by any of the three men on the poop deck. Scarlett felt a warmth growing in his right palm and the fingers still wrapped around the hilt of the dagger. He instinctively raised it for inspection and discovered that the silver webbing was glowing a luminant sapphire blue. Curious, he withdrew the knife from the scabbard to find that the intricate engravings on the steel blade were glimmering in the same bright colours. He held it up towards 'Paws' and 'Mumbles'.

"The fuck do you make of this, lads?" asked Scarlett.

Curiosity dawned on the men's faces and an answer would surely have been forthcoming for their captain, but words and faces were suddenly engulfed in a swirling dark mist pouring over the starboard gunwale. The black weirdness consumed them; it was frightfully cold, arid dry, and textured with strands of pure hatred, but as quickly as it had rolled in, it maintained a course to the north across the beam of the deck, disappeared over the port side gunwale and was absorbed once again in the motionless grey mist of the night's tropical air. The knife in Scarlett's hand grew cold in his palm, and its webbing returned to plain silver.

The lanterns ceased flickering and returned to their former soft, warm glow.

All three men stood in silence and solidarity, hoping whatever that thing was, it was sailing on over the ocean and would never return to the *Maiden Bride* and the good souls aboard her.

29

Fetch Me the Sugar

9th November 1587

M atheo y Valois was the most gifted knight in the Spanish Realm, a devout Catholic, and the adopted son of Philip II, who was King of Spain, Portugal, Naples, Sicily, and Lord of the Seventeen providences of the Netherlands.

Matheo loved his father, and the feelings between them were mutual. But he was not his real father. He was just an old man.

The tournament being held was in honour of Philip's late third wife Elizabeth of Valois, for she had adored the excitement and passions generated by the brave contestants and their skill with swords, bows, spears, horse, and lance in the jousting, and, well, all of it. The chivalry and pageantry. The colours. The cheers of the crowd. The song and dance and revelry.

Matheo had loved his adopted mother, too. And she had adored him. But the truth was he had been a difficult child for her.

That had changed when the court Scribe had blessed him with charms of his making. The spells had been more than enough but had come a little too late. His mother had died when Matheo was five. Old enough for him to remember the pains he had caused her as a cantankerous little brat. But too soon for him to make it up to her as a growing boy. He was now twenty-three.

Regret. A powerful reminder of the fragility of life. How easily it can be taken away. These tournaments were living proof.

Sitting atop his horse, a powerful, pure white stallion of the Lipizzan breed, named 'Mono' – the beast was indeed a bit of a monkey times – the pair were some distance away from the fray, beside the peaceful Rio Eresma, looking down at the steady flow of purity held in its waters, and Matheo was readying his mind for the forthcoming day's events.

For you mother.

Matheo turned his horse away from the tranquil scene and galloped off. The shadow of the great castle, Alcázar of Segovia, loomed above him and a three-thousand strong crowd attending in the arena, and he was promptly met in earnest by his loyal servant, confidant, friend and second for the games, Antonio de Guevara.

"*¿Estamos listos, Antonio?*" said Matheo cheerfully, enquiring in a shorthand the two men had long since developed, if everyone else was ready for them.

"*Sí, mi Señor,*" Antonio replied, with just a hint of a wink.

Out across the arena from them, King Philip was presiding in the Royal box, central to the pomp and circumstance, surrounded by other dignitaries, of course. Matheo knew many of them. Some he liked. Some he didn't. And he trusted none. His father had tried to change his opinion on that many times.

His father was a good man. A noble man. But too trusting. And too loving.

Matheo looked up at his father, and down over the crowd. He could feel the animal tense underneath him. Its hunger for battle.

Matheo sensed the mood of the arena change as he accepted the first lance of the day from Antonio. Spain's first knight was going to war, and the crowd hushed in anticipation.

He focused downfield and looked over his first opponent, sitting atop his horse. A disgusting Italian no-name, wearing inferior armour, accepting an inferior lance from his peasant second.

Matheo waited for the flag to be raised and thought of his mother. Regret.

He slapped the visor of his steel helmet down, dug his heels solidly into his stallion's flanks, positioned the lance in his arm and was on the move before the flag had even been fully lowered.

The two knights drove at each other with courage and precision, horses snorting, hooves pounding, straw and mud flying. Complete focus now. Time slowing... and slowing...

CRUNCH!

Matheo drove his lance straight and true, firmly into the heart of his opponent, knocking the man clean off his horse and winning the bout outright. Just like that. Too easy. Next.

He slowed his horse and tossed the shattered lance to the ground as he reached the end of the run. The crowd was cheering their champion once again and it felt good.

But something was wrong.

Matheo snapped his visor open and could sense something in the contrite expression on his second's face as Antonio looked up at him. He jumped down from his horse, gave a cursory wave and bow to his audience in the arena, but his focus was on Antonio.

"What is it?" Matheo demanded in his native tongue.

"Well, Sire... there is news."

Matheo took the man by his elbow and urged him aside, away from the masses, towards several tents set up for the contestants and their teams. Matheo's tent was obviously the largest as he was on home ground. It was his castle that formed the dramatic backdrop. He pushed through the door of the dwelling and addressed several servant staff inside. "Leave us."

The room emptied, immediately.

"What news, Antonio?" Matheo questioned.

"Lady Katherine Cecil..."

"Yes?"

"Our network informs that she is to be, or is betrothed already, they say..."

"Spit it out man," snapped Matheo.

"On New Year's Day, the announcement will be made by the English that she is to be wed to the Scarlett Buccaneer."

Matheo stared blankly through his servant for a few seconds. "We are sure of this?"

"The source is most reliable, Sire. Our best man at Windsor."

Matheo turned away and paced aside for a moment's thought. "Lord Burghley is a two-faced piece of shit."

"Yes, Sire. It would seem so," said Antonio, the colour draining from his face.

"Seem so? I fucking know so. I'm going to the homage," Matheo said, "get me out of this armour."

"But, Sire, you are due with swords in less..."

"Now!"

Antonio began helping his lord and master out of his armour and was dragged out of the tent with Matheo's urgent fury to leave. They pushed through a few people milling about and made their way to Mono who was standing patiently, probably wondering what was happening next, more jousting, or just swordplay.

"Help me with this," said Matheo, as he started stripping his horse of its shiny steel set of armour clothing. Antonio was quick to step up to the task.

"Horse up and follow me to the castle," said Matheo. "Fetch me the sugar and make it the good stuff. Silver shit and everything. I'll meet you at the tower of homage."

"Sure thing, Sire."

When the last plate of armour dropped to the ground, Matheo jumped onto Mono's back, and drove the animal away from the masses, back towards the river, before galloping for the castle, with its massive stone walls and fairy tale turrets. Though the edifice was approximately a mile away it towered above the racing duo, and it was all uphill for the poor animal doing the running, as it was constructed on top of a huge rock formation cut by the convergence of the Rio Ciguinela and the Rio Eresma. At this point, all that was going through the horse's mind was, *Thank Helios I'm not wearing that clunky tin suit for this one!*

The edifice was a fortress surrounded by woodlands, with deep moats cut all around to make the chances of enemy infiltration an impossibility. As castles went, this had to be the most secure in all of Europe.

Matheo and his four legged 'monkey' raced for the drawbridge, slammed over its wooden planks, crossed the moat, and entered the castle. The imposing two hundred-and-forty-foot-high tower of Juan II loomed above them. Matheo dismounted and immediately dashed through the entrance vestibule, dog-legged through to the 'patio de armas', where he completely ignored all the stunning archways he used to dance in and around as a child, carried on through to the clock yard and slowed down at the far west end of the castle and its tower of homage so he could catch his breath. He propped himself with his back against a wall and focused on calming his fury.

Antonio arrived five minutes later, flush faced, carrying a circular silver platter covered in an extraordinary display of sugar-coated sweetcakes, shaped into tiny sculptures inspired from the animal kingdom; lions, tigers, a bear on its hind legs, a monkey, and others. What made the whole thing perhaps more art than a lunatic's dessert menu was the peak of perfection in this delicate confectionary; a gilded dragon swooping down over a gleaming crystal blue and silver pond made of melted sugar.

"Jesus, brother," said Matheo, "the little prick is going to think it's Christmas."

"You said lay on the silver shit," said Antonio, chuckling.

"Catch your breath," said Matheo, taking up the weight of the tray in his hands, "I'll see what he's got to say."

Matheo crossed to the west side of the room and approached a wooden door. He knocked out of politeness but didn't wait for an answer before opening the door and entering. He faced a modest sized semi-circular room with two windows and a fireplace with glowing embers alive. The space was warmer than other rooms in the castle and smelled of orange and burnt oak. The walls were lined with shelves from floor to... well, roof, as the crown of the room was domed and covered in ornate timber carvings of sinister little gremlins, demons, and devils. The shelves were stacked with all manner of books and rolls of parchment. The stone floor was covered in a dark red rug inlaid with numerous symbols, pentagons, and circles. An elaborately carved desk, with a gently sloping top, and what looked to be snakes and other slithery serpents for legs, sat between the windows. A small side table sat beside the desk. Sitting on a stool in front of the desk was a nine-year-old boy with white hair, who was scribbling on a substantial roll of heavy parchment, with a quilled feather pen.

"Katherine Cecil is to marry the Scarlett Buccaneer," said Matheo, firmly.

The boy looked up from his work. He had a cute face and was wearing rounded spectacles.

His eyes were a deep shade of pure amber, and he was smiling.

"Is she?" said the young Scribe.

"Yes, she bloody is! Our spies are all over it and..."

"And this vexes you, got it," said the Scribe. "What are those sweets?"

"Don't you get it?"

"I might, but come, lay the tray down here," said Scribe – for unsurprisingly that was his name, though in Spanish it would of course be 'Escriba', so let's give him due respect – "I'm hungry."

Matheo closed the door behind him, crossed the room and placed the saccharine breakfast on the table beside the young academic's desk. Escriba raised his glasses and leant over to peruse his food choices.

"Oh, come on, you have all day to eat. We can't let this happen, I want her as my Queen and you know it," barked Matheo, with increasing frustration.

"Aren't you supposed to be in a battle or something today?"

"Yes," said Matheo, "and with you I feel like I'm in a worse one."

"I must say, the kitchen has outdone itself with the drag-on. How have they made it look like it's flying?" mused Escriba, lowering his spectacles, leaning right in, and looking for the answer to his question, not Matheo's.

"It would be good for the English Realm, I suppose," said Escriba, nonchalantly.

"What? That's what you've got!" cried Matheo. "There won't be an English bloody Realm when I'm done with the war, and I need her as my Queen, you idiot! Over here and over there!"

"Speaking of Queens, I should be certain that Elizabeth is making Katherine's decision for her. Good for the people and all that type of whatnot."

"Fuck the people," snarled Matheo, turning away.

"You say that now because you desire the girl," said Escriba, "but you'd do well to learn from Elizabeth. She's very canny."

Escriba ran his fingers over the little sugar animals, opted for a small owl-shaped delicacy, and bit off its head. He savoured the taste for a moment before continuing, "Have you proposed marriage to Katherine yourself?"

"Well, no not yet, not formally," admitted Matheo.

"Then perhaps you should bend a knee, or have lunch, or dinner with her, or whatever it is that you kids do these days to get laid in eternal bliss," said Escriba, before chomping another bite from the owl. He went for the feet this time, leaving behind a little feathery torso with wings.

"And how might I best do that?" enquired Matheo, "If you would be so kind with your eternal wisdom."

"Greenwich at New Year's, of course," said Escriba. "And if Katherine herself doesn't want to marry this Scarlett fellow, then maybe you have a shot, if you're charming... no, let me correct myself, if you don't fuck things up."

"Greenwich, huh?" mused Matheo, "And if she says no?"

Escriba munched the last of his bird-cake, wings-and-all, and held up a finger requesting a pause while he chewed and swallowed.

"Let me put it to you this way," said Escriba, "a yes or a no is irrelevant. Would it not be better for you to be wed with her back here in Spain, under the true guidance of our Catholic Pope?"

Matheo squinted his eyes at Escriba for a moment until the facts clicked in his brain and his eyes opened fully again.

"I think I have a few battles I must get on with," said Matheo, "mustn't keep my people waiting. Enjoy your breakfast."

Matheo left the room. Escriba got back to his breakfast, smiled and his eyes became flickering stones of amber with pupils resembling those of a cat...

Twenty minutes later, Matheo was back on his horse by the river, both fully clad in shiny silver-plated armour, staring at the calm, clear water running past, cleansing his mind, and centring his focus for his next challenge in the arena. He was about to get to the part about his dead mother and regret and killing and all those good things, but the water below him became darkened and cloudy and smothered in a swirling inky mist that rose and swept slowly up the bank towards him, engulfing both he and his stallion. It was frigid cold, arid dry, and interwoven with fibres of pure hatred that cut into his mind and every sinew of his body and soul. Mono bucked up violently on his hind quarters and Matheo tumbled backward, crashing to the ground.

30

The Love Rule Book

9th November 1587

Rosa's Galley was under oar heading north with the rising sun burning through the last of the night's mists shrouding the starboard side of her ship. William was sitting on a small open deck at the bow with his back against the fore facing wall of a three demi-cannon turret housing. He was literally under the gun. *El Libro de Reglas de Amor* was in his hands, and he still hadn't figured out how to unlock the silver clasp on the little book. He was fighting the urge to toss the damned thing overboard when Aletha dropped down from the gun housing and landed with a delicate thump beside him. She was carrying a silver carafe and two copper cups in her hands.

"*Buenos días Señor,*" said Aletha, "*¿Puedo ofrecerte un café?*"

William looked up at the girl and was about to answer *'yes'* – or possibly, *'oh, shit, yes, that would be fantastic, and I'll pay for your entire university education'* – when Rosa presented her beautiful face between two of the cannon above William's head.

"Aletha, use your English tongue, *por favor*, it's not every day we have an English pirate scallywag of a man to practice with."

"Sí, Capitana," said Aletha looking up, before returning her focus on William, "Mister William, would you, care for, a cup..."

"Fresh cup..." corrected Rosa, from above.

"...would you care for, a *fresh* cup of coffee?" Aletha finished.

"Ah, sí eso seria excelente..." said William, smiling for the first time in a long while.

"William!" Rosa bellowed, for she understood sarcasm as well as any other female capitana with a crew of ninety-six women, even though she was, technically, the only one on the planet.

William looked overhead, "Sorry, couldn't resist," and when refocusing on Aletha he said, "Thank you, that would lift my spirits this morning, Aletha. It is very thoughtful and kind of you."

Aletha smiled a bright, beaming, innocent smile. If she knew how powerful a tool it would be in her future, she would probably spend more hours practising it than her command of the English language, but that was not her natural way of doing things and she would never need to, so she simply handed one of the cups to William and filled it from the steaming carafe.

William took a sip of the much-needed refreshment. "As beautiful as your smile this morning, Aletha, thank you."

"Willlliiiaaamm," came as a warning, before Rosa jumped down and landed on the bow deck beside Aletha. She had a steaming cup of coffee in her hand.

"What do you say, Aletha?"

Aletha thought about it for a moment. "You are most welcome, William, and stop flirting with me, you are too old for me, and you maybe are, as a, pervert."

Rosa howled with laughter, in full appreciation of her protégé. "Nailed it, girl, goodness me, you buried him right there."

William burst out laughing. "Alright, you got me, Aletha, bravo."

"What is, bravo?" asked Aletha.

"A word for approval, and good, and he's right, well done," said Rosa, "you've filled my cup already, fill your own."

Aletha, who was clearly no slouch, immediately filled her copper mug.

"My angel," Rosa said, "William, Aletha's here to check your wounds. The coffee's got rum in it, just in case..."

"The rum's got coffee in it, I noticed," said William, "and sure thing, Aletha."

William twisted to place 'The Love Rule Book' and his coffee mug down beside him on the deck and inadvertently spilled some of the hot brew onto the cover, "Oh, shit," said William, naturally, before wiping his hand across the spillage instinctively to limit any stains on Carlos' prized treasure. The leather cover of the book became translucent in the places smudged with the hot liquid. William squinted, then blinked to clear his eyes, to be certain he was registering the transformation. The semi-transparent smudges revealed a spiral maze of silver walls perhaps an eighth-inch high with a tiny iridescent blue pearl caught inside. A freaking puzzle after all!

"Shit!" exclaimed William, "Look at this."

"What?" asked Rosa.

"Sit down."

Rosa did so, taking a seated position beside William on the deck. William snatched up the book, but by the time he presented it to Rosa, the cover had completely returned to its normal scruffy leather appearance, with its embossed spiral and title.

"What am I looking at?" asked Rosa.

"Wait a second."

William stretched out his legs, laid the book in his lap, grabbed his hot mug of rum/coffee, and dribbled a helping of the dark liquid over the book's cover. Once again, the cover became translucent, and the full spiral maze was re-vealed.

"Wow, that's...", gasped Rosa.

"I know, right," said William, as he picked up the book and wobbled it gently in his hands. The blue pearl followed his movements, skirting along the pathway of the maze, before the cover gradually turned completely opaque and reformed as beaten leather once more.

"Is it the heat or the rum?" asked Rosa.

"I don't know," said William.

"It must be the heat," voiced Aletha, who was peering intently at the curious proceedings.

"Why, angel?" asked Rosa.

"The rum, it is just alcohol, it will, *evaporar*, in air with heat, no?"

"Evaporate," said Rosa.

"*Sí, sí*, evaporate, *evapora, cualquiera*," said Aletha, rolling her bright adolescent eyes, "it's still gone, no? Elim-ination processes, means, heat, hot, not rum. *Sí*?"

"Never let her marry," said William, turning his head to Rosa.

"What? Why not?" questioned Rosa.

"Because her future husband is fucked already," said William, with a broad smile.

Aletha burst into giggles and turned away.

"I very much doubt I can stop her," said Rosa, conspiratorially.

William raised his cup, "To Aletha, may she marry the right fellow."

"Aletha, and her tortured man," pronounced Rosa, clinking her cup with William's, before they took healthy gulps of their drinks.

William placed his all but empty cup down on the deck and concentrated on the small, mysterious volume in his lap.

"Aletha, would you like to see a parlour trick?" asked William.

"What is parlour trick?" asked the girl.

"It's like magic," clarified Rosa.

William stretched his arm out and offered his hand up to Aletha, "Take my hand in yours."

"William." said Rosa.

"Sshhh."

Aletha put down the carafe, crouched beside William and took his hand in hers.

"Do you want hot or cold?" asked William, innocently.

Aletha thought about the question for a few seconds and answered with a mild trepidation in her voice, "Cold."

"Thus, shall it be," said William.

Aletha stared first into William's eyes then instinctively down at their locked hands. A tingling sensation entered her palm and spread out to the tips of her fingers.

"Aaahhgghh," voiced Aletha, and almost pulled away.

"It's fine, stay with me."

Aletha bit her lip and relaxed a bit. William smiled. Aletha felt her hand begin to grow cold from within. Like diving deep in the ocean in winter, but her hand was steadily becoming colder and colder. The feeling began to trace up her wrist and into her forearm.

William unlocked his grasp.

Aletha immediately felt a normal return of heat pouring back into her fingertips and palm. William smiled and flicked a charming, raised eyebrow in the girl's direction. Rosa simply shook her head and drank a slug of rum from her cup.

"How do you do that?" asked Aletha.

"Honestly, I don't know, I just think it," said William.

"You must, to show me how, please," said Aletha.

"When you get married, William will show you, it will help cool the temperature of your home, how's that?" said Rosa.

William laughed. Aletha pouted, then relaxed into a smile.

"How's the Spaniard?" asked William.

"Sleeping. Sophia's lying down too," said Rosa, "she bumped her head last night."

"Is she alright?"

"She's breathing. Doesn't follow that she's ever alright."

William smiled, placed his hands on either side of the book, thumbs wrapped onto the edges of the cover and held it firmly over his outstretched legs. A few seconds passed and the same transformation began across the book's cover, the spiral gradually being revealed, with the translucence edging in from both sides. William concentrated, tipped the book gently, this way and that, such that the blue pearl in the maze made its way inwards to a central vanishing point. The pearl dropped into a tiny hole, disappeared, and the silver clasp on the right-hand side of the book gave a firm... 'CLICK'.

"Well, open the thing!" exclaimed Rosa.

William released the pressure his thumbs were exerting and opened the book's cover.

There were no words. No lettering. No symbols. No numbers. Nothing, but...

A small, shoulder height portrait of a stunning young woman, captured in rich oils on canvas with a darkened background, an emerald light enhancing her warmth, beauty, and the unfathomable depths of her sage green eyes.

William knew her well, once upon a time, in a land, far, far away... *Katherine*.

31

Her Nose is a Bit Off

The morning mood aboard the *Maiden Bride* was not what it should have been, given that the majority of the day had been assigned to transferring an absolute fortune in gold, silver, gemstones, and other riches from the *Santa Oscuro's* hull to the *Bride's*. Roger Prowse was having a tough time, partly because there were very strict protocols in place regarding the separation of the Queen's treasure and that of the fresh bounty. In part, because there were myriad complex repairs to attend to before they could be underway and heading across the open Atlantic Ocean. Partly because the bow of the ship had been shot to shit by the Spanish. But mostly because the men undertaking those tasks were quibbling like a hundred-and-twenty-four teenage girls on a school field trip to a slaughterhouse, not that 'Paws' ever had the pleasure of managing such an excursion personally. He knew this though; the *Bride's Banter* was lacking, and the insults had moved far away from the natural slagging of each other's sisters, mothers, brothers, race, colour, or creed as a mechanism for distraction, or letting off emotional steam. The normal tiredness, frustrations tempered with humour, and kindness in unification had jumped the gunwales of the ship. The pettiness between the crew was becoming divisive and just plain mean as the sun slowly rose above the isle of Saint Kitts and the broken lower yards of the foremast.

Old 'Paws' had a fair notion of the reasons for the men's behaviour.

Phases, cycles, stages, call 'em what you will. All connected, innit.

Their captain was bedridden, struggling to move from a fever that had broken out and completely incapacitated him. His collapse on the quarterdeck, during his usual jovial address to the men of the morning watch had seriously hurt morale, for sure, yet was understandable given that the man had been gut shot the previous day. Preemptive grief perhaps.

Shaky territory as moods will have it.

Notwithstanding, it was the loss of the captain's First Mate, William, the crew's inspiration, and anchor in the daily perils at sea that was perhaps – no not perhaps – it fecking well *was* the reason the crew was having a collective cycle with the worst outbursts that 'Paws' had ever known a crew to inflict upon each other.

Denial stage of grief perhaps. Givin' up too soon by my reckonin'.

The answers, or mysteries, to most things at sea were generally attached to cycles; in time, tides and luminance of the moon.

How do I sets about explainin'? Can't hardly holler, 'Ere boys, gather round, men got monthlies too you know', can I?

All the same 'Paws' was in charge for a phase and he sought out John Prior, before pulling the man aside quietly, "Now quietly John, walk with me fer a spell, if you would."

John fell in line with 'Paws' as the men cut a crafty tack amidships to the leeward gunwale.

"Ere, John, now what if I was to sets about explainin' cycles to the boys as part reason fer their bitchin?"

"New moon; floppy cock. Full moon; stonker on proper, like?"

"Well, I wasn't gonna go there, per se."

"Oh, right, good. Had me worried you might be losin' yer..."

"I ain't lost nothin' o that sort yet as far as I remember," said 'Paws'.

Prior smiled, "Been a while fer us all ain't it, Mister Prowse."

"Times, tides, and light by way of the moon. The effect on the boy's synchronised mood cycles," said 'Paws'.

"Synchronised. I likes that 'un. I'll save that up fer Bately, see if he thinks it's some sort of beaver's nest or such," said Prior, before thinking through the connotations of 'Paws'' question. "Well, I suppose it's worth a go an' all. Men ain't so different as to women in moody cycles. Fer mostly I'll say. Not sure we should be talkin' about it today or any day like this 'un min'. Hardly stuff or season to toughen em' up this mornin' like, is whass I means."

"Aye, yer right. I was just..." started 'Paws'.

"Oh, we're all at a loss, Mister Prowse. But I'll say this, I fer one ain't grievin' yet. William's a wily bastard."

'Paws' half smiled and nodded, "Thanks, John."

"Thank you, Mister Prowse," said Prior before taking his leave from the Boatswain and moving off across the deck.

Martin 'Mumbles' No-Name was one of only two crewmen that seemed to be unaffected by the crew's seemingly collective 'menstruation'. He was steadfastly working through his little journal and documenting every single move of the Spanish treasure's relocation from ship to ship. 'Paws' and 'Mumbles' had agreed that the most unmistakably valuable chests be stored first. They'd wait for Scarlett's instruction on the expensive silks, spices, dyes, and the like. 'Mumbles' was as proud and happy as 'Paws' had ever known the old boy to be. The challenge was rejuvenating him. He was either consumed with happiness because of it, and the fact that he was now a rich man, or because he knew that 'menstruation' was derived from the latin word *'mensis'* and related to the moon phase through the greek word *'mene'*, and just like every other cycle in life, all things would eventually come to pass. 'Paws' also considered that technically 'Mumbles' must surely have long since hit 'men-o-pause', so his hormones had levelled out and he no longer gave a fuck.

The only other merry seaman aboard seemed to be Head Carpenter, Robert 'Chips' Stuart. A tall, lean, man of forty years, with white-grey hair, keen blue eyes, and a complexion that never suntanned past rose-pink, 'Chips' was of Scottish Protestant descent, from a family that had emigrated to the Irish Midlands generations ago. He could drink any Irishman under the table with his own whiskey, and never seemed to be affected no matter how much he consumed, which was a proven fact that the big fella Shamus O'Reilly had learnt the hard way.

'Paws' made his way forward across a main deck teaming with activity and landed in beside 'Chips', who was overseeing two men cutting through a busted pine yardarm to form new planks that were needed to repair the prow of the *Bride's* hull. A six-foot by four-foot hole had been made in the deck, which allowed two men, one on either end of a six-foot long-toothed ripsaw to push and pull their way through the length of circular pine spar. A normal enough operation, requiring a degree of skill and plenty of elbow grease. The thing is that, to operate the saw efficiently, one man had to be the 'Top dog' and enjoy the pleasures of fresh air on the open main deck. The other man, technically the 'Underdog', was a deck below with his hands on the opposite end of the six-foot-long saw, pushing and pulling in unison with the 'Top dog' and that was, in short, the shit end of the stick, because most of the rough sawdust and chips from the cutting ended up in the man's mouth, nose and eyes. And for Dye Bant, the 'Underdog' situation he was in was very much to his disliking, as he looked upward through the dust and flakes, through the hole in the deck.

"Aaarrraghh, pppeeecckkkaa, fuck, shit, purrggghhh," said Dye, for the umpteenth time, "It's not right, see, not, ppeecckkka, not that I'm begrudgin' but you're a bastard, your sister's a bastard, and your mother, well, she's...atichewww... well, she's a total bastard for birthin' you in the first place!"

"Stop your whinin', Taffy, sooner we get this done, the sooner we goes home," said Jim Dolby.

"Fuck... you, aarragghhh, jackoff codpiece... peecckkka, shit," spluttered Dye.

Above deck, 'Paws' tapped Robert 'Chips' Stuart on the shoulder, "Walk with me, Robert."

The two men stepped away from the saw cutting duo and made their way east along the keel, fore of the mainmast.

"I need an estimate. When can we be underways?" asked 'Paws'.

"Okay, erm, Jees, hard to say, you know," said 'Chips', "the men ain't on form, you know."

"I know that, but I need somethin' fer the Captain," said 'Paws'.

"Okay. Okay. Well, maybe three days," offered 'Chips', "maybe, you know."

"Bugger," said 'Paws', "I was hopin' on two."

Robert twisted his lips, focusing his craftsman's brain, and scouted the various labour activities taking place all around them. 'Paws' did the same.

"Okay, well, we'll see, but..." said 'Chips'.

"But what?"

"Well, we could probably stow some repairs for during the sail, but..."

"But what?"

"The Captain," said 'Chips'.

"Aye, he's not goin' to set out without a tidy *Bride*," said 'Paws'.

Robert twisted his lips again, this time by way of expressing "exactly", and the two men walked fore along the deck where they arrived beside a seven feet high temporary timber box-scaffold. The *Maiden Bride's* figurehead was centred within the framework. It had been damaged in the cannon fire and removed from its location underneath the bowsprit of the ship for repair.

"Captain ain't goin' anywhere 'til she's mended," said 'Chips' to Roger Prowse, before looking up and addressing the two men sitting atop the scaffold. "Okay, how's the progress on the Captain's *maiden*, boys?"

"Slow, bein' honest," said Ted 'Tumbles' Turner. "Capt' gave us order not to use timbers from the dark, so we've had to..."

"Okay, yeah, I know, I know," said 'Chips', 'she's comin' along though, is she?"

Robert launched himself onto the lower stages of the scaffold and turned back, looking down at the Boatswain, "I'll have a better answer fer ya in a while, Roger."

"Aye, get on there Rob, I'll be, here, somewhere," said 'Paws', before turning aft and stomping away.

Robert climbed up to the work deck of the scaffold and sat down beside 'Tumbles' and Richard Bately, both of whom had tool belts around their waists and chisels in hand. A scattering of off-cuts of various woods, saws, hammers, and pots of glues, paints, and brushes lay around them.

"Okay, Jees, she's not lookin' too shabby, boys, you're doing alright, you know," said 'Chips', coming face to face with the statue. "Something about her nose is a bit, off, maybe."

"I said that just now, didn't I Richard?" offered Ted 'Tumbles'.

"He did, you did, we've been trying to figure it," said young Bately.

"Okay, hand me the picture there," said 'Chips'.

Bately offered up a portrait of a lightly dark-skinned young woman done in oils, on a small stretched-linen canvas. She had long dark hair, pale, ice-blue eyes, full lips, and was wearing several chains of dark-coloured pearls around her neck.

'Chips' studied the image closely.

"We thought it best to use teak, but we'd have to be pullin' the Capt's cabin apart," offered 'Tumbles'.

"Okay, no, not a reasonable option," said 'Chips', maintaining his gaze on the portrait.

"We got some elm from the stores," Bately said, "but we wasn't sure how to splice it in across her right cheek."

"We was sayin' that just now, wasn't we Richard?" said 'Tumbles'.

"Truth is, we wasn't wantin' to cut into her, fer fear of feckin' her face up worse."

"Okay. Okay, we'll go with the elm then so," said 'Chips' looking up from the portrait. "Hand me the old mallet, and I'll need a half inch curved chisel."

Bately snapped to it, and scurried across the boards of the temporary platform, digging into a bundle of tools wrapped in a waxed-cloth bag.

"SHIP AHOY!" came a voice from the crow's nest, braced high up between the mizzen topmast and the mizzen Topgallant mast.

"SHIP AHOY!" came another voice from the crow's nest on the mainmast.

'Chips', Bately, and 'Tumbles' all did the same instinctive thing in unison; first looking straight up at the crow's nests, observing the direction in which the 'watchmen' were pointing and then turning their heads south to look out over the starboard gunwale of the ship.

"Can't feckin' see anything. Can you?" asked 'Tumbles'.

"Nope. Not a thing. Mist is well clearing though," said Bately.

"SHIP AHOY!" came another blast from above.

"Okay, jump down lads, let's see what the fuss is about to be about," said 'Chips', calmly, "and maybe ye should fetch a couple of swords in case, you know."

"Aye, we should," said 'Tumbles', "Richard, maybe you should go find old 'Paws' and see if the Captain's in need of anything."

"Okay, good, come on then so," said 'Chips', sliding his backside from the platform and slithering down the scaffold. Bately and 'Tumbles' followed and were soon heading aft across the main deck. Many of the crew were already lining up against the starboard gunwale. Others were darting around handing out swords, cutlasses, knives, and muskets, readily on hand from the armoury.

Bately spotted 'Paws' on the quarterdeck near the helm and he skipped aft. He stopped at the foot of the main stairs that normally were out of bounds to the crew, except for Scarlett, 'Needles', and William of course.

"Mister Prowse!" yelled Bately, "Mister Prowse!"

"Come on up with you, Richard!" shouted 'Paws', "It's alright, lad!"

Richard darted up the stairs and landed in beside 'Paws', who was staring out over the starboard gunwale.

"Can you see anything, Mister Prowse?"

"Aye, lad, I can, though for the life of me, I reckon I can't believe me feckin' eyes."

Richard stared out over the ocean and spotted the bow of a ship maybe just less than a half-league out.

"What do you mean, Sir? Is there cause for alarm?"

"Well, that depends, lad. Mostly, on the time of the month," said 'Paws', casually, whilst maintaining his gaze across the water.

Richard followed his lead, straining his eyes against the blinding refection of sun bouncing off the glassy sea. The ship had two masts, and her sails were clearly furled, which was no surprise as there were no winds to catch. Hadn't been since the storm. It was a Galley-Frigate, and it was cutting across the water towards them, because the ship was under oars.

32

She's in Danger. Terrible Danger

M aria Castella, Rosa's First Mate, was pacing the central isle of the *Doncella Escarlata* keeping a sharp eye on the crew. The numerous women aboard were three to an oar and putting their backs into each stoke. Or, more specifically, their thighs, because most of the power transferred to the lengths of each oar was generated in the leg muscles, and it was thirsty work in the humidity of the Caribbean. Two younger, slighter girls were pacing the lengths of the ship handing out ladles of fresh water from barrels on rickety wooden carts with wheels. In another age they might have been considered stewardesses, cabin staff, or even flight attendants, but as the only thing in the sky that day had organic wings, they were simply, 'water-girls', and they were critical elements of the crew, very popular with the rowers, let it be said.

Maria skirted one of the water carts, making her way purposely fore of the craft to check in with her capitana.

She found Rosa climbing up onto the gun-housing from the bow-deck of the ship.

"Capitana. The girls are tired," said Maria, in her native Spanish tongue, "permission to rest for a spell."

"Sí, otorgada," said Rosa.

Maria about-turned and yelled, *"¡Cesar los remos!"* before turning aft and pacing down the central isle of the main deck.

The command was taken up and the ninety-odd rowers came to a graceful, well-practised, gentle relaxation of their movements. It was quite pretty to watch if one enjoyed such synchronicity.

William joined Rosa atop the gun-housing, followed by Aletha, carrying her carafe and three empty cups.

"Oh, Aletha, you need to check William's wounds," said Rosa.

"I'm fine," insisted William, "why are we stopping? We need to get to Kitts…"

"Calm, yourself. The girls need a rest," said Rosa, firmly. "Sit down. Kitts will still be there in an hour."

William breathed and took a seat on one of several large coils of rope on the foredeck. He held the portrait of Katherine on top of Carlos' little leather book.

"Aletha," said Rosa.

The girl placed the carafe and mugs down on a nearby chest and approached a somewhat frustrated William.

"You must relax," said Aletha, "and please, re...re..."

"Remove," interjected Rosa, whose attention was drawn north across the sea way out towards the horizon. She smiled yet remained silent.

"...please remove your shirt," said Aletha.

"Yes, sure," said William, shaking his head. He placed down the items in his hands on the deck at his feet and pulled his shabby blouse over his head. Aletha drew close to inspect the cuts on William's head, neck, and shoulder.

"Jesús. ¡Que mierda!" exclaimed the girl.

Rosa, snapped her head away from the bow of her ship immediately, "Language, Aletha!"

"Lo siento Capitana, but look! What is this?"

Rosa stepped the few paces needed to draw in close. She looked over William's upper body and ran her hands through his hair where the gash had been in his head the previous night.

"What in Christ is with you?" exclaimed Rosa, "Aletha, what did you do?"

"I did only as you taught."

"What's the problem? I feel fine," said William.

"There isn't a mark on you, is the problem!" said Rosa.

"What can I tell you, I don't drink, I don't smoke, and I swim a lot," said William, brushing off his own concerns. He really had been well busted up last night from what he could recall.

"Horseshit!" exclaimed Rosa, "What's happening to you?"

Below, and aft of the ship, an excited Carlos dashed from the door to the stern castle, followed by a lively, Sophia, "You must remain lying down, Carlos!"

"I don't want to lie down!" cried Carlos, who sped up his walking, or trotting, or part limp, part trot, part speed walking up the central isle – it was nigh-impossible to truly define his gait – and Sophia nearly had her hands on him, when he deftly skirted one of the water carts. Sophia was less fortunate and slammed right into it before toppling sideways into the isle.

Carlos kept coming, pushing past a confused First Mate, Maria, who landed in the lap of one of her rowing crew.

"Stop him, he needs to lie down!" yelled Sophia, who was picking herself up from the deck and stumbling forward, but had there been wind in the air, her words would have been carried quickly away and probably mean as much to Carlos as they did now, for he kept limping forward. When he reached the gun-housing near the fore of the ship, it became evident that he was unsure of the appropriate way to mount it and reach the deck above, where Rosa, William, and Aletha were watching proceedings unravel with heartfelt curiosity.

"I must see my book!" yelled Carlos, "You have opened it, yes?"

"Carlos, are you alright?" questioned Rosa, for lack of anything else to say in the moment.

William swept up the book and Katherine's portrait and approached the aft guard rail of the small gun-house deck. "It's here, Carlos. Calm your nerves and lend me your hand."

The Spaniard offered up an outstretched arm. William hoisted him up easily – the man barely weighed ninety pounds – and Carlos landed with his feet on the deck. He immediately snatched the book and the portrait from William.

"Which of you opened it?" Carlos asked, casting his eyes between William, Rosa, and Aletha.

"I did, Carlos," offered William.

"This woman. She was inside?" asked Carlos.

"Just her portrait," William clarified.

"Good. Good. She's in danger. Terrible danger, but she won't know it," said the Spaniard, while fixing his eyes firmly on Katherine's portrait. "Her brother will kill her, or wed her, he's evil with evil spirits. And war is coming. She must not die. You must do something. I can help. I can. I can help... it's all wrong..."

"Carlos, slow down, breathe," said William, the latent irony of his remark crossing his mind as the words escaped his lips.

"Yes, yes. I will breathe, as you say."

"Carlos, you need to lie down!" yelled Sophia, arriving at the forecastle gun-housing and launching herself upward, climbing the five-foot-high wall to the deck. She perched with her hands on the guard rail and her toes shoved between timbers.

"I will, I will, good woman," said Carlos, "I remember things today. I must have time to explain. I was trapped a long time ago in Alcázar. And banished. I was trying for Seville. To return. I knew who you were, who you are, William. But now I must journey to England. That is my purpose. Can you help me? I must find my Elizabeth."

"Carlos, why don't you sit down for a bit?" said Rosa, placing her arm around the Spaniard.

"Yes, yes, I will sit," Carlos said, "I'm not making sense. I'm not, but I will."

Rosa guided the crazed little man to one of the coiled ropes and urged him to sit.

"William, Elizabeth is to me, as this woman is to you, don't you see?" said Carlos, holding up Katherine's portrait.

"It's alright Carlos, perhaps the girls here are right," said William, "stay your thoughts for a moment."

"Aletha, give the man some coffee," instructed Rosa, "it may calm his nerves."

Aletha, took up her cue, poured out a cup of the rum-based brew and handed it to Carlos. Sophia, climbing the remainder of the gun-deck wall, vaulted over the guardrail, and stomped forward, pushing her way past William and Rosa, to gaze fore of the ship and out over the open sea. "Ha, I can see our destination," she said, "that's some good navigating, Capitana. Very good, but do you know what you are getting into, I wonder?"

"I think so," said Rosa, quietly.

William paced forward and set his sights across the water. And there she was, less than a half-league ahead, anchored against the backdrop of Saint Kitts Island. His home. Finally. But something was drastically wrong. He concentrated on the waters, the air, the energies emanating from the far-off Island.

Ah, smart move. The Spanish crew are pissed.

William concentrated his thoughts on the *Maiden Bride*... Then Scarlett...

"Set sail, Rosa," William said.

"There's no wind today," observed Rosa, acutely.

"I'll take care of it," said William.

"What are you talking about?"

William turned towards Rosa, "Please, just do it, we don't have much time. And set oars, again."

Rosa caught the determined intent in William's stern expression, and, though she was fairly certain he'd lost the plot in much the same fashion as the deranged Spaniard,

Carlos, she turned aft and yelled out, "Maria! *Zapar, por favor.*"

Maria was quick to attend her capitana, "*¿Qué? Estás loco?*"

"*¡Solo hazlo ahora!*"

"*Sí, Capitana,*" said a confused Maria, but as instructed she bellowed out orders for the crew to unfurl the large lateen sails carried by the ship's twin masts.

"*¡Y remar ahora!*" yelled Rosa.

Maria nodded, "*Sí Capitana,*" before bellowing the order to begin rowing again to the crew.

William vaulted from the gun-housing and returned to the bow deck, resuming his earlier seated position with his back to the wall underneath the three cannon, and there he sat for several minutes with his eyes closed and his mind wandering through the minutes spent with the strange man named Arthur, who had saved himself and Carlos from the sea.

"You're coming of age", the stranger in the habit had said.

William concentrated more deeply on his surroundings; the movement of the bow as the oars pushed though the water below and propelled the ship forward in steady increments. The boundary of air cushioning the surface of the calm sea. The human energies aboard Rosa's Galley; the confusion, anticipation, and anxieties of the unknown ahead. The sounds of the sails now unfurled and being tied off.

Scarlett.

A splitting headache cut through William's skull. His eyes began to burn. His breathing slowed. He could hear the rhythm of his heart slowing in his ears. He opened his eyes. The colour of the landscape had changed. The air was a liquid mass of tiny crystal particles suspended above a sea of green and blue. He saw the stagnant lack of interaction between the vibrant grains, and it annoyed him deeply to the core of his being. So, there and then, he decided that he would feckin' change it.

Then he felt wind ruffling his hair.

William pushed on with his focus, banishing the pain in his head and eyes. The inert grains in the air began to collide and bounce between themselves. Not good enough.

William breathed, forcing his mind to see a river of sparkling particles moving in a single direction: The *Maiden Bride.*

And the *Doncella Escarlata* gained momentum across the waters. William could feel her sails swelling, dragging her forward, her oars becoming redundant. The muscles in the arms, thighs and backs of the rowers aboard loosening into a state of relaxation.

Minutes or hours passed, and William maintained his focus, until Rosa popped her head over the guardrail above his head, "William! William!!"

He broke focus and tipped his head backwards looking directly up.

Rosa recoiled in sheer terror, for William's normal ocean-blue eyes were luminescing as cobalt/sapphire gemstones.

William snapped out of his trance immediately and was heartened to discover that they were less than fifty yards off the *Bride's* starboard side. The crew were waving and yelling, but he couldn't hear them, so William changed that, took the volume off mute, and decided it would be just as handsome a decision to drop the winds around him, for fear that Rosa's ship might actually ram straight through the side of his own ship. Well, Scarlett's ship. But his home too.

Scarlett.

As sounds rushed back into his ears, William leapt to his feet and the momentum of Rosa's ship slowed in the water.

"AHOY, there!" yelled William, waving an enthusiastic arm above his head, "Rosa, get down here."

William turned to see Rosa leaning over the guardrail again. "What the fuck was that?"

"Get down here, I'll explain later, if I can," said William. "Right now, I need you to meet Scarlett's crew."

"I'm not supposed to be here, William."

"Yeah, well, all that's bullshit. Scarlett protecting the bloody Realm," said William.

"He told you such things?"

"Of course he feckin' told me. Don't know why you put up with it, quite frankly."

"Maybe love."

"Maybe," said William with a wry smile, "listen, I need you to come aboard with me."

"No! Absolutely no."

"Just you. Leave your crew here. Have Maria come about, draw alongside and weigh anchor," said William, broadening his smile, "we'll wing it from there, after we see Scarlett."

"No," said Rosa, firmly. So firmly she crossed her arms in the saying of it.

William ignored her protestation and turned back towards the *Bride*.

Sophia stepped forward and nudged Rosa, "I've got this, young one, you must go."

Rosa, though unsure of just about everything, turned towards the bow of her ship and stepped up beside William once more.

The *Bride's* crew were all jeering and yelling. Seems they were pleased to see William, at least. A Jacob's ladder was unfurling from the gunwale to the water directly beneath

'Paws' who had stationed himself centre mass of the throbbing hordes on the main deck.

The 'beak' of Rosa's Galley was gliding slowly forward and would kiss the centre of the ladder in eight feet...seven...six...

"Ladies first," whispered William. "You can jump, or I can throw you, which is it?"

"You're a pig," said Rosa.

William smiled and focused on the *Bride's* Boatswain. "Permission to come aboard, Mister Prowse!"

"Ha ha! Duly granted lad!" yelled 'Paws'. "Took yer feckin' time. We was about to send out a search party!"

William laughed, "Found my own!" he shouted, indicating Rosa.

"Permission to come aboard, good Sir?" yelled Rosa.

"Aye, miss! It's about bloody time!" called 'Paws'.

Five feet...four...three...

Rosa leapt elegantly from the bow of her ship, caught the Jacobs perfectly, and climbed effortlessly upward.

"Give her some room lads!" yelled 'Paws', "Backup and show some respec' fer the Capitana of that there ship."

The men obliged willingly, separating, and creating space all around Roger Prowse, and the head of the ladder.

Rosa deftly vaulted the gunwale, and 'Paws' stepped in with a chivalrous helping hand as she gracefully dropped to the deck.

"It's a fair wind that brought you, miss. Welcome aboard," said 'Paws'.

"Thank you, Mister Prowse."

When the crew set eyes on Rosa, every single one of them fell completely SILENT. Not a whisper. Not a murmur among them. A few heads were turned to neighbours, seeking confirmation that what their eyes were seeing was to be believed. The rest were just plain awkward, simpleton, staring dummies.

A simple explanation for their collective behaviour could have been that the visitor was a woman, and quite frankly that never happened aboard the *Bride*.

Ever.

But that wasn't it.

A better explanation for the stunned silence and confusion was buried firmly in the fact that the beautiful lady now standing in the centre of the main deck was the absolute spitting image of the ship's figurehead. Which, if any of them were uncertain of comparison, was standing high in a scaffold, just fore of the mainmast, looking down over all of them.

Heads were turning left, right and centre, but not a sound was uttered...

She is the Maiden bloody Bride!

William vaulted the gunwale and landed with a thump on the deck breaking the silence, "Where is he, Roger?"

"His cabin," said 'Paws'.

William nodded, and turned to the crew, "Hey, lads, we'll parley it some in a jiffy. This is Rosa, and she needs to see the Captain, comprende?"

John Prior was first to catch on, as usual. "Right nice to have you back Will, we'll break out a glass or two fer later. If thass 'right with ye, Misser Prowse?"

"Aye, John, course it's right," said 'Paws', "cut a path there lads, you heard Master William."

"Come with me," said William, tucking his hand underneath Rosa's elbow and prompting her aft across the deck, "you too, Roger."

"Aye, William," said 'Paws', stepping in smartly.

The two gents and the lady skipped quickly up the stairs to the quarterdeck and stopped in their tracks at the helm, when they found Trevor 'Needles' Neary exiting the ornate door to the captain's cabin.

"William?"

"The very same, Trevor, long story. Is he inside?"

Trevor nodded and was about to say something but pulled up short...

"What?"

"He's not up to conjugal visits, let me put it that way," said 'Needles', before turning to Rosa, "Meaning no disrespect to you, miss Rosa, none at all."

"None taken," said Rosa, masking little of her concern.

"Rosa, stay with the gents here," said William.

"Alright, William."

"Roger, just, do the..."

"Aye, Will, no problem, be glad to." said 'Paws', effortlessly.

William was already pushing through the door to Scarlett's cabin. He crossed the outer room, skirted the central table, and knocked on the inner door to the captain's bedroom.

A gentle coughing could be heard, before the single word, "Enter".

William pushed the door open and stepped through the threshold. There was a stale, dank smell pervading the air. Scarlett was lying atop his bed at the stern end of the room propped up on a pile of cushions.

"You're alive," said Scarlett, weakly.

"Aye, somewhat. Are you?" offered William, as he crossed to Scarlett's bed.

"I'm suffering, to cast approval on your casual appearance, Master Hope," said Scarlett and lurched into a fit of coughing.

"I'm struggling to cast approval over yours," said William, as he pulled up a nearby chair and settled into it.

"Our plan of attack was a bit off, do you think?"

"Very likely," chuckled William.

Scarlett smiled and broke into another fit of wheezing and coughing. His skin was grey in pallor and sweat was dripping profusely from his brow. His eyes were dull and glassed over. "I've lived an amazing life," said Scarlett, relaxing back into the pillows, his gaze far beyond the oak ceiling above.

"Past tense," quipped William.

"Lord, what will become of me, once I've lost my novelty?" said Scarlett, weakly.

"Novelty? The fuck are you talking about?" asked William.

"I do not fear death," said Scarlett, "I only fear that I didn't do enough in life."

"Past tense, with melancholy," said William.

"Oh, shut it. Allow a dying Captain a little peace of mind."

"Sure. You carry on in your head, and I'll see if I can find a dying Captain," said William, rising from the chair.

"Is Bazán aboard the *Oscuro*, or on Kitts with his crew?"

"Neither. He's in Spain. It was Recalde that shot me, the sneaky bastard."

"Well, fuck him too, I'll be back, though I can't promise his peace of mind," said William, stepping away towards the door to the outer cabin.

Scarlett, smiled, and coughed some more. He grabbed a wad of the sheets on which he was lying and covered his mouth.

William stopped pacing and half turned back in concern.

When the spasm in Scarlett's lungs subsided, he relaxed back, revealing blood splatters on the bed linens.

"I have gold I don't want. I never wanted it. Do you understand?" said Scarlett.

William returned to his chair and sat down beside Scarlett's bedside once more as he gently replied, "Sure. I got no problem with you being poor," said William, "Pisses me off when you lie to yourself though."

"I'm not lying, damn you. I see them. The men I killed. I didn't know them. I might have liked them. I didn't care. I couldn't care. Wasn't allowed to care. All for gold and silver and bloody trinkets. For what? Don't you see?" questioned Scarlett. "Do you see their faces, Will?"

"Nope. Never killed anyone," said William, "never had to."

"All gold is blood red to me now," said Scarlett. "What good did it ever bring?"

"Oh, I don't know, the lives of countless orphans in London, the wellbeing of the English Crown and the millions of families freed enough from poverty's noose they could feed themselves. Their children inspired to better by the kind, generous, fearless, valiant, daredevil, Scarlett Buccaneer."

"I never had a family, William," said Scarlett.

"Is that from your heart or your head?" asked William.

Scarlett ran a hand through his hair, thinking about William's question.

"The heart has its own brain, you know," said William, "people touch their heads when they're thinking. They cup their hearts when they're feeling."

Scarlett smiled, "If the heart is a brain, then every man has three brains."

William chuckled, "Uh, huh, and most women. You should try listening to the one in the middle for a change. Where'd the fecker shoot you?"

Scarlett twisted to pull up his shirt and reveal the wound in his abdomen. A yellow/green sepsis was livid in his skin.

"Jesus, what was 'Needles' playing at?"

"No! Not his fault," said Scarlett, "I didn't take his... I wanted to stay sober. There were things..."

"Fuck. I can't do anything about what's in your heart, but I need to touch you," said William, as he placed his hand on Scarlett's wound.

"Did you think I was dead?" asked William.

"Not really."

"What did you feel?" asked William, "Truth."

"I don't know, loss. Grief."

"Oh, ye of little faith, right there," said William, smiling.

"I'm not myself. I just... I regret the things I've done. And I'm struggling with the things I haven't. The things I won't get to do. It's a blackness consuming me. It's making this feckin' wound worse, I know that."

Scarlett, spasmed into coughing again and grabbed for the sheet. William watched carefully but maintained his focus on the wound in Scarlett's abdomen. Aletha had been privy to his earlier parlour trick with the hot and cold. This was much the same, but different. This time William was purposefully killing harmful organisms in Scarlett's rotten muscular tissues and blood. And his intent was merciless. Not a feeling he enjoyed. His head began to ache again, though he didn't let on to Scarlett.

"You alright?" asked William when Scarlett's coughing subsided.

"I don't think I treated some of those women well at all sometimes. I didn't think of the consequences. The hurt I caused. But it didn't stop me. I was playing. It was just play. And company. Good times. But I was drunk. I was mean. Well, not entirely mean, that's harsh, but ignorant. I was ignorant to the hurt. I'd play. I'd leave. I'd play again. Leave them behind. Give them a few jewels, for Christ's sake. Like that would absolve me of their... disappointments or feelings... I'd make promises I could never keep," continued Scarlett. Had he been relieved of his delirium and looked up from his inner self he would have seen William's irises spiralling with a dull cobalt luminescence.

"I caused fights where there needed to be none. I ran. I always ran, back then. Mostly to the bottom of a bottle. It was dark. It was night after the sun rose. Every day, all those years, but I needed to be, well, I had to be the stupid legend the people wanted, William. The Scarlett feckin' Buccaneer. And it means nothing I say. Nothing. It just caused hurt. I caused so much hurt."

William removed his hand from Scarlett's wound and sat back in his chair. "You done bitching?" William's irises had returned to their usual deep ocean blues.

"I think I am, yes," said Scarlett, "for now at least."

"Present tense," said William, "that's gotta mean something."

"If I don't die tonight, I shall have you whipped tomorrow, Master Hope."

"I'll look forward to it, Captain."

Scarlett smiled and relaxed back into the pillows once more. He took a long, deep breath, sighed, and closed his eyes.

"Family, huh?" prompted William, gently.

"Yep. I'm not sure I'd have been a good father," said Scarlett, "probably for the best I never was."

"Past tense," William said, "There might be a few dozen little Scarletts running around out there somewhere. Perhaps you should track some of them down."

"Don't be a dick. What would I even tell them?"

"Don't tell them shit, just give them your gold. Can't take it with you where you're going."

"Truly, don't be a dick. That's an order," said Scarlett, his eyes still closed in repose.

William smiled and glanced over Scarlett's wounded side. It was healed of infection. The scarring from the gunshot and 'Needles' handiwork remained, but only as a dull rose colouring on the skin.

"What do you feel about Rosa?"

"The Queen would never allow the match. You know it, and so does Rosa."

"I didn't ask that. I asked how you feel about her."

Scarlett remained lying down with his eyes closed. He drew another breath and sighed.

William allowed several moments of surrendered silence.

"Hope," said Scarlett, gently. "With Rosa, I feel hope."

William smiled again and raised himself from the chair. He crossed to the starboard side of the room, opened a wardrobe, and then a chest of drawers adjacent.

"You need to wash up, and get dressed in your finest," said William, "I can't bury you looking like that."

"I don't want to be buried," said Scarlett.

"I know. That's why I brought you a wedding present."

Scarlett opened his eyes and sat up in his bed. William noticed that the usual vitality had returned to his complexion and the clammy sweating had ceased.

"What? Who's getting wed?"

"Get dressed. The crew needs you. And so does she."

"What have you done?"

"I listened," said William, "come on, get dressed. Go be the Scarlett you haven't been."

Scarlett placed a hand to his side and inspected his wound. His confused expression betrayed most of his thinking.

"I... what did you?" said Scarlett, "Ah, shit, you have to stop with the parlour tricks."

"Clothes, finest, now," said William with a smile, then turned and made his way to the outer chamber of the cabin. He crossed to port, grabbed a bottle of rum and a glass from a sideboard. He sat down at the dining table, poured himself a large one, and chugged it like it had been a long day.

Scarlett presented in the doorway separating the two rooms. "I honestly wouldn't know where to start," said Scarlett.

"I do. She's right outside that door."

"What?"

"Just get your clothes on and don't fuck up, this time," said William, nonchalantly pouring himself a second glass of rum, and offering up his glass by way of a toast. "Oh, and long live the Queen."

"Lizzie can kiss my pert dying arse," said Scarlett.

"Nope. That's the old Scarlett talking."

"I don't give a toss what the Queen thinks," said Scarlett.

"Better. I'm counting on it. Cheers Captain," said William, before he swigged from his second glass and offering up the rum bottle in an outstretched hand. Scarlett shook his head, snatched the bottle from William and disappeared into his bedroom.

33

Things at Sea that be Magic

The quarterdeck held shadows of concern that couldn't be missed by the crew on the main deck, all staring up to Roger Prowse, Trevor 'Needles' Neary, and Rosa Brizuela, who were stationed in a huddle beside the helm of the ship.

"I should have knocked him out, with rum, with anything, but he wouldn't have it. He cares too much for the crew than he does for his own good," said 'Needles'. "Miss, he's dying. He won't last the night. No point in me coatin' it with sugar. Sorry. I couldn't have..."

"Stop. Control what we can. Not what we can't. Not your fault. Mister Prowse, your men are freaking out," said Rosa, "my face is on your figurehead and as far as they know, their Captain won't wake up."

"Miss, have faith. There are things at sea that be superstition. There are things at sea that be magic. And then there is, Scarlett."

"You mean William."

"No, I mean, what you mean to Scarlett," said 'Paws'. "And who can understand William? Now, right there, I've said too much for an old man."

'Paws' turned away from the conversation and made his way fore to the railing separating the main deck from his position on the quarterdeck. He looked out over the men. What the Christ was there to say? They needed guidance, for sure. In all his years at sea, he couldn't remember a moment so keen in ambiguity.

Scarlett opened the ornate door to his cabin, waltzed out on the quarterdeck – in his finest garments noted 'Paws' – picked Rosa up in his arms and spun her around in a joyful seven-hundred-and-twenty degrees spin.

"Bear with me here, for a beat, eyes upon us, and I would have liked to do this another way, but will you marry me?" whispered Scarlett.

"What?" gasped Rosa. "We can't."

"Can."

"We're not allowed to," said Rosa.

"You're right, as always, but what if I put it to the crew? Will you play along?"

"If my crew have a say also, sure."

"Very good. Gotta go be Scarlett for a bit. Are you on board?"

"Yes. How many babies?" asked Rosa.

"Seven."

"Three," said Rosa.

"Four."

"Alright, four. But the *Maiden Bride* remains in port."

"You'll come with me to England?" asked Scarlett, "No pressure, but the men are counting on you to lift their spirits."

"So are the women," said Rosa.

"Naturally," said Scarlett.

"Carnage?" questioned Rosa.

"Better a bang than a whimper," Scarlett said, the broadest grin apparent.

The captain of the *Bride*, gently lowered Rosa from his arms to the deck. With a smile and a wink, she let him step forward to the main staircase and the new Scarlett took a position he'd never rehearsed in a mirror.

"Abew yer eyes me hearties, yer Captain's on the quarterdeck and ye're all rich men, but what of riches without love?!"

He waited for the full attention of his crew. He didn't have to wait long, so he continued, "Are ye lily-livered bilge rats, or gentlemen o' Fortune?"

"FORTUNE Captain!" came the unanimous reply.

"Now I might point out that there is a ship full of good women off the starboard gunwale, and each one of them needs your full attention and kindness, for they are no different in these times than are you. I might point out that there is a Spanish galleon off the port side that is full of rum. I might also point out that you are the very best of men that I have had the pleasure of sailing with for the Queen's cause. But I'm not going to do that. You already know it. So, I'm asking this of you. If I propose to the love of my life. If I disown Queen and Country. If I get down on my knees, and ask a better person than I to wed, will you see to it that we shall have a festival of kindness and beauty? For this I will tell ye, she encourages me to be who I am, little though it means in a cosmic context, but only good will come of it. Are ye up fer a celebration of goodness?"

SILENCE again aboard the crew and the ship. Are we bound fer home? That had been one question a crew would never hear. Are we to decide the fate of our captain's heart? Well, that was quite another.

So, naturally, the crew of the *Maiden Bride* made a unanimous decision.

"AYE, AYE, CAPTAIN!"

Scarlett listened. In the same way William had taught him to, perhaps.

He turned about, and motioned Rosa to step forward with an outstretched hand. She did so, somewhat bashfully.

As soon as she met the head of the main staircase to the main deck, Scarlett dropped to one knee and took Rosa's right hand in his. "What say you, good lady? I would love to be yours and yours only. Will you see to it that you might wish the same? I love you more than time and tide. Will you marry me?"

Rosa turned from Scarlett's earnest face to his crew, "What say ye, lads?"

"AYE!!" came the shout, "AYE, LADY!"

"AYE, MISS. You can put up with him."

"AYE, AYE, maiden," came another.

Rosa looked out over the masses on the main deck, took her time and offered, "Very well, I'll agree, *IF* and only if, you all see to it that my friends are invited aboard and ye all get up to no good, and do some good between yerselves! What say you to that?"

"AYE, FUCKIN' AYE, MISS CAPITANA!"

Rosa took stock of the crew for a beat and returned her full attention to Scarlett. "Yes." Scarlett bounded up from his knees, kissed Rosa, swept her up in his arms once again, and without dropping her feet back to the deck, he addressed his crew once more. "Get them ladies aboard my ship, get a wedding prepared, and get yourselves drunken. I wanna hear music. I wanna hear song. And I want each and every one of you to love each other. Is that clear?"

"AYE, AYE CAPTAIN!" was all that could have been said, and so it was, loudly!

William was standing in the threshold of the door to Scarlett's cabin, watching events with a broad smile. The crew on the main deck, who were no slouches when it came to priorities, split into two groups. The larger of those groups dashed to the starboard gunwale and began to politely aid Rosa's crew up the Jacob's ladder. The first aboard was Sophia, quickly followed by Aletha, Maria, and the other women. The second group of men were already over the port side gunwale and heading out on the gangplanks, crossing to the *Santa Oscuro* to empty its hold of rum and champagne for the evening's entertainments. Martin 'Mumbles' was with them, light of heart, journal in hand, bellowing instructions on where to find the 'good stuff'.

Robert 'Chips' Stuart had seen plenty in life, but rarely such wild and innocent enthusiasm from a crew or crowd. He dropped his chisels, slid from the scaffold surrounding Rosa's image, and dashed aft towards the quarterdeck. He met 'Paws' midway up the main stairs, "Mister Prowse, I'll have it that we may need an altar!"

"Aye, Jesus, we do, I didn't think fer it, Rob," said 'Paws' "what do you recommend?"

"Few timbers, nicely shaped on the forecastle," said 'Chips' "make for a proper setting, with Kitts in the background."

"Right, you'll need your men," said 'Paws', before turning aft and shouting up the stairs, "Trevor! A word if I may be so bolden."

"Aye, Mister Prowse," said 'Needles', stepping past the helm with a quick step.

"Rob's got an idea fer a ceremony on the foredeck, what say ye?"

"How're ye Rob?" said 'Needles', "I'm liking your notion. We'll need two rows of pews on the main deck. One side for the bride and the other fer the groom."

"Jesus, we do, ye're right, and before sundown," said 'Chips', inadvertently looking out over the main deck whilst scratching his chin.

And thus, it was feckin' ON. Ninety-four sex starved, fiery, women meeting a hundred-and-twenty-four equally sex-starved foolhardy men, all passionately setting about organising a wedding between their respective captains.

"Mister Prowse, a quiet word," said William, as he casually descended the central stairs to the main deck.

"Aye, William, o' course' what d' ye need?"

"I'll need access to the *Bride's* jewels in the hold," said William, "and a bit of quiet."

"The Queen's jewels?" said 'Paws'.

"Aye."

"You don't need my permission fer that, Will," said 'Paws', smiling.

"Just letting you know."

"Aye, righty oh, I'll see to it that 'Mumbles' drops by with a skite of rum," said 'Paws', with a broad smile.

"My thanks Roger," offered William. "Oh, there's a nice woman, I'd like you to meet, walk with me."

"Oh, I don' know, Will," said 'Paws', "I ain't too clever when it comes to them lot."

William headed aft and veered towards the starboard side of the deck, followed by a hesitant 'Paws'. William spotted his target, "Sophia, I'd like to introduce you to Roger Prowse."

"Alright, why not?" said Sophia.

"Roger... Sophia, Sophia... Roger," said William, nudging 'Paws' forward.

"Ma'am, right nice to make yer aquaintin'", said the Boatswain, holding out his right paw.

"Hello," said Sophia, shaking his hand, "though you know we've met before."

"Well, I'll be, and can't say that we have," said 'Paws', "fer sure I'd 'av' remembered, what with the likes of your beauty."

"Oh, rugged and charming, hey," Sophia said, "we met in two of our last lives, you see."

"Never, I'll be buggered," said 'Paws', "how's about a glass of rum and you can tell me a bit about it then?"

"That would be wonderful...", was the last William heard of the conversation, as he tactfully stepped away, proceeding towards the forecastle of the ship.

"Richard!" shouted William, passing the temporary scaffold surrounding the ship's figurehead, as young Richard Bately was sitting with paint brush in hand, touching up

Rosa's statue. "Get your arse down here, there's someone I'd like you to meet."

"Oh, no, I can't do that, Master William," said Bately, "Mister Stuart, said I gotta be finished up here..."

"That was an order, Mister Bately," insisted William, "I'll see it put right with 'Chips'."

"Well, alright Master William, if you say so."

Bately slid down from the scaffold and landed beside William, who was straining sightlines through what was quickly becoming a crowded deck. Flagons and cups of rum were being passed around, chairs, benches and barrels were being hauled from below decks and moved about. The lower shrouds on the main and foremasts had dozens of men and women clinging comfortably, chatting, drinking, and let it be said, flirting handsomely.

"Where is she?" mused William, rhetorically.

"Where's who?" asked Bately.

"Ah hah!" declared William, as he stepped aft and dragged Bately along with him. "Two cups and a bottle of rum if you please, Mister Prior!"

John Prior was centre of the main deck, having set up something of a makeshift bar. Quite how he and Jim Dolby had rallied so quickly about it, was both a mystery and no feckin' surprise at all, given the men's enthusiasm for life in general.

"Aye, aye, Will," said Prior, smartly handing William the required items. "Still wanna hear about your findin' a bloody ship full of women mid-ocean, after you was left fer dead, mind."

"You wouldn't be complaining, John?"

"Christ no!" said John with a smile, "Just wonderin' how the fuck, is all."

"We'll parley soon enough," said William, stepping away. He handed the cups and bottle to Richard Bately and shoved him aft once again. "You'll be needing these."

Aletha was sitting on large barrel, port side, resting her back on the lower shroud netting of the mainmast. She had her knees tucked up and her arms wrapped around them, looking somewhat out of her element, with all the adult activities unfolding at pace around her.

"Aletha!" said William, "I'd like to introduce you to a friend of mine. My guess is you're gonna like him. You've both got a lot in common."

Awkward silence between the two adolescents, prompted William to push Bately gently in the back, "Manners, Richard" he whispered.

"Hello miss. Would you care for a drop of rum?" asked Bately, quietly.

"I'd, yes, I think I would," said Aletha, "after I know your name, perhaps."

"Oh, sorry. I'm Richard. Richard Bately."

"Aletha. Would you care to sit down?"

William smiled, fashioning that Bately's sitting down was a cue to vacate the scene. He stepped quickly to the forecastle and entered the ornate little door to the crew's quarters, where a dozen injured men were laid out on cots, most of them holding fresh cups of rum. He made his way down ladders and stairs, passing through the upper, and lower, gun decks, with hammocks strewn between cannon, onwards through the galley, storerooms, the base of the jeer capstan, and on down more ladders to the orlop deck, stepping around, or between, coils of rope, food stores, animal pens, barrels of fresh water, and some of the ship's diagonal bracing and ribbing timbers. He stopped amidships in the hold, technically below the waterline, at the door to his chosen destination. He stepped inside revealing a room, some sixty feet in length with a central isle and long rows of floor-to-ceiling shelves stitched to the sides of the ship. Barrels of spices, sugar, dyes, plants, salt, tobacco, and hemp were crammed between the shelves or stacked on top of each other. A multitude of rolls of various coloured cloths, cotton, silks, and fine linens were stowed in every spare nook and cranny. At the aft end of the stores, dozens of chests were stacked, and it was among these that William landed.

He took his time opening several of the chests, sifting through a variety of gold, silver, and gemstones. He settled upon a delicate rose gold bracelet, a pale sapphire the colour of Rosa's eyes, a greenish-blue aquamarine stone, almost matching Scarlett's eyes when he had set his sights on a conquest of some kind. He sorted through some opaque stones and picked out a turquoise pebble. He rooted around further and extracted several small uncut diamonds, before wrapping his booty in a leather cloth and setting himself down comfortably on a large coil of heavy rope. He laid the stones and chain on an upturned barrel beside him.

"Find what you wanted?" came a voice from the doorway.

William looked up to see Martin 'Mumbles' ambling into the central isle, carrying a crystal glass and a bottle of rum. The outside of the bottle was adorned in an elaborate motif done in silver leaf.

"I think so, Martin," said William.

"Brought you some of the good stuff," said 'Mumbles' holding up the bottle.

William smiled, "Join me, won't you?"

"Oh, well... alright. Don't mind if I do. Hang fire a tick," said 'Mumbles', as he began to rummage around in a couple of chests. He pulled out a silver goblet, before plonking his backside down on a stack of rolled up cloths. He handed William the crystal glass, then filled it with rum from the bottle. After that he poured a good measure into his newfound goblet.

"Cheers," said William.

"Aye, cheers an' all, Will," said 'Mumbles'. Both men enjoyed a decent slug of their spirt. "It's good."

"Bloody good," said William.

"Whass we got going on here then?" asked 'Mumbles', indicating the small array of gems atop the barrel.

"Wedding rings," said William. "Thought I might fashion them for the happy couple."

"Oh, right, oh. Thass nice thinkin', that is," said 'Mumbles'. "How the bloody hell's you gonna do that then?"

"Don't quite know yet," said William, "I'll think on it for a spell."

"Right, makes perfect sense," said 'Mumbles' before taking another swig from his cup. "You gonna take a woman, Will?"

"I have one already," said William. "You?"

"Arrghh, I ain't got the energy fer the likes, these days," said 'Mumbles', "might play me some music instead on me lute. Least I know whass to pluck on that thing."

William smiled, and raised his glass, "To pluckin' strings, not hearts."

The two men clinked cups and downed their drinks.

"Well, I'd best be headin' upstairs, Will. The young 'uns are gonna need lookin' after while they're on the piss, least I would have a long time ago."

"Do me a favour, Martin?" asked William.

"Aye, Will, name it."

"Get a hold of Roger. See to it that the Spaniard, Recalde, and his officers are fed and watered and firmly locked in his cabin for the night," said William.

"No invite to the wedding, got it," said 'Mumbles'. "Get em' hammered?"

William smiled, "You and I are in accord."

"Now, forgive me ignorance here, Will, but what of the bloody crew on the island?"

"Read my mind," said William, "round up a dozen kegs and have Shamus O'Reilly and Dye Bant take an armed yawl-boat to shore. Dump the rum with the Spanish men."

"The best way of squishin' a rebellion is to drown it," said 'Mumbles', "I'll see to it."

William smiled again, "Good man."

'Mumbles' nodded, and stepped away aft, then paused, and opened one of the chests on the port side of the isle. He rummaged around for a few seconds and withdrew a gemstone of his liking. He turned back to William, "Ruby is fer the heart."

'Mumbles' tossed the stone to William, who caught it. "My thanks, Martin."

'Mumbles' turned about and disappeared into the depths of the hold.

William returned his attention to the jewels laid out on the leather cloth before him. He added the ruby to the mix and settled his mind. He concentrated on his environment. The lanterns attached to the stanchions in the room. The mild crackles of their oil-fired flames. The smell of seawater pervading the space and the gentle lapping of the waves against the hull. The reverberations of laughter – and now song – emanating from the main deck three flights above him. The enthusiastic joy of the crews mingling in banter, bashfulness, flirtation, and, most of all, hungry anticipation of the unifications to come. The union of captain and capitana. William breathed deeply. His eyes began to burn. A headache blossomed, probing his frontal lobes.

Scarlett and Rosa... Rosa and Scarlett.

William took up the bracelet of rose gold and settled it atop the palm of his right hand. He smothered it with his left hand, cupping his palms together. His headache increased in strength. A dull rose-coloured glow began to emanate from his hands, and William smiled.

He unclasped his hands after several stationary minutes. Three rings were sitting in the palm of his right hand. One, thicker than the other two, had a robust crowned setting. The other bands were narrower; one a plain hoop, the other with a smaller crown setting. William placed the rings down on the leather cloth, picked up several uncut diamonds, using the tips of the thumb and index finger of his left hand. He laid the stones in the upturned palm of his right hand and cupped his left palm down over the gemstones. A dim white light leaked from between his palms, and, minutes later, William separated his hands to reveal a sparkling powder of diamonds, each the size of grains of sand on a beach.

"You *are* one of them," came a small voice from shadows towards the aft end of the room.

William snapped his head around, to see the delicate form of the Spanish man, Carlos, limping his way forward down the central isle. He was clutching his little book, as usual.

"How long have you been here, Carlos?" William offered, gently.

Carlos watched the luminescence in William's eyes dim, revealing their normal navy colouring when in the shadows of a ships hold.

"I don't mean to bother or hurt your, your, workings," said Carlos.

William smiled, "You're not. I'm glad to see you. Please, sit down with me."

Carlos, looked unsure for a beat, cast a furtive glance behind himself, and shuffled forward. He sat down on the same stack of rolled up cloths, previously occupied by Martin 'Mumbles'.

William brushed the diamond dust from the palm of his hand carefully onto the leather cloth. He then grabbed the bottle and poured healthy rations of rum into the silver goblet, and his own glass. He laid the bottle down beside him and offered the goblet to Carlos, who accepted it.

"Salud," said William.

Carlos raised his cup and smiled. Both men sipped.

"You're not enjoying the fun upstairs?" enquired William.

"I like the music. But I am too much in the sun, I think. Many people," said Carlos.

William nodded.

"There is one of you in Alcázar. Though he is not like you," said Carlos. "He hurt my head so much I could no longer see. He is young. And his eyes are cold amber fire. He writes books of magic and darkens them with sugar. Every day he does this. I remember these things."

William opened his mouth to speak, but stifled his words, for lack of anything appropriate to say. Confusion wracked his mind, yet he masked it in neutral expression.

"This belongs to you," said Carlos, offering up the portrait of Katherine.

"It came from your book, Carlos."

"Please. It is yours. You chose it," said Carlos, "I should like to meet her. I think I have things to tell her. I think she has not been told these things."

William leaned in and received the little oil painting from Carlos.

"Will you help me get to England, William?" asked Carlos. "Do you think your Captain would mind? I will work to cover my board. I promise. I just... I must find my Elizabeth."

"Elizabeth. Yes, you mentioned her, I'm certain."

"I have not seen her since the night of your birth," said Carlos.

William stared at the strange man before him, wondering whether to press any line of enquiry that might reveal even the least semblance of comprehension.

"Will you ask your Captain? I will work my way for the journey."

"Yes, Carlos, I will gladly ask him. But let me tell you this...", said William, "his answer is already yes. Glad to have you on board."

Carlos, choked, half chuckling, and doubled forward clutching his little book tight in his lap. "You mean it? I will get to see Elizabeth?"

William smiled, "Certainly, Carlos, you can be sure of it."

"Thank you. Oh, and you say, Cheers. So please, Cheers," said Carlos, raising his cup.

"To your Elizabeth," William put forth, clinking his glass on Carlos' cup.

"Yes. Yes, thank you," said Carlos, throwing his head back and downing his rum.

William was quick to offer the bottle a second time. Carlos held out his cup and William filled it.

"Elizabeth," Carlos said, standing. He tipped his head back and downed the second cup, before stumbling sideways. "With your permission, I will leave you in peace, I must find the sun."

"You don't need my permission. Your Majesty," said William.

Carlos gave William a double take, before limping aft down the central isle and disappearing into the shadows once more. William waited for him to vanish and returned his attention to the assembly of jewels beside him.

34

Wilt Thou Have Thee?

As the sun lowered below the ship's mizzen topsail yard, aft to the west, the *Maiden Bride* was lying naked, all sails furled, her hull steady on the calm sea with her bowsprit overlooking Saint Kitts and long shadows rolling in over the island's green hills.

Scarlett's *maiden* wore an ankle length dress of fine white linen. It was embellished with a thick leather waistband highlighting her tiny waist and accentuating her athletic curves. A cutlass hung at her left side. Her hair was adorned with a selection of dried flowers weaved in and around a white bandana. She was standing on the forecastle of the ship facing south, and, more importantly, facing Scarlett. The two of them were standing beneath an altar of dried flowers, jewels, and silver chains wrapped around wooden arches. Lanterns were flickering all around the altar and foredeck.

Trevor 'Needles' Neary was standing fore and between the two captains, dressed in a grey robe with a gold sash draped around his shoulders. He held a book in his hands. He would have preferred that book to have been a bottle of rum, but a small sacrifice was necessary in taking up his role as pastor of the hour.

'Needles' gave a gentle nod to Martin 'Mumbles' who was sitting unobtrusively on the starboard gunwale, plucking a gentle melody on the strings of his lute. The tune was more akin to 'Stir it up' by Bob Marley than any tune ever written or played in the sixteenth century, but, as Bob wasn't around, and 'Mumbles' had never heard of him, he felt sure the merry rhythm was appropriate for the occasion and free of copyright complications.

The crews of Scarlett's and Rosa's respective ships formed a congregation on the main deck, separated by a central isle with men on the right side and women on the left. The only exceptions for the ladies were Maria and young Aletha, who were both on the foredeck standing close by Rosa. Exceptions for the men were William and young Bately, who stood on Scarlett's side of the ceremonial gatherings.

In tune with gentle undercurrents in the audience, 'Mumbles' ran over the last few bars of his tune and gently tickled his fingers to a pleasing fade on his instrument.

Silence beckoned anticipation, so 'Needles' cleared his throat and said, "I'd normally set about tellin' ye all that 'we are gathered 'ere today, now, to celebrate the union...

and blah, blah, blah, the joining of these two souls, etcetera, etcetera', but the looks shared between them means I can't speak much more to ye all, but to say forthwith, the space between them is blessed and pure, and formed in the bonds of true love, and that is a rare and wonderful thing. Now, the Lord has seen fit to see to it that I unite these two children in the sacrament of Holy Marriage, and it falls upon me to begin with this; is there anyone present here today, man, woman, child, or beast that has good reason that these two lovelies should not be united in love and marriage under the eyes of whatever Gods you are all choosin' to be believing in?"

'Needles' looked out over the main deck and filled the attending silence with a dramatic silence of his own.

"Anyone here, now, have good reason to believe these two beautiful reprobates are not madly in love with each other?... Anyone? Please bear in mind, I hates to see anyone flogged."

Not a word spoken.

"Good. Ye're all on board," said 'Needles'. "Right then...", he continued, looking down at the book in his hands and purposefully flicking through a couple of pages.

Scarlett's left and Rosa's right wrist were wrapped in a loose, pure white silk cloth, for they were holding hands.

"Wilt thou, Scarlett, have this here girl to be thy wedded wife, to live hereafter in the holy estate of matrimony?"

Scarlett looked deep into Rosa's eyes, "I will."

"Wilt thou love her, comfort her, honour her, keep her safe in sickness and in health and bring her all the rum she ever desires?"

Scarlett smiled, "I will."

"Wilt though love her kindly, gently and passionately when her desire calls upon it for babies and such, and for as long as ye both shall live?"

"I most definitely will."

"And wilt thou bang her in the arse on occasion if the mood takes her in that direction?"

"None of your bloody business", said Scarlett, shaking his head and chuckling.

"Rosa Brizuela, wilt though have this charlatan of a man to be thy wedded husband, to live together after God's ordinance, in the holy estate of matrimony?"

Rosa looked deep into Scarlett's proud eyes, "I will."

"Wilt thou love him, comfort him, honour him, and keep him, in sickness and in health?"

"I will," smiled Rosa.

"Wilt thou keep him, forsaking all others, put up with his nonsense, and listen to his tuneless music and unfunny jokes with patience, for as long as you both shall live?"

"I most definitely will," said Rosa.

'Needles' laid his book down on a nearby stand. "Methinks, this is going so well, we should set about an exchange of rings."

Scarlett suddenly looked mortified, "Oh, shit," he whispered, flashing his eyes apologetically towards Rosa, who, in turn, shook her head and shrugged with wide eyes.

William simply said, "Kids."

Aletha stepped forward to Rosa and presented her with a rose gold ring. It held an emerald, infused with aquamarine and a tiny red heart of ruby buried deep within its crystal surface. A dusting of diamond grains bound the central stone to the ring's band.

Richard Bately stepped forward with two rings held up in his outstretched palm. Scarlett tentatively picked up the rings in his fingers. One was a simple band. The other held a pale sapphire, infused with aquamarine and a tiny ruby heart buried within the crystal's centre. A dusting of powder-like grains of diamonds fixed the stone to the rose gold ring.

"Well, let's have it then, the good Lord ain't waitin' fer his rum any more than me," said 'Needles'. "You got anythin' you wanna say to each other in front of these good people?"

"Rosa, I will love you every sunset and sunrise over all horizons. I take thee as my wife."

Scarlett took Rosa's left hand in his and placed the two rings upon her third finger.

"Scarlett, I will love you beyond our horizons, to the moon and stars and back. I take thee as my husband," said Rosa, lifting Scarlett's left hand and placing the emerald ring on his third finger.

'Needles' gave it a beat before continuing, "Grand, this is lovely, now, ye have declared yer intents before Gods and everyone. And may it be that the good Lord strengthens your consents with rum and blessings, fer what He has joined no man, woman, child, or beast has a right to pull asunder. Amen to that. And so, by the Power invested in me from above, I now pronounce you, Man and Wife!!"

Scarlett and Rosa came together in a loving, lengthy, cuddling, passionate KISS.

The crews ignited in "CHEERS!" Men and women throwing caps, rice, beans, flowers, and most other things they could lay hands on.

Scarlett swept Rosa up in his arms and the kissing became even more passionate.

'Needles' stepped away with the bottle of rum firmly to his upturned lips and set his sights on Maria Castella, First Mate of the *Doncella Escarlata,* for his subconscious desires had noticed her during his ceremonial articulations, and he was now dead set on putting his role as pastor to bed and taking up his role as ship's naturalist by studying her mating habits as soon as possible.

Scarlett and Rosa descended the stairs and landed in the fray on the main deck. 'Paws' and Sophia had come together having been parted by a frustrating, but respectful three feet of space, in the foremost pews of the congregation. They passed the first of numerous glasses of champagne to the newlyweds and hugs and cheers were abundant.

The 'band' struck up their instruments on the quarter-deck, with lutes, guitars, violins – known as 'fiddles' aboard the *Bride* – trumpets, a harp, various drums, recorders and Scarlett's very own harpsicord, which had been moved from his cabin. It was clear that the unpractised jamming was yet to find an accord, or a chord of any kind, suitable to the mix of Creole and Irish jigs exploding with enthusiasm from the mix of male and female musicians, all of whom were concentrating less on the music and more on the tones of each other.

Shamus O'Reilly held two women, literally, one in each arm, each sitting comfortably in the nooks of his elbows, as he greeted Scarlett and Rosa in the central isle. "Congratulations, Captains!" bellowed the big Irishman.

"I think we should be congratulating you," quipped Scarlett, as he and Rosa made their way aft doing the rounds.

Ned 'Toes' Williams was just fore of the mainmast with a section of a broken yardarm held above his head by way of a show of his considerable strength, and to be sure it was a handsome showing, as there were six ladies of Rosa's crew sitting on top of it.

"Givin' these girls a better view of the happy couple, Captains, they had seats in the back," said 'Toes', customarily unabashed, "didn't think it was fair, like."

"Your kindness will no doubt be appreciated," said Rosa.

"I'm hoping it goes a long way, miss. Congratulations to you," said 'Toes'.

John Prior and Jim Dolby had their makeshift bar in full swing once again, as Scarlett and Rosa approached, only this time they were fully staffed with eight of Rosa's crew lending helping, if not entirely wandering, hands.

"Hey, Capt', I'll fancy you and your maiden might put those glasses down when I replace them with these," said Prior, reaching underneath the bar and pulling out two bejewelled golden goblets, "Special recipe, and I'll cop a lashin' tomorrow if it don't put a length in your strokes on your wedding night."

"Hardly appropriate, Mister Prior," said Scarlett, before turning to Rosa, "what d'you think my dear?"

"I think Mister Prior is my favourite among your crew this evening," said Rosa, receiving both cups from Prior, giving him a wink, and passing one goblet to Scarlett.

"Link arms now, luck will follow," said Prior, with a smile.

Scarlett and Rosa hooked elbows, with both drinks in their right hands, and downed them in one go.

"Jesus," said Scarlett.

"Holy crap," said Rosa, "what's in that?"

"Ask me again in the morning, miss," said Prior with a wink. "Congratulations to you."

Scarlett and Rosa moved on as Prior was engulfed by patrons demanding attentions. Further aft, Robert 'Chips' Stuart and Dye Bant were to be found. They had jerry-rigged a swing set high up off the mizzenmast. Lads and ladies were climbing the shrouds and plonking their arses in the seat, arms wrapped around each other, before a tug on ropes sent them flying into the air, off the starboard gunwale and into the calm waters some forty feet below. Their screams and laughter resonated along the entire ship.

"Wanna have a go, Captain?" asked Dye, as Scarlett and Rosa approached.

"What do you think, my dear?" Scarlett asked of Rosa.

"I'm already wet, my dear," said Rosa, "perhaps a little later."

"You heard the lady, Mister Bant," said Scarlett.

"Congratulations Capt," said Dye, "and I sees you've got him under control already, miss, he couldn't have asked fer a better friend than you, fer sure."

Rosa blushed a little as Dye returned his attentions to his makeshift fairground attraction, and the next happy flirting customers in the swing.

Scarlett and Rosa made their way up the main stairs to the quarterdeck.

William was still atop the ship's forecastle watching events unfold across the ship and enjoying the energies of the various couplings aboard, and the antics unfolding. He caught sight of Scarlett and Rosa as they paused beside the band on the quarterdeck.

Scarlett never disappointed, that was for sure.

William maintained his gaze as Rosa and Scarlett disappeared, arm in arm, behind the door to the captain's cabin. He smiled. Job well and truly done.

35

"For England, Yar!"

10th November 1587

Rosa awoke to her surroundings, unaware of exactly where she was. She sat up quickly.

A swift transition to consciousness was alarming for a few seconds and surely attached to the beginnings of a hangover from hell, but as her heart rate calmed the darkened cabin became clear in her mind.

It helped that Scarlett stirred in bed beside her. Rosa smiled as he came to and fumbled his way to leaning across her thighs. His hand stroked her soft skin and made its way from her knees, upward along her inner thighs and...

"I need to squirt," Rosa exclaimed.

"Beg pardon?" questioned Scarlett.

"Unhand me you brute."

"Is it not I that has been ravaged this night?"

Rosa leaned forward and kissed him, "I really need to pee."

"Very well," said Scarlett, removing his weight from her legs, "I need to pee, too, truth be told."

"Outside," said Rosa as she shifted from the bed, and made her way across the room to a chamber pot tucked away on the port side, behind a small blind, "this chamber is taken."

"I can wait," said Scarlett.

"Outside!" said Rosa, "I'll not have you contaminating my efforts. This pee is gold."

"Fine," said Scarlett, rising from the bed and wrapping a cotton towel around his waist, "That pee is pure rum, I'm certain of it."

"Out!"

"Yes dear, I'm going," said Scarlett, dragging his feet across the room, through to his outer cabin. After a minor stumble he found the outer door, opened it and stepped through onto the quarterdeck. He closed the door, made his way to the port side gunwale, stepped up on his toes and set about his business while casting an eye over the length of his ship. The evidence of a solid celebration was obvious. Couples and threesomes and the likes were under blankets here, there, and everywhere. All passed out, sleeping soundly. A sliver of a moon cast tired joyful shadows over them all.

William was sitting on the foredeck, on a bench. Upright. Awake. Alone. Staring up at the sky, with his back resting against the ship's starboard side.

That boy thinks too much.

Scarlett finished relieving himself, tightened the towel around his waist, and made his way east, skipping lightly around bodies and carnage. He grabbed a bottle of rum from Prior's bar and continued to the forecastle.

"Sleep not your friend tonight I see," whispered Scarlett as he stepped up to the foredeck and approached William.

"A man doesn't need sleep to dream."

"Ah, quite so," said Scarlett, taking a seat beside William, "what's on your mind?"

"Not sure how it's going to play out."

"With the Queen, you mean?"

"Uh, huh," said William.

"We'll figure it out. Here," said Scarlett, handing up the bottle of rum.

"Thanks," said William, placing down Katherine's portrait on the bench between them and accepting the bottle. He chugged a decent helping.

"This is Katherine," said Scarlett, taking up the portrait for inspection.

"So I'm told," said William.

Scarlett nodded while continuing his observance of Katherine.

"Haven't seen her in ten years," said William.

"I'm aware," said Scarlett, "how'd you come by this?"

"Carlos had it in his book."

"So, she was on that ship," said Scarlett.

"Uh, huh," said William, "after a fashion."

Scarlett smiled. William handed him the bottle of rum. Scarlett chugged a healthy gulp.

"I never thanked you for the rings."

"You never need to."

Scarlett smiled, "I said I'd see you in England before I'm sober, Master Hope."

"I guess you will."

Scarlett scrunched up his left eye, leaned forward, raised the bottle, and placed his heart in the tones of the *Bride's Banter*, "For England, Yar!"

"For England, Yar!" said William, grabbing the bottle from Scarlett once again.

The End

****

Acknowledgements

For your priceless encouragement: Rory, Mel, Neil, Nikki, Mike, Georgina, Sara, J.C., Jason, Penny.

Agata Broncel, for your bewitching cover design.
Elizabeth Ward, for your insightful editing.

Robert 'Chips' Stuart. Ya Bollix.

Oh, and cheers to you Roger 'Paws' Vance may you R.I.P.
with a pint and a smile.

About the author

George Christopher Vance was born in London in 1971 and spent most of his childhood in Bristol, England. He graduated Newcastle University with a degree in Civil Engineering. Chris spent eight years transitioning from construction to entertainment and became an actor/producer/writer in Hollywood. The William Hope stories were spawned in a pub in Clapham, London when Chris was 29 years old. He has bounced around the world, living and working on five continents, with these tales knocking about in his grey matter ever since.

You might recognise Chris from his TV roles in Prison Break, Mental, The Transporter Series, Hawaii Five-O, Rizzoli and Isles, Bosch and Supergirl.

Here are links to Chris' website and IMDb pages:

https://chrisvanceauthor.com

https://m.imdb.com/name/nm0888496/

487

Also by Chris Vance

The William Hope and The Princess Tales

Part One – "For England, Yar!"
Part Two – An Implausible Nascence
Part Three – Murder in the Green Reach
Part Four – The Princess and The Prince

*****

The William Hope and The Alchemist Tales

Part One – "For Algiers, Yar!"
*****

For more information visit: https://chrisvanceauthor.com

Oooh, Arrr, You Might Also Wanna Read This 'un...

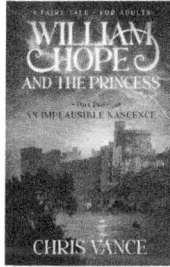

William is born with a cowl.

Katherine is born with a silver spoon.

And who the fuck is Matheo?

*****

READ ON FOR THE OPENING CHAPTERS...

Anus Anomalous

29th October 1564

Some fifty years of good living had left no doubt in Nicholas White's mind that he was more than capable of distinguishing good from evil. Were it any other time in said fifty years, he would have expected his command of this capability to guide him steadily through the woes of his present predicament. As it was, the only thing he could discern with any degree of certainty, was that his present predicament was particular to someone with no sight at all.

Which made the whole good and evil thing considerably more unnerving.

He was not a brave man. By his own admission, he was not. He had realised certain accomplishments throughout his life by way of the odd courageous choice. But truth be told, his hindsight had surpassed his foresight in each one of those choices. Opportunity had played its part, as luck would have it. But right now, he was not a brave man, and he was feeling none too lucky, either.

He had strained his mighty gait before, of course he had. Though of late, it was in times of need only. His current anus-anomalous-affliction was a compelling reminder that seats in general were not intended as a luxury, particularly if they came with a hole in the centre. But, right now, he wished he were sitting, for the strain of merely standing was enough to make him cry.

White had spent a great majority of his adult life establishing, investigating, or simply exploring matters of fact. A pursuit that was not altogether necessary, but also not uncommon, for a Judge. That said, he, like the great majority of his peers in the legal profession, always held a soft spot for matters of fiction. It had grown to become the only truly amusing part of his work. Those all-too-familiar exaggerations and deceptions presenting in every courtroom drama. His one true gift, however – and White had never been shy about declaring this in public – was in his ability to appreciate the intricate shades between imagination and actuality in any given argument, which, in turn, White argued, gave him his unparalleled talent to distinguish between truth and bullshit. In a perpetual darkened moment, in the Long Gallery of the private apartments of the Upper Ward of Windsor Castle, with a porcelain bowl resting between his outstretched palms, his nightgown consuming what he hoped was urine spilling down his left thigh, a twisting fibrous darkness of arid cold ripping into his soul, and a lurid strobing image of a white-haired, boy/gremlin, wearing horn-rimmed glasses over burning amber eyes, leering at him, chewing his way into White's mind, the judge came to understand that he could no longer call upon his great gift for disparity betwixt fact and fiction.

In point of fact, he couldn't fully understand anything at all, except perhaps that there was good and there was evil.

Somewhere.

But this fact, whilst testifying to his profound vulnerability as a human being, was somehow, he felt – though he was at a loss to confirm it – the only thing keeping him alive.

Flirting With Gravity

C arlos was waiting. Waiting since Tuesday. This day
was Thursday – almost Friday – for it was well into
the Protestant hours of the night. Ordinarily the application of such inactivity would have settled securely with
Carlos, but not tonight.

He had retired from the entertainments audaciously early, sound in the belief that his protest would occasion her
presence.

It had not.

Most certainly it had not, for his stomach was now
bound closely with the repercussions of his wilful display.
It was not the first time in his seventeen years that he had
left a party early, but the reason as to why he had he been so
compelled to leave this party when he did was now defeating him. For all his good intentions in moments just past,
he had achieved nothing more than the surety of ventilating
his father's immeasurable stale contempt beyond the un-
speakable closet in which it had always lived.

493

And, worse than that, he hadn't even got the girl.

Carlos was more than defeated… he was positively vexed.

He peered at the floor between his feet. Rather, he peered at the carpet, for his feet were resting on it. Swirls of leafy things wound around flowery things that covered every gaudy part of it. It was horrible. Nothing in its design inspired distraction. No good. Reliving the moments of his undoing had never offered absolution in the past. Carlos lay back from his sitting position on the edge of the ample bed and stared absently at the lavish ceiling tableau, his hands automatically seeking his genitalia and comfort.

It is at least a month's journey back to Madrid. No doubt a further week before I am summoned before my 'sap' of a father. Plenty of time for a decent excuse.

He had time for amends. The panic retreated.

Decorative figurines in the composition above him began to flicker in the inadequate candlelight of his extensive surroundings and morphed with the tones of revelry ongoing in his absence, distant, in the largest of the Staterooms. His vexation increased as his mind laboured once again through the all-too-recent moments of his undoing…

The Great Hall of Saint George was alive with colour and warmth. The light of a thousand great candles and a hundred great flambeaus bounced off every great arch in the ceiling and every great column below. A profusion of paintings, tapestries, and coats-of-arms dangled from each of the great walls. A legion of swords, shields, and spiky things perched precariously from everywhere else.

As Don Carlos entered the Great Hall, his entourage fanned out behind him and he knew that his timing was impeccable; simply perfect, *'absolutamente perfecto.'*

His unfashionably late arrival at the head of the Great staircase secured appropriate attentions – albeit more slowly than he had anticipated – from the entire room.

He paced forward to the very edge of the top step on the staircase and revelled in the moment. Five-hundred people, hand-picked from the upper echelons of the English aristocracy, were staring straight up at him. Each of them was adorned in red. Reds of the most delicate silk and reds of the finest cottons and velvets; their garments cut together in designs that represented the height of English fashion. They crowded the Great floor below him. In that crowd a dozen privileged foreign nobles added yet more gravitas to an already grand occasion, and it had hardly begun.

Thus, safe in the knowledge that the party couldn't really start without him, Don Carlos drew a satisfied breath in all that was laid out beneath him and envisaged with some pride the next impeccable steps of his graceful and dignified entrance.

It was either the impossible volume with which his introduction was delivered, or his proximity to its delivery, that took the young prince by surprise...

"LORDS, LADIES AND GENTLEMEN!"

Legs that had previously been attuned to Don Carlos buckled in objection...

"HIS MOST NOBLE ROYAL HIGHNESS!"

His princely head jolted sideways such that his eyes might fully attest to the broadsword of a voice now compelling his ears to detach. The rotund little munchkin that accompanied the prince's introduction was clearly in his sixties and no more than four feet tall. The portly little figure delivered again...

"DON CARLOS, PRINCE OF ASTURIAS, FROM THE HOUSE OF HAPSBURG!"

Toes that had previously been attuned to Don Carlos' legs now found themselves in air that had never been occupied by stair. Both toes and he with them, teetered for a moment...

"FIRST-BORN TO KING PHILIP!"

His arms reached out involuntarily, grasping at the barrel of voice in front of him.

Too late... "HEIR...

APPARENT...

..TO

...THE

......KIN

...........G

..............D

................O
....................M
...........................OF
................................S
....................................P
....A
....I
....N!"

A fall down a flight of some twenty steps is rarely a uniform matter, but it does have rules, and individuals who take it upon themselves to enjoy the experience generally abide by them:

1. One's limbs should thrash about wildly such that the momentum of the falling body is impeded at every opportunity.

2. One should never allow one's head to contact the more prominent features in any given banister.

3. One's buttocks should be used to provide for adequate inertia when the foot of the stairs is reached.

4. One should take the lessons learnt at the foot of the stairs, and, prior to any given future stair falling opportunity, apply with common sense.

Most other boys of his age have had such an experience at one time or another, they fall, they play by the rules, dust themselves off at the bottom and walk away wiser.

Don Carlos did not abide by the rules.

In fairness to him, the breaking of rule two caught him entirely by surprise. His first experience of a similar tumble had happened two years' prior whilst he was chasing a handmaid around the servant's quarters of his father's palace, and that set of stairs was devoid of any banisters at all.

Rules one, three, and four were somewhat beyond his grasp for differing reasons: to appreciate, if not understand rules one and three, a person must be relatively familiar with the laws in Newtonian Physics. To appreciate rule four, one must be inherently blessed with common sense.

This was way before Newton and Don Carlos had no common sense.

So, Don Carlos was in submission – much to the relief of his ears – fully prostrate at the foot of the Great stairs, as the last echoes of his announcement faded into the depths of the Great Hall like a shockwave across the faces of the five-hundred or so distinguished guests. A splatter of nervous giggles took hold of a few, but not many. Then they quickly faded.

Then the paradox set in.

Don Carlos' first attempts to re-coordinate his limbs were not going well. Faces that looked upon his struggle shared unbroken completeness with that of their neighbours as the paradox set in.

How could anyone possibly describe the... the... well, the... *spectacular* fall they had just witnessed? It would do no good to be honest; who would believe you? It would do no good to lie; who would believe you?

In fact, therein was the paradox:

Sure, you could say, "Sir, you should have seen Don Carlos falling down the stairs, it was... *unbelievable,*" and seek a reaction to your anecdote. Or you could talk it up, "My word Madame, I have never witnessed such a fall as Don Carlos, it was simply... *hilarious,*" and seek a response, but inevitably a disappointment would set in, as the required reaction would never, ever, equal the first-hand experience. This, coupled with the undeniable fact that a prince of the Spanish Realm *never* takes to falling down a staircase, most certainly not whilst engaging in an ambassadorial role, and lest one should lose one's head in the telling of it, such a fall *never* happened.

No. The fall of Don Carlos at the October Masque of Her Royal Majesty Queen Elizabeth I in 1564 A.D. was possibly the first true paradox in history that was never recounted.

You simply had to be there.

Some say that had she been present, it would have helped poor Liz's affliction, for a good laugh was known at the time to cure many an affliction. Whether it would have worked on her smallpox, or not, is a different matter. But surely it would have done her no harm. And surely, she doesn't have smallpox. Long Live the Queen...

When Don Carlos finally reclaimed his footing – un-aided of course – he was, after all, still a prince – it was immediately apparent that he was unaffected by the fall.

"*Gracias. Gracias.* Thank you. *Estoy bien. Él está bien. Continúan por favor.* Please continue," offered Don Carlos in a relatively regal fashion.

He was mentally unaffected at least. It was impossible to discern if anything was physically altered. It was not to suggest that his physicality was the result of inbreeding, but Don Carlos had only four Great-grandparents, two of whom were sisters. Let's say, then, he was delicate, in physical form, and let's say then, that after the fall, nothing about him looked more unusual.

No one was moving.

As embarrassment exceeded relief, Don Carlos felt his cheeks turning to a brightness matched only by the crimson clothing of the onlookers. He snarled at the closest few, "*Continúe, continúe, por el amor de Cristo, déjeme solo* and continue."

Thus instructed, the crowd dispersed and re-immersed in the polite conversation of earlier. Men that were not flirting with another man's wife flirted with another wife's husband. Ladies simply flirted with anyone of more wealth than their own useless husband. The ruse for all flirting; the political and social application of the allegory behind the evening's Masque, about which no one knew anything, but the saccharine tongued architect who had designed it, and even he altered its theme depending on whom he was speaking to.

So, the flirting was outrageous.

Music had returned to the air, and Don Carlos had returned to his feet.

For the first time since his arrival two days ago, he was glad that she was not in the same room. Though he was certain she would hear of his entrance.

But how bad could that be? What would they say? He had slipped: ¿Así que lo que? He had fallen; She would only be concerned for my safety. Is she not in love with me, too?

He snapped a look at the doors, to see if anyone might be leaving to relay the tale of his downfall to her. They were not, as far as he could tell.

There must be a dozen secret passages leading away from this room. Bloody English and their bloody secret passages. It's a wonder anyone sees anyone at all in this bloody country.

The sycophants suddenly consumed him. Flattery for hire. The devil's own creatures. Protestants all. It made him sick to his sphincter. That, and the boring, boring adumbrations that graced the tongue of every stupid metaphor touting individual in the room.

When all he wanted to do was talk to her...

Although relatively innocent of years, the young prince was well rehearsed in the tradition of Masque in the English court as a complimentary offering to dignitaries of his standing. He had accompanied his father on numerous visits to England in the past, and, after all, it was his great-great granddaddy Max that had first taken a liking to the art form, back in the day, when Max had ploughed half the family fortune into the stupid things.

Don Carlos had forgotten the number of times he'd sat through dinner listening to tales of his Max's triumphs on the stage. His 'Julius Caesar' had been simply *sublime*, apparently. His 'Mark Anthony' considered *powerful* beyond measure. How he managed to play both in the same Masque had always been gilded over at the dinner table, and always, the conversation would then swing to Max's greatest accomplishment: the role of Holy Roman Emperor Maximillian I, in a four hour, five-act piece penned specifically for the original Burgundy stage. It had been an audacious move for the time, and the nation's critics had responded accordingly, lacking foresight by citing that Max's representation of the emperor lacked the *tenacity* of the real man. In short order they had crucified his accomplishment.

It was a one-off performance.

Max, who, incidentally, was Holy Roman Emperor Maximillian I at the time, took certain umbrage with the critics in question and had them crucified in return. Without the reviews they of course had no audience, and everyone knows that a Masque without an audience is both a soul-destroying and most unprofitable enterprise...

Don Carlos was aware then, that the Masque presenting that evening was in his honour, and, to this end, he took his appropriate seat in the front row, when a costumed imbecile appeared on stage accompanied by a gentle run on several stringed instruments.

It was undoubtedly the most ill-favoured Capricorn that Don Carlos had ever set eyes on, and why it should be chosen to narrate the forthcoming tale in October he could not fathom, but he settled himself in polite preparation, and issued permission for the continuance of the performance with a gentle nod of his brow.

The goat took up his cue, and began speaking:

"Wherein these giusts that foorth will surely follow,
I choose a suddeine marke to add my claime,
Let ear be used to haste bothe joy and sorrowe,
Lest eye be blinde to pleasure or to paine,
In truthe a life and loue shall neuer remaine,

A truer knight to euer upheld the Realm.
May nought be fonde in tales of ought afore..."

It was becoming apparent to Don Carlos that the present state of verse in the Elizabethan court had a merciless quality that strained the ear rather than gracing it. Certainly, he felt, there was opportunity should a half decent writer come along.

He was not alone in his thinking, for all in the room, except for Sir William Maitland of Lethington – who was recovering from a severe infection of both ears – shared empathies with poor Don Carlos as he continued to endure woefully inadequate verse from the mouth of the poorly attired goat:

"His loftie deede and word will ride the helm,
Of euery vertuous tale layn down in lore.
Peruse infernall feends with foule vapore,
Euerin a Glorious Queene of Faerie lond..."

At last: A mention of the Queen. Surely this is the cue for her entrance.

It was unconventional, he couldn't think why the Masque would begin in her absence, but he was not a stranger to the complexities of the Tudor court. Don Carlos strained nervously around the room.

Nothing.

All eyes were fixed eagerly on the babbling goat with the expectation of children.

She's not coming, she's not bloody coming, yet she insists that I endure this, this... second rate pantomime. Does she not love me as I do her? Does she not ache in my absence as I do for her? I should have sent the letters, I knew it. I knew it: I should have been brave... I should have sent all of them.

Don Carlos kicked out in disdain. His foot inadvertently connected with the head of a lesser sycophant stationed on the floor by his feet... no matter... he clutched at his toe, anticipating the pain that would follow.

It didn't.

A conflagration of light and sound thrust an effectual attack on his senses, and he raised his head towards the stage, facing onslaught. Some fifty or more revellers bounced into view, their costumes alive in the light of a hundred flambeaus. Fauns, satyrs, and unicorns followed witches, fairies, and... more fauns and satyrs onto the stage, hordes upon hordes of them, prancing and dancing and laughing and singing, as every conceivable instrument charmed in accord, bringing yet more joy to the already whole-hearted ensemble. Thunder and lightning respectively pounded and flashed as all the Gods of Olympus gloried above the affray. The monsters of Tartarus twisted the view, scratching and scraping and screaming in disdainful harmony as the dragons ignited the stage. A rage of white light banished the dragons and the music slowly dispelled, leaving just one angelic note, and a single, breathtaking, maiden, alone on the stage, transcending the forest behind her. A mist of pine scent bewitched every nose in the room as her endless gown willowed in a breeze from the heavens. A magnificent display, truly surpassing the maturity of the adult mind.

Don Carlos was not yet an adult.

He raised himself from his chair, simply turned, and walked out of the room. Though it was more of a slight stumble really, as the pain in his toe announced itself upon his standing, not to mention a grumbling coccyx, from his earlier fall.

Not that anyone else in the room would have known he was stumbling, the difference between his new stumble and that of his normal limp, would have only presented in earnest to the most highly trained medical eye, and this was way before medical training. But they did realise he was leaving, and they did recognise an insult to their Queen when they saw one.

Particularly when dealt by a foreigner.

In truth, only three of the great crowd felt no indignation at all towards the young Don Carlos, who was clearly to them upholding a bloody-good-effort, as he hobbled his way out. Three gentlemen of considerable standing, stationed shoulder-to-shoulder, incognito at the rear of the room, just left of the Great staircase, eyes fixed on the beautiful young woman on stage, who was clearly to them upholding another bloody-good-effort, in her all-but-see-through nightgown.

Flirting With Swords

An atmosphere of suspicion pervaded the sodden stillness of the soupy mist that veiled the Thames River and its banks. The odd, dank gurgle lofted in, faintly, from the north, sounded no doubt by some ongoing revelry within one of the closed taverns on Eton High Street. Nothing could be heard from the town of Windsor to the south.

The occasional suppressed moan swelled from below the planks of the bridge deck as the creaking wooden piers attended their timeless struggle with the passing current. Two indistinct lanterns marked each of the bridge's abutments. Two other lanterns marked the centre of the bridge's railings.

"*¿Herminia, qué es el tiempo, por su reloj?*" whispered the capitán.

Herminia de Torquemada placed herself beneath one of the centre lanterns and peered at her clock. She peered at her 'pocket clock', actually. To give either the woman or her precious instrument less than due credit would not have pleased Herminia on a good night, and she presently suspected that this was not such a night.

Herminia's gaze departed the single hand on the enamelled face of her pocket clock and landed on the face of her capitán, as did her monotone response to the latter's former question, *"Reloj de doce o, o un poco más adelante."*

Of the sixteen horses standing patiently in the centre of the bridge only fifteen had riders astride their backs. Of those fifteen riders, only the Englishman spoke, "What did she say?"

Silence.

William Allen made a second attempt to alleviate his increasing anxiety, "What d...d... did she say? God d...d... damn it."

Diego del Talavara graced the inquisitive man with a translation, "She says twelve o'clock governor, or a bit past if you'll have it."

Though grateful of the answer, Allen found to his considerable surprise, that his anxiety had not been eased in the slightest. The incongruous scarring on the otherwise quite-beautiful face of del Talavara was disconcerting enough, but the perfect cockney accent that graced the tongue of the Spaniard was downright intimidating. Allen's body, and his horse with it, backed away a fraction by way of instinct.

His attention was immediately drawn to the amusement that washed across the faces of all but one of those surrounding him. As Allen ceased his retreat, his horse did the same. Allen spoke again, "She is sure? How can she b... be so sure?"

Any remaining expressions of mirth faded around him. Herminia delicately closed the rare timepiece with her left hand and admired the elaborate engraving that embellished its golden casing. She laid it against her slender bosom and left it to dangle from the substantial chain around her neck.

Herminia de Torquemada's right hand flashed in a near perfect arc.

The point of the sword now resting gently beneath the left side of Allen's chin pressed home a feeling of woeful consternation, and let's just say, it did nothing for his anxiety.

Capitán Luis de Requesens y Zúñiga, the one man who had not shared in the enjoyment of Allen's question on the matter of Herminia's timeless integrity, whispered one, rather simple, word, "Belmonté".

Another hand flashed, this time in an absolutely perfect arc.

The sword that had previously harboured a state of quiescence against Allen's chin found new rest upon the planks of the bridge deck. The point of a second sword – unparalleled in its making, perhaps the finest sword since Excalibur

– now found perfect poise beneath the right side of Herminia's chin. The sword objectively balanced such that each pulse of her jugular vein sent a tremble along the length of the cutting edge, into the exquisite handle, and on into the skilful digits of the hand of the man that influenced the blade:

The left hand of Maestro Ignacio Belmonté de la Vega.

Who, apart from holding his sword, was doing no more at this time than staring calmly over the black waters flowing eastward away from the bridge. The slightest of wry smiles slipped across Belmonté's lips. He hadn't flirted like this in a long time.

Herminia was now fully persuaded that this was not a good night.

Luis de Requesens y Zúñiga stroked the reins of his animal. The horse adjusted its position slightly so that his master might face the man, Allen.

Zúñiga spoke in his customary whispered tones, "*Señor* Allen, you have your answer. Be assured it is, *un pequeño...* a small, amount of time past twelve tonight. We have come a long way, and my men are, anxious to continue." He did not take his eyes off Allen, who, in fairness, was not missing the irony of the capitán's words.

"You should know this, *Señor*, as you impart the, *detalles,* that you have promised." Zúñiga's eyes remained on Allen, while he whispered again, "Belmonté."

Belmonté returned his sword to his scabbard without a moment's hesitation. He continued to look out at the water and wondered – as he had every night for the past five years – if this would be the night, he would find the four-eyed woman.

If Herminia's relief was palpable, it was not apparent in her face.

Zúñiga maintained his susurrant tone, "You must play your part as a traitor, no?"

Allen recognised his cue, "B... b... by the south bank, f... f... follow the river east for a sh... sh... short time. The r... round tower will form a silhouette you cannot miss. Th... the path will split in f... front of you. You will l... l... leave your horses there. The right of the t... two paths will lead you to the north wall. G... g... go w... west along the w... wall until you reach the c... c... curfew tower. It will not be g... guarded. There you will find a d... d... door. It will be unlocked for one hour. Make your way inside but be..." Allen's voice defeated him.

"¿Qué? Señor? You are doing well, no? Diego, Señor Allen does well, yes?" Zúñiga turned his head to Diego, "You are with him, no?"

"All the long way, Guvnor."

Zúñiga returned to face the Englishman, "You do well Señor. Continúe, por favor."

Allen meant to continue, but the Spaniard's compliment came as something of a fright.

Zúñiga sensed Allen's reluctance to remain quiet and his struggle within. It was the same reluctance that grabs a rabbit in torchlight on a night's shooting.

The capitán sought guidance from his interpreter, *"Escupida?"*

"Spit, gov. Spit," said the cockney, Diego.

"Speeett?" enquired Zúñiga.

"Spit... S..p..it."

"Sp..et? Speet? Speet."

"Good enough, Gov," confirmed the mockney cockney.

Zúñiga was reassured, *"Señor* Allen, you must speet, *sí?* And say what you intend."

Allen sucked in a deep breath and expelled thus, "The... the door on the north w... wall w... will b... b... be unlocked for one hour, but it would be b... b...b...better if you are quiet, if you d...d... do not all b... barge through at once, is what I mean."

His relief, at having successfully imparted his chosen words, was little compensation for the panic that accompanied his certain collapsed lungs. Allen sucked at the cold night air once again. It now seemed too thin to provide his lungs with sufficient volume.

Zúñiga burst into a whispered cachinnation. Part snigger, part wheeze, part Christ only knows, but the impulse providing the ungodly mechanism was clearly laughter.

In his thirty-two years on the earth Allen had never heard anything like it. He felt his lungs were slowly inflating, but his anxiety was turning to cold sweat.

The capitán stopped his elated rasping, "He means us to suck eggs, yes?"

The other Spaniards reacted in a variety of ways. Some shuffled on their horses, smiled as warmly as they could, others simply bowed their heads in acknowledgement. All were still reeling from the disgusting noise that had just graced their capitán's throat.

Zúñiga pressed on in his secret voice, "Now speet *Señor* Allen. Speet."

"P... p... pardon me?" Allen enquired, using as little breath as possible.

"Speet. Speet, on the floor *Señor*. Your words did not come so easy. They were stuck, no? You must speet on the floor so they will not get stuck again. Speet."

Allen's fear of failure in upholding the capitán's request ensured that he was perhaps a little over-zealous in his attempt. It began with an extended snort that half ingested what felt like two thirds of his brain and ended with a truly gruesome expectoration that lacked sufficient velocity for the entirety of the mucus to reach the floor. That which did not escape, was shared between his beard and his doublet. Without exception every head on the bridge was compelled to turn away, and that included the horses.

Allen, unaware in the moment that a month's bile and snot was suspended beneath his chin, forced himself to continue, "M... m... my man will be w... waiting for you in the cloister. He will show you the w... way to the Upper W...Ward. It is th... there you will f...f... find the infant that you seek."

Zúñiga was fighting hard to regain his composure. His eyes were fighting just as hard not to stare at Allen's chin and to his dismay he quickly found that this battle with Allen's mucus was bettering him. Zúñiga retreated, forcing his eyes to avert by dismounting his steed and landing on the bridge deck with a thump of his sturdy feet.

He addressed Allen indirectly, "Be assured Señor Allen," he said, whilst pacing away, "all will be well." He stooped to retrieve Herminia's fallen sword. "All will be well," he repeated, as he rose and paced slowly towards the sword's owner, "if what you have told us is truth," he said, as he held up the handle of the blade to Herminia. "If your present looks are a measure of your integrity in this matter."

Herminia recovered the sword and returned it to its scabbard as she whispered gently, *"Gracias, mi Capitán."*

Zúñiga smiled and allowed his eyes to linger on the woman's face for an inappropriate moment longer than they should have, for good form's sake. He felt the strength of his full composure return in the instant. He turned and mounted his horse with a flourish, rounding on Allen at the same time, "You will wait here, *Señor.*"

He waved his right hand to his conscripts. They, their horses with them, along with the unmanned mare, spiralled southward in an impressively choreographed display, rattled off the bridge and dissolved into the darkness.

Zúñiga paused as they departed and addressed Allen for the last time, "If all is not well, we will alter your looks to suit the outcome when we return, yes? Now clean yourself you miserable wretch."

Then, he too, was heading into the vaporous night and on towards the castle.

Cast of Characters

Crew of *Maiden Bride*

William Hope – First Mate, Enhanced human, Arthur and Abbey's son

The Scarlett Buccaneer – Captain, Most successful privateer in the English Realm

Roger 'Paws' Prowse – Boatswain, Protector, Sly old dog

Ted 'Tumbles' Turner – Clumsy Sailor

Ned 'Toes' Williams – Legend with the Ladies, Sailor

Martin 'Mumbles' No-Name – Elderly Sailor

Robert 'Chips' Stewart – Sailor, Head Carpenter, Some might say Genius

Dye Bant – Taffy Sailor

Shamus O'Reilly – Mighty Sailor

Richard Bately – Young Sailor, Protégé of Scarlett

John Prior – Unassumingly smart Sailor

Jim Dolby – Shy Sailor

Trevor 'Needles' Neary – Ship's Doctor, Philosopher, Naturalist, Opiate-Chemist

Jonsey – Sailor

Mister Thomas – Sailor, Assistant to 'Needles'

Mister Johnson – Sailor, Assistant to 'Needles'

Mister Powell – Sailor

Tim Darley – Sailor, Night watch

Crew of Santa Oscuro

Capitán Juan Martinez Recalde – Capitán

Pedro Garcia – First Mate

Diego Vázquez – Ship's Doctor

Luis Sánchez – Sailor

Crew of *Doncella Escarlata*

Rosa Brizuela – Capitana

Maria Castella – First Mate

Sophia – Bohique Lady, Mystical Healer

Aletha – Young Sailor, Protégé of Rosa

Mariana Canimao – Sailor, Rower, Tobacco chewing pee lady

Valeria Canimao – Sailor, Rower, Tobacco chewing pee lady

Castora – Sailor, Rower, Tobacco chewing pee lady
Atala – Sailor, Rower, Tobacco chewing pee lady
Charo – Sailor, Rower, Tobacco chewing pee lady
Jaidyn – Sailor, Rower, Tobacco chewing pee lady
Marquesa – Sailor, Rower, Tobacco chewing pee lady
Romula – Sailor, Rower, Tobacco chewing pee lady

English Royal Court at Theobalds

Lady Katherine Cecil – Daughter of William and Mildred Cecil, and William's sister, maybe

Queen Elizabeth I – Virgin Queen of England, maybe

Francis Bacon – Cousin to Lady Katherine, Scientist, Philosopher, Gambler, Politician, Not a cider drinker by choice

Sir William Cecil – Lord Burghley, Advisor to Elizabeth, Katherine and William's adoptive father

Lady Mildred Cecil – Lady Burghley, Katherine and William's adoptive mother

Robert Cecil – First born son of William and Mildred Cecil

Sir Flemington James of Bon – Privateer, Mentor to Scarlett, Advisor to Queen Elizabeth

Sir Ignatius Jones – Privateer, Advisor to Queen Elizabeth

Lady Destiny Jones – Wife of Ignatius Jones

<u>Brethren of the Coast at Tortuga</u>

'Black Teeth' McCarthy – Pirate, Musician, Solid friend of Martin 'Mumbles' No-Name

Jimmy Wily – Pirate, Musician, First Mate to 'Black Teeth'

<u>The Spanish Royal Court</u>

King Philip II of Spain – King of Spain and all its Global Domains

Sofonisba Anguissola – Advisor to King Philip, and honestly not Sir James of Bon's Lover

Carlos – Prince of Asturias, Son of King Philip II of Spain

Matheo y Valois – Adopted son of King Phillip II

Antonio de Guevara – Aide to Matheo

Mono – Matheo's horse

Escriba – 4,000-year-old enhanced human, Advisor to King Philip, Psychopath

<u>Other Players</u>

Arthur Hope – 5,174-year-old enhanced human, Philosopher, Gatekeeper, William's dad

Thomas Wilson – Groundskeeper, Stone Mason, Carpenter, Barkeep, Butler on rare occasions at Theobalds House

Sister Agatha Templeton – Nun at Alms House

Chaplain Joseph Hardwycke II – Priest

Timothy Killiam – Curate

Giles Winterbottom – Head Gardener at Theobalds House

Michael I – Valet

Michael II – Valet

Tarquin Smedley-Smythe-Smythings – Captain of the Queen's Body Guard of the Yeomen of the Guard

Raine – Captain Smedley-Smythe-Smything's horse

Walters – Adjutant in the Queen's Body Guard of the Yeomen of the Guard

Bertram – Private in the Queen's Body Guard of the Yeomen of the Guard

Vessels of Fortune

Maiden Bride – Scarlett's equal

Santa Oscuro – aka *Dark Saint*, Spanish Naval Tall-Ship of Doom

Doncella Escarlata – Rosa's Galley Frigate

Printed in Great Britain
by Amazon

61855326R00302